Dream Girl

It was just *music*, after all, just a woman howling *Don't take it for granted/We'll eat you like air/It's one thing to want you/Another to care* and he felt the rhythms driving down through his body, feet twitching, shoulders jerking, and it was like warm golden air moving through him. He was feeling that happy. It was that kind of bliss.

At some point he must have dozed off without realizing it, because he was in the middle of a wasteland. No signs of life at all, just the sweep of beige-orange sand enclosed by jagged rock.

"Are you ready?" a woman said from behind him.

He turned, and there she was: the hitchhiker, the girl from the CD cover. Her hair was white-blonde, sticking up around her head in windblown tufts. Hip bones jutted above her low-slung jeans. You wanted to hold and protect her; only, Ramsey thought, she might shatter in your arms, cut you up with her broken pieces.

Ramsey said, "Who are you?"

She didn't seem to be looking at him but through him. It was as if he wasn't talking to a real person but some kind of random impersonal holograph, projected into his mind. "Come to the desert," she said. "I have something to show you."

"Who are you?"

He didn't expect her to answer. But suddenly her eyes shifted, and she seemed to look directly at him. As he opened his mouth to ask another question, she faded.

"Don't go," he said  of loss.

BloodAngel

JUSTINE MUSK

A ROC BOOK

ROC
Published by New American Library, a division of
Penguin Group (USA) Inc., 375 Hudson Street,
New York, New York 10014, USA
Penguin Group (Canada), 90 Eglinton Avenue East, Suite 700, Toronto,
Ontario M4P 2Y3, Canada (a division of Pearson Penguin Canada Inc.)
Penguin Books Ltd., 80 Strand, London WC2R 0RL, England
Penguin Ireland, 25 St. Stephen's Green, Dublin 2,
Ireland (a division of Penguin Books Ltd.)
Penguin Group (Australia), 250 Camberwell Road, Camberwell, Victoria 3124,
Australia (a division of Pearson Australia Group Pty. Ltd.)
Penguin Books India Pvt. Ltd., 11 Community Centre, Panchsheel Park,
New Delhi - 110 017, India
Penguin Group (NZ), cnr Airborne and Rosedale Roads, Albany,
Auckland 1310, New Zealand (a division of Pearson New Zealand Ltd.)
Penguin Books (South Africa) (Pty.) Ltd., 24 Sturdee Avenue,
Rosebank, Johannesburg 2196, South Africa

Penguin Books Ltd., Registered Offices:
80 Strand, London WC2R 0RL, England

First published by Roc, an imprint of New American Library,
a division of Penguin Group (USA) Inc.

First Printing, October 2005
10 9 8 7 6 5 4 3 2 1

For Elon

Acknowledgments

Thanks goes first to Shirley, Terry, and Erin Wilson, my family; to Mark Clements and Donna Levin, whose respective excellent workshops saw me through the first pages of the early drafts; to Marta Zieba, Tiffany Ward, and Mary Beth Brown, whose critiques proved invaluable; to Hugh Hodges, my favorite accidental professor; to Andrea Somberg, Jennifer Heddle, and Liz Scheier, for their charm, intelligence and professionalism; to Terri Brown–Davidson, Jim Ruland, Tony L Hines, and the rest of the talented Zoetrope crew, for their continuing support, advice and inspiration.

Since this is a book in which music features prominently, I'd also like to acknowledge Alabama 3. Their albums *Peste, Power in the Blood*, and *Exile on Coldharbour Lane* were all played obsessively during much of this writing.

And finally, the song lyrics attributed to my character Lucas Maddox were written by Hugh Hodges.

Prologue

The Summoner

Crowe's Crossing, England, 1399

Death came to the village, and the tall man followed.

He was no longer a prince. He had let his old name go, with grief and reluctance, and had not yet chosen another.

He stood in the shadow of an old twisted elm, his hood pulled low on his face, and watched as they buried the bodies. These people were still odd to him: so many of them so pale and ruddy, so coarse in manner, and short. Short-lived.

The air reeked of sweat and sewage and rotting flesh, of smoke curling up from stone chimneys.

The magic shifted inside him. Soon, he knew, these corpses would be remembered differently. The villagers— the men raining dirt into the mass grave, the women and children who stood back and watched—would forget the clawed-out chests and throats, the strange deep marks of teeth.

They would recall bubonic welts that had never been, testify to spells of sickness that had never happened.

Or rather: had not happened here.

Not here, where the demons had been.

I

Dark Muse

One

Lucas Maddox

California, Spring 2005

The girl came from nowhere.

The Chevy crested the hill and she was there, walking alongside the highway, duffle bag slung across her shoulder. She held out her thumb. Lucas thought of a trigger cocking back.

"You like that?" said Brett Carmichael, the driver. He glanced at Lucas and grinned, light sparking off his steel-rimmed glasses. Tom Waits drifted from the car speakers: "Romeo is bleeding . . ."

Yeah, he's bleeding. The thought gave Lucas a melodramatic pleasure. *He can't stop himself.*

He said, "Don't stop. Pass her by."

"What the *fuck*?" Brett was guiding the car to the shoulder. Yellow grass sloped away from the road, thinned out to sandstone cliffs. "I think she'd be a much more stimulating companion than *you*, my friend. No offense."

"None taken." Lucas unrolled the window, breathed in salt mist air. He was starting to feel as jagged as the coastline. *Not just yet,* he told himself—told the fat-bellied monkey sinking claws into his back—*not just yet. Just wait a bit.*

The girl was studying them through the windshield. She wore beat-up jeans, a too-big leather jacket. Her white-blonde hair was cropped short, mussed up. Lucas saw the razor cut of her cheekbones, the long line of her throat. He turned away.

"Hey," Brett called out to her. "Where you headed?"

She stepped around to Brett's window. Her voice was too low for Lucas to hear.

Brett said, "What a freak of a coincidence. So are we."

The girl opened the door and tucked herself into the backseat.

"I'm Brett Carmichael," Brett said, smiling at her in the rearview mirror.

And they were on their way again, eating up the sweeping coastline lengths of Highway 1.

"This guy beside me is Lucas Maddox. You'll have to forgive him. Lucas is kind of a loser now—no offense, Lucas—"

"None taken."

"—But he used to be in a band called Slippage, you remember them?"

The girl's voice was flat and hoarse. "No."

"They had this single, "Black Box." Really cool lyrics, you know, a bit morbid, inspired by some plane crash—"

"Trans-Unity Air," Lucas said. "Went down off the coast of South Africa. Lots of people died." The song, that music, those days in Seattle: stained futons and cockroaches, peanut-butter dinners, streaming backbeat of rain. Paula in his arms, her warm, honey skin.

"You'd recognize it if you heard it—Lucas, sing it for her."

"No."

"Just a bit of it?"

"No."

"I'd sing it," Brett said, "except I'm a shitty singer. Couldn't do it justice."

No response from the girl. Lucas shifted in his seat and glanced back at her; she was huddled up against the window, hands pressed between her knees as if trying to warm them. She was very thin. Breakable. "You okay?" he said.

She didn't answer.

Glancing again in the rearview mirror, Brett said, "What's your name, honey?"

She shrugged.

After a moment, she said, "Asha."

"No last name? Like a supermodel. Like one of the fabulous people. You're pretty enough to be *fabulous,* you know."

The girl was looking directly at Lucas. Her mouth twitched.

Brett said, "So what's a slip of a thing like you doing alone on the big bad road?"

"I'm looking for someone."

She was staring at him, at them both, her head cocked to an unnatural angle.

"A boy," she added.

Brett whistled. "*I'm* a boy. And you're looking right at me."

Her eyes closed and she leaned her forehead against the window. Beyond her, on the other side of the highway, the bald, lion-yellow hills ranged on and on.

"Here we are, buddy," Brett said, guiding the car into a roadside rest area. "Here we are. You can go set yourself right again." He turned off the engine. He was looking in the mirror at the dozing girl.

Lucas grabbed up his knapsack and got out of the car. The mist was thinning, burning off. Blue and yellow flowers pushed up through the ground, and the air exploded with the cannonball-boom of the surf. He walked to the low-slung building that housed the restrooms. Hunkered inside a stall and unzipped the bag.

Ah, ritual. Watch the stuff dissolve: bubbling amber in your spoon. Summon up the vein: blue-green worm against your skin.

The spider-bite of needle.

The plunger beneath your thumb. The push. The downward glide.

And then.

Float off.

You are smooth and creamy again, you are smack-dab in the caramel center.

The world tilted away from him and slowly, slowly tilted back. He wandered back out into the sunlight. The day had turned very bright.

The car was empty.

They were gone, the girl's leather jacket husked off in the backseat.

Once, in Reno, Lucas had surprised Brett with a girl in a motel room. He saw the glint of the knife and the blood on her breasts and got the hell out of there, sat down heavily on the curb of the parking lot. He even considered the police, but briefly, because he was a one-time drug offender with stash on him, enough to feed that fat-bellied bitch of a monkey until he hooked himself up in LA. Police were not Lucas-friendly. And he had done enough kinky shit of his own—*not like that,* a voice kept yammering in the back of his mind, *she's just a baby*— that he was hesitant to draw such hard-core conclusions.

So he did nothing.

Later—he didn't know how much later—Brett found him smoking in a corner of an all-night coffee shop. Brett dropped down beside him, plucked the cigarette from his fingers and stubbed it out in the green plastic ashtray. *It was a fantasy thing,* Brett said. *A role-playing thing, you know?* He studied Lucas for a moment, then said carefully, *She's a lot older than she looks.*

Right, Lucas said, and took a sip of cold coffee. And realized, with a knife-edged clarity he had not experienced since Paula died, that once upon a time he would not have tolerated the company of a shit like Brett Carmichael. Once upon a time he would have bashed the fucker's head in.

Now, as gulls wheeled and surf shattered on the rocks, Lucas tugged off his shirt, let the sun bake down on his body. He leaned against the car. He had been waiting for maybe fifteen, twenty minutes when he caught movement from the corner of his eye.

He turned.

Saw an animal in the yellow grass.

He blinked twice, looked again.

Skittering crab-like on all fours: animal-girl in jeans and stained white T-shirt, sun glinting off her pale hair—

He thought: *No.*

And the girl stood in front of him.

Smiling.

Everything was becalmed, everything was creamy. *Run,* his brain was screaming at him, *this is fucked up,* but the connection between brain and body was cut. He stared at the girl and could only think how cute she looked, innocent, as she took the dripping knot of dark-purple muscle out from inside her T-shirt and held it in blood-soaked hands, as she lifted it to her teeth. She tore off a piece, chewed and swallowed as if eating a roast beef sandwich. "Hey," Lucas said again. His voice like fluff in his mouth. "That's his . . . That's . . ."

She ran a hand across her mouth, smearing blood like lipstick.

"That's his goddamn *heart*. His *heart*. His *heart*—"

"Lucas," she whispered, and reached up to touch his face.

The pressure of her fingertips, her deep carnal breath.

"Lucas," she said again. He unloosed a groan, felt his legs melt away from him. He was on his knees in the

dirt and the girl was stepping behind him, slipping her
arms beneath his shoulders. He had the strange sensation of being lifted without effort.

In the arms of a slip of a girl.

"Lucas."

And in the moment before he blacked out, Lucas
Maddox seized on the impossible fact this was not a
dream, not a drug.

She had come for him.

He woke up in a hotel room, the cheap kind where
the television remote was bolted to the nightstand.
Someone—he didn't think *who,* wasn't ready to think
who yet—had left him a glass of water. Lucas fumbled
it to his mouth, took sloppy gulps. He leaned over and
vomited. The glass rolled from his fingers, his head
crashing back to the pillow . . .

. . . Floating through memories gone warped at the
edges. Back on the road with Slippage, the grind of the
early days: Bill Clinton still rising, grunge and heroin
chic and Gulf War aftertaste and *Pulp Fiction* and
"Smells Like Teen Spirit" and "Jeremy" and they were
living off music and coffee and cigarettes and tequila
shots lined up in seedy Seattle bars . . .

When he opened his eyes again, something was missing from him but he couldn't pinpoint what that lack,
that absence, actually was. His hands flew to his chest:
seeking the wound, the blood. But he was intact.

Lucas gasped for air like a swimmer breaking surface,
pushing up against the headboard, thrashing off the
sweat-soaked sheets.

Asha was waiting at the foot of his bed.

He wasn't sure he was seeing correctly. He couldn't
be seeing correctly—

Because the girl was perched on the bed's footboard,
her bare, long toes curled round the edge, gripping it,
her body hunched and balanced in a way that didn't
seem, couldn't be, *possible,* her arms crossed loosely

over her knees. She wore a white cotton shift with dark stains on the front. The cropped, tousled hair gleamed in the light shafting in between the curtains. Her lips were wet and red.

She said, "Hello, Lucas."

His mind buzzed with static; it was a moment before it cleared enough to send up a thought, a transmission—

"What the fuck?"

Asha cocked her head to the side.

"What the fuck are you?"

She only looked at him.

He didn't think it was that complicated a question.

"A fucking vampire? Just tell me—"

"No," she said. "Although it's the same kind of hunger."

Her skin was so white it was almost translucent; there was something bruised-looking beneath her eyes, and the rest of her face had a raw, naked look to it.

"I've been away for a very long time," she whispered.

She looked at him, eyes shining.

He said, "You killed Brett."

She shrugged.

"Not that I care," he added. "The dude is not worth crying over."

She ripped out his heart and ate it. She ate his fucking heart—That voice in his brain spiraling upward, starting to scream again—*Do you understand the depth of the bizarre shit you are in here? Do you?*

But even if he was going to die, get ripped apart like Brett, he was no longer sure he cared much. The good parts of his life were done. The pain would suck, certainly, but it would end soon enough. The world wouldn't waste time crying over him, either.

He sank back into the bed.

"Tell me what you are," he said wearily. "And what the fuck you want from me."

"My full name is Bakal Ashika." She was smiling a little. "I have reinvented myself. That is the American

way. I have watched many hours of television." The
smile opened up into a grin. "I'm looking for someone."

"A boy."

"Yes. Mine. They owe him to me."

"Who—"

"But I will share him with you. And with others."

He didn't see her move. She was just, suddenly, *there*:
crouching above him on the bed, crouching *on* him, except he couldn't feel her at all; she was weightless, she
was gossamer, the sun-shaft breaking like waves around
her pale head. *Oh you angel,* he suddenly thought—it
was from a song he'd written but never recorded, a song
for Paula, dying Paula, who took the gun one bright
Spanish morning and walked down the path, out of view,
and he broke as he watched but knew enough not to
follow—*you're a bad, bad angel.* He had thought of it as
a love song, a pleasingly twisted one. Except it was no
longer for Paula, and it was no longer a love song.

"You need to sleep," Asha whispered.

She placed her hands on his face, experimentally.

"Let your body recover."

And it was then he realized what he had only sensed
on waking: the absence of addiction. For the first time
in a decade, his body felt cleansed. He didn't *need* anything, nor was the monkey-part of him plotting the
where and when of the next fix. Inside this new, shiny
lack, he felt . . . at peace.

"Sleep," Asha whispered. "And then we can make
music."

"I don't do that anymore."

Her green eyes fixed on his. Something sparked inside
him, jolted through his veins. Maybe the monkey hadn't
left him after all, had morphed into something new. He
felt the floor of his consciousness crumbling away beneath him; poised over the fall, he mumbled, more from
curiosity than anything, "What did you do with his
body?"

She looked at him, chewing on the knuckle of her baby finger.

"Brett's body," he said.

She took the knuckle away from her mouth.

"I was very hungry."

He heard the answer without registering it. He was falling into dreamland: warm beach and Paula on the sand, her blonde hair lifting in the breeze, her hand resting lightly on a picnic basket filled with fruit. She was healthy and smiling and waiting for him. He sank down beside his woman and fed her chunks of papaya and watermelon, keeping his gaze away from the bloodstained horizon and the dark things that stalked it.

Two

Jessamy Shepard

New York City, summer, 2005

On the subway, darkness flashing past the windows, Jess Shepard noticed the ad. A model was holding up a credit card. Some fervent anticapitalist had vandalized the girl's face, red paint streaming from the corners of both eyes. The model smiled on, showing all her perfect teeth, as if she didn't know she was bleeding.

"Someone was looking for you."

They were preparing to hang the *Heir of Nothing* show, paintings spaced out along the polished parquet floor. Jess was stepping around their edges, sipping coffee from a stainless-steel travel mug, examining the paintings in this new context. Ejected from her studio, finished and framed: they were Art now, they had prices and promo material.

Nicky was the gallery assistant. He said again: "Someone was in here last night, looking for you. Seemed to know you."

"Can you be more specific?"

"A man."

"Good start. More specific?"

"A *god* of a man. Perhaps an ex?"

Jess thought for a moment, then shook her head. The lovers before her current relationship had been casual at best; chosen for their angular, hipster beauty, their faux vulnerability, and sent on their way when their ability in bed could no longer atone for their inane conversation. No reason why any of them would come looking for her.

"So if you don't want him," Nicky chirped, "can I have him?"

"He might be a serial killer."

"But you should have seen his *eyes*. And his *shoulders*."

Jess turned, rising up on her toes and stretching her arms above her head. The place was shaped like a cul-de-sac, steel stairs going up into the back. The artist showing there did ancient Egyptian–inspired collages with the inevitable postmodern, pop-culture twist. Her own work would fill the lower level.

Her gaze fell on *Heir of Nothing,* the title piece of the series, propped by the door.

The boy.

Her boy.

He filled the foreground, his slanted, glowing eyes staring out at the viewer. Behind him, the desert swept up to a line of mountains. Jess imagined that beyond those mountains the desert dropped away altogether. Because this world was flat, and if you weren't careful you would step over the edge, you would never stop falling. The sky was a pale, apocalyptic red. In the boy's thin body and sweep of landscape were shards of mirror, embedded in the paint. Jess saw herself reflected in bits and pieces: fragments of a tall lean body in jeans and a vintage-rock tee.

There were odd moments, like now, when she didn't feel like she had created him. He'd emerged from some dreamlit inner space, and she'd been smart and quick enough to get out of his way—to get to paint and canvas and let his image rise up through her. Usually Jess spent months planning a painting, assembling notes and photographs and rehearsal sketches; only when the image was locked down in her mind did she take it to canvas, starting at six or seven in the morning and continuing straight through until twilight, or longer, working in the white glare of spotlights, stereo blasting, until she stepped away ravaged with hunger and fatigue.

But the paintings of the boy—seven of them in all, forming the core of her first one-woman show—had been different experiences. She couldn't plan him out or lock him down; he was just simply, suddenly there, springing full-blown into the center of her mind, and it was a question of getting him down—of nailing the image—before he slipped away from her.

She'd never experienced anything like it. Like him.

Her nomad. Her archetype.

"So no idea who he is?" Nicky's low honeyed voice was suddenly in her ear. "Does he even exist? Or is he just a figment of our collective imagination?"

Jess glanced away, self-conscious. "It's just a painting."

"Silly rabbit." He was looking at her with a self-satisfied smile, the backs of his hands on his hips so that his arms made off-angle wings. "I meant the guy who was in here before, claimed to *know* you. Was he faking us out? Was he full of shit?"

She was tired of this topic; her mind had jumped to other things. She shrugged.

"It's about time you got your first stalker," Nicky mused.

The boy was still returning her gaze.

Jess Shepard sipped her coffee and turned away from them both.

Three

Jess was behind the bar, hanging up wine glasses, when she saw Michelle Hathaway, her closest friend and boyfriend's twin sister, coming down the stairs. "You," Chelle said, collapsing on a chair. "I'd hug you like mad, except I'm too frigging tired. How've you been?" The votive candles on the bar flickered shadows on her cheeks.

A girl's voice squealed, "You would not fucking *dare*," and the group in the far banquette shrieked more laughter. Kevin, the model-actor-waiter still on duty, was shooting them murderous glances. Jess could read his mind. He wanted them all to spontaneously combust so he could cash out and go home. "How was LA?"

"I started smoking again," Chelle said, slapping down a pack of Marlboro Lights, "so don't give me shit about it, I feel like a loser as it is. I got the job."

"Yeah, well, that's why they flew you out there, isn't it? To woo you."

"I was wooed," Chelle muttered. "All they want is my soul. They'd pay a good price for it."

"So tell them to go to hell. You don't need that kind of income."

"I *like* the income. I just don't want to be a lawyer

anymore." Chelle flicked ash into the ashtray. "So fuck all those episodes of 'LA Law' I saw in my formative years."

"The evils of eighties television," Jess agreed.

"I want to be like you. Pursuing what I love."

"I was lucky."

She had come to the city as a seventeen-year-old runaway. She'd been lucky to have Chelle, then a law student at NYU, to run to; lucky that her uncle had never come looking for her; lucky for those friends and mentors who taught her what they knew, shared supplies and studio space, let her sleep on couches and floors in their cramped Lower East Side apartments; lucky to get discovered by her dealer at an obscure group show in a Brooklyn warehouse.

Chelle rested the cigarette on the edge of the ashtray. Her sleeve fell down her left arm. Jess saw the pale network of scars there, hard to see if you didn't know to look. She glanced away. Kevin came by the bar. "Another round of martinis for the rat bastards," he said.

As Jess shook them up and filled the glasses, she could sense Chelle's eyes on her. Kevin sighed heavily, dramatically, and trotted off with the tray. Jess grabbed a cloth, wiped down the bar and said without looking up, "If it's about Gabe—"

"He says you're *in angst*."

"In what?"

"Playing the brooding *artiste*—"

"I'm not *playing* anything—"

"Distant and secretive and won't tell him why."

Jess rolled the cloth through her hands. She was finding it difficult to meet Chelle's gaze. "Maybe I can't," she muttered.

"Maybe you should try."

Jess tossed the cloth in the sink. "What should I say, Chelle? That I'm on the verge of some kind of . . . break with reality?" She was smiling as she said it, but the undertone of her voice was serious enough.

"Jess, are you—"

"No. No. I'm exaggerating."

Chelle leaned in towards her and placed her left arm on the bar, inner forearm turned up for full exposure. She had not missed Jess's earlier glance at those decade-old scars, Jess realized. And now, targeted in that calm, hazel gaze, Jess felt her walls going up, her expression turning blank, her gestures and inflections betraying nothing. If Chelle excelled at reading people, Jess excelled at being unreadable.

Jess said, "Chelle. I just—" She rubbed her eyes. "I'm anxious about the show. I'm a mess, I admit it, but it's just the show. I can't focus on anything else."

They looked at each other for an oddly helpless moment. Chelle drew in breath to speak, when her gaze shifted towards the stairs.

Jess looked over.

The man had paused on a middle step, shadows slanting over him; but Jess saw his height and strength, his dark hair, the bronze shade of his skin. He wore a dark suit that was loosely, beautifully cut, jacket open on a dark silk shirt.

He was looking straight at her. Even through the shadows, though she couldn't see his face, she felt their gazes connect. It was like a snap of cold electricity at the base of her spine.

"Jess," Chelle said, but Jess was only vaguely aware of her. Something was pulling too fiercely at her memory: salty taste of tears, high shelves filled with books, a man in a gold and green uniform holding a porcelain teacup, and someone else—

—Yes, someone else, there in the room with her, sitting in the plush armchair as she slowly circled round it, someone with long legs extended, one large hand falling on the armrest as a body leaned forward and a deep voice spoke her name, spoke it as if he knew her—

The man in the suit turned and went back up the stairs, out the door, swallowed by the summer night.

Someone was looking for you.

"Jess? Honey?"

It took a moment to focus on her friend.

Chelle said, "You know that guy?"

"He was just . . . He was reminding me of—" Another memory came to her, but this one was full and intact: standing on the Cape Town harbor looking over the water, to where dark shapes of ships moved in the distance. She had watched those ships without knowing what they were doing, searching for the wreckage, the bodies. She had been six years old.

They never found the black box; they never came to a satisfactory conclusion about why the plane went down.

Your parents are dead. You are my child now.

"He was reminding me of something," Jess said. "I don't know why. I don't know that guy."

Chelle looked as if about to say something, then closed her mouth, stubbing out her cigarette with small, precise motions.

Four

That night, Jess Shepard had dreams:

She's in the desert, some kind of ghost town: wooden buildings, sun-bleached and wind-beaten; bars with no one inside them; broken windows streaked with grime and dust.

"Hey. You."

She turns.

He's standing about twenty feet away from her, hands hooked through the belt loops of his jeans. He wears a white shirt that hangs off his tanned chest. He is lean, wiry, maybe five-ten. His hair is sandy brown and longish, his jawline rough with stubble.

"I know you," he says.

And grins.

It is a hard, fierce thing, that grin, and yet there's charm in it.

"About the boy," the man says. "Thought you should know. We're going to find him first. Ready or not, we're getting all ready."

She has no idea what he's talking about.

"Stay home, girl," the man says, and smiles. "You'll

*get everything you ever want if you just stay home.
Wouldn't fuck that up if I were you."*

*A shadow falls over him, and he looks up into the sky.
The air shimmers, thins, and Jess Shepard steps through
the membrane separating the dream-life from the other.*

She was not in her bed.

She was in the bathroom, crouched in the corner, the
tile like ice beneath her feet. She glanced at the forms
that surrounded her, found comfort in their banality:
claw-footed tub, sink, blue shower curtain. *Get a grip.
Get a grip. People sleepwalk all the time.*

Only dreams. They couldn't hurt you.

There was a cosmetics tube on the floor. It was un-
capped, the lipstick broken off and blunted. Slashed inside her arm in dark red lipstick, in handwriting she
recognized as very much her own, were the words: RE-
LEASE THE BOY.

She bit back a shriek; it emerged from her in a stran-
gled half-cry of repulsion. Fumbling at the taps, she ran
her arm through the water, scrubbing until the lipstick
marks blurred and smeared and faded altogether.

She glanced at herself in the bathroom mirror.

Does your brain work right, girl? Her uncle used to
say that to her, those years she lived with him and his
whisper of a wife in their elegant Georgetown town-
house. *Are you stupid, or just crazy?* Sometimes accom-
panied by a slap to the face, a punch to the back or
sometimes the stomach. His name was Claude Harker,
although everybody called him the Judge. She hadn't
talked to him in a decade, didn't even know if he was
still alive; but she could still hear his voice in her head.
Some voices never left you.

"You're okay," she muttered to her reflection. "A bit
fucked in the head, maybe, but so what. You're fine."

*Somebody drop you on your head when you were just
a wee bitty baby? Scramble things up in there? Is that
what happened? Or were you born a fucking imbecile?*

She left the bathroom.

The words were written all over the scratched hardwood floors, the mirrors and windows, in marker and lipstick and paint.

RELEASE THE BOY RELEASE THE BOY RELEASE RELEASE RELEASE THE BOY

Eventually, when Jess felt she could move again, she set to work scrubbing, washing, and rinsing.

Five

The night of the show, she stayed in the bathtub for close to an hour. She closed her eyes and searched for the image. A familiar image, a valuable daydream. Jess hadn't used it in a while, but she located it with ease, let it flesh itself out:

She stands on a balcony in a hammerfall of sun. A lizard dozes along the ledge, one pale eye opening to look at her, then closing again. Beyond and below, the city rambles on: zigzagging sunbaked walls, turrets and domes, the fringed green of palm trees, winding out into the desert. The sun hammers down on glazed tile, stained-glass windows, courtyard mosaics. Music floats from below—stringed instruments, flutes—and she breathes in the drifting scent of incense. She feels all anxiety ease, draining from her like water through a sieve.

At once, she felt better. Calm. Jess pulled the plug and stood, water sluicing off her body. Reached for her robe.

She was ready.

"Jessie, sweetie," Timothy Clayton was saying, "why the hell are you still with Taylor-Taylor?" He had a habit of sidling too close to her, so that she was subtly but constantly backing away. "Have you seen the place that Damon Oaks just opened in Tribeca? Now *he* would know how to show off a great young prize like you—"

"I like Taylor-Taylor," Jess murmured. She caught fragments of a conversation going on behind her, a dealer and art writer discussing the new wave of artists coming out of Africa. That was the conversation she wanted to join, but it was breaking up now, the art writer drifting away. As Clayton yammered on about the latest renovations to his house in the Hamptons, Jess scanned the gallery for Chelle.

The crowd was a curious mix of uptown and downtown, dressed in New York black and holding glasses of red wine: socialites and creatives, Wall Street types and their well-manicured significant others. Sara Nolan, the gallery owner, flashed her a discreet smile, talking with a black-haired collector in the corner.

"—Art as an intellectual exercise," Timothy was saying now, "and not just a *scene,* although God knows there's nothing wrong with a high-caliber guest list. Tell you the truth, I wish there was a magic spell you could cast on people, so you could tell at a glance who's worth talking to and who's simply—"

Chelle was standing alone in front of the *heir of nothing* painting, sipping wine.

"I'm sorry, Timothy," Jess said, and gave him her best smile. "Would you excuse me? Thanks for coming."

Chelle glanced over as Jess fell in beside her. "The ones with this kid in them—this character you've created—they're different from your other works. There's a different feeling to them."

Jess glanced at the youth in the painting. The sleep-written words in red lipstick flamed through her mind; she felt the urge to look away from this painting but forced herself not to. It was ridiculous to be so unnerved by an image of your own creation, as if he were about to breathe himself to life, step down from his framework of paint and canvas, challenge her right there in the gallery.

"Duende," Chelle said.

Jess glanced at her sideways. "Isn't that the Spanish word for demon?"

"The poet Lorca used it as a metaphor for artistic expression." Chelle had done her undergrad degree in literature. When she talked books or writers she slipped into a professorial mode that Jess found amusing, even as she listened intently. She would never admit how deeply she envied her friend's education. "The *duende* is kind of like a dark muse—artistic inspiration in the presence of death. It's hard to explain." Chelle paused, frowning. "You know, I've always thought you're so talented it's scary. Especially considering you had so little formal training. But these paintings—"

"Duende," Jess echoed.

"That feeling of apocalypse," Chelle agreed. Then: "Hey. There he is."

Her brother was angling his way towards them. He was dressed more casually than the people around him, in jeans and an olive-green cotton sweater, his strawberry-blond hair in need of a cut. Gabe was the black sheep of the Hathaway family, who had elected not for law or medicine but designing and building furniture.

As he looked at her now, he wasn't smiling. "Jess," he said, and was about to say more, when she gave herself over to impulse: stepping forward, touching his chest, saying, "I've been unfair. I'm sorry." His nearness unleashing something inside her, like rain. "I've been—"

His hand closed over hers, tightened.

"Let's talk," he said.

"Not here."

She put in her appearance at the afterparty and left as early as she decently could. She and Gabe walked through the quieter streets of the Village, railings glinting in the near-dark, thin young saplings spaced out along the sidewalks. They ended up at one of those places that manage to be crowded and mellow at the same time: candles flickering at high round tables occupied by a mix of gay and straight couples. A white-haired woman in a fedora played Gershwin at the baby grand.

Jess said, with some difficulty, "I do love you."

He downed the rest of his beer, signaled the waiter for another.

"I do. I'm just not very good at it."

"You know what it's like, sometimes, being with you?" She waited.

"It's like—it's like standing in fucking *shadow*. It was intriguing at first, your aloofness and everything, but it gets old, Jess. It's not what I want."

"But you—" She paused as the waiter set down another beer. "You know me."

"Christ, Jessie, what makes you think you even want to be *known*?"

She was slightly bewildered. "Doesn't everyone?"

Gabe rubbed his hand along his jaw, snorted.

She felt herself go into a kind of free fall. "There's something inherently wrong with me." She realized how vague and melodramatic that sounded. "Shit," Jess sighed, and pushed her hands through her hair.

But Gabe was looking at her closely now.

He spoke abruptly, surprising her. "I don't know anything about your life before New York. You never told me and I didn't ask."

"You know the important parts."

"I know your parents' plane fell out of the sky. I know your uncle put you in a psych ward. Where my pre-Prozac sister happened to be at the time. *That's* what I know." He set down his glass, cleared his throat. "And I know your home life was—"

"No," she said.

"Christ, Jessie. Kids don't run away from happy homes."

"I mean," Jess said tiredly, "let's not go there. It's not worth talking about."

"What if it is?"

"Who are you, my goddamn shrink?"

He rose. "I'm out of here."

"I'm sorry. Don't go."

He dropped back into his chair.

"I'm really sorry. I am." She was smiling. "Still love me?"

He looked away from her, across the room, to where people in black leather coats were pushing out through the doors. He looked back at her and grinned. *"Sometimes."*

She grinned back at him, lacing her fingers through his, touching her lips to his scarred knuckle. "So take me to bed."

They made a sleepy, dreamy love, in the darkness of Gabe's Chinatown apartment, the sounds of night traffic grinding through the open windows. After, he kissed her shoulder and hugged her close.

Jess was tired, but afraid to sleep, dream, wake up somewhere else with strange writing on her body: those messages sent up from her other, sleepwalking self.

She suspected, at times, that she needed her *angst*, those tough painful parts of her that fueled her work. If those wounds healed, what if her talent closed over as well? Without that, she was nothing.

She got out of bed. Gabe slept on.

She found his Marlboro Lights on the windowsill, muttered, "Fuck it" and slipped one out of its pack. Standing naked beside the iron-guarded window, she smoked her first cigarette in two years, wincing at the taste but smoking it down to the filter, remembering the pleasure the act used to give her. She stubbed it out in the ashtray, dressed in the stiletto boots and black pantsuit she'd worn to the opening. She hovered over Gabe a full minute, her heart a swollen thing in its bone cage.

She touched his cheek, then left.

Six

She stepped inside the loft, switched on the lights. Touched the bronze sculpture by the door for luck, tossed her keys in the Chinese bowl on the bookshelf.

The air seemed wired with a strange, shadowy energy. Her gaze traveled over the reach of space, the books and dark corners and sparse furniture. The loft wasn't hers; she was house-sitting for a professor-sculptor friend in Europe for six months.

Ash-taste of cigarette in her mouth. She passed through the loft, flipping on lights as she went—suddenly needing the place to be blazing with light—and stepped down into her work space. Darkness bunched against the windows, backdropped by the rise and fall of roofs, the cold scattered glow of city lights. Panes of mirror leaned against the far wall, waiting to be broken up, put to use in her work. She saw her reflection, stretched-out and made off-kilter by the angle of the glass.

She saw herself.

And the man who stood behind her.

His height, his fine dark clothes, his blazing eyes.

"Jessamy," he said quietly. His voice was low and hoarse. "Jessamy Shepard."

She whirled, light blurring at the corners of her vision. He watched her with a calm expression, stepping down into her studio.

Nicky, the other morning in the gallery: *a god of a man.*

His face angular and high-boned; his eyes wide-set, almond-shaped, tilting up at the corners. They were a deep, glowing amber, the color of melted lava; *nobody has eyes like that,* Jess was thinking even as she backed away from him until her hip jammed against the edge of her worktable and a can toppled over. Water spilled along the newspapers, dripped onto the floor. *Nobody could possibly have eyes like that—*

"I'm not here to hurt you," he said.

"You were in the gallery," Jess said. "You were in the bar."

"I know this must seem . . . uncivil." He lifted his hands, palms up. He had the skin of a youngish man, but something about the way he held himself, looked at her, something in his voice and eyes, suggested he was older.

Much older.

"I have stalked you," he said. A confession. "I had—I have—no choice. Otherwise I would have left you to your life." He tilted his head. "How are the dreams, Jessie? Are they just about the boy, or is there someone else in them as well?"

She bolted, then, hurling herself past him and up the steps. She got to the door, fumbled with the dead bolts. Her hands on the doorknob, twisting, pulling, almost enough space to slip out into the hallway, almost enough breath in her lungs to scream—

When the door ripped from her hands and slammed itself shut with such ferocity that the very wall seemed to rattle. She grasped at the knob but the door would not move. "No," she muttered, but when she turned around the man was still standing there, watching her, and no matter how many times she said *no* she knew she couldn't change it. Any of it. Not the dreams, not the boy, and especially not this man—

"Jess. I'm sorry, but I can't let you go."

And she saw her life as she'd known it slipping away. He stood in front of her, and he eclipsed everything.

"You were in the library," Jess whispered, acknowledging it now, truly, for the first time. "The library of the hotel. In Cape Town. The day they fished my parents' bodies from the water."

"Yes," he said.

"Jesus Christ."

"Hardly." He tilted his head. "We've been mistaken for vampires in the past. Do you believe in vampires, Jessamy?"

She shook her head. Although in that moment he could have told her he was a vampire, an alien, anything, and she was prepared to believe him.

She didn't answer. She couldn't find breath to speak. He stepped closer. He was very close now. She pressed back against the door that would not open. There was nowhere for her to go. His eyes moved across her face as if studying, memorizing, comparing it to something in his mind. His gaze lowered to her body, assessing it in a way too abstract to be sexual. He was close enough so that she could breathe in his scent, which reminded her of burnt matches. *As if he's just walked through fire,* she thought wildly. *As if he's just come from hell.*

He said, "Do you believe in demons?"

"Is that what you think you are?"

"No. But I do know a few. My name is Kai Youngblood. You might remember me, if you think back a few years."

"You'll have to refresh my memory."

"The balcony scene," Kai said, and the words were like an electric jolt going through her. She knew at once what he meant.

"The balcony scene," Kai said. "The vision of the old desert city, the Labyrinth. I gave that to you, when you were a child, to help you through your grieving."

She wasn't sure she'd heard correctly. "What—"

"You thought that was just something you'd dreamed up on your own?"

"I thought I saw it in a movie, or a storybook." She was stammering. "A picture I saw when I was little. I thought—"

"It was a memory."

Kai tapped his temple. His fingers, she noticed, were long and tapered; the nails had a metallic sheen.

"My memory," he said. Then added, as an afterthought, "The lizard was a boyhood pet. His name was Tapaku. He lived a very long time, for a lizard."

Jess was shaking her head. "There is no city like that," she said evenly, "anywhere in the world." She knew she was right. The place—even though she had only gotten a sliver of a glimpse—had felt like too much of a dream, too far outside of ordinary life.

"Not anymore."

He turned away from her and walked into the kitchen. Her hand slipped behind her back, grasped at the doorknob. It did not move. It seemed frozen in place.

"It's a very easy casting," Kai said casually, as he opened the refrigerator. Cold light washed out from the interior. "You mind if I help myself?"

"A casting," Jess echoed.

"The door you're so quietly trying to open. A casting. A spell."

"You're saying you're some kind of—of magician?"

"Magician," he mused. He drank down a swallow of beer. "Now that's a quaint little English word. You mean the kind that entertains at children's parties, pulls bunnies out of hats?"

He was coming towards her again. A wry smile was twisting his mouth, but the amber eyes reflected something else: a fatigue, Jess thought. A grief.

"Or the kind that puts on big shows in Vegas," he continued, "with costumes and tigers and pretty girls?"

The slanted amber eyes, the silvery nails, the height

and strength of him. The faint, burnt-match scent that rose off his skin. She stepped away from him, suddenly afraid that he might try to touch her.

"Tell me about the boy, Jess. How long has he been in your dreams?"

She said, "Maybe a year."

"Have you dreamed of anyone else? A female, perhaps, green-eyed?"

A thought nagged at her, was gone. "No."

"The boy is real, you know. As real as you are."

Her knees were threatening to buckle beneath her; she had to focus on standing upright.

"We don't know his name," Kai continued. "We don't know where he is. We only know that he is out there. But he can't hide from you, although I'm sure he'll try."

"No," she said. "He's just a painting. A dream. I don't know anything—"

"The boy doesn't know what he is, the entity he carries inside him. We need him, and he needs you. You think you can allow yourself to walk away from that?"

"You're not making any sense to me."

In two swift strides he had closed the distance between them. He grabbed her face, his fingertips pressing in beneath her cheekbones. She was too stunned to react. "I see," he said quietly, more to himself than to her; and let go.

"Get out," she said. "Get out."

"Don't you want to *know* yourself, Jessamy? Don't you want to know what you can truly *do*?"

He held out his hand, long fingers opening like petals unfurling. Two objects lay on his palm. One was a purple box of matches with an address printed on it in black type; the other was a disk of hammered dark metal about the size of a silver dollar. Two images were etched into the metal, facing each other: a serpent on one side, a bird on the other.

"Take them," Kai said quietly, and she did. The disk was thin and cold. The address on the matchbox was in

the meatpacking district, not too far from the Taylor-
Taylor gallery.

He said, "The floating Masquerade. Come see for
yourself. And then, I think, you'll be ready to believe."

She looked up, into the man's amber eyes. He touched
her face, and now she did not flinch or back away.

"Meet me tomorrow night," he said. "Bring the crest.
Show it to the pretty ones at the door. They'll play you
a little, but they'll let you through."

"And if I don't?"

"The boy dies horribly, and the whole world goes to
hell. Many hells, actually." His eyes flashed in the half-
light. He turned away. "Good night, Jess."

Her own voice sounded strange to her, as if echoing
down from a very great distance. "Sweet dreams," she
said.

He laughed, briefly, and was gone.

Seven

I remember you.

He had never forgotten her.

That first encounter in the Cape Town hotel, Table Mountain throwing its shadow over all of them. He had been following her bloodline for the past five centuries, through all its permutations: the ones who lived long and the ones who died early and the ones who carried the Binding deep inside them, always unknowing, passing it on to the next generation like a latent disease.

So as soon as Jessamy Shepard, six years old and newly orphaned, had stepped into the sunlit hotel library, as soon as he saw the fair skin and black hair and blue eyes, something thudded home inside him. In the far corner, an elderly gentleman in a white linen suit dropped his tea, china breaking on carpet, the man in the hotel uniform quickly putting a hand on the old man's arm, then stooping down to pick up the pieces.

The little girl didn't seem to notice. She came into the library, eyes wide and glassy, wiping her hands along her shorts as if desperate to rub something off them.

Kai was sitting in an armchair in the shadow of the

bookcase, windows casting bright squares of sunlight to either side.

He called, "Jessamy."

She didn't seem to hear.

"Jessamy."

The girl looked over, puzzled, then came to him. She was tall for her age, lanky, in denim cutoffs and a red T-shirt emblazoned with a cartoon lizard.

"Oh," she said. "It's you."

Kai leaned forward in the chair, elbows on knees, trying not to startle or scare her. He wore a white cotton shirt, khaki slacks, tinted glasses that concealed the peculiar color of his eyes: just another affluent European. He smiled and said, "I've been in your dreams. Haven't I?"

The girl nodded. He wondered how much longer before the blood-truths, so natural to her now, would seem like nothing more than fancy: the play of a talented child. Jessamy's mother had buried the Binding deep within her at a very young age, bent her life around a definition of "logical" and "normal" that precluded such truths. Kai had not found the mother very interesting, of course, but she had been spared the nightmares and paranoia and bizarre, unseemly "incidents" that had ruined so many of those who'd come before her: those who had been tortured, burned at the stake, locked up and lost in asylums or prisons.

Now he looked at this little girl, wondering how she would grow. She had an athletic quality to her, a proud way of holding her head. A bit of the warrior in this one, or maybe that was wishful thinking. If he ever had to come for her—which was unlikely—he would need a warrior.

"I heard about your parents," he said.

"My parents are dead."

"I know that. I'm very sorry."

Her voice had a flat, numbed quality that matched the expression in her eyes. "I'm my uncle's child now. That's what he told me."

"You are your own child," he said.

She looked at him and nodded. He didn't know if she was placating a grown-up or if his words resonated.

"I want to give you something," Kai said. "Can you come a little closer?"

She eyed him warily.

Kai said, "Am I such a stranger, Jessamy?"

She considered this, hooking a finger over her lip. Kai spread his hands in the air, smiled a little, waiting. The man in the hotel uniform was watching them from his corner, not quite sure what he was seeing. Kai shut him out, focused on the girl. "Jessamy," he said, and took off his glasses. The color of his eyes shifted with his mood; he felt peaceful now and knew they'd be a deep, mellow color, the shade of a setting sun.

She met his eyes with her own and smiled, clapped her hands once, and came forward.

"It is you," she said. "It is you."

"I've been in your dreams."

She nodded, touched his hair experimentally.

She smelled like butter and coconut. She had a sunburn on her shoulders, the skin just starting to peel. His reaction to her surprised him; he was no longer an affectionate man, and he had never been a sentimental one. Children in general had little effect on him. But he had the inexplicable urge to pick up this little girl, promise her the father's love and protection now denied her.

She said, "I don't mind." Hunching up her shoulders. "You can share my dreams if you want. There's space."

Kai was genuinely touched by this. "But you'll grow up," he said. "And I'm not supposed to be a part of your life. I'm not even supposed to be talking to you now."

"Who says?" A glint of steel in her eyes; a hint of the rebel her mother never was. Warrior, Kai thought again. Maybe not wishful thinking after all.

Kai said, "It's best that way. I'm very different from you. I just need to check in on you now and again."

"Why?"

"It's complicated."

She plucked at her lip, unconvinced.

"Here," Kai whispered, and touched the tip of his thumb to her forehead as if baptizing her. The transfer of memory took only seconds; he wasn't as out of practice as he thought. Her eyes widened as the single memory vaulted inside her, braided itself into her own net of imagery.

"The lizard's cute," she whispered.

He touched the lizard appliqué on her shirt. "I thought you'd like it."

The man in the corner was watching them more closely now.

"When you feel scared," Kai said, "when you feel sad, that's the place in your mind you can go. It's a little trick you can do to make yourself feel better. Okay?"

She nodded.

"Go back to your uncle. He'll be looking for you."

"No," Jessamy said, and shook her head. "He doesn't care."

"You'd better go," Kai said gently.

She looked at him, beseeching. He didn't change his expression. She blew out air and spun on her heel and walked away from him. For a moment—just a moment— he thought about taking her with him. A simple invocation, a brief focus of energy, and no one in the hotel would remember that he, or the girl, even existed. He would say, *Come with me,* take her hand, lead her into a different mode of existence.

But if he was going to share a stretch of time with anyone, it would be under different circumstances. He had no wish to play father.

Jessamy turned and hit him with one last, blue-eyed look, as if to reprimand him for the decision that had whistled through his mind in less than a second. "My parents are dead," she said, as if hoping he would tell her that her uncle was wrong, her parents were sitting in a restaurant somewhere, sipping martinis, laughing, oblivious to the sea-soaked grief and wreckage of Trans-Unity Air Flight 242.

"Yes," Kai said to her. "They're dead."

She lifted her chin, then turned and ran out of the library. Kai reached out his mind a little and traced her presence through the hotel.

Yes, she'd gone back to the suite.

He stood up and stretched and slipped on the tinted glasses—the room shading fractions darker—then walked to the tea table in the corner and poured himself a cup. The man in the uniform handed him the sugar, looked as if he wanted to say something but didn't. As Kai took the sugar he brushed the young man's hand with the tips of his fingers: something had happened to the man's little sister, Kai sensed, something that had twisted and darkened this man's entire family. He could have probed further but didn't. Best to respect a person's privacy.

He sipped the tea.

He never expected to talk to Jessamy again.

He was living in Barcelona, dealing in a range of antiquities and rare books, drawn to old things, old beauty. He was amused at how some things, like some people, found their way back to you, winding down through space and time like a dog searching out a beloved owner. A saber he'd purchased in Peking in 1700 and given away years later had come into his Barcelona shop at the end of the last century, wrapped in bubble paper, from a bespectacled young man who wanted to go to California and start up a dot.com. A first edition of *Childe Harold* that the poet himself had given him those years in London, and that Kai had sold off with his other belongings in one of his sporadic "deaths" (after which he reinvented himself somewhere else, in an ever-shifting game of identity). He stumbled across the book two hundred years (and one more death) later, in a dusty little bookshop in Rome, and when he saw his old name inscribed inside the front cover he felt his own ghost reach out from those Regency days, stroke his throat with unseen fingers.

Other objects, too: a silver Byzantine goblet he had favored for years, a minor Van Gogh in a scratched wooden frame, a fur jacket a soon-to-be-legendary stage actress had left behind in his Paris hotel room.

They showed up in museums, catalogs and auctions, private collections, eBay. When you lived as long as he had you could not afford sentiment, nostalgia, or else the gathering weight of your memory would crush you (as others of his kind had discovered), but as his memory broke apart over the years, a book or art object or faded sepia-toned photograph could bring a lost shard of time into focus. *Yes, I was there, I watched them storm the Bastille. My friend Alexandre was imprisoned and beheaded for some senseless bullshit reason. I had an affair with a married woman named Marie-Thérèse, who had a strawberry birthmark above her right breast, and when they came for her as well I smuggled her out of the country.* He would see the thing—the Chinese saber, the book of poetry, the goblet—he would hold it if he could, let the memories pass through him, associations of a life now lost. And then he would put it back, give it away, or sell it: release it into the world and idly wonder when he'd meet up with it again. His own treasured collection was not one of things, but lives—men he had been, roles he had played—and his recent, deepening wish to remember them was, he supposed, a sign of aging, a sharpening awareness of his own mortality. The Summoners lived long—sometimes very long—but not forever.

He had been aware of Jessamy Shepard from the day she was born. When he was capable of it—the strength of his abilities fluctuated—he would look in on her life through dreamshaping or remote viewing. He went to Cape Town to find her, to give her some comfort if he could, and also to satisfy his own curiosity. To see her in the flesh. Her mother, Rachel, had been a gentle woman, highly intelligent, but weak, dominated by her father and her brother.

And as another century moved toward its end, spinning out the fears of doom and apocalypse characteristic of such periods, he thought back to Jess and to that moment when he had actually (seriously?) considered taking her with him to Spain. A foolish impulse, and he was glad he'd overridden it. Still, he found himself wishing he had taken something of hers—a little talisman— although the thought of what that could have been (the plastic watch on her wrist?) made him smile and shake his head at himself.

But after Cape Town, he was restless again. He closed up his shop, sold the Barcelona apartment, stored some of his things in the house outside London and gave away everything else. He went to the Caribbean, traveling through the islands, pausing unexpectedly at St. Martin when he became involved with a woman there, an expat named Celine who had a six-year-old son. And he found himself playing *father* after all.

Until Ashika found them.

Until Ashika changed everything.

Now, in New York, he had taken a suite at the Four Seasons. He dropped his card-key on the table, walked through the sand-and-bronze rooms to the terrace. He stepped outside, sliding the door shut behind him. The air swept his face. He looked down into the city. Once, he had stood in this same spot and watched horses and carriages. That had been a time when a young and provincial New York worshiped the great European cities. Now it worshiped itself.

Kai took off his gloves, took a pocketknife from his coat pocket. The knife was a pretty thing with an ivory handle. He hesitated for only a moment before slashing open his left palm. He lifted his hand, turned it over. Blood dripped onto the stone. "Shemayan," he called.

Sending his voice, his thoughts, out into the darkness.
"Shemayan."

The air slipped over him. But there was something
else that edged the wind now: a smoky, spicy scent, a
hint of something darker than the shadows. His blood
began to disappear before it hit the stone, as if the air
itself were drinking it in. Kai watched as a new shadow
formed, grew into the shape of a man as tall as himself.
The shadow-hands reached up to the shadow-head, drew
aside the shadow-hood.

Kai said, "Welcome back, my friend."

Shemayan's face was pale as moonstone, as gently luminescent. His features were sharp and thin, his eyes
hooded in deep sockets. Colorless eyes. Death had
leached all color long ago.

—Greetings, Your Highness.

The words were diffident; the tone was not.

—The Pact is broken. The others no longer trust you.

Kai drew his wounded hand against his chest. "I found
her," he said.

—My prince. You must reunite your Pact. You can't
accomplish this alone.

Kai ducked his head in acknowledgement. But he did
not want to talk about the group of spellcasters with
whom he had crossed into Summoning, all of them
bound to each other through blood and deep magic. Kai
knew that the Dreamlines that linked them, and gave
them greater power as a group than they possessed as
individuals, had been thinning for years.

And instead of dealing with the problem, he had
turned a blind eye, dropped out of the Dreamlines
entirely.

—They will think it was you. You've been too aloof,
too enigmatic, for too long. You were unwise, my prince.

"We all came undone," Kai said, the words painful,
"in one way or another. We neglected the rituals. We
broke away from one another. The Pact turned corrupt
a long, long time ago."

—Regardless. You are easy to accuse, and you made yourself more so.

"Yes," Kai admitted, and then, "She grew up beautiful, Shem. You'd be proud."

—The damage?

Kai paused. He thought of Jessamy's mother, Rachel, the placid, productive life she had led. "That depends, I suppose. If circumstances were different—"

—But circumstances being what they are. She's cut off from her own nature.

"Our nature. Yes."

Shem's mouth pursed in distaste. Even now, he was reluctant to concede that a descendent like Jess Shepard had the right to her own humanity.

—I sense your plan. It is right. Take her to the creature Del.

Kai was quiet for a moment, his gaze shifting beyond Shem to the near-distant silhouette of the Empire State Building, rocket-shaped tip blazing with light. He was surprised by the weight of his own reluctance. The same plan that had seemed inevitable a few days ago now seemed dangerous, foolhardy.

He didn't say anything; he didn't have to; Shem could sense his second thoughts.

—There's no other choice. Time moves quickly, princeling, and the woman herself is of small consequence. It is the Binding we need.

"The Binding would be useless if she's too traumatized to—"

—You don't think you're being just a little condescending?

A wry smile twisted the colorless mouth. Only Shemayan could have addressed him as *princeling* without giving offense; likewise, only Kai could have so openly questioned Shemayan's judgment.

—I suspect that my child is made of strong stuff. Take her to Del.

"Del can't be trusted."

—He will help her for his own reasons.

"Which is what concerns me."

—The woman must be tested sooner or later, my prince. If she doesn't have it within her to handle a trickster like Del, then we are all lost, and can spend these last days wallowing in our little lusts and hedonisms.

Again, the pale smile.

—So we might as well know now.

Kai absorbed this in silence. Shemayan was right, of course; he always was. In his time he had been the greatest mind in the Labyrinth, employed by the king himself to tutor the royal sons. As an impatient child-prince, Kai had not liked his tutor: thought him too cold, sardonic, lacking emotion and passion. Shem wasn't fun to be around, like the jesters and entertainers; he wasn't stylish like the courtiers, or romantic like the poets. But then the slavegirl-demon and her "children" had come with their dark blazing wrath, rampaging through the city, leaving it broken and smashed. The actors and courtiers and poets were lost, scattered or killed, as were Kai's father and brothers. It was Shemayan who had saved him. It was Shemayan who had saved so many of them.

Now, on this twenty-first-century Manhattan terrace, Kai ducked his head in acknowledgement and surrender. "I'll take her to Del."

—Bakal Ashika is out there even now, my prince. Gathering strength and energy. Soon she will release her children, and she will be powerful again. And they will seek to complete what they started so many centuries ago.

"I know," Kai said.

He felt the blood from his hand soaking through his shirt, warm and moist against his skin.

—Save the woman if you can. But if her life must be rendered forfeit, you must not stand in the way of that. We all pay our price in one way or another.

He paused.

—As I did. As you did.

"She's an innocent," Kai said.

—Not for long. Make me proud, my prince.

Shem's eyes turned flat and hard.

—Both of you.

He folded himself into the shadow, disappeared.

And Kai was alone on the terrace, with the wind and the skyline and the drifting sounds of traffic. Loneliness shafted through him, cold and clean as moonlight. It was always like this following a Contact, as if the honed awareness of his solitude was part of the price to be paid, along with the wound.

He glanced at his hand, opened and closed the fingers.

There were things he could have said, but hadn't. He never did. Things like: *I miss you. My friend. My mentor.* It was not the kind of thing to be given voice, by either of them.

One other thing he could have said, there on the stone-and-cast-iron terrace pitched seventeen stories high in the New York night. *I could fall in love with her.* The idea of saying that to Shem—to anyone, but particularly him—was unthinkable.

It's forbidden, I know, and wisely so. But I could fall in love with her.

Eight

Ramsey Doe

Dearmont, Minnesota

The boy was flying.

Sunlight shattering over him as he skimmed the iron railing, body leaning into perfect balance, harmony, and then he was in the air, trees shivering their leaves at the edges of his vision; and then the *cra-ack* of impact as pavement flew up to the board and Ramsey Doe, fifteen years old, was gliding, smooth, standing easy on the Tony Hawk as it took him to where tarmac met grass, to where Abe and Tim waited on the wrought-iron bench, Abe's own set-up flipped over by his feet.

"Nice, bro," Abe said.

Ramsey grinned and joined them on the bench.

A midsummer's afternoon: the light slanting low in that way he liked, mellowing out the sky, burnishing grass and trees and the red-and-yellow metal of the kids' jungle gym.

". . . Swimming with the dolphins," Tim was saying. Ramsey could tell he relished the phrase. Tim used it again, tilting his broad, ruddy face in Ramsey's direction.

"You interested in swimming with the dolphins, my brother?"

Once a month Tim visited his older brother in Detroit and came back with several CD cases filled with ecstasy, the pills arranged and pressed beneath layers of Kleenex. It made him very popular at the middle-to-affluent suburban high school they attended.

"Nah," Ramsey said. "Not today."

They walked out of the park, down O'Henry, past ranch and split-level houses. A beagle, tied to a frontyard oak, barked at them and leaped against his leash.

And then Tim said—as Ramsey had known either he or Abe finally would—"So what's the deal with Lauren? You think of her like a sister yet?" The grin on his face as he said this suggested the impossible nature of such a thing. Lauren Campbell, with her dancer's (now exdancer's) body and waist-length river of hair, her full-lipped mouth and the small perfect mole beneath her right eye.

"Lauren," Ramsey mumbled. He stepped on his board, pushed off, wheeling over the sidewalk cracks and bumps. Abe yelled at him to wait. Ramsey only grinned and stepped up the pace.

The Campbells lived in a renovated Victorian near the city limits, where the suburbs bled out into fields and the woods opened out onto the interstate highway. You couldn't see the highway from the Campbells' property, but Ramsey had dreams about it. Stark deep-sleep visions of half-starved dogs barking at him from the woods, as some unseen enemy hunted him down the swath of concrete. The more he tried to run, the more he realized the weight of his own shackles, the long chain dragging out behind him.

Ramsey had been with this family for eight months now. He was slipping up, thinking of this place as *home* instead of what it truly was: a living situation, not his first and not his last. Because these situations never lasted. Sooner or later something changed, and the family ejected you: sometimes with tears and apologies, sometimes with naked relief.

His foster mother was in the living room, reading.

"Hey," he said. He saw the gleam of her crucifix against her freckled collarbone.

"Hey," Dorrie said. "John gets home at seven. So dinner's at half-past."

They all ate together, almost every night, sitting round the table like one of those families on TV.

"Cool."

"There's a letter for you. On the hallway table."

"Cool."

Ramsey tended not to keep in touch with people—tended not to get close to begin with. But he was surprised by the number of people who kept in touch with him. He picked up the letter en route to the stairs. But then Dorrie said, "Ramsey," and he doubled back to the living room doorway.

Dorrie had closed her book, marking her place with her finger. She was looking at him with a troubled expression.

"About Lauren," she said. "I know that since she got back, she hasn't been—She hasn't been very welcoming to you—"

"It's okay," Ramsey said.

Girl comes home from ballet school with her knee ripped up and her dreams stripped away, finds some bookworm skate-punk foster kid embedded in her house, her family, her life, as if he had every right to be there. He wasn't sure what Dorrie had expected. Lauren didn't owe him anything.

"She'll come round," Dorrie said, "just give it time, just don't take it personally."

And in that moment, Ramsey felt it: that strange, hot flash of clarity that sometimes overcame him, whispered through his blood, his bones, pulsed up behind his eyes and altered the way he saw the world. He looked at Dorrie and grasped (in that instinctive, sudden way he had that he didn't understand but accepted as part of him, like his gray eyes or skinny-boy build) her daughter's aloofness, restlessness, raging need for life outside Dearmont. He saw how these things cut against Dorrie's own nature, made Lauren an enigma to her. Dorrie loved the girl with all her heart, but she wasn't quite the daughter that Dorrie had expected. Or wanted.

The moment passed.

That hot, alien feeling left as quickly as it had come. Dorrie was still waiting.

"I'm not taking it personally," he told her. Which was true. Whenever he sensed Lauren's gaze on him, Ramsey did not feel himself an object of hostility but more like some kind of equation she was trying to solve. For that, he could hardly blame her. If Lauren Campbell was an enigma to her sweet, schoolteacher mother, Ramsey Doe was an enigma to himself.

His upstairs bedroom was small, the angled ceiling making it smaller. But it was his, and the door locked, and that was all that mattered.

Besides, he didn't have much stuff. Jeans, T-shirts, a battered army jacket hung in the closet. A college-store print of Gauguin's *Where Do We Come From? What Are We? Where Are We Going?* hung on his wall. Secondhand paperbacks filled the bookcase: thrillers and some horror, but he was also reading his way through a list of novels that had been banned or challenged in high schools across the country. *The Color Purple. Foxfire. A Clockwork Orange. The Handmaid's Tale.*

Add in his notebooks and journals, and that was it for worldly possessions. A person should travel light, he figured (as if he himself had any other choice). You never knew what you might pick up along the way.

He walked to the window and lifted the blind.

They were in the backyard, as they often were, be-

cause Dorrie wouldn't allow smoking in the house (a
rule that Lauren often violated late at night, the scent
of the smoke seeping into Ramsey's room). They sat on
lawn chairs facing the woods, Lauren's injured leg
propped in front of her. The air was soft with late June.
Paul Andes was leaning over Lauren, whispering in her
ear, and she was laughing.

When school was in session Paul Andes was part of
the foyer crowd, so called because they hung out on the
benches in the school lobby, beneath the skylights, as if
the sunlight itself were officially anointing them. Andes
had a reputation among the more marginalized kids as
one of the decent ones. Friendly with different cliques,
never bullied or taunted anybody.

Now, he tipped back the lawn chair until he was looking up at the house. His eyes made sudden contact
with Ramsey.

Ramsey stepped back from the window. He had nothing against the foyer crowd. They thought they were
movie stars, rock stars, CEOs. But high school would
end soon enough. The real world was coming for them.

The letter was still in his hands. His name and address
were printed in block letters in black felt-tip pen. No
return address. He ripped open the envelope and a
folded slip of paper fell to the floor. Ramsey stooped to
retrieve it and as he plucked the paper off the hardwood
a sense of *wrongness* flooded through him, even before
he turned the paper over and saw more words printed
in black felt-tip, stark and cold as any ransom note:

I know what you are.

*The world will burn
because of you.*

The breeze moved in through the window, carrying the
scent of Lauren's cigarette. His hands went cold. The

cold slipped through his body and hollowed out his stomach.

He ripped up the letter and envelope both. Went into the bathroom, rained the pieces into the toilet. It was only then he realized he should have checked the postmark.

Nine

Cocooned in the tiny second-floor study, Ramsey checked his e-mail, sent off a few replies, then surfed some music and skateboarding sites.

But the real, the important business was darkhouse.com, a site for fans and writers of goth fiction. Whenever Ramsey lay in bed, insomniac, the way he'd done the last night, he passed time by writing something in his head. Now he went into the "poetry" room and dumped his latest from mind to keyboard. He was too lazy for titles.

Untitled
By Nemesis

This is the battle of longing and belonging.
(the nest that cradles and protects you
vs. sunstroked highway)
You long for home and the leaving of home.
For the highways/roads and avenues/trails and pathways
Sun a hand on your neck that guides you
Night a thing that comes down soft
like cashmere.

You long for pretty girls and silken adventures
For a world that cracks at your feet like an egg
You long to lose yourself.
You long for the one who will find you.

Ramsey went from there into the site's chat room, where he found some of the usual suspects.

Lizardking: *. . . nemesis, my man, you're back. I really liked that last piece you posted, that untitled thing on apocalypse? It rocked. Seriously, man.*

Nemesis: *thanks. I just put up a new one*

Tigerlily: *. . . . are u a night writer, nemesis? . . . you seem so in touch with the ebb and the flow of the night. . . . its energies, its powers. . . .* ☺

Flake: *your stuff's a bit obscure for me. Sorry, Nem.*

Nemesis: *don't worry bout it*

Lizardking: *Are you ever gonna get your work together? Send it out for publication or something?*

Nemesis: *no*

Tigerlily: *but writing should be your LIFE. Writing is your SOUL & u should commit to your SOUL! What do we have in this life if we don't have our SOUL?*

Flake: *. . . pizza . . . beer?*

Voices were rising from elsewhere in the house, catching his attention. He glanced up from the monitor. He heard Lauren say clearly and loudly, "Why can't you just respect my decision?" followed by a low, male voice he assumed to be Paul's.

Not his business. Ramsey swiveled back to the screen. The chat was going on without him; Tigerlily and Soothsr were arguing over a plot point from a vampire TV show Ramsey never watched. He was scrolling through the lines of transcript when a dialog window opened up in the corner of the screen:

Lizardking (*whispering*): *Nem baby? You there?*

Lizardking (*whispering*): *These idiots are boring the crap out of me. I wanted to chat privately for a moment. . . .*

Ramsey grinned, touched fingers to keys.

Nemesis: *What up, dude?*

Lizardking: *something you might be interested in. your apoc. piece made me think you'd like this. Go to bloodangel.com and check out the song. then e-mail me. Tell me what you think.*

Nemesis: *is this you or your band or something?*

Lizardking: *I wish. A friend turned me on to it. Fucking amazing. You seem pretty cool so I thought I'd pass it on. . . . You should come into the desert with us. I'm putting this group together. I'm in San Francisco, where are you?*

Nemesis: *the desert? camping or something?*

Lizardking: *check it out and get back to me. my e-mail's carma@quicktime*

Nemesis: *ok*

Lizardking: *shit. out of time, out of money, and this place is closing anyway. Gotta go.*

Nemesis: *ok see you*

Lizardking: *I think so yeah*

Ramsey returned to the main chat room to say good-bye to the others and then closed it down. He typed in bloodangel.com. In the moments the website took to load he listened to the sounds of the house: a car starting up in the driveway, the *da-da-dum* of the theme music from "Law and Order," clinking sounds from the kitchen.

And then.

Stark black letters on an acid-green background:

TRANS
(under construction)

And below that, drawn in stark, simple lines, a road winding off to a vanishing point and the silhouette of a hitchhiker.

And below that:

ARE YOU READY FOR YOUR JOURNEY?

He ran the cursor over the image of the road and clicked.

Nothing.

He clicked on the hitcher's silhouette.

A dialog box appeared on the screen, image of little papers flying out of a little folder as the song downloaded. Ramsey waited, tapping his fingers on the desk. He heard screams coming off the television in the den. Someone had just discovered that episode's dead body.

The downloading completed.

The song started: drumbeats rising up, stark and tribal and catchy.

Then the heartbeat of a bass line.

Mournful swell of lead guitar. Keyboards.

It was interesting. A hard-core violence of guitar and drums, nailed through with fat juicy beats. Definitely not radio-friendly. MTV wouldn't be playing it either. It didn't really work, except . . . except, well, yeah. It worked. It worked *fine*.

And then, after long minutes of just music: the voice.

Her voice.

You were screaming and dreaming when you fell, she sang, but on that first listen—and then the second and the third—Ramsey wasn't listening to the lyrics. She could have been singing in Swahili for all he cared; what mattered was that melody, stark and brutal and haunting

and pounding, stabbing through his skin, amping up his
heart; what mattered was that voice, like honey mixed
with broken glass, raw and rich and sweet and deep and
thick and wounded, starting out soft and rising into the
bridge and exploding with the chorus while the guitar
throbbed and wailed behind her and the drums counted
out an otherworldly heartbeat. Ramsey fell back in the
chair, closed his eyes. He let the song go through him.
Go into him. That female voice like nothing he'd heard
before, that didn't seem fully human, a disembodied
thing drifting up out of the computer like magic. A voice
of pure magic, singing just for him.

The song was still thrumming in his veins when he
went upstairs.

The door to Lauren's room was open. She was sitting
at her vanity table, wearing low-slung pajama pants and
a snug black tank, and she was looking straight at him.

"Ramsey?"

He didn't respond. His mind was too full of the song.
*The world is breaking down/There are dark things on the
wind/And the wild cry inside you just gets stronger . . .*

"You seem different," Lauren said.

She was studying him in the way he now found so
familiar: as if he were a question that needed an answer.
He wondered if she was any closer to finding one. Her
hair was braided into two plaits, hanging down along her
shoulders. It was an odd look for her. She was holding
her left hand beneath the table, out of sight.

She said, "Come here."

He had not been in her room before—at least, not
since she'd moved home and reclaimed it with her
things, her light vanilla scent. There was a pair of ballet
slippers on the windowsill. They were crushed and
broken-looking: the satin worn through, discolored, the
blocked-off toes stained with blood.

Lauren lifted her hand from beneath the table, displayed a pair of scissors. "You haven't been very friendly to me."

"You haven't been friendly to me."

She snipped at the air, then set the scissors on the table and fiddled with one of her braids. "I guess that's right," she admitted.

"I guess so."

"I heard a story about you." She watched him in the mirror. "I heard you don't remember anything about your life before the age of seven."

He shrugged.

She continued, "I heard you, like, just wandered into a police station in St. Paul and your clothes were covered with blood. And you wouldn't say anything. People asked you what your name was, where you lived, where your parents were, and you didn't say anything. You didn't answer any questions."

That wasn't true, exactly. When they had asked him how old he was Ramsey had held up seven fingers.

Lauren said, "So that really happened? That's not just some kind of, you know, urban myth?"

"Who told you this?"

"Paul. He used to live there. I mean, my parents must know, from your file and everything—but it's not the kind of thing they'd talk about. Paul said he remembered it from the papers, TV, because his mother used to talk about you at dinner, she felt so sorry for you."

"It wasn't my blood," Ramsey said. "They ran tests. It wasn't my blood."

"And you couldn't tell them what happened to you?"

"No." His voice sharper than he'd intended.

"You didn't remember anything." She sounded awed. He could tell what she was thinking: *Like something from a movie.* Except it wasn't any movie, it was *him*, his *life*. "You didn't even remember how to speak?"

"I remembered how to speak. I just didn't *want* to. I didn't *want* to speak for two years." He had drawn a lot of pictures. Everybody in the world, it seemed, had wanted him to make pictures, sitting him down again and again in front of crayons, paper, paints.

"And so they never figured out—"

"Your walls are bare," Ramsey said.

She was so startled she left off her question. Ramsey glanced round, taking in the empty walls, the off-color rectangles where posters had been. He could feel that hot wave of clarity breaking over him, washing up through his very bones. "They were dance posters. Baryshnikov, right? I bet you loved Baryshnikov. I bet he was your first big crush when you were a little girl, even though he was already kind of old by then. I bet you saw, *White Nights* fifteen times."

"Nine," Lauren said. She swiveled in the chair and looked at him. "Nine times. You get this stuff from my mother?"

"You took down all those posters the night you got back, right? 'Cause your knee hurt so bad and you were so pissed off. And I bet you did something dramatic with them. It wasn't enough to just throw them out. You had to take them somewhere and . . ." He paused, then in his mind he saw it: the leap of flame, the curling and charring and crumbling of glossy paper.

". . . and burn them."

Lauren's mouth had fallen open, her head jutting forward: a graceless pose of incredulity. Ramsey barely noticed. He was following it through in his mind, trying to think of where she could burn the posters. "The barbecue on the patio," he said.

"It was five in the morning," Lauren said. "I thought I was being quiet."

She had tucked her good knee against her chest, her slippered foot balanced on the edge of the chair. She hesitated, then added rather dryly, "And then I roasted marshmallows for breakfast."

"Because now you can eat what you want."

"I can get as fat as I want and no one will kick me

out of anything." Her eyes narrowed a little. "So what
are you, Sherlock Holmes?"

"Hardly."

"You *spying* on me?" But from the puzzled expression on her face he could tell, even as she said it, that
she didn't believe it.

He didn't bother to answer.

She persisted, "Then how . . . ?"

"So what are the scissors for?"

"Why don't you tell me? You figured out all that
other stuff."

"Are you really going to cut off your hair?"

Lauren hugged her knee to her chest. Then she picked
up the scissors and held them out to Ramsey. A new
expression opened up through her eyes: a mixture of
daring, delight.

She said, "Do it for me."

He looked at the scissors, then back at her. Her mouth
was curved in a smirk . . . or the beginning of a genuine smile.

"You can't be serious."

"You can figure out that stuff about the posters," she
was baiting him now, enjoying this, and he found himself
ducking his head in response, "but you can't figure out
if I'm serious?"

"Go to a salon. Get it done by a pro."

"No. I mean, a salon wouldn't . . . Having it done at
a salon just wouldn't . . ."

He picked up the thought for her.

". . . Be *symbolic* enough," Ramsey concluded.

A moment passed when she didn't say anything. And
then the smirk opened up into the smile, going into him
like sunlight. "Well," she said. "I guess you kind of understand. I didn't think anyone would."

He took the scissors from her.

"You have beautiful hair," he said.

"I've had it like this since I was ten. For *dance*. You
know? It was for *dance*."

"There's a poem by Robert Browning." He felt uncomfortably close to babbling, but couldn't seem to stop himself. "About this guy who goes psycho on his mistress and wants her to stay with him forever, you know, be *his* forever, never ever ever leave him. So he strangles her with her own long hair. So that way he gets his wish."

"All the more reason to cut it off."

"Your mother will kill me," Ramsey muttered, and something about the way he said that made her laugh, and then he laughed as well. He picked up her left braid, felt the weave of it between his fingers, then scissored it off at the base of her neck. The braid came away like a cord unplugged. She watched in the mirror. Her eyebrows lifted a little. He picked up the remaining braid, worked the scissors through it, and then it was done.

Lauren leaned towards the mirror.

Thick, choppy hair ending just above her shoulders. She shook it out, ran her hands through it. Her whole face seemed different: older, angular, less pretty, more serious. "I like it," he told her.

"I feel like I just got hatched," she said, "from all that hair. Now I'm shiny-new."

"You're an odd one, Lauren Campbell."

Her grin widened. "So are you."

"I'm a freak," he admitted.

She was looking at him as if that wasn't a bad thing.

"I fought with Paul," she said, a while later.

It was past one in the morning, and they were talking in hushed voices. Her parents were asleep at the other end of the hall. She had stolen some scotch from the downstairs liquor cabinet. "Single malt," she informed him. "Twelve years old. Never drink it younger." She was smoking a Marlboro Light, tapping ash into a coffee mug, her body angled so that the smoke drifted out the open window. He refused her offer of a cigarette. He wasn't touching his scotch, either, but she didn't seem to notice.

"Paul wanted me to go to his parents' cabin this weekend," she said. "His parents are going to be there, right, and they know my parents and my parents trust Paul and everything, so it's no big deal."

"But you said no."

"I didn't expect him to be so *pissy* about it."

"Be careful with him."

The words slipped out before he even realized he was going to say them. Lauren squinted at him, laughed a little. She flicked ash into the coffee mug. "You sound *parental*."

"Sorry."

"No, it's fine. It's cute, even. What have you got against Paul?"

"I don't know. Just a feeling. It sounds stupid, I know—"

"I respect feelings. *Intuition*. It's not just women that have it." She extinguished the cigarette and lifted the mug to the windowsill, out of sight, as if the remains of her smoking disgusted her.

Ramsey said, "You don't want to go to the cabin because of your injury?"

"Maybe that was part of it," Lauren said. "But it's something else. I wouldn't tell Paul what it was and that's why he got angry. I haven't told my parents either. My father would say I'm wasting my money and my mother . . . God knows what she would say. She has some strange ideas." She looked directly at Ramsey. "They think I'm going shopping with Aimee tomorrow."

"I won't say anything."

"I know. Otherwise I wouldn't tell you."

"So—"

"I was thinking you might like to come along."

He was too surprised to respond.

"This person we're going to see? Maybe he could help

you, your mysterious past and all." Lauren scratched the
back of her neck, said, "You know something? I haven't
told anybody this, but for a while I got—I got kind of
obsessed with tarot cards. Look." Using her bed for support, she hopped over to the night table, opened the
bottom drawer, and removed a bundle of yellow silk scarf.
She brought it back to Ramsey, unfolded the sunny
fabric.

"Tarot cards," she said again, fanning them out along
the floor. "The funny thing is, I don't believe in them.
But after the thing with my knee—I got addicted to
them. I never gave readings to anyone. I just did them
for myself. Over and over."

The cards were medieval in theme: characters in long
flowing clothes who had slipped out of an Arthurian ro-
mance. Cups and wands, swords and pentacles. They
meant nothing to him.

But one card snagged his eye like a fishhook catching
seaweed. A dark-haired woman in a long blue dress sat
between two pillars. She clasped a book with a scarlet
binding. Her eyes were very blue.

". . . Just felt panicked," Lauren was saying. "And
looking for answers, I guess . . . You know? . . . You
ever get like that?" She paused, then said, "Priestess."

The word startled him away from the card.

"Necromancer," he said, and he didn't know why.

Lauren frowned at him. "Priestess," she said again,
pointedly, and tapped the card with her finger. She
closed her eyes and recited from memory: *"She holds
secret knowledge and wisdom, the mysteries of which will
only be revealed when the candidate is properly ready.
The veil between the pillars represents the darkness before
dawn, the state before enlightenment."* She paused,
opened her eyes, took a sip of her scotch. "The promise," she said dramatically, "of revelation."

Ramsey picked up the card and turned it facedown:
turning that fierce blue gaze away from him, that book
so heavy in her lap. *Lauren is wrong.* The voice rose up

inside him like a dark, secret fish. *Lauren is wrong. She isn't a priestess. She is—*

His chest tightened.

She is—

Lauren was looking at him.

She is part of the betrayal.

"Ramsey?" Lauren said.

"I'm sorry," he said. "I just—" He pressed a hand against his temple. *Sometimes I think crazy things,* he wanted to say, but did not. *Sometimes I hear this voice, this dreamvoice, I hear it so clearly, even when I'm wide awake.* "Headache," he said instead.

"I've been talking too much," Lauren said. "I know that. I'm sorry."

"Jesus Christ, Lauren, don't apologize. I'll listen to you anytime."

She looked at him for a beat, said, "You really mean that, don't you?"

He glanced away from her. Said quickly, "This thing tomorrow. You're going to see someone who . . . reads tarot cards professionally?"

Lauren tilted her head to the side, the chopped-off hair brushing her shoulder.

"Not quite," she said.

Ten

The address was an effort to find: an unmarked steel door at the end of an alley. Only the faint thump of music suggested life behind the brick wall. Jess tried the door, half expecting it to be locked, half expecting some avant-garde type to rise before her and thunder *Thou art not cool enough* before casting her outside. But the door opened easily. She went up two inside steps, opened a second door.

Stepping into a small white hall that reeked of fresh paint. A staircase to her left led upwards and down.

"My girl, you're not prepared for this place."

Tucked against the wall opposite the stairwell was a reception desk. Two tall, slender women stood behind it and looked at her. One had purple curly hair cascading to a narrow waist. She wore a shiny bronze jumpsuit that laced up the sides. The second was a platinum blonde squeezed into a vinyl corset, long legs balanced on deadly stilettos. She held a switchblade in one hand, using the tip of the blade to clean her long fingernails.

"Stop," the purple-haired one said to Jess.

"In the name of love," added the blonde.

They looked at each other and giggled.

Jess said, "I'm looking for Kai Youngblood."

The purple-haired one snapped her gum. "A lot of people are looking for God, honey, that don't mean they're ever gonna find Him."

"Or Her," the other one added.

"You're very cute," the first one said generously. "You're just *savagely* underdressed. Go down the street, maybe Sweet Zone will take you."

"I have this," Jess said. She was starting to feel like a fool. But she fished the small silver disk from her pocket, held it out for them to see.

Purple Hair plucked it from Jess's fingers. She studied it. She showed it to her companion. They studied it together. They looked at Jess. Something new surfaced in their expressions . . . something that looked very much like awe.

"If your man is around," said Blonde, "he's downstairs."

Purple Hair was still staring.

Blonde pointed at her with the switchblade. "So don't just *stand there*. Take your fine self downstairs."

The staircase was narrow, dark and winding, thumping with bass.

Someone was slumped on the bottom step.

She thought he was unconscious, until he stirred and lifted his head. He was maybe sixteen, naked from the waist up, rib bones pushing against his skin. A blue, glistening powder decorated his chest and back, looping up from the ragged waistband of his jeans to the base of his throat. His eyes were bloodshot, heavy-lidded.

"Jax it with me," he said softly, and held out his hand.

Cupped in the palm was a mound of blue powder.

"We can jax it together," he whispered. He gave her a moist-lipped grin, dipping his fingertips in the powder and drawing them down along both cheekbones. She thought of fairy dust mixed with war paint and had no idea what the hell it was. Her knowledge of the club scene stopped with ecstasy (and she herself had preferred cocaine, before giving it up—in one brutal swoop—with cigarettes).

"Maybe next time," Jess said, not unkindly, and side-stepped him on the stair.

As she walked towards the heavy curtain that blocked off the end of the hall, she heard him call, "Gotta be careful, big sister. All the pretty things gotta be careful . . ."

She swept back the curtain and stepped beyond.

Her first thought: it wasn't a club.

It was a spectacle.

The cavernous space was made more so by the heavy gilded mirrors that leaned against the walls, reflecting the room and multiplying the population. Iron staircases wound up into balconies where sinewy figures leaned against railings and sipped from long-stemmed glasses, gazing into the sea of bodies below. Above them all, two voluptuous women sat on swings suspended from the ceiling, describing wide arcs in the haze-filled air. Their long white hair trailed behind them, blew back against their bodies, streamed out again. Ropes hung in a far corner, small lithe figures twisting and slithering along their lengths like snakes. On stainless-steel pedestals throughout the room, girls and boys were posed like living art, rendered immobile by the white leather straps that crisscrossed their limbs and bodies, forced them into contrived, unnatural positions. As Jess watched, a woman in a red sequined catsuit climbed onto a pedestal and crouched beside a boy-sculpture. She held a chocolate to his mouth. After a moment, he accepted, the chocolate disappearing between his lips; she waited a moment and then offered him another.

Savagely underdressed, Purple Hair had called her. She saw men and women alike dressed in lush, flamboyant styles: feather capes, gleaming snakeskin bodysuits, elaborate ensembles of silk, velvet, fur, leather and vinyl, that clung or draped or fell to the floor. Some wore masks—exquisitely crafted masks studded with stones and feathers. As they danced—everyone dancing—to a world beat–techno fusion, bass and flutes and pulsing, thrumming rhythms.

She felt eyes on her—crawling across her—as she angled through the crowd to the bar. Yet when she sought to return the looks, gazes broke away from her like thin bones snapping.

And it was then she started to see the marks, like pale, glittering tattoos. The same blue substance on the boy in the stairwell now surfaced on a man's inner wrist as he lifted his drink; glistened on the back of a woman's naked shoulder; described a cross on a laughing man's cheek. Jess passed beneath a wrought-iron cage that hung on chains from the ceiling. She turned and looked up through the bars: a girl contortionist was standing on her hands, bent neatly in half, the top of her head nestled against her buttocks, her small bare feet pointed through the bars. In the flickering light, the glittering blue streaks on her face and body were so wide and thick they looked carved into her skin. The girl's eyes were hollowed out and haunted.

A hard edge slammed against her; Jess realized she had knocked over a martini glass, pink liquid spreading onto the bar's beaten-metal surface. The owner of the drink didn't appear to be anywhere. The bartender was at the far end, serving a woman in a purple dress with a mandarin collar. Jess felt a quick shock of recognition: wasn't she that blonde supermodel, the one in the Versace ads . . . ?

A tall blade-thin man stepped into her line of vision. He wore old-fashioned velvet coattails, rather tattered, braided long black hair draped along his shoulder. His eyes were dark, but had the same shape, same uncanny luster, as Kai's. "I have something for you," he said, smiling at her, as he lifted a walking cane and placed it on the bar. It was tipped with a heavy silver death's head. He took a silver cigarette case from his pocket, opened it, and held it toward her. "Have some," he said generously. "You look like you're in need."

The case was filled with more of the blue powder. The man repelled her, but she couldn't help her curiosity: "What is it?"

"A taste of the Dreamlines."

"Of what?"

He grinned. "You must be new. Careful. These are deep, deep waters for a novice." He paused. "My name is Salik. And you are . . . ?"

"What are the Dreamlines?" she said.

"Oh," he said, still grinning, "the Dreamlines are a place of power—*first* power, *original* power, if you go deep enough. They bridge all the realms."

"The realms?"

He waved a hand. "Realms, worlds, dimensions, call them what you want."

"Oh . . ."

He grinned even wider. "This"—he gestured with the powder—"will catapult your mind straight there. Want to try?"

"What's the downside?"

"It turns your brain to sludge. Eventually. But a small price to pay, I assure you."

"I like my brain the way it is."

"What a shame."

She was turning away from him when he said, "But wait. Doesn't this belong to you?" He held out the silver disk Kai had given her. His nails were long, curved, and silver-tinted. His other hand was encased in a black glove, held to his side as if it were wounded.

She reached for the disk. She felt the small cold weight of it in her palm—and then nothing.

The coin was gone.

The man grinned again and plucked it from the air.

"I haven't seen this crest in a long, long time. So what's your connection with our beloved Kai?" Twisting his mouth on the word *beloved*. "His *royal highness* Kai? He's been gone a very long time, you know. Some of us were starting to wonder."

Ignore him, a voice warned, but again, the surge of curiosity: "Wonder what?"

"What he's been up to. What he might be responsible for." The man's smile widened. "Perhaps you hadn't heard. The official ending of things has officially begun."

Her mind flashed on Kai's words: *The boy dies horribly, and the whole world goes to hell. Many hells, actually.* Jess felt her eyes itch and water and as she closed them, rubbed them, she had the sudden tilted feeling that this club and this man Salik and her desire to find Kai were already a memory sunk deep in the past, that she would open her eyes to a future made present, to a series of blasted, twisted landscapes, everything burning, screaming, and dying.

Her eyes snapped open.

"You can see it, can't you?" There was a glitter in Salik's eyes, in his voice: *This man,* Jess realized, *this man is not fully sane.* "You can see it. Can't you?"

She said nothing.

"There will be a whole new world order," the man went on. "And it won't belong to your kind, or even to Kai's. So you might want to form a more strategic alliance."

The man leaned towards her, smiling. His teeth were crooked and uneven. "Kai Youngblood," he said distinctly, "is spoiled weak royal scum. But myself, well, I could be your friend. It will be good to have friends in the days ahead. Why don't you come with me for a bit?" His grin widened. "In fact, you look familiar—"

"Fuck off," Jess said, and moved away from him.

Except his hand slipped out, thumb and fingers encircling her wrist—a light, slithering touch, there and gone.

"Quite familiar," the man said. "You're a painter, aren't you? That delicious young thing in Sara Nolan's stable. I was at your show the other night. This is getting more interesting all the time. What could His Highness possibly want with you?"

The feeling started in her wrist, swarming up her arm

like light. She stumbled, grabbed the edge of the bar to steady herself.

The man stepped closer to her, humming beneath his breath. He said in singsong, "Why don't we go awwwaaaaaay . . ."

The alien warmth was moving through her body, eating up her strength.

". . . and *chat* for a while? You can tell your new friend Salik everything you know about absolutely everything . . ."

Thought became an elusive, watery process. Her knees were dissolving beneath her; she couldn't hold on to the bar; she was going down—

Except then the man closed in on her. "No," Jess muttered; her vision clicked back into focus and she pulled away from him. His eyebrows went up in surprise. Jess stumbled back from him and he didn't make any move to go after her. She turned—

—And realized people had drifted in from the dance floor to watch them. The supermodel from the Versace ads was among them, lifting her drink to collagen-enhanced lips. Jess stumbled, nearly fell, as that alien light began slipping up inside her head now, trickling through her mind. "Excuse me," she muttered to a man in a fur-and-feather coat, "let me through—"

The man said, "Aren't you supposed to stay?"

She tried to shove her way past him and he grabbed her shoulders and pushed her back with such force she felt the floor disappear beneath her feet. Then she was on the ground, and hurting—except, no, the pain was dissolving, there was no pain anywhere. The light and warmth were all through her now, taking the strength from her body, taking over her body, and that no longer seemed a bad thing. Salik was bending over her, his black-gloved hand tucked against his side, his other hand gripping the walking cane. "I'll return you to Kai"—and his breath was hot on her face—"eventually. In some form. I promise."

"Wait a minute." Another voice. The supermodel, kneeling beside Jess, eyeing her with what seemed to be genuine concern. "She really doesn't look well. I think she needs a—"

"She only needs me," Salik said. He lifted his cane and shoved it against the model's chest—against and through—and Jess heard but couldn't believe she was hearing the wet crunch of bone and gristle, saw but couldn't believe she was seeing the end of the cane emerge from the woman's back, as her voice lodged with a grunt in her throat and she looked at Jess with widened eyes, her hands scrabbling at her chest, at the cane that impaled her, before she slumped to the ground and began to convulse.

The bartender looked on, drying a wine glass.

"Let's go, little girl," Salik was saying to her, grabbing at her shoulders, lifting her up, when a voice said, *"Salik."*

Salik looked up, mouth twisting into a hard smile.

"It took you long enough," he said. "You missed the good parts."

He let her go. She felt herself fall; heard the sound as her head hit the floor; none of it seemed to mean much. Her vision was dimming at the edges. She saw Kai stepping through the crowd, staring at Salik. They were both saying things, but the words were so distorted (through this haze of beautiful, floating light that was about to carry her off), that she couldn't make sense of them, didn't want to, didn't care.

Then Salik yelled, "You think this world's worth saving? *You think it ever has been?"* when his body lifted and slammed back against the bar as if he'd been picked up and thrown, except no one had touched him. He clapped both hands to his eyes and screamed in fury. Blood dripped between his fingers. Then Salik's shoulders started to shake; he was laughing. "Oh, I forgot you can still do this," he said, taking his hands away. His eyes were blindly staring orbs, leaking blood. "I trust the effects are still temporary?" Then the warmth and light and bliss swallowed his words entirely and Jess's gaze fell away from him. Her own eyes were closing.

And then Kai's voice in her ear, as clear and sharp as January cold: "Jess."

She struggled to hold on to the last shard of consciousness.

"You'll be fine," Kai was saying. He was crouching next to her. "Just ride it out. But don't believe in it—it's an illusion—it's false—"

But the light, she wanted to say. It was as if the whole world were splitting open, corridors of light stretching on in all directions, and all she had to do was follow those corridors until they led her to the source of everything, the answers to all the questions she had ever wanted to ask. And it would feel so very, very good.

Kai was still talking except now she couldn't hear him; his lips were moving with no voice attached. She smiled at him and closed her eyes. He could go away now. She was fine. But then she heard his voice in his head, inside her own thoughts, startling her away from the light and the bliss: *I need to know,* Kai said. *Do you trust me? Will you come with me?*

The man who had been in the library all those years ago, who had looked at her so sadly, who had given her the memory of that warm perfect hour on the balcony, a lizard asleep on the ledge. *His name was Tapaku.*

"Yes," Jess said. Or thought she said. She was aware of someone—Kai?—picking her up in his arms, moving faster than she would have thought possible. She was aware of people falling away to either side of them, making room for them, watching in awe from behind their artful masks.

That was all the awareness she could manage. She felt herself shutting down.

The world disappeared. Everything was light and darkness, both.

Eleven

They waited on the porch steps. Lauren was dressed in shorts and a tank top, the brace enclosing her left knee. While other girls wore platform sandals or flip-flops, Lauren wore sneakers. She never went barefoot, even in the house; she padded around in socks or slippers or ballet flats. Ramsey knew without asking that it was the dancing; it had banged up her feet, and she was self-conscious.

"That's her," Lauren said, slipping on sunglasses. "That's my girl."

A battered-looking Mustang convertible swung into their cul-de-sac. The girl at the wheel was the same age as Lauren. Ramsey knew her from around school: her name was Aimee Reed; she was in all the school plays.

"It's Ramsey, right?" Aimee was looking at him with a friendly expression. "Are you coming too?"

"He is," Lauren said.

She got in the front, Ramsey in the back, crutches angled through the gap in the front seats. The Mustang pulled away from the curb. The suburbs thinned, the road turned pitted and bumpy, houses yielding to trees and grass and sloping fields.

They were on the highway.

Ramsey settled back against the faded leather. He didn't know where they were going—Lauren had refused to divulge information, saying instead that it was a "secret," and even though secrets of any kind made Ramsey uneasy he had nodded and smiled and gone along with it—but he wasn't sure he cared. It was enough to be riding in a convertible on a summer day like this, sun and wind slipping over your skin. Lauren's presence so close: he could reach out and touch her hair, her bare olive-skinned shoulder. *This is the battle of longing and belonging.*

But at that moment, he wasn't battling anything at all.

They exited the highway where a sign announced LESTERTON, POP. 15,000. They followed a road that wound through more fields. It was midday now, elms and maples and oaks casting the shortest of shadows. Ramsey saw a hawk wheeling in the distance. It folded itself into a cannonball and dropped: a hunter's plummet. He wondered what small startled creature had just been sacrificed. The air was warm and dry in his lungs. Aimee and Lauren were listening to the radio, turning it up when the news came on about the disappeared supermodel, then switching it off.

"Are we there yet?" Aimee asked playfully, and then answered her own question. "Indeed, indeed we are."

There was a whitewashed wooden farmhouse with a wraparound porch, a large white cat sprawled on the step. Cherry trees and rosebushes grew in the front yard. Aimee cut the engine and they got out of the Mustang, doors slamming. The sunlight, drone of bees, simple beauty of house and yard and fields, the lethargic heat of early afternoon: he didn't know why, but everything felt tilted, off-angle, washed through with the surreal.

He glanced at Lauren. She was balancing on her crutches, looking at the house with an intent expression.

As if this were an equation she had to solve or die trying.

The front door opened and a man appeared on the porch.

"You're here for Munroe," the man said, "are you not?"

"Yeah," Lauren said.

"I'm Sebastian. Munroe's half-brother. I translate for him."

They gave him their names. Sebastian was maybe five-eight, five-nine, dressed in white slacks, white shirt, dark glasses, sandals. He had a pale, freckled complexion and his coppery hair, brushed back from his forehead in waves, shone in the sunlight. "Come in."

The interior was breezy, minimalist, with pale wood floors and simple furniture, cut-glass vases of white lilies placed around the living room. A silver pitcher of lemonade, a plate of pastries, and several glasses were arranged on the coffee table. Sebastian beckoned for them to sit down, poured them each some lemonade, said, "You are all first-timers, yes?"

Nods all around.

"Then," Sebastian said, and settled into the armchair across from them, "I would like to talk with you a bit first, so that you understand the process involved."

Aimee said, "Where's the—where's, uh, Munroe?"

"Preparing," he said. "My brother becomes very light-sensitive at such times, so when you go into the room you will find it quite dim, the shades drawn. *This* room is much too bright for him." Sebastian took off his glasses. His eyes were a pale, washed-out color, his eyelashes so faint they were almost invisible.

He said, with the air of someone launching into a speech he had given many, many times before, "My brother is a psychic, yes, but he doesn't gaze into a crystal ball. What he does is shift his mind into a different place, where the past and present and future interweave in strange ways."

"A different place," Ramsey said.

Sebastian looked at him. The pale eyes sharpened . . . then a strange light came into them, and for a moment Ramsey felt as if he'd been—

As if he'd been—

Recognized.

Sebastian smiled, his teeth small and white and sharp. "We call it the Dreamlines. You may think of it as the Twilight Zone if you wish. What my brother learns there, he brings back and shares with us."

Aimee interrupted, "Another reality? Like, a parallel world or something?"

"Think of the Dreamlines as a passageway that connects all the different worlds."

"How many worlds are there?" Ramsey asked.

"Too many to count, or even know. Far too many."

"And your brother can just—fly up to this dream-place, hang out?"

"There are a handful of ways to access the Dreamlines, one of which is through profound meditation. Many of us," Sebastian said, turning towards the two girls, "are psychic in some way, still retain the thinnest of talents that we have lost the ability, the *knowledge,* to train and develop. But people like my brother— it is a shame, a genuine shame, to think what he could have been. If he had found a proper teacher. But those teachers disappeared long ago."

"Teachers?" Ramsey said. "Who were they?"

"A race of men and women with a special relationship with the Dreamlines," Sebastian said, "who can channel the energy of the Dreamlines through their own blood and use it to perform what we think of as magic." He glanced at his watch. "It is time."

"Wait, wait. This is really cool. These people were, like, aliens or something?"

"I'm sorry, young man, but it is time—"

Ramsey said loudly, "Who were these teachers and where did they go?"

Silence in the room.

Only the sound of the grandfather clock, tick-tick-ticking.

"I've heard different things," Sebastian said. "Some people say they withdrew into their own secret cities. Some people say they stayed among us, mingled and mated. So it's possible they disappeared . . . into us."

It took a moment for Ramsey to work this out. "So if their bloodlines mingled with our bloodlines—and this Dreamlines mojo thing was somehow in their blood—then maybe it passed down into some of our blood, too?"

Sebastian shrugged.

"Like a magic gene," Ramsey marveled. "So other people can do what your brother does?"

"There are people who have the potential. But potential on its own is not enough. It must be quickened."

"Quickened?"

"Awakened. And then it must be trained, developed. These things require a proper teacher."

"So how did your brother get . . . *quickened*?"

"He refuses to say. And if he won't tell me, he won't tell anyone. And now, young friends, it really *is* time. It's *past* time. Aimee, my dear, care to be first?"

"Sure," Aimee said. But she got up from the couch a little shakily, as if she were about to enter the lair of a person who was, at best, a nutcase; at worst, a serial killer.

Or else, a voice whispered inside Ramsey, *Munroe is exactly what Sebastian says he is. What if this is true, every bit of it? What then?*

And then Aimee paused in the doorway to the hall. Ramsey saw her shoulder blades stiffen beneath her T-shirt. She turned and murmured something to Sebastian, who nodded.

"Lauren," he said, "would you like to come with me?"

"Sure thing." Lauren stood up, grabbed her crutches,

and swung herself out of the room; they heard a door open and shut from elsewhere in the house.

Aimee sank down on the couch next to Ramsey. She was hugging herself. The skin of her upper arms had erupted into gooseflesh. "Freaking hell," Aimee murmured, although to herself or Ramsey, he couldn't say. "Freaking me *out*."

"What happened?"

She turned to him. "Are you believing any of this?"

"Why didn't you go through with it?"

"Because—" Aimee looked into space, hugged herself again. "Because I just had this feeling that—that this guy, Monteroy—"

"Munroe—"

"—Whatever the fuck his name is, he would tell me how I'd die. And when I'd die."

Through the open windows came the mingled scent of roses and fresh-cut grass, the faint unending drone of bees.

Aimee said, "I came here for fun, but this isn't fun. This is creepy."

"How did you even find this guy?"

"Some friend of Lauren's from New York referred us. You have to get *referred*. He doesn't see many people." Aimee rubbed her upper arms. "He sure as hell's not seeing *me*."

She sank like a stone into her own silence. He felt an itching along the back of his shoulders. He wrapped an arm around himself, tried to scratch it away. Wondering if he'd picked up a mess of mosquito bites without realizing.

The creak of a floorboard made him look up.

Sebastian stood in the doorway, tall cool figure in white, hands folded in front of him.

"Ramsey," he said quietly.

The world will burn because of you. The words— printed in stark black felt-tip—floated in front of his eyes. Ramsey blinked them away. He stood up, and the itching spread across his shoulders and deepened, became something much closer to pain.

"Come with me, please," Sebastian said. "We need your assistance with Lauren."

Three kids, Ramsey thought, *in a house in the middle of nowhere. It's the perfect setup for a slasher flick. Does anyone know where we are?*

He followed Sebastian.

But this was not the den of a serial killer, or killers. Lauren was not hanging from a meat hook while the brothers closed in on her with carving knives.

The room was small and bare and shuttered. Thin blades of sun slipped through the blinds, offered enough light to see by. There was a small round table and three chairs. Lauren sat in one, her face pale and apprehensive.

In the chair across from her sat the person called Munroe. He was a small, compact figure, taking up much less room than Ramsey had expected. He had a baby-cheeked face with a tapered, pointed chin; his complexion was pale and freckled, his hair redder and thinner than his brother's. His small hands rested on top of the table, as if he were eager to prove he had nothing to hide.

"Ah," he said pleasantly, and his eyes shifted to Ramsey. They were large and slanted down at the outer corners, giving his face a melancholy cast. But the thing Ramsey noticed most was how colorless they were.

Eyes as pale as glass, as ghosts.

"Ramsey Doe," Munroe said. He gestured to the empty chair. "Usually my brother sits there, but for the moment he'll simply have to stand. Please."

Ramsey sat down, keeping his eyes on the small, strange man. Munroe's smile was as thin as his brother's. "I was sharing some information with your sister," he said, "when I sensed something strange. Something lacking. I understand what it is now. It is, quite simply"—and he turned his hands palms-up on the table—"you."

Munroe closed his eyes.

Ramsey waited. Lauren still wouldn't look at him. He could hear the tick-tick-tick of someone's watch. Munroe opened his eyes, and now they were no longer colorless; now Ramsey understood the tension in Lauren's face and body, as his own breath was sucked away from him.

Munroe's eyes had turned into something not human, at least not in any way Ramsey understood the word. The whole of his downward-slanted sockets were filled with a molten sheen. They cast their own, silvery light into the room.

And Munroe began to speak.

Words that were not English, not any language Ramsey could recognize, poured fluidly, breathlessly from him. *". . . Sentika niosl maladyic sheritoka vyuorikiano . . ."*

Sounding like gibberish, a child's pretend language, yet spoken with the authority of an adult.

Sebastian also began to speak, his voice deeper and rougher than his brother's, the two like rivers intersecting and overlapping and dividing again:

". . . He will go," Sebastian said, in a perfect monotone, *"as he is meant to go, he has no choice, and you must not follow. It is death to follow. For there will be a stage that awaits, blood in the desert, blood and music and war, for the one who wrought the plague walks again, sings again, and has begun to harvest her children . . ."*

Sebastian paused, and listened to his brother in silence for several moments before chiming in again:

" . . . The winds of the labyrinth blow again, but the song is a dark one, a corruption of praise, a corruption of power. The friends of Salik will come looking for you and you must not let them catch you, or they will use you as bait and you will cross over. You will cross over. You may help him then . . ."

Sebastian paused again. Munroe was no longer speaking but whispering.

" . . . There is death ahead but it is not what you think it is. So don't be afraid. Don't be afraid. For Del will

*play his game, Del will be the wild card. There will be a
great, strange gifting, there will be another Teaching, and
a new kind of necromancer will rise to walk among us.
Will defend us . . ."*

And now the words falling from the small man's lips
had grown too faint for his brother, for any of them, to
hear. The smaller man opened his eyes, and Ramsey saw
again the strange silvery color, shifting like liquid in the
hollows of his face. Munroe continued to whisper, and now
it seemed as if the bees from the front yard had taken
up residence inside Ramsey's skull, buzzing just behind
his eyes. He pressed his hands to his temples but kept
his eyes on Munroe, unwilling to miss even a half-second
of this—

—And now the backs of his shoulders no longer itched
but *burned,* as if someone were peeling away his skin,
layer by layer—

The whispering stopped.

Munroe's eyes altered their blind, preternatural gleam
to the colorless gaze of before. *Contacts?* Ramsey
thought. *Does he manage that with contacts? Does he—*

And the voice from before, like leaves rustling inside
him: *What if it's all true?*

"Now," Munroe said, as smilingly pleasant as a host
offering coffee, "I would like some moments with Ramsey alone. Lauren, that is all I have to share with you
today. Thank you, and you may go."

Lauren pushed back her chair with such force it nearly
toppled over. She muttered something beneath her
breath and left the room.

"You too, Sebastian," Munroe said quietly. "I know
this is an unusual request on my part, but Ramsey Doe
is an unusual boy."

"As you wish," Sebastian said.

He stepped from the room and closed the door behind him.

Ramsey said, "You know my last name."

"Or rather, the true lack thereof." Munroe smiled

again. He folded his hands on the table. "You long for home," he said quietly.

Ramsey shrugged. "Not really."

"You are nostalgic for the lost paradise. You long to return, but you cannot escape your chains." Munroe's eyes assumed their silver sheen, opaque and glinting in the half-light.

"You sound like a bad poem," Ramsey said.

The eyes narrowed.

"You are double-named, double-souled, but your vessel is poor and unfit. You were not meant to carry what you carry. That is why the pain has started. It will only grow worse, and you will have no choice but to wither inside it. You are running out of time, Ramsey Doe. And it was borrowed time to begin with."

"I don't know what the hell you're talking about."

"Your moment is coming for you."

Ramsey started to speak, but Munroe cut him off.

"You are a danger to yourself," Munroe said, "and to her. You have to go away."

"What—" Ramsey tried to keep still, say nothing, but the word came from him again. "What"—and he couldn't help exploding: *"What the fuck is going on in my life?"*

"I'm sorry. I see only glimpses." He raised a finger in Ramsey's direction. "You *want* to go," he said. "It's the only way to uncover the truth of yourself."

"What did all that stuff mean, the stuff you said earlier? Blood in the desert—"

"There are some places, mystical places, where windows open up between realities and creatures may pass between. Where many things are possible, dark and light things both. I was speaking of such a place."

"Creatures from another world can live in ours?"

Munroe frowned. "No. There are always exceptions, but—our minds may travel places where our bodies may not follow. Our bodies are bound to the physical laws of our home-realm."

"You said there are exceptions," Ramsey said.

"There are always exceptions."

Munroe leaned forward in his chair. His pale eyes gleamed.

"You should be dead," he said. "I've never encountered anything like it."

Ramsey wasn't sure he'd heard correctly.

"When you were a very small child. It is written all over you, that death. But something interfered."

"I don't understand." But Ramsey felt something inside him, an echo of deep recognition. *Yes. I was dying. I was dying.*

"When your father shot your mother," Munroe said, "and then you, and then himself. There's a mark on your chest, where the bullet went in. You should have died. But something interfered."

"That's not true," Ramsey said. "That can't possibly be true."

It wasn't my blood. There were no wounds on me. It was someone else's—

"It was someone else's blood," he said.

"Your blood," Munroe said quietly, "changed. And your body tells the story. Bodies often do. Those marks on your back, for example. They serve as a kind of symbol. Stigmata."

"There aren't any marks on my back," Ramsey said. He felt an odd sensation in his hands. He realized they were trembling.

Munroe was silent a moment. Then said, his voice thoughtful: "Not yet."

Ramsey tried to get out of the chair, so he could get out of the room, but there was no strength in his legs.

"There are others," Munroe said, "who could tell you more. Who could maybe tell you what you are."

"Others . . . like you?"

"Better than me. Stronger than me. I'm only a seer, and a middling one at that."

"Your brother said they've all disappeared."

"I love my brother," Munroe sighed, "but he doesn't know what he's talking about."

"How do I find them?"

"They will find you eventually. Some of them are already looking."

"Can I trust them?"

"You can trust one." Something faint and metallic shifted through his eyes, like quicksilver, there and gone. "A woman. There's someone with her—a man. You can trust him as well."

"What more?" Ramsey said.

Munroe was silent.

"*What more?* Is that all you can tell me?"

Munroe shrugged, lifted his hands a little, as if to say *C'est la vie.* Ramsey felt as if he'd hiked to the edge of a cliff, about to see the landscape below for the first time—only to have a blanket of fog drop down and smother the view.

"You, dear boy," Munroe said quietly, "are beyond my capabilities."

Twelve

Awareness came like light filtering down through murky water.

She thought, *A plane?*

I'm on a plane?

A man's voice said, "You're awake."

Memory bolted through her. She opened her eyes and sat up, the wool blanket slipping off her legs to the floor.

She was in some kind of private jet. The couch and seats were done in a deep creamy leather. Kai Youngblood was sitting across from her, holding out a bottle of water. Behind him she saw the closed door to the cockpit. The drone of the engines filled the air.

When she spoke, her voice didn't sound like her own. It was too hoarse, scraping off the base of her throat. "What is this? Where—"

Kai's face was smooth and calm, but his eyes were as bleak as a bombed-out building. There was a cloth bandage wrapped around his left hand.

"I'm taking you abroad," he said. He capped the bottle, placed it by his feet. "To someplace very high and very cold."

"You're joking."

"Does it look like I'm joking?"

Her head filled with white noise, fuzzy static. The only thing she could think of to say was, "I don't have my passport."

Kai reached into the pocket of his overcoat and produced the slender document. "You do."

"How . . . ?"

He shrugged, looked innocent, sipped water.

"Is this your jet?"

"On loan from a friend. As are the pilots."

Kai's eyes were on her, the color of dark fire. He glanced pointedly at her right wrist.

She followed his gaze and saw the faint blue line that looped the skin. She flashed back to the youth at the foot of the stairs, the glittering lines that overran his chest and back. She remembered the symbols glimpsed on men and women as she navigated her way through the club.

Kai murmured, "I apologize for what happened with Salik. He and I have known each other since childhood. There are tensions."

"Tensions," Jess echoed. "He said you were scum."

"I am not."

"That you're weak."

Kai shrugged.

"He's insane," Jess said flatly. "I saw it. I felt it. Did he really . . . Did he *kill* that woman, or was I just on a bad bad trip?"

Kai looked away. "Things have changed. I didn't expect that place to be dangerous."

She was conscious of all the dark empty space rushing past the windows.

"You . . ." She could feel the words deflate inside her throat. "So what are you? How old are you?"

"Seven hundred."

"Years?"

"Give or take." He looked at her wearily. "The magic

changes you physically. It changes your life span. You yourself will discover this."

He leaned forward and showed her his hands, palms up. That night in the loft, something about them had struck her as odd, and now she realized precisely what it was. Not just the metallic nails. His palms were smooth, unlined, like blank paper. No heartline, no lifeline. No fortunes there to tell.

Jess whispered, "So what were you before the magic? Were you just a normal guy?"

"I am a Sajae," Kai said, accenting the second syllable.

"And your people—the Sajae—all use magic?"

"Abilities vary."

"But you. You're pretty good, right?"

"I'm a Summoner," he said quietly. "I crossed into deep magic when I was thirty-six."

"So that means you're powerful?"

"Used to be." Kai looked at her directly and said, "I have a story to tell. Do you think you are ready to hear it?"

She said, "I don't know."

The sound of the engines roared in her ears.

She said, "Try me."

"Some of my people believe that we are direct descendents of the Watchers, those angels who came down to mate with human women."

Jess gulped again at her water. *"Angels,"* she said, and couldn't stop some nervous laughter.

He brushed his knuckles against his mouth. "Those women gave birth to a race of giants. I don't know if you ever heard this story—"

"The giants ate everything: the animals, their parents, each other. I thought it was just a—"

"A myth. A story. It might well be, Jess, but it might be seeded in some truth, however distorted. Most of these children—these giants—were destroyed in a great flood. The survivors scattered throughout the world and continued to mate with humans. A segment of that group became isolated high in the mountains and slowly evolved into us." Kai spread his hands a little. "So we were a people of great wisdom and power . . . and appetite, and lust. There is a dark side to our nature that must be controlled. And we controlled it for a very long time.

"We were nomads. Our name—Sajae—translates roughly as 'wandering ones.' We mingled freely and openly with the world. We—or at least, the majority of us—promoted peace, knowledge, and healing. It was a good time for us. When we were at our finest, our highest.

"At least, that's how the stories go.

"After Rome fell—although it didn't really *fall,* it was a much more complicated process than that—the Sajae went deep into the desert and created our own city. The Labyrinth. There was little plan to it, little order. It had its own magic. It grew as it would, and we grew along with it. And it's not in our nature to be very . . ." Kai thought a moment. "It's not our nature to be very *ordered*. The scientific method was very much a human invention, something your kind taught us, to the extent that we can truly engage with it. But the Labyrinth— our little kingdom—was . . ." A look of longing passed across Kai's features.

"But it was the great mistake," he said. "The Sajae became rooted, no longer nomadic, no longer centered on anyone or anything except ourselves. The old values—of teaching, healing, learning—fell away. Our darker appetites began to assert themselves. And those who were powerful began to separate themselves from those who were not.

"And through the generations, the magic changed as well. It became more and more a commodity, a marker of power and status. No longer taught freely, no longer shared without price. The ruling bloodlines had established themselves.

"The Labyrinth was founded on magic. But as magic became more and more confined to a power-elite, people were forced to live much differently from before. Manual labor became necessary.

"And that brought in the slave trade.

"There was one slave," Kai said. "One young bondgirl. She was sold into the city by one of the barbarian tribes. No one guessed she was as tremendously gifted as she was. And somehow she learned magic. Somehow she entered into a Pact with six other Summoners who opened up one of the oldest, highest, and most forbidden forms of magic. They summoned demons. They took—they took the demons inside them, and became—"

"Possessed," Jess said.

He smiled a little. "You're thinking of that movie. *The Exorcist.*"

"My frame of reference is pretty damn limited."

"I've seen that movie many times." Kai smiled wanly and shook his head. "It wasn't like that," he said. "Bakal Ashika and her followers were very willing. And they were transformed. And the things they could do. They could rain blood. Open up the earth. Spread disease. Spread illusion, delusion, insanity—

"They destroyed the old city, the Labyrinth. They turned it to sand. Many of us escaped into the outside world—into Europe and Asia—and they followed.

"They hunted us down.

"They slaughtered much of the world, as well. Just for fun, I suppose, although Ashika's vision of what she wanted—of what was *possible*—was changing. Or maybe she had always been . . . so ambitious.

"We fought those demons for almost one hundred years. We were forced to use magic that we had never—never known. We could not kill them," Kai said, "so we banished them to seven prisons, in seven different points around the globe. And we have been guarding them there all this time."

Jess was shaking her head. "What you're saying—"

Kai lifted his eyebrows.

"—There would have been *evidence* of this. Demons and Summoners stalking each other in the Middle Ages—I mean, no offense, but someone would have noticed. At the very least, history would have recorded some kind of massive death toll—"

The realization struck her, then, and she felt a dark space open up inside her.

"A massive death toll in the mid–thirteen hundreds," Kai agreed. He looked at her steadily. "The equivalent of a nuclear bomb. A strike so massive it took centuries for the human population to replenish itself."

"I can't—" Jess pressed her hands to her temples, rocked forward in her seat. "You're talking about the plague."

"Yes."

She looked up at him. "The goddamn bubonic—"

"Yes. The Black Death. It was one of the weapons they used." Kai paused to sip some water. Then: "It was a spellcasting. A very powerful one."

"But—"

"What is history, Jess, but memory? What we remember, how we remember it. What we write down. Seven hundred years ago, my colleagues and I were still strong in our power—"

She sensed a skip of the narrative needle: one moment Kai's people were exiled, hunted down like deer; the next they were powerful enough to rewrite history. *There's something he's not telling me,* she thought. *Hell, there must be all sorts of things he's not—*

"We were strong enough to play with human memory," Kai continued, and she refocused her attention on him. "With collective human memory."

"So you cast a spell," Jess said. "You cast a massive amnesia spell over the whole world—"

"Easier than you might think. At least back then."

"—And so people just pieced that part of history together, from rats and fleas and all those corpses?"

"We traveled. We talked to people, we planted suggestions. For a long time it was also our mission to find and destroy certain documents. Keep in mind the true plague was a cyclical disease that occurred every now and again. So we disguised our war as one of those outbreaks and concealed it among the periodic real ones." He paused, then added, "But then the Western nature worked to our advantage. Welcome to the age of rational thought, the great enlightenment. Journal entries, stories, paintings, anything that depicted Sajae or the demon battles or the things that truly happened—were soon regarded as nothing more than lunacy. Art. The whims of a more *primitive* age."

Jess realized she hadn't stopped shaking her head.

"Jessamy," Kai said, and there was something new in his voice. "Bakal Ashika has escaped. She's in the world again. After centuries of imprisonment she will be weakened and disoriented, but if she regains her former strength and finds and releases her disciples—"

"The world burns," Jess murmured.

"This realm will become one of the hell-realms," Kai said, "and she and her consorts will rule."

She was silent. She was aware of herself in the plane: the earth cut out from under her, the air too thin to breathe, as time rearranged itself between departure and destination.

"I don't want to believe you," Jess said. "I'd rather we were both crazy."

"You know that's not the case."

"I do?"

"The knowledge is inside you," Kai said. "It's in your veins. It shapes your art."

"My art," Jess said. "You mean the boy."

He lifted an eyebrow.

"Where does he fit into this? And *me*. God, why me?"

She heard a change in the pitch of the engines. Kai glanced out the window, said mildly, "We're beginning our descent."

"So where the hell are we *going*?"

"I'm going to introduce you to someone. A demon."

He was looking at her with an odd, enigmatic smile.

She gave a short, sharp laugh. She said, "No way on earth you're serious."

"His name is Del," Kai said. "You might like him."

Thirteen

To: Nemesis
From: Lizardking
Subject: present for you

NEM.

    *What up. The voice is named Asha. She came
out of nowhere. The dude behind Trans is Lucas
Maddox. They made a CD you can't download all
of it. But give me your snail mail and I'll send
you a present.'Cause I'm that kind of guy.*

Lizzie

Not even the Internet could yield much information
about the band. They had come out of LA less than a
year before. Ramsey found Internet listings of gigs
they'd done at Sunset clubs, a scattering of mentions in
obscure e-zines. A search engine led Ramsey to the website of a Los Angeles writer who called himself the Poet:

    . . . . *Humid strung-out Friday night. I go to the
Strip. Sidewalk rolling with the hipsters and wan-*

nabes, guitar kids, girls in little tops and tight jeans
with flesh squeezing out above the waistbands,
girls with long streaked hair and heavy eyeshadow.
Cars cruising past, tops down, blaring rap music,
blaring hip-hop, blaring classic rock. Clubs and restaurants a glittering, ramshackle line set against
the shadowed hills, where multimillion-dollar houses
nestle in folds and crevices.

I see a crowd gathered outside this club called
Snakecharmer, never been there before, bored
dude in black T-shirt sitting on a stool by the door.
Barely flicking glances at the IDs flashed before
him. I pause outside the rope, call out, "Who's
playing?"

He doesn't even look up. "Trans."

Never heard of them. But there's a vibe, a snapping restlessness, to this loose line of people and
so I figure what the hell.

And then inside, a dark hot small space packed
with people. Fight my way to the bar for a beer,
fight my way back to a table. The band comes on.
Two guitars, drums, keyboard, vocalist.

And they play.

How can I describe this? The singer. Oh God, the
singer. A raw ripping wail of a voice. Voice that's
been to hell and back, seen everything in between.
Small skinny girl getting bigger with every beat,
veering wildly between broken tortured tenor and
sweet cajoling croon, she bends as if injured, let-
ting the words out, getting the songs out, as if the
act demands nothing less than every atom of energy she has in that small formidable surprising
body.

And then it's over, they pack up and they're gone,
not even acknowledging this audience still hungry, desperate for another feeding. I track down the
club manager, ask them, Who are they? He says
it's Lucas Maddox's new band. He can't tell me

*much. They come, set up themselves, don't really
speak to anybody, blow through this amazing set,
and then they're gone (although sometimes the
singer—Asha—deigns to mingle with the commoners
outside). They've been gigging pretty regularly at
Snakecharmer, other places. Some major-label dude
was in last week asking questions about them, but
Maddox shut him down real quick. He won't go that
route again.*

That night Ramsey had his old dream of the highway.
It was cold and dark. Feral dogs rushed from the woods
and barked at him (but they wouldn't come too close,
kept a respectful distance) and a moon the color of
blood burned through the sky. His wrists were clamped
and weighted with shackles, and his back was burning
with pain.

But this time he wasn't alone.

He turned, and although he saw no one he could sense
a presence, *her* presence, like the feel of mist on skin.

Let me help you, she said, and her voice was unmis-
takeable, honey mixed with broken glass, *let me free you
of these.*

There was a click. He glanced down at his wrists, saw
the shackles unlock, fall away. They clattered to the
pavement.

A dog howled at him from the edge of the wood.

All I ask, the voice whispered.

Rain fell, darkening the pavement, slipping down his
face.

All I ask

But the dream, the highway, ended there.

Lauren wasn't seeing Paul anymore. She refused to answer the phone when his number flashed across the caller
ID screen. "Well, Paul," Ramsey overheard her mother
say awkwardly, "I guess maybe you two should take a
break."

He could only imagine Paul's response.

Wednesday evening he knocked on Lauren's door. She called out a halfhearted "Yeah," and he opened the door partway. She had cleaned and organized her room, which surprised him. The vanilla fragrance was gone. Now the air was scented with lavender.

" 'Law And Order' just started," he said. "Want to watch?"

"It's a rerun of a rerun."

"Okay," he said, but as he was about to withdraw he heard himself say, "Was it something Munroe said?"

She narrowed her eyes at him.

"Why you suddenly broke up with Paul," Ramsey said.

"We weren't *going out*. We weren't *boyfriend and girl-friend*. So it's not like I *broke up* with him."

"Okay. Whatever."

She had refused to talk about their experience with the odd little psychic in the farmhouse in the middle of nowhere. Afterwards, they drove home in silence. Ramsey was wrung out with exhaustion, as if he'd run a marathon; he could tell from the girls' expressions that they felt equally drained. Lauren broke the quiet only once to mutter, "That was . . . that was *insane*."

Now, she only said, "That guy . . . Munroe . . . had nothing to do with it."

"Okay."

"Absolutely nothing. Munroe is *whacked*. And so is his brother. Didn't you think so?"

"No," Ramsey said, then closed her door and went into his own room.

She appeared in his doorway a little later. "Ramsey," she whispered, and he shifted beneath the thin cotton sheet that was all you needed on a night as humid as this. He opened his eyes, squinted against the flood of light from the hallway.

"Ramsey," she said again.

"Yeah?" Other images of Lauren, dream-images whispering words the real Lauren would never say (not to him), pressed against the edges of his mind; he felt his body grow hot. He forced those images away. *Foster sister. Parents down the hall.*

Besides, it's not like Lauren would even—

And yet, as she fell back against the doorframe, hair falling forward to veil her cheek like a forties-style movie star, he could have sworn she was posing.

"I just wanted to say," she said. She cleared her throat. "I mean, what I said about him. Being insane. Maybe I shouldn't have said that."

Ramsey had to focus a moment to understand the reference.

Lauren shifted a bit in the doorway. "You seemed to take offense."

"I didn't take offense," he said. "I just disagreed with you."

"You must think I'm a bitch."

"Lauren."

"I can be bitchy, sometimes."

"I don't think you're a bitch. I just think you're unhappy."

She was silent again, then said, "You sure you're only fifteen?"

He didn't know what to say to that. He didn't get a chance to say anything. Lauren slipped away, pulling the door behind her. He heard the soft sound of the latch, and then he was alone again, sealed inside the darkness and the quiet.

He closed his eyes and waited for the dreams.

Lizardking was as good as his word. Ramsey came home from working a lunch shift at the diner, the smell of the tuna-fish special still in his nostrils. He was kicking his shoes into the hall closet when he noticed the flat brown envelope on the mat below the mail slot. His name and address were scrawled on the front.

In the high left corner, a second name and address:

L.K.
C/o King's Way
132 Leary St.
San Francisco, California

He picked up the package. Usually he took any mail directly to his room, waited until he was behind that closed door: a leftover habit from the boys' home, where privacy was something you fought for and hoarded. But now, standing in the front hall where people could assail him from three different directions, Ramsey ripped open the envelope and tilted the contents into his hand.

A CD. The cover art was roughly, brutally painted: a desert setting. Black mountains carving out a jagged horizon. A slender woman knelt in the sand, her face turned away from the viewer. Black, ragged wings sprouted from her shoulders. Her body was cut and bleeding, her hands out in front of her. Her fingers were tipped with long silver blades.

Below the image, a line of type said simply, TRANSGRESSIONS.

He went to his bedroom. He plugged himself into his Discman and curled up on his bed.

It wasn't music you listened to, exactly. It was music you fell into. It opened itself up, beckoned you to the precipice, and then either you jumped in or the music just reached up and pulled you down; either way, it swallowed you whole. One song bled into the next, into the next, into the next, and the more you listened the more you got the sense that it wasn't just the beats that mattered, it was the spaces in between where something else was happening, some deep primal code tattooing itself into your brain, into your being, some message that, if you listened closely and often enough, you would crack wide open.

And there would be discovery.

There would be revelation.

And then he would suddenly shift out of this kind of thinking and wonder at himself, shake his head—what the hell?—it was just *music,* after all, just a woman howling *Don't take it for granted/We'll eat you like air/It's one thing to want you/Another to care* and he felt the rhythms driving down through his body, feet twitching, shoulders jerking, and it was like warm golden air moving through him. He was feeling that happy. It was that kind of bliss.

At some point he must have dozed off without realizing it, because he was in the middle of a wasteland. No signs of life at all, just the sweep of beige-orange sand enclosed by jagged rock.

"Are you ready?" a woman asked from behind him.

He turned, and there she was: the hitchhiker, the girl from the CD cover. Her hair was white-blonde, sticking up around her head in windblown tufts. Hip bones jutted above her low-slung jeans. You wanted to hold and protect her; only, Ramsey thought, she might shatter in your arms, cut you up with her broken pieces.

Ramsey said, "Who are you?"

She didn't seem to be looking at him but through him. It was as if he weren't talking to a real person but some kind of random impersonal holograph, projected into his mind. "Come to the desert," she said. "I have something to show you."

"Who are you?"

He didn't expect her to answer. But suddenly her eyes shifted, and she seemed to look directly at him. As he opened his mouth to ask another question, she faded.

"Don't go," he said, and woke up with a keen sense of loss.

Subject: eternal gratitude
LK,
   Wow. It's like the movie of my life just found the perfect soundtrack. Thanks.
Nemesis.

Subject: re: eternal gratitude
Nemesis—
   You really mean that you should come down this
way. Prove your devotion. ☺ *Word's out that*
Trans is cooking up something BIG and once-in-a-
lifetime special, out in the Mojave, and I'm put-
ting together a group of people gonna go out and
take part in it. You're totally welcome to join us.
King's Way, San Francisco. Go there. Ask for me.
Someone will give you directions.
LK
P.S. Did you dream about her?

He had Friday off. Abe got his driver's license, which
they celebrated by driving out of town and spending the
day at the skate park. Ramsey came home flushed, exhilarated, blowing hair from his eyes.

When he stepped inside the house, it felt empty and
silent. He remembered: Dorrie and John had gone to a
wedding in Ithaca, would not be back until the next
morning.

The door to the den was partly open.

Lauren was on the couch, her good leg pulled up
against her chest, TV light flickering across the high
rounded lines of her profile.

On the screen, a young ballet dancer performed alone
in a studio. She was very thin, long-legged, dressed in a
white nightgown with her hair loose to her waist. She
held a candle out in front of her, like a gothic heroine
moving through a haunted house.

It was Lauren as she'd been as a dancer, before the
knee injury.

When the dance ended, Lauren pointed the remote
like a gun at the screen and rewound the tape. She
played it again. He watched along with her, secretly. His
gaze kept shifting from the Lauren on the TV screen to
the Lauren on the couch. The dancing girl seemed so
ethereal; it was hard to believe she could emerge from

the dance and turn into someone real. She seemed . . .
doomed was the word that came to mind, but he shook
it away. He turned his attention to the Lauren in the
room with him, sharing this near-darkness: the sun-
tanned healthy girl with a sensuality the dancer on the
television was too stripped down to possess.

When she finally glanced over at him, the light
streaked off her tears.

"Hey," he said.

"I'm not crying." She was wiping at her eyes. "I will
not fucking cry."

"Hey," he said again. He sat on the couch beside her
and patted her back. She turned to him and put her
head on his shoulder. And suddenly the gesture seemed
easy and natural: he put his arms around her, and held
her.

Too soon, she pulled away and stood up and left the
room. His body still savored the feel and scent, the imprint of her. He needed distraction. He'd go online,
maybe, or go finish his Robert Cormier novel—

She reappeared in the doorway, a glass in one hand
and a bottle of scotch in the other. "This one's mine,"
she said, lifting the bottle. "Aimee's sister got it for me.
You want some?"

"No. Take it easy, okay?"

She grinned at him, limping into the room. She had
traded in her crutches for a cane, and could go short
distances without it. "Worried I'll end up in AA?"

He shrugged. "You know what they say . . ."

"Huh. What do they say?"

"It's one thing to drink with others. It's another thing
to drink alone."

"I'm not drinking alone. I'm drinking with you." She
poured some scotch into the glass and sipped. She
looked at him and cleared her throat and started to say
something, then paused, then cleared her throat again.
"I don't want you to go," she said.

Ramsey absorbed her expression, her words, for a full

moment and then laughed. "I'm not going anywhere. I have no plans."

"Munroe said . . ."

"Munroe said what?"

She looked down at her glass. "Forget it."

"Lauren—"

"Forget it."

Aimee's words suddenly coursed through him: *He would tell me how I'd die. And when I'd die.* Looking at Lauren now, for a moment, half a moment, he thought he saw death in her eyes.

No way, he thought, and felt a stab of panic in his gut. *No.*

The night deepened outside the windows. Lauren talked about the first time her aunt took her to a ballet, when she was five years old. She talked about how much she missed her dance life, her life in New York. She talked about how difficult she found it to make friends.

"But you're beautiful," Ramsey blurted.

She laughed at him. "So?"

She talked, and he listened; she talked as if she hadn't had the chance to say any of this to anybody, not even Aimee; and he hung on every word. He began to realize that she was fascinated by his fascination with her.

Finally she said, "Enough. Enough. Now you talk."

Ramsey grinned. "Me?"

"Share something," she said. "I've, like, spilled my guts. Now it's your turn."

"I'm not a big talker."

"I noticed."

"In fact, I'm a pretty quiet guy."

"You don't have anything to say?"

"Guess not."

"Liar."

"There is something . . ." But it seemed so daring, so exposing. He had never shown those pictures to anybody. And yet, he wanted to share something of his life, himself, the way he really was; and he knew if he tried to use words he would only fuck it up. "Upstairs," he mumbled. "In my room."

At once he wished he'd kept quiet. But Lauren was grinning, pushing to her feet. "Show me. Lead the way."

He had never shown these drawings to anyone except Dr. Ryan, who had counseled Ramsey for four years, right up until his heart attack in a Tex-Mex restaurant five blocks from his office. Ramsey had felt that death like a knife slipping into him. He wasn't sure why he'd held on to these drawings (Ryan had kept some of the others, and Ramsey had no idea what had happened to them), why they had traveled with him through the years, the ever-shifting living situations.

So how to begin to explain them to Lauren?

He couldn't think of anything to say that didn't sound hopelessly lame. He handed her the sheaf of papers and let her sift through them in silence.

"So you made these?" Lauren said finally. "When you were a real little kid?"

"The shrink wanted me to. He was looking for clues, you know, to piece me together."

"So who is she?" Lauren said. "Someone you used to know? It *is* the same woman, right?"

"The shrink thought so."

"Your mother?"

"No." For all that he couldn't remember about himself, Ramsey was sure of that. The blue-eyed, black-haired female figure he'd outlined and colored in so many times—crayons gripped between his clumsy little-kid fingers—was not his mother.

"So why draw her over and over?" Lauren leafed through the drawings again. "In this one," she said, "she's some kind of a—what's that word—"

"Falconer. Something I learned about at school."

In the picture, the woman stood flatly, without depth or dimension, and held out her right arm. A chain looped her wrist and traveled up into the sky, tethering the stick-thin

ankle of a large white bird. The bird's wings were straining
for flight, its eyes like dark lonely wounds.

Lauren said, "And you have no idea who she is."

"No. But the bird is me." Ramsey touched the white
wing. "The bird is somehow supposed to be me. I
know that."

Lauren gave a low whistle. "Pretty heavy."

Ramsey said nothing.

"So you think, whoever she is, she played a key role
in whatever happened to you, your family?"

"I don't know." Frustration in his voice, but it was
thin and worn after years of not knowing. He could be
looking at an entire lifetime of not knowing. Ramsey
knew he had to come to terms with that, or go crazy.

He remembered what Munroe had said:

*Your father shot your mother, and then you, and
then himself—*

Your body tells the story. Bodies often do.

There was an odd little birthmark in the center of his
chest, about the size a bullet might make. But that was
just a birthmark. *It wasn't my blood.*

"I don't understand." She put the drawings on his
desk. "Why be so secretive about this?"

"It's just private, Lauren, that's all—"

"It's you, your past. Nothing to be ashamed of.
Or . . ." She tilted her head as a new thought occurred to
her. "Or does the woman in the pictures *frighten* you?"

Her brown eyes scanned his face, and Lauren's own
face showed a turn of understanding.

"That's the secret," Lauren said. "She frightens you."

Held inside the scrutiny of that fine dark gaze, Ramsey didn't say anything. He felt himself cracking open;
felt that gaze slipping in, like cool air on sunburn.

"You're frightened," Lauren said again. And then
added, rather wonderingly, "You really are so alone in
this world—"

And with that, she'd gone too far. "Lauren," he said,
annoyed, except then—

Except then she was kissing him.

He was too stunned to react. She'd taken him by surprise. She'd taken his very breath: her lips soft against his own, her body moving close, her hand coming up to the back of his neck. The warmth of her tongue, at his lips and darting between them. She tasted of scotch. She backed him against the bed until they had no choice but to fall across it, tangled in each other. Lauren laughed. He smiled helplessly back at her. He didn't have the breath to laugh. She lifted herself on her elbows, dipped her head so that her soft thick hair brushed his face. And they were kissing again; such bliss, this kissing; he'd fooled around with girls before, clumsy groping in the back seats of cars, basements, beneath the bleachers, that kind of thing, and all of it so stupid, really, because it didn't compare to this at all, he'd never been kissed like this before, he'd never even *known*. This was what it meant to want someone. The hunger in his body so streamlined, so focused on her. It couldn't be any other girl. It had to be her.

And then he felt the descent of another kind of clarity: the hot wave of insight and understanding storming through him. *Ah, no,* Ramsey thought, as Lauren pushed up his T-shirt and laid a trail of kisses across his chest and belly. *No, no. Let me have this.* He didn't know whom he was addressing—not addressing, but *begging*— perhaps just his own sense of decency. Or something else. Something that lived deep inside him, that whispered against his bones.

She was tugging at his belt buckle.

"Lauren," he said.

She grinned, her eyes open and bright. He grasped her wrists in his hands.

"We shouldn't do this," he said.

"Ramsey." She blew a strand of hair off her face. "I know what I'm doing—"

"You're drunk. Your judgment is impaired."

"Not that impaired," she said evenly.

Something new came into her eyes. Ramsey recognized it for what it was: a touch of predator. He drew back a little, not from fear but from surprise.

"You lied to me," she said suddenly, savagely. *"You're not fifteen—"*

"You stopped seeing Paul because you slept with him and regretted it," Ramsey said. "And you didn't want to do it anymore."

"You're ages and ages older than that—"

"Because you can't go back to just holding hands with him, can you?"

Her lip trembled for a moment—half a moment—before she pulled away from him.

"So is that it?" she said. "You don't want to skip the holding hands part?"

"That's not—"

"You're right. What the hell was I thinking. Christ, you're a *kid*." Lauren said the word with disdain, although she herself was only one year older. She balanced on her good leg, looked around for her cane. "I'm a frigging *child molester*."

"Lauren—"

"Someone should *lock me up*."

"I don't want you to regret me," Ramsey said, but her only response was her body retreating. And then a slammed door.

Fourteen

They landed somewhere in the mountains.

A pale-haired man in a uniform boarded the plane. He and Kai exchanged a few words of Spanish. The man glanced at both passports so briefly that Jess had to wonder why they'd even bothered to bring them. The man nodded at them both, then stepped down from the plane. Jess glanced out the window and saw him striding towards the small white terminal at the edge of the airfield.

She felt hands at her shoulders. Kai was draping the wool blanket around her. "You'll want this. It's cold outside."

"So what nationality is your passport?"

"Which one?" His eyes gleamed with what might have been humor. "I have ten."

The car climbed higher into the mountains, narrow road shearing off into rock-tumbled gorges. Silence ran vast and deep. This was a land, she thought, that belonged only to itself.

They turned into a narrow road that cut into the mountainside. And then, perched high on a ridge, the chateau came into view: a rambling building of dark stone, a pitched and shingled roof.

Jess said quietly, "What is this place?"

"A prison," Kai said.

The Cherokee traveled up the driveway, loose stones crunching under the wheels. The driver said nothing to either of them as first Kai and then Jess got out of the car, doors slamming.

Jess stood there, numbed, watching the Cherokee fade down the road. Last chance, she couldn't help thinking. Except her last chance had come and gone while she was back in New York, and perhaps before then. *I need to know,* Kai had told her, as if the choice were hers to make. Something huge and dark was closing over her, and one person's will seemed a small thing in comparison. It was like standing on the beach with your arms spread, trying to hold back a tidal wave.

Hang on, she told herself. *Watch and listen and stay low, until you start to figure things out. And then go from there.*

A woman was waiting for them.

She was standing on the porch: a tall, statuesque figure with thick red hair that fell almost to her knees. She wore jeans and a fur jacket and held herself so still she seemed to seal off the space around her, untouchable as a princess in a glass coffin.

"Mina," Kai called out, and the joy in his voice was undeniable. The woman gave him a smile, but there was caution in it. He leaped up the steps. She moved towards him, allowed herself to be embraced. She kissed him on the mouth and then stepped away.

"Mina," Kai said, "may I present Jessamy Shepard. Jessamy, this is Mina Rakalas, a very"—he looked at Mina and grinned, and her dark eyes flashed in response—"a very old friend of mine."

Mina said, "I was hoping you'd be older."

"Maybe I'm like you," Jess said. "Older than I look."

She seemed to consider that a moment, then laughed. "I doubt that very much. Come in."

The interior was bigger than Jess had expected. Dark

wood floors layered with threadbare Persian rugs. A high, raftered ceiling. A fire snapped and sizzled inside the stone fireplace. The walls were draped with medieval tapestries, yet the furniture was an eclectic mix of styles. Sleek contemporary couches mixed with leather armchairs from the 1930s, pulled around a marble-topped coffee table inlaid with onyx. There were wall-to-ceiling bookcases where antique leather-bound volumes pressed against current best sellers. It was a room designed for comfort and visual interest. Nothing about it suggested prison.

Or demons.

A short young man in jeans and a sweater entered from the opposite door. He carried a tray—coffee mugs and plates of cheese and bread—which he placed on the table. "Anything else?"

"That's fine, Jack. Thanks."

He left the room.

"He's new," Kai observed.

"He arrived eight months ago. Siobhan recommended him."

"I remember Siobhan."

"She's in Amsterdam now." Mina folded herself into one of the leather armchairs, Kai into the one opposite her. Jess sat on the couch, feeling awkward and out of place, and much too light-headed. It seemed entirely possible that she was asleep on the plane—or back in the loft—dreaming this.

Kai was already helping himself to the bread and cheese. She reached instead for one of the mugs. Hot chocolate, rich and creamy with a cinnamon tang.

"You look like him." Mina's voice was thoughtful. "You look like Shemayan."

Jess's eyes shifted to Kai. "Who?"

Kai said, "Jess is still learning her own history."

"*Kai.* Look at her true. She's a child—"

"I'm twenty-eight," Jess could not help retorting. "That's hardly—"

"—And you want to put her down there with Del?"

"She can handle Del."

"Listen." Mina tilted her head to the side. Her expression grew dreamy. "He senses you. He knows you're here. He's been waiting."

Jess felt her own senses heighten, and she heard it: a faint, droning sound that rose and fell in atonal chords. The air seemed to vibrate with it.

"It's a song," Mina informed her, and Jess detected a note of pride in the other woman's voice. "Demon song."

Jess's numbness broke a little, and a shaft of fear slanted through, but she blocked it off. Better to be numb. Better to get at least some degree of orientation, before the fear smashed in and sent her spinning.

"So this is one of the seven places," Jess said. "A demon is imprisoned here."

"Below." Mina gestured to the floor. Her smile was tight. "Far below."

Kai said, "Del isn't quite like the others."

"This is true," Mina acknowledged. "Del never was, and he's become less so. Five hundred years of boredom and solitude can play with your mind a little." Her voice turned wry. "It can't be easy for a demon."

"Del's full name is—or was—Delkor Lokk," Kai told her. "He was an artisan in the southern part of the Labyrinth. He seemed harmless enough. He did not own slaves; he did not seem to care about the excesses of court or the corruption of the Academy.

"But he fell into Ashika's circle of influence. We think it was because"—he exchanged a look with Mina—"he was not just amoral, he was *bored*. The dark magic excited him. War and annihilation amused him. And when he grew distasteful of the slaughter, he all but surrendered. He was the only one who went easily."

"He lives in the moment," Mina said, "and for the moment. Kai thinks you would amuse him. He thinks this is why Del would help you." Her eyes shifted to Kai. "And also because—"

Kai raised a hand. "Mina," he said tiredly. "Is it necessary to—"

"—Del has a *crush*."

"A crush?" Jess said.

"Mina."

Mina laughed. "Relax, Kai. I think it's rather cute."

Jess glanced from one to the other. "Why do I need his help? What is this?"

"Even imprisoned," Kai said, "a demon's abilities are strong. Del can quicken you with a speed that I can't. We don't have time for other options."

"*Quicken* me?"

"There's a great talent sleeping inside you. We need to wake it up."

Her gaze drifted beyond Mina's shoulder to the tapestry on the wall behind. Jess rose from the couch and went over to study it. A battle scene was woven into the cloth. Trees and crude houses suggested a peasant village. Dead bodies lay scattered in the road, while surviving villagers crouched and watched with awestruck faces.

In the foreground were two figures.

They were not human.

They had stepped from the realm of myth and nightmare. The first was female, silver-skinned and silver-haired, her eyes like gashes of green flame in her face. Her mouth was open, showing rows of jagged teeth. Blood spilled down her chin. In one hand, she had what seemed to be an apple until Jess took a closer look. *A heart,* she thought. *Human.*

Squared off against the demon was someone, something else.

It was a thin, almost insubstantial figure that cast off a vivid white light, its arms flung out and its head thrown back. The silver-skinned demon was retreating before it, fire-pitted eyes blazing hatred.

"We never knew his true name," Kai said. "We called him Innat. After my teacher Shemayan's firstborn son."

He was directly behind her. She had not heard him approach. She felt his breath against her cheek, heard him say, "We beat back Bakal Ashika and the demons because of him."

Jess touched the cloth.

"This is an idealized depiction," Kai continued. "In reality the two were much more closely matched. We suspect they had their own private battle, the two of them, in the Dreamlines. Bakal Ashika nearly tore him apart."

Jess said, "But what is he? What . . . ?"

"A war-angel from a very distant realm."

He put a hand on her arm to steady her. He spoke in an absent tone, as if concluding a dialog he'd been conducting in his head. He nodded towards the tapestry. "Innat was summoned—pulled—from his own world and into ours. The man who did it was my teacher, Shemayan. No one else could have done it. No one had the capability."

"Shemayan." Jess clicked into the name. "The one I resemble."

"Shem bound him to his bloodline. Innat fought for us, but he did not serve us; he served only Shem. And when Shem died, the blood-link, or Binding, passed down to his children. And his children's children. And so on through the generations.

"And finally to you, Jess.

"It has come down to you."

She took a step back, as if she could put some distance between herself and the things he was telling her. When she spoke, her voice sounded strange to her, faint and tinny: "How does a person accomplish a thing like this? Capturing a—an entity like this?"

"It's complicated. It takes great skill and power. And sacrifice."

"Sacrifice," she said. She felt too warm, too close to the fire. "What got sacrificed?"

He held his breath for a moment, and she thought he

would refuse to answer. But then he said, "His son. He bound the creature to his bloodline through the body of his firstborn son.

Another log collapsed inside the fireplace. She was conscious of Mina watching them, curled inside the leather armchair.

"Shemayan is your ancestor," Kai said. "On your mother's side."

"That's impossible," Jess said. "That would mean I'm part—Like you. And her." She jerked her head towards Mina.

"You haven't figured that out yet?"

"I'm—"

Her voice, her words, just stopped.

"You paint brilliantly," he murmured, "especially for one with so little formal training. You never required any."

"That's hardly proof of—"

"Shem's line is particularly gifted in such ways."

"I'm not like you," Jess said. She didn't say it in protest; simply as blunt, self-evident fact. "Look at me. I don't look like you. I can't do anything paranormal, for God's sake. . . . I know what I am. I *paint*. I'm a *painter*."

Kai sighed. Said tonelessly, as if reading off a prompter, "You have a psychic link to Innat and the ability to command him the way Shemayan did. And that's why you're so important. Bakal Ashika does not know you exist. She thinks she slaughtered all Shem's children, thinks the bloodline ended with Shemayan himself. You, and the ones who came before you, are the secret I've spent centuries protecting. In case I was ever to need you. Like now."

The bones in her legs were turning to dust. She put a hand against the wall to steady herself. "It's the boy," she said. "Not this—this thing—" Her eyes fell again on the shimmering, elongated figure in the tapestry. "I'm linked to the boy." It was an important distinction to make. The boy in her paintings (his ancient grieving

eyes) was the person who needed her, haunted her. It
was the boy who compelled her. Not this shimmering,
otherworldly warrior.

"Jessamy. The boy *is* the warrior. Or partly. After
Shem's death, Innat lived within the Dreamlines—"

"The Dreamlines," she said. That word again.

"—Caught in a kind of limbo, unable to return home.
At some point he came back down into this world.
We're not sure why. It's possible Innat knew of Ashika's
impending escape; it's possible they were in some kind
of psychic communication. Innat knew he was not strong
enough to survive another encounter with her. So he
went into hiding the only way he could."

Struggling to follow this. "He's hiding *inside the boy*?"

"Yes. In this realm Innat is like a ghost, Jess, he can't
exist in the same physical way that you or I do. But
inside human flesh, human soul, Innat is concealed from
us all. From us, from Ashika, from everyone but you.
You alone can recognize his true nature, can see the
face and name of the one who carries him." He paused,
then said, "Your paintings."

"And the boy himself doesn't realize?"

"He would know he's not exactly normal. He wouldn't
know why."

She was aware of Kai and Mina exchanging long
glances. She was aware of the wood snapping in the
fireplace, and the faint droning song—*demon song*—
thrumming up from unseen depths, through floor and
faded carpets, into her own body.

Kai was still speaking to her, but she must have missed
a step in the conversation because she didn't, couldn't
know what he was talking about. This was a game, a
dream, a storybook. She was ballooning out of herself,
gazing down. None of this was real. Couldn't be. "You
can heal him. Make him strong again. If you can only
get to him. Del can help you awaken your own power,
Jessamy. That's why I brought you here."

"Why can't you do it?"

His eyes flicked aside, as if he were ashamed.

"I think you should rest, now," Kai said.

"You realize you have this habit of not answering my questions?"

His eyes darkened. She was fascinated all over again by their rich amber color. "I think you're very tired, now. You need to sleep."

"No," she snapped, but the sleepiness was already working through her. *Wait,* she wanted to say. This fatigue was not her own, not natural, as it spread through her body like heavy syrup. Jess felt Kai's hand in the small of her back, steering her from the room.

Down a short hallway, up stairs to a lofty landing that overlooked the living area. She saw Mina curled in the chair, staring into the fire. But then Kai was opening another door, guiding her through it.

Her eyes were so heavy.

Vague impression of a bedroom: shades of blue and yellow, a big four-poster bed. "Sleep deeply," Kai was murmuring to her. "I'll come for you tomorrow. I'll even serve you breakfast in bed."

And then she was nestled beneath soft covers, as sleep steamrollered over her. She fought against it, struggled to speak through it: "Kai."

In the doorway, he paused.

"Don't ever use magic on me again."

If he made any reply, she didn't hear it. Sleep took her deep and far, and she did not dream that night.

Fifteen

Mina said, "You haven't told her, have you?"

It was a strange kind of fatigue, grinding in his bones. He had sleepspelled Jessamy not so much because she needed the rest—although she needed all the rest she could get while she could get it—but because he no longer had the energy to deal with her questions, the stream of explanations.

Mina said, "You haven't told her what we need from her. What it will cost her."

"Mina."

He didn't want to deal with Mina either. He sank onto the couch. Good to be here in this warm, familiar room, fire blazing orange and yellow behind the iron grate; good to be sipping fine port from this cut-crystal glass. Mina had the young man—Jack—go down into the cellar and fetch another bottle. As Jack placed the bottle and glasses on the coffee table, Kai glimpsed the edge of a tattoo above his neckline. He cast a startled look at Mina, for a moment thinking she'd lapsed back into the old tradition of branding, ownership. But this was a personal tattoo, he realized; even clean-cut types were into them nowadays.

Jack, like his long chain of predecessors, earned a lucrative salary as Mina's assistant, but that wasn't the most interesting reward of the job.

Time moved differently in the demon-prisons. The places themselves were chosen not just for their remoteness but because they were innately, naturally powerful: they were *sorenikan*, sacred places, crossroads of energies that could be channeled and learned from and manipulated and exploited. *Sorenikan* formed their own secret pockets of space and time. Even people completely lacking any trace of Sajae blood were affected. They did not physically age for as long as they remained in this chateau. Mina chose for her assistants people who were lost in some way, who needed a different perspective on their lives before plunging back into the fray of the world. Some stayed for a few months or a few years, while others—like Siobhan, the woman now in Amsterdam—stayed much longer. Siobhan had been twenty-six when she came to this mountain. Three decades later, when she left, she was from all outward appearances still twenty-six.

"Kai," Mina said again. Her tone was patient. She was used to him, his silences, knew how to coax his attention as if it were a wayward dog.

He looked at her, and said, "I have to take it in stages, Mina. She has to be . . ."

"Broken in? Like a wild little pony?"

". . . properly prepared."

Mina looked into the fire. "Is it possible you're wrong about her?"

"No."

"You're so certain."

"You should have seen her paintings."

She didn't answer this. She said instead: "We are not what we were."

"You think I don't realize this? I realize this every hour of every day—"

"We can do tricks." Her voice was edged with scorn

and something else: loss, Kai thought. A knowledge that ran deep and vast, that continued to bind them.

What they had lost. What they were losing.

"Sleepspells," Mina continued. "Memory tricks. A little bit of levitation, a little bit of dream- and mindplay, and some of us can no longer do that. And one pretty descendent is supposed to make up for all this? Forgive me, my prince, but I am dubious."

"Mina," he said, but he didn't want to argue. Mina could be difficult for the sake of being difficult: her nature for as long as he'd known her.

He changed the subject. "I saw Salik in New York. He killed a woman for no reason. Because she annoyed him."

Amid the shifting firelight, Mina's expression was implacable.

"He asked me if I thought this world was worth saving."

"What did you answer?"

"What do you think?"

She looked away from him, sipping at the port that gleamed so richly in the glass, then murmured, "What if it's time?"

"Time?"

"What if it's time for this world to enter a new era? And for the Sajae to just quietly, finally . . . desist? What makes you think we're so special, so *right,* Kai? Why should the world belong to us and not to them?"

"You're not serious," he said flatly. "A new era of what? Disease and destruction?"

"And then a rebuilding," Mina said. "A re-*creation.*"

"Oh, yes," he said. "A brave new world authored by fucking *demons*—what is it, exactly, you think they would create? A more effective political system?" He waited a beat, as she shifted in the chair, her hair a deep auburn in the firelight. "They don't *create,* Mina. They *can't.* They need humans to do that work for them."

"Kai—"

His hand was shaking. He set down his glass. The glitter in Mina's eyes had unnerved him. "Is it *Del,* is he getting to you? You're been here with him for such a long time—You've grown inbred, my lady, you're losing all reason—"

"That's absurd." She vaulted from the chair, moved in front of the fireplace. He remembered—with a clarity that took him by surprise—how that rich, tumbled hair had once felt in his fists. Remembered her naked body against silk pillows.

But that had been many, many lives ago.

She said, "People come through here, for one reason or another, bringing me news. Bringing rumors. And you. *You.* You went too far, too long. You disappeared."

"I was traveling the Pacific. It's not like I was on Mars."

"You took yourself out of contact."

"That was the bloody *point.* Some people might call it a vacation."

She laughed. "A vacation from what? Yourself?"

He didn't answer.

He had felt his own sanity slip, from time to time. There were occasions when he had to go save it.

Mina was smiling. "So tell me, dear prince, how *did* that work out for you?"

He thought of Celine, the Parisian expat he had lived with in St. Martin. She was thirty-seven, ripe and soft and tanned and freckled. He stopped his memory there, before it moved any deeper, before it presented Celine and her son the way he had left them—

"Some of it," he murmured, "was lovely."

—But memory can be relentless:

He returned to the villa and searched the rooms for Celine, yelling her name all the while, and found her in the kitchen. She was on the floor, rocking back and forth, cradling the severed head of her six-year-old boy. The side of her own head was sunken and bloody. And she keened, keened, keened like an animal until she sank into his arms and finally died.

He went out into the rain-lashed courtyard and screamed for Ashika, and her voice drifted back on the wind: Did you love them, Kai? I hope you did. I hope you love again. So I can find them and kill them with pleasure.

"So you reappear," Mina said, and Kai forced himself back inside this moment, "and attempt to claim your old authority, and expect us to rally behind you? Things have changed, Kāi. The world is not what it was seven hundred years ago. *We* are not what we were seven hundred years ago. And . . . there are suspicions." She seemed to struggle for a moment, looking for a softer way to phrase it: "*You* have become an object of suspicion."

Behind her, the fire was dying out; he flung his hand toward it in annoyance and the flames blazed up again.

"There is talk," Mina said slowly, "that you released Bakal Ashika. That you set her loose in this world."

"Mina, that's utterly absurd."

"I'm only reporting the rumors. To someone who's more *out of touch* than he realizes."

"Who is suggesting this? Salik?" Mina's silence was her answer. "Is he saying this because he believes it or because he just wants to destroy me?"

She jerked her head impatiently. "Does it matter?"

He coughed, touched his sleeve to his mouth. "Bakal will want me first," he muttered. "Those twisted ideas she has about atonement. She'll arrange for me to *atone* in some bloody, spectacular fashion. Would that be proof enough, you think, I'm not in allegiance with her? Or would I still be an *object of suspicion*?"

She didn't answer. Kai motioned at the fire again and the flames surged with new intensity.

He wanted the old powers back; wanted them with a ferocity that unsettled and depressed him. *So do we just give up, hand the world to Ashika? She thinks it is her due. Do we save ourselves by agreeing with her? Is that our only option?*

It is not. It is not. I will not accept that.

Kai said, "If I told you that we can be restored to ourselves, to what we were, would you believe me?"

"No one can soulcast that deeply into the Dreamlines," Mina said.

"But if I was willing—"

"Is Bakal truly the threat you think she is?"

He was too stunned by the question to answer.

Mina said, "She was imprisoned for over five hundred years. She has not attempted to release any of the others. Surely she would have done so by now . . . ?"

This was a question that had troubled him as well. Ashika had gone to America. Following Innat, Kai knew, and yet he wasn't sure why. She was weaker and more vulnerable alone. They all were.

"She didn't try to free them," Mina said, "because she *can't*. In her own way she's as crippled as Innat. She's confused and lost out there." Mina's eyes locked with his. "That's what the others are saying."

"They're wrong. If she's weak, she won't remain so."

She looked away.

"Trust me, Mina. You know me better than anyone. And I know *her* better than anyone."

"You've fallen from grace. I don't think you realize."

"I realize—"

"Your own Pact doesn't trust you. They won't follow you. They'll keep on living as they're living and they'll listen, and they'll watch; and if Bakal comes to power like you predict, they'll hide. Or die. Some of them might even join her, if she'll take them." Mina's eyes turned flat. "A lot of them just don't care anymore. We saved the world once, and for what? What's become of it? Or of us?"

"Do you?" he said. "Care?"

She didn't answer.

"Mina," he said quietly. He stepped closer. "Mina." She wasn't looking at him. But neither did she move away from him. They stood there together, breathing together, as the wood turned to ash and the firelight died.

She had been in this place, now, for four hundred years, her devotion to Del's Guardianship as single-minded as her devotion to pleasure had been, a long time before. He had been one of those pleasures. Hair falling over him like auburn rain. They'd been so young then, swallowed whole by palace life. So easy to forget the layers of society that churned beneath, studying you because they couldn't afford not to: their lives were balanced on your whims. They learned you, they learned your every nuance, and they despised you. While you played away at court, self-satisfied and oblivious. That kind of power was only interested in itself. Everything else fell away: unseen, unregistered. And then you were blind.

"You are fond of her," Mina said suddenly. "Of Jessamy."

It was not what he'd expected her to say.

He said, "I've watched that family for centuries. It's only natural."

Firelight flickered, shadows weaving and dancing on the tapestries.

"You must step carefully, my prince. For so many reasons."

He thought of Jess Shepard curled on the bed. He had assumed she was asleep, until her voice caught him in the doorway: *Don't ever use magic on me again.*

"I know that," he said wearily. "Mina, I know that."

Sixteen

And when the house of cards that was his time with the Campbells came tumbling down, it happened swiftly and bloodily and without warning.

Ramsey wanted to wipe that late-night encounter from memory and go on as if nothing had happened. But as soon as he came downstairs the next morning and caught eyes with his foster sister—she was leaning against the kitchen counter, plucking shell off a hard-boiled egg— he knew, in the space of one burning glance, that she was feeling too rejected, that it made her ashamed and angry.

And he couldn't look at her without remembering her tongue in his mouth, her hair in his face, her bare, silken breast in his hand.

They were civil to each other, like courteous strangers.

That evening he practiced jump shots, hook shots, from different points on the driveway. The feel of the ball in his hands, the sight of it swooshing through the nylon mesh, calmed him a little.

There was the squeak of the screen door opening,

Dorrie's plump, friendly body appearing on the porch: "Ramsey? Run to the store for me?"

The ball got away from him, bounced twice and rolled into grass. "Sure," Ramsey said.

She gave him a short list of items and some money. And then paused.

"You know," she said, as if clarifying something in her own mind, "you are a good kid."

He thought of her long-legged, brown-haired daughter, straddling his body and pulling on his belt buckle.

He turned his face away.

"Thanks," he muttered.

"So don't let them tell you any different."

He walked down to Samson and Peninou, passing beneath tangled, shadowy branches that arced over the sidewalks. This was where the town thinned out, giving way to the woods.

The convenience store's was the only lit window in the strip mall. The plus-size boutique, martial-arts academy, and town's only (and failing) sushi restaurant were locked up and empty. The clerk sat behind the counter with a magazine open in front of him. He glanced up as Ramsey entered, seemed to consider saying hello, changed his mind and returned to his magazine.

Ramsey cruised the aisles. He picked up the chips and went to the refrigerated section at the back of the store. He tucked the chips beneath his arm and picked up some low-fat milk and a foil-wrapped brick of butter. He closed the door—

—And found himself looking into the face of Paul Andes.

"Hello, Ramsey," Paul said quietly.

Paul's brown hair was rumpled and greasy, his eyes threaded with blood. He had his hands shoved deep in the pockets of his light cotton jacket.

Ramsey nodded at him. "Paul." He was surprised by the other boy's appearance—Andes was usually so styled, so golden-boy immaculate. But now the odor of unwashed skin and hair lifted off him. His arms wrapped round the groceries, Ramsey said, "Well. See you around." He tried to edge around him.

Paul stepped in front of him.

Over the other boy's shoulder, Ramsey could see the clerk, sitting behind the counter and turning a page of his magazine.

Ramsey shifted his gaze back to Paul. "Something I can do for you?"

An odd, eager light came into Paul's eyes.

And he said, in that same quiet voice that didn't sound at all like the Paul Andes Ramsey had heard bellowing across the football field, or murmuring with Lauren as they sat together on the couch: "Did you guess it was me?"

Ramsey tried to step round him but Paul moved with him, blocked him, as fluidly as any ballplayer. "I said," each word carefully enunciated, like a drunk man trying to sound sober, "I said, did you guess? Did you guess it was me?"

"What the *hell*," Ramsey said in wonderment, readjusting his hold on the carton of milk that was threatening to slip from his grasp, "have you been *smoking*?"

Paul's voice dropped an octave and something moved through his eyes, something dark and glittering and not sane. Ramsey felt his stomach twist in on itself.

And then came the bloom of realization.

The note that he'd ripped up and flushed away, and forced himself to forget.

"I've seen it in dreams," Paul muttered. "These dreams, Ramsey, I'm having such crazy dreams—"

"It's okay, Paul," Ramsey said quietly. He glanced again at the clerk, who remained engrossed in his magazine. "The dreams can't hurt you. The dreams—"

Paul took his right hand from his jacket pocket. Ramsey saw the gun. It happened so quickly, so casually, Ramsey's first thought was that it had to be a toy.

"The world will burn because of you," Paul whispered, "—so it's up to me to do this. I am not afraid. I am *not* afraid."

The milk, the butter, the cellophane bag of salt and vinegar chips: they all slipped from Ramsey's arms. The carton made a loud, moist, thwacking sound as it hit the tile.

That got the clerk's attention. He lifted his head and said, "Dudes—"

Paul swiveled on his heel and shot him.

He did it as casually as tossing a Frisbee. The clerk's head snapped back and he slumped off the stool, vanishing behind the counter. They heard the clumsy thump as his body hit the floor.

Paul turned and aimed the gun at Ramsey.

Ramsey didn't know anything about guns. He couldn't have identified the make and model of this one if his life had depended on it (which it *doesn't,* a wild little voice shrieked in the back of his mind, it doesn't because Paul will shoot you *anyway*). The barrel was looking straight at him, into him. He kept himself perfectly still, as if face-to-face with a wild predator that, at the slightest sign of movement, would leap and tear out his throat.

Paul Andes just shot that guy—

Paul Andes from the town's golden circle of athletes and rich, pretty kids, holding Ramsey at gunpoint, Ramsey the quiet loner with the much more fucked-up past (*And so shouldn't this be the other way around? The shrieking, wild little voice in the back of Ramsey's mind wouldn't shut up. Aren't you supposed to be the one opens fire on his peers?*).

Paul Andes just turned around and shot that guy.

Ramsey swallowed—tried to swallow—and said, "Paul. Dude. C'mon."

"I have to do this," Paul said. "You have to understand. Nothing personal, Ramsey, but"—and again, the dark glitter in his eyes—"they will *find* you, they will *devour* you, they will plunge the world into a *Dark,* a *Darker* Age—"

"Paul," Ramsey said, "Paul," the name banging around his skull like a caged hysterical bird.

"—The world will crawl with disease," Paul said, "Oh such great disease, such decay, and the demons, oh the demons—"

"Paul, please, listen to me, they're just dreams, just dreams—"

"That's not true! Don't you understand that's not true?" The corners of his mouth were twitching. "People crucified on telephone poles up and down the highways. People bleeding from every orifice, people eating the brains of their children, people melting and twisting in the flames. People vomiting blood and shitting out their organs. Don't you know what you are? She's going to use you, Ramsey. She's going to use you! *Don't you know what you fucking are?"*

The gun was trembling in Paul's hand. Ramsey was close enough to see the stubble that bristled along the boy's jaw, breathe the stink of the sweat that had darkened his T-shirt.

Ramsey said, with all honesty, *"No."*

But the voice at the back of his head whispered, *He's right,* the words like cold poison injected in his veins. *He's gone crazy and he doesn't understand. But he's right. You know it.*

Paul gave a small nod. "I'm really sorry," he said, and there was a click as he pulled back the trigger, "but you have to die. Or the world will burn, Ramsey. It will all burn away."

What happened next happened very quickly.

Ramsey felt a blossoming deep inside him, something so cold it burned through him like hellfire. Whatever it was—whatever force—it ripped up and through his body and blasted out from him, and Paul's eyes went very wide as something unseen snatched him off his feet and slammed him against shelves of boxed sugar doughnuts and stacked rows of Pop-Tarts, and the gun went off in a whip-crack of a sound.

—And Ramsey felt the world go away from him for a moment—

—And he was on his knees, staring down at cheap speckled tile, and his shoulder was alive with pain.

Paul was crumpled on his side, unconscious or dead, the gun on the floor beside him. Ramsey cried out. He scrambled to Paul's body and kicked away the gun, the way cops did in movies and TV. Paul still didn't move. Ramsey stood there, hunched over, one hand pressed to his right shoulder, liquid heat soaking through his army jacket. He watched the other boy until he saw his chest rise and fall and knew he wasn't dead.

The clerk was, however.

Splayed out on the floor between the counter (with its glassed-in shelf of lottery tickets) and the back wall (with its stacks of cigarettes), the clerk stared glassily up at Ramsey. There was no fear on his face, just a naked confusion.

Ramsey snatched up the phone behind the counter, called 911. "Sir, sir, please calm down, I need you to calm down—" the operator was saying, but Ramsey could barely hear her. He rambled on until he was pretty sure he had said everything he needed to say, then let the phone hang off the counter so they could trace it if they had to. There was a blazing in his veins, licking the underside of his skin; he could not stay in here, it was much too *hot* in here, dead clerk behind the counter and maybe-dying golden boy crumpled amid boxes of chocolate fudge Pop-Tarts and Ramsey flung himself against the door, spilled out into summer night, air washing over him as he stumbled through the parking lot.

His first instinct was to go back to the Campbells. He could not deal with police or ambulances with red sirens flashing, but he was pretty sure he could deal with Dorrie. She would calm him, would explain to him what had *really* happened, because surely he had not just fought off Paul with some invisible force blasting through him like he was a character in a comic book, surely he had not done that, for God's sake, it just wasn't possible.

He reached the sidewalk, turned in the direction of home.

Then paused.

The street was abandoned. On the other side, the woods began: dense and tangled and darker than the shadows that enclosed them. But up behind the little strip mall, a scattering of houses. Someone had surely heard the gunshot . . . ? But there was no sign of activity or alarm. Silence lay on the neighborhood like fallen snow.

And then Ramsey heard the footsteps behind him.

He whirled, felt the scattered beat of his own heart, expected Andes to be there with the gun again, like the monster in a horror movie that just kept getting up and getting up again—Where was the gun? What had happened to the gun? Ramsey couldn't remember. But there was no one behind him—not Andes—not anybody. He was staring at an empty expanse of parking lot, the dark facade of the martial-arts school, the clothing boutique, summer dresses hanging off the plus-sized mannequins in the window.

But then the footsteps sounded again, distinct and unmistakable in the clear evening quiet. Pain beat inside Ramsey's right temple. He pressed his hand—palm warm and sticky with his own blood—to his head.

The footsteps sounded across the pavement, stopped beneath a streetlight.

Ramsey trained his gaze on that patch of light and sidewalk.

"Help me," he whispered.

A figure was forming inside the pool of artificial light, forming tall and slender and female. Ramsey drew closer. The pain in his shoulder no longer seemed significant.

The woman on the sidewalk said, "Come here. Let me see you."

Ramsey stopped. Her voice was familiar but wrong.
Not the singer's voice.
Not Asha.
The woman said, "Let me find you. Tell me where you are."
He took another step towards her, was about to speak when he noticed the color of her eyes—dark blue, navy blue—and recognition slammed home. She was the woman from his drawings and the tarot card, the Priestess and the Falconess, while Death rode his pale horse and the sky burned just like Andes had said it would and it was all because of him—
—*Him and the green-eyed thing that clawed and ripped at him as they fought in a realm outside this one, and the monster was tearing him apart but he couldn't get away from it, he was bound, so bound, and from somewhere far below he heard the rattling of a chain and understood it to be his own—*
"No," Ramsey murmured.
—*But he was tumbling through cold dark space, teeth ripping into him and nails sinking deep into him and salty coppery blood rising through his mouth—*
—*OH IT HURTS IT HURTS SO MUCH—*
Do you know what you are?
"No," Ramsey said. Speaking to her, this woman, this *presence,* standing in the ghostly pool of streetlight. "Stay the fuck away from me. *I was promised my release, do you understand? Do you hear me? I was promised.*"
He felt, again, the stirring of hot winds inside him.
All around him.
The woman disappeared.
She was there, and then not there.
Ramsey broke, then, and ran across the street. He stepped inside the dense, rustling air of the woods just as the sound of sirens—four minutes after he'd made the 911 call—rose into the dark.

*   *   *

He stooped and rubbed his hands in the dirt, trying to get the blood off. He rubbed his hands again on his jacket, then gently probed the wound. He had been shot; he should be feeling more pain than this.

He made his way deeper into the woods, following the sound of trickling water until he found the creek. It was churning and gleaming in the shadows. He followed it for what seemed a very long time, the moss and leaves and loose-packed earth muffling his footsteps. He listened to the sounds of his own breathing, to the soft wind knocking branches above. He felt hollowed of all thought and feeling, yet by the time he broke free of the woods, stumbling onto highway asphalt, he knew he'd made a decision.

Something choked up his throat and he doubled over, coughing. He coughed until the sheer force of it brought tears to his eyes, his hands grabbing at his throat. And then something was in his mouth—cold and splintered and coppery-tasting—and a shudder ran through him.

He spat it out.

The bullet.

It lay on the road, wet from his own saliva.

The world was tilting and weaving all around him. He looked at the stars, the woods, the bleak unraveling highway. He didn't feel like Ramsey Doe anymore. He felt as if he were losing his mind.

"Screaming and dreaming as I fell," he muttered.

Drained, hungry, dirty, Ramsey began to walk along the highway. And when he heard the car sweeping up behind him, he turned, squinting against the bright gash of headlights.

He did what seemed the natural thing.

He held out his thumb.

Hours later he stopped by a roadside phone booth. He dropped in quarters, dialed the number. Through the dirt-streaked glass he could see the dawn, sky like dirty cotton above the cluster of telephone wires and fast-food restaurants. He waited, prepared to hang up if the wrong person answered.

But it was Lauren's voice: anxious, breathless. "Ramsey?"

He said nothing.

A semi rumbled by, clanking hot air in its wake.

"Ramsey. Please. I want you to know—"

"I love you," Ramsey said, and hung up.

Seventeen

He brought her breakfast as promised, on an antique Japanese tray. "Tabasco sauce," Jess mumbled, forking up some scrambled eggs. She didn't remember when she had last eaten.

He sat on the edge of the bed. "I'm sorry?"

She was wolfing down the food. "Thank you."

"My pleasure."

She tore off a piece of toast, met his eyes with her own. Cool snowy light shafted through the windows behind him.

Kai said, "I won't, you know."

"Won't . . . ?"

"Use magic on you. Not unless your safety depends on it."

His eyes had darkened to a deep auburn. His facial expression rarely changed, but his eyes reminded her of those mood-stone rings she used to wear in grade school. She would watch him carefully, then, learn to gauge him through those eyes.

Kai said, "How do you feel?"

"Well-rested," she said. This, at least, was true. She felt part of herself going away again, detaching; she gazed at Kai with calmness, as if he didn't really exist, as if she were still dreaming.

"What were you?" she said. "In your old life, in the Labyrinth? You said the magic was restricted to the elite. So you—"

He shrugged. "I was a pampered rich kid."

She studied him for a moment. "You were more than that."

"Eat your eggs."

"Tell me what you were."

"Crown prince."

She dropped her fork. It clanged against the plate.

"So when Salik called you *His Highness,*" Jess muttered, "it wasn't just sarcasm."

"Yes and no. Jess. No more questions."

"I have the right to question—"

"You have every right." Kai handed her a folded sweater. "It's big for you, but you'll need something warm."

The sweater was blue cashmere, soft in her hands. "It's mine," Kai said, "but there are more clothes in the wardrobe. You can meet us downstairs when you're ready."

"Are you really going to take me to a demon?" Jess said flatly.

"You thought I might be joking?"

The wardrobe—a hefty antique—held jeans, T-shirts, drawstring pants, all pressed and clean and perfectly organized. They were all brand-new, all her size. As if someone had prepared for her coming. As if someone had assumed she'd be there for a while.

They were waiting for her in front of the stone fireplace. Mina nodded at her. The other woman was simply dressed, in a wool caftan and leggings, her long hair braided and wound around her skull. "This way," she said.

Jess looked at Kai. He gave a small nod. The gesture comforted her, and she felt again her depth of confidence in him. It unnerved her to be this trusting, leave herself open for such a deep and easy wound.

He said, "You need to seem innocent. Which you are. So listen to him, play along with him. That's all he requires. His first exchange will take place with me, so stand back and listen and follow my lead. Understand?"

"Seems simple enough."

"You will see a ring of colored, broken glass around his cell. He's very proud of this little collection of his, but it serves another purpose. You must not step beyond it, even when he asks you, no matter what he promises. Understand?"

Do not feed the animals. She had to swallow a laugh.

"Yes," she said.

He looked to Mina and nodded.

Mina led them from the room, down a hallway that ended in a wood-and-iron door. Mina laid both hands on the wood, murmured words beneath her breath, and the door shifted open.

She stepped through. Jess glanced uncertainly at Kai, then stepped across the threshold, aware of Kai's broad-shouldered presence behind her.

A dry, cold, narrow stairway, winding down into rock. They did not talk. A couple of times Jess glanced over her shoulder; Kai's face was devoid of expression, his eyes dark and hard. Their footfalls echoed and faded. Old-fashioned torches were spaced along the stone walls. Mina flicked her fingers at them as they passed, pale blue flames slipping up to light their way.

Time shifted away from Jess. She felt as if she had always been doing this: descending stone stairs, caught between individuals who claimed and seemed to be more than human. Except suddenly there were no steps left. They entered a tunnel, dark curve of stone above, pale form of Mina ahead.

And then Jess heard the rise of song: the atonal humming from the night before, filled with an urgency, an eagerness, shoring up the very air.

They came to another stone door. Mina touched it with her fingertips, murmured more words, and with a deep groaning sound it shifted open.

They stepped into a cavern filled with blue light.

Something that was not human said, *"Oh, my friends. Welcome."*

And in that moment, Jess believed everything.

Reality wrenched loose from its moorings and broke apart. She touched the cavern wall, steeling herself for the impossible thing that lay before her. And all the things that lay beyond that.

The light that swirled around them was ghostly and blue, like the firelight in the stone stairways, charged with an energy that hummed through her whole body. A mosaic of stained, broken glass was laid out in the center of the floor, curving around the blue sphere that hovered three feet off the ground.

Kai touched her shoulder, whispered, "That glass. Do not step beyond it."

She managed a nod.

The sphere was large enough to accommodate a full-grown man, but the thing that moved inside it and watched them through the glistening wall was not—or was no longer—a man.

It pressed long, spidery hands against the sphere wall, hissed, *"Kai."*

There was delight in its voice, its slanted red eyes. Its body was that of a human male, but one that had been distorted, elongated. It was moving, undulating, inside the sphere, long curving nails scraping across the rounded walls. And Jess saw that it had a tail: long and tapered, hairless, like a reptile's.

"My prince," it whispered. "You've come back to me."

Kai drew something from his pocket: a circle of glass, stained in a geometric design of red and blue. "Hello,

Del," he said quietly, then stooped to place the glass within the mosaic. The action reminded Jess of a person paying homage. The demon crouched and watched, wrapping its tail around its legs, red eyes following its new piece of treasure.

"Don't put it there," it said suddenly, urgently. "Move it to your right!"

Kai shifted the glass.

"Between the purple and the yellow! Yes. Good. Good!"

Kai moved several steps back.

"Very nice, Your Highness. Thank you. Thank you so much. You look very good, my prince. Very handsome." The demon grinned, revealing rows on rows of dark jagged teeth. "Every inch the image of your illustrious father. Don't you think so, Mina-Mina?"

Mina chided, "Be nice, Del. Or we'll leave you all alone."

"And take away my pretty glass? Oh, Mina-Mina. You are so very cruel. Very cruel to your little pet Del."

Kai said, "This is Jessamy Shepard. I thought you'd like to meet her."

The demon's attention shifted to Jessamy. She felt pinpricks of heat on her skin as the thing's gaze moved along her body.

"Pretty," it murmured. "The prince has found himself a nice little toy. Just like in the old, old days. Right, my Mina?"

Mina said nothing.

The demon clucked its tongue, stroked the tip of its tail. Its voice turned honeyed. "I know. The same insults, the same little barbs. But I'm trapped in here with so little to play with. Only my memories." It sighed, and rolled the red eyes back toward Jess, as if angling for sympathy. "Only memories. It's your own fault, Mina-Mina. You don't provide much in the way of stimulation. How is your little pet Del to amuse himself?"

It stuck its head forward and leered at Jess. "A pretty

little—" it said again, then cut itself off and pressed its long, rippling body against the sphere wall.

"Come closer," it barked. "Come closer, little girl. I need to smell you."

Jess approached the ring of colored glass. She could have been viewing an extremely rare animal at an extremely odd exotic zoo. But running just beneath the detachment and shock and growing curiosity was a charge of emotion. It took a moment for her to recognize it as anger.

Her life, her sense of the world, based on quicksand. And now sucked under.

The air held the sharp scent of smoke, something burning. The demon grinned. Its skin looked slippery-rubbery-smooth, pale lips wrinkling back from dark gums, dark teeth.

"I smell your blood," Del said. "I smell the blood of Shemayan."

It tossed its head back and made sharp, barking sounds, tail slapping against the curved floor of its cell. It lowered its head and looked again at Jess, and she realized it was laughing. "How interesting," it said. "How very interesting. I thought—we all thought—"

Del's gaze shifted over to Kai.

It said softly, "Well played, my prince. *So* well played."

"You thought they had all been destroyed," Kai said.

Del's face scrunched into what seemed to be a frown. "Shemayan had three children. One-two-three children. We pulled the head off the second one, gutted and ate the third. The third had pretty eyes and *such* a piercing scream. It hurt my dainty ears. And the first one." He snickered. "We know what happened to the first one. The vessel. Does *she* know?" He pointed a talon at Jess. "Have you told her everything? Or anything at all?"

"There was a fourth child," Kai said. "An infant daughter born outside the marriage."

"Our noble Shemayan an *adulterer*? So very very naughty."

"His wife made the arrangements," Kai said. "They knew they needed another child. A secret child."

"To carry the Binding," Del said. The fierce gaze returned to Jess. "And so this little one is the result. The secret progeny. How very clever. Well done, well done. I didn't know the old guy had it in him." It paused, then said, "Shem was an easy kill, you know. It was very very disappointing." It flicked its tail, body rippling back and forth in the sphere. It seemed agitated, pacing. "Why have you brought this little daughter to me, my prince? May I venture a little guess?"

Kai's voice turned wry. "Please."

"I can smell the Binding, but it's very very deep within her. Do you need me to dig it out? Open her up, so to speak? Show her around?" The demon's voice spiraled up an octave. "Has your kind grown so weak?"

"Yes."

Behind them, Mina drew in breath. Kai continued, his voice smooth and untroubled: "Bakal will crush us with ease. It won't be much of a show, Del, not for an audience as demanding as you. No suspense, no plot twists, no sense of climax. No fun."

He glanced sidelong at Jess. Glanced away.

The demon appeared to be musing to itself. "Innat, poor crippled hurting Innat, concealed in human flesh." It stroked the tip of its tail. "Hmmm. The Sajae scattered and fallen and some of them, like Mina-Mina here, even resigned to their own defeat. The Binding buried deep in the contaminated blood of a descendent. Oh my. Oh my, no." It glanced back at Kai. "But Bakal must gather her strength, her bearings, in this strange new modern world. Do you think she's found her special friend yet?" Del grinned. "There is *always* a special friend."

"Odd," Kai remarked, "how demons can't stand to be

alone. As if you find your own company rather loathsome."

"I find myself enchanting," Del said, and thumped its tail. "But we digress. So you require just a touch of demon magic, do you not? And I, the only demon *foolish* enough to help you, *selfish* enough to risk the wrath of my colleagues." It giggled. "Do I have a crystal-clear understanding of the situation?"

"Beautifully clear."

"You expect me to betray my own kind?" Del hissed. "Betray *Bakal*?"

"I think even Bakal Ashika would like a good game," Kai said. "Once you annihilate us, what will you do for fun?"

"You know what Bakal has planned for you? Quite gruesome. You could save yourself, Your Highness, if you would only—"

"Is that what you want to see happen?" Kai said.

Del ducked its head, peering up at Kai, stroking its tail.

Jess thought: *My God. It's flirting with him—*

"You should probably die, Kai." But the demon was plucking its tail with both taloned hands, turning away from the Sajae prince, as if it was unsure.

"Everyone dies. It's just a matter of time and place."

"And how much pain."

"Don't you want to make things interesting? You can be the wild card."

"The X factor." The demon was pleased. "The random element."

"That makes you very powerful."

"Whatever I do," Del said, "is meaningless in the end. What good is a blood-link to a warrior made crippled and cowardly?"

"I don't know. Why don't we find out?"

The demon paced inside the sphere for several moments, and the high, sweet, burning smell grew stronger.

Del grew very still, looked out at them again. "She

will win, in the end," it declared. "It is a matter of destiny, it is the way of things. But you have learned me very well, sweet prince. I want a *good* game. I want a *fun* war." The red gaze shifted slowly across them all. "Leave the little one with me. Let us get to know one another."

Mina said, "Are you prepared for this, Jessamy?"

Del laughed. Jess did not flinch or look away. Her fear was a thing she had cut away from herself; she could feel it, floating nearby, tethered to her but not *of* her.

"I can handle this," she said.

"*Can* you?" Del said. He sounded happy, gleeful. "Let's find *out*."

Kai's hand on her shoulder, his voice in her ear, one final repeated warning. *"Don't go beyond the glass."*

Jess nodded.

"Ten minutes," Kai said to Del.

And then Kai and Mina withdrew. She heard the shift and thud of the stone door behind them.

Del spoke first. "Mina once read a story to me called *Alice in Wonderland*. Do you know it?"

"Yes."

"It was very *trippy*. You can play Alice. Is Kai your White Rabbit?"

"Mina reads to you?"

"We enjoy each other. We keep each other company. It's a twisted demented relationship. It's *lovely*."

"Kai said you could be charming," Jess said. "I'm still waiting."

"Did he?" Del chuckled, deep in its throat. "Maybe in my finer days. But charm is such a cheap and shoddy thing. Easily put on. Easily taken off. Never trust the things that charm you. The man is enchanting, don't you think? Even in the old old days, when he was just a spoiled little princeling. He was a wild, beautiful thing. Someday you should open him up—not literally, of course—and get him to tell you stories. If he still remembers. *I* could refresh his memory." Del paused, scratched his chest with one long, tapered finger. "I smell him on you. That sweater. Is he courting you? Romancing you? Is he scr—"

"No."

"Shame. I imagine he's a wee bit different from *other* men. Do you find that difference repellent, pretty Jessamy?" He paused. "Or are you . . . in love"—he batted his eyes and made fluttery motions with his hands—"with someone else?"

She didn't react; or at least, didn't think she reacted. Yet he had already picked up the answer.

"Ah," he said.

"Is this really what you want to talk about?"

Del giggled. "It is, actually. But I see your point. Time is ticking, ticking, tick tick *tick*. So come closer."

She was caught by his voice, his eyes. She moved towards the sphere, until her chopped-up shadow fell across the circle of broken glass.

"It was slave magic," Del whispered. He covered his mouth with his hand, looked around him with big eyes; then he giggled. "That's what they called it. Bad magic. Illegal magic."

He pressed his hands against the sphere, looking at her. His eyes sparked and flamed. She was drawn in by that gaze, fascinated by it.

He said, "Driven underground, practiced only by outcasts like me, and slaves like Ashika, who kept it concealed from the overclass, the ones who ran and ruled the city. But magic becomes rather *twisted* when you have no wise one to guide you. And *our* teacher was Bakal Ashika. She wasn't a very good influence." He giggled.

"Who taught Bakal? How was a slave able to grow so powerful?"

"That's a dark, perverted, *fabulous* story, but we'll put it away for a rainy day. Look here. I'm going to put on a show for you."

He pointed one long curving fingernail to the stone wall on their right. Images appeared on the stone, flickering there like a film with the sound turned off.

"Pay attention," Del ordered. "This is important."

Jess saw a high, sunbaked city wall, wrought-iron gate swinging open. A caravan entered the city, dark-skinned figures in bright robes and scarves filing through on camels and horses. And behind them, Jess saw the slaves: men and women of different ethnicities, roped together by wrists and throats, bare feet shuffling in the sand.

At the end of the line was a small, thin girl, a mass of blonde hair hanging down her sunburnt back.

"That is her."

Del's voice was reverent.

"That's my lady."

It sounded as if the demon were whispering right against her ear. Jess started, wheeled round: but Del was only watching her from inside the sphere, hands flattened against its chest.

"She was twelve," Del said. "Look, look."

The scene changed to a cool, luxurious interior, walls of red silk undulating in the breeze. Half a dozen Sajae—all tall and lean, with high-boned features and tilted, luminescent eyes—sat in a semicircle, smoking and making comments to one another, their eyes on the event taking place in front of them. Two of the men were taking turns with the blonde slave girl. She was on her hands and knees, matted hair swept over her shoulder, face wrenching with every thrust. Jess saw the girl's eyes, the expression in them: selfhood burned away, nothing left but animal pain, animal fury.

Twelve.

"The idle aristocrats," Del observed. "The cultivated elite. This was before they discovered she could sing. Then they would make her perform for them, and *then* they would fuck her."

The images flickered again and disappeared.

"The dark-haired Summoner using her from behind,"

Del said casually. "Years later, Bakal force-fed him his own testicles. But she fried and buttered them first, while he looked on, still bound up and bleeding. It was funny."

Jess said quietly, "Was Kai . . . ?"

"You mean, did the *prince* ever put the slaves to such purposes?" Del grinned, licked his lips. "No. Alas." A note of pride in Del's voice. "He was growing a social conscience, if you can believe that. The city was on the verge of revolution, wanting a return to the old ways: equal access to the Academy, the magic, that kind of thing. Kai was starting to be involved with it—secretly, of course, otherwise his father would have slaughtered him. But the revolution wasn't happening fast enough, it would not have gone far enough. Not for *us*. We wanted some *fun*."

"So Bakal and her followers destroyed the Sajae—"

"Can you blame us? Or at least, can you blame *her*? She tore apart every man who ever violated her. She slaughtered their wives and children. We helped. And, well." Del shrugged his bony shoulders. "We ended up killing everyone, actually. Sometimes these things happen."

"So why not take your revenge and *stop*? Why—"

"Because bloodshed is *fun*," Del said, and thumped his tail. "It's *tasty*. And the hunger. The demon-hunger. The hunger goes deep, so deep, never stops, never *stops*. My colleagues developed all sorts of plans." Del thought for a moment, then shrugged. "They all want power, of course. Ultimate domination, godhood, that kind of thing."

"But you don't?"

"I think their goals lack imagination, myself." He pressed his face against the sphere wall. "Myself, well, all that hunger made me *tired*. Enough chitchat. Come closer."

She was so focused on him that she automatically stepped forward; when the glass crunched beneath her boot she was surprised. She froze, one foot still in mid-air, as the demon tilted its head at her like a curious terrier.

"Kai told you not to go past the glass?"

She didn't answer.

"Aw, *shucks*," he said. "I could do all sorts of things if you got close and cuddly. All *sorts* of things." Del sighed. "But we'll have to work from here. Now, what do you have to give me in exchange?"

But her wall of detachment was thinning and crumbling, streaks of true fear ripping through her. She lifted one foot to step back off the glass—

—And it felt as if someone had taken a sledgehammer to her head. The pain knocked her sideways, her hands coming down on broken glass, shards scattering beneath her body. She kicked out, scrambling away from the demon, but she realized the demon, the entity, had just reached *inside* her, filling up her head until her skull was close to exploding; she cried out, clutching her temples. Opened her eyes, saw the demon sitting inside the sphere, perfectly still, eyes closed, and when it spoke again its voice came from *inside* her, booming and echoing like a voice in a dream. *I need some memories, pretty Jessamy. That's all I want. You can spare a few memories for a poor, bored demon, can't you?*

Fragments of her life were raining through her mind, the demon overturning desk drawers of memory: road trips with her parents when she was very small; her encounter with Kai in Cape Town—*How interesting,* the demon said, and *Weren't you just the little cutie*—and then the years that followed, shell-shocked with grief and displacement. New girl in school; older boys coming round, sniffing out her vulnerability, angered by her resistance, *Are you frigid, bitch? Are you a lesbian?* The times with Harker, her uncle. *Not exactly what I'm looking for,* the demon said. *Really, Jessamy, don't you have something a little more . . . feel-good?*

Images of her life in New York.

Better, the demon said approvingly.

Gabe.

Gabe, the corded strength of his arms, the way he murmured her name as he moved his hips against her. *Much better!* the demon chirped. Candles by the bed, by the bathtub. The discussions they had over coffee and pastries, steaks and martinis: books, movies, her art, his plans for his own line of furniture; the five-day getaway to Santa Fe they took last April; the bookshelves they built together for Jess's last apartment; the time they tried to run the New York City marathon and dropped out halfway through, went for nachos and beer instead; the fights, the makeup sex that quickly followed; reading the newspaper together, jogging together, watching TV together; his habit of whistling the classical music he never listened to anymore but had been inundated with as a boy; his love for fantasy and comic-book art; all the details that knit up into a thing more profound, mysterious, than the sum of their everyday parts.

I love you.

The demon took it all.

No, Jess cried. Stop. But the demon ignored her, and she felt the memories peeling away and out of her and coldness, emptiness, rushing through the vacant spaces. *I love you, Gabe.* The history and emotion behind those words thinning to nothing—

I'm just not very good at it.

—Until the words themselves collapsed into ash.

Oh, grow up, the demon said impatiently. *It's nothing you can't live without.*

Look what I offer in return.

She no longer knew if she was dreaming or awake.

Because now she stood in a hallway lined with closed doors. The hallway seemed to go on forever, unreeling all the way down to its vanishing point; the lines of the doors were at weird angles.

They're all shut, she told Del. She was sure that she had been here before. *Those doors are all locked.*

Not anymore, Del said.

The demon had transformed. He now looked like an ordinary man, dressed in a rough brown cloak and sandals. His face was lined and tanned and friendly.

She asked him: *Where do those doors lead to?*

Yourself. He looked at her intently. *This is what Kai could not do for you. This is what you could not do for yourself. Remember that.*

He grinned, cupped both hands around his mouth, and blew.

The door closest to them flung open; light poured forth like fire. And Jessamy heard a name, carried high on the wind and the light, spoken in a voice that was eerily familiar—

Ramsey.

His name is Ramsey.

—A voice she recognized as her own.

She approached the first door, shielding her eyes. Del stayed behind, hands clasped in front of him, like a parent waiting patiently while his kid went trick-or-treating. Jess turned in to the doorway, into blazing, blinding light, and stepped across the threshold—

—And into a deserted parking lot.

She saw the parking lot, the strip mall, the night sky overhead, the dark woods rising across the road. She took a few steps, tested the feel of the pavement beneath her, the air on her face.

And she saw the boy.

He seemed to come from nowhere, lunging towards her. He was hurt. She stared at him, and he stared back with the same stunned expression. Blood was soaking through his army jacket. His face was blanched, eyes glassy. She had painted him so many times that now, to see him living, breathing, hurting, she felt as if she had authored him: he had stepped from her mind through her paintings into life. She knew that was not true, and yet could not shake her sense of power over him.

She spoke to him. Jess could barely remember her own words—*Let me find you. Tell me where you are—*

because the expression on his face rolled over her like
lava, taking all her words away.

Terror.

The boy was terrified of her.

She felt a hot wind rising, stirring the leaves in the
trees, sending an empty can scuttling across the
pavement.

Wait, she tried to say, but heard the sound of a door
swinging shut.

It all went away.

When she opened her eyes, Jess Shepard was back
on the floor of the chamber, the chill seeping through
her clothes.

She looked up.

Del gazed at her. He had moved back from the sphere
wall, sitting cross-legged in the center like a yogi, his tail
tucked neatly around him. "Please come again," he said.

And then: "You owe me. You all do."

He wasn't speaking to her.

Footsteps behind her. Strong hands beneath her shoulders, helping her up. Her hands, she saw, were bleeding,
blue glass embedded in her palm.

"Jess," Kai whispered, and the guarded expression in
his face gave way to concern.

"She stepped on the glass!"

This time it was a higher, thinner voice that broke out
from the demon. Del pressed himself (and Jess realized
that her concept of the demon had at some point shifted
from an "it" to a "he") against the sphere wall, staring
at Kai. "She stepped on the glass! It's her *own* fault! It's
your fault! You should have warned her!"

"I did what you said," Jess said hurriedly. "I didn't
go beyond the glass. I—" Her mind felt strange, it felt
changed, as if a splinter of glass had driven deep into
the core of it.

She said, "I need to get out of here."

But Kai was staring at her, and at the demon, and didn't seem to hear.

The demon squashed his face against the curved wall, grinned, waggled his fingers against the glass. "I did it for you, princeling! I gave her a gift!" His voice rising, shrieking, hurting Jess's ears. "I gave her a GIFT! Now the game is interesting! *Now* the game is interesting!"

"We're leaving," Kai muttered.

Mina was waiting for them outside the chamber. She said nothing, turned and walked down the tunnel. The demon's voice boomed around them.

"Remember, princeling! You owe me for this! Remember, remember, sweet prince!"

II

All the Pretty Ones

Eighteen

In the dream, Jess thinks she is alone in the building.
Until she hears the singing:

> *I'm slap happy*
> *I'm punch drunk*
> *Got a sinking feeling I'll wake up on Monday*
> *With a suitcase full of nothing*
> *Ain't it funny?*

A raspy baritone, set to the melancholy strumming of
guitar. Jess walks down the hallway. It is lined with
doors: some of them closed, some of them swinging partway open, none of them she wants to go into.

> *But I can't believe*
> *I'm getting away with this*
> *Junkies' parade through lover's town*

When the hallway joins up with another she turns left,
towards the singing, the deep lonely sound of the guitar.
She comes to a door. It opens easily.

The room is empty: white walls, dark wood moldings,

a bay window that looks onto a brick wall. In the middle of the room a man in a white T-shirt and jeans and motor-cycle boots sits on a stool with his guitar. His light brown hair falls across his face, but she knows that face, this man, even before he looks up.

You're my little handful

He's looking at her now. His eyes brown and gentle, but flecked with slyness.

I'm your handful of dust.
Isn't it ridiculous
What love's done to us?

His hands still against the strings.

He says, quietly, "I'm in too deep. Can't get out now. How 'bout you?"

"I've dreamed about you before," she says.

"Actually," he says, as he frees himself from the guitar and places it inside the case, "you've been dreaming about me for years. You just don't remember in the morning."

"Why the hell would I dream about you?"

"I'm hurt." He kicks shut the guitar case and looks at her, boots hooked round the rung of the stool, hands clasped between his knees. Suddenly he reminds her of a repentant schoolboy, sitting out detention. He says: "She scares me."

"Ashika."

"She fucking *eats* people."

She only stares at him.

"But I can't let her go. She's in me now. She's chang-ing me. And I like it. I like the power it gives me." He pushes the hair back from his face, light glinting off the rings on his fingers.

"Then is it true?"

"What's true?"

"There's going to be an apocalypse?"

"Well, yeah. There's no getting 'round that. It'll start soon and go on for years." He smiled at her. "Interesting times, don't you think?"

"I don't want to die."

"That's not the only option. Come with me."

"Why would I do that?"

"I'm hurt," he says again. Then: "We know each other, you and I."

"We don't."

"We know each other well."

"Not in this lifetime."

"No," he agrees, surprising her. "Not in this lifetime. Not yet."

Nineteen

They were waiting for him in the parking lot of the motel, clustered around the curb, sitting cross-legged on the grass. Lucas wasn't in the mood for this. He was too tired, his ears ringing from the mediocre band he'd gone to see in the downtown blocks of whatever town they were in tonight; he no longer bothered to remember the names. He wanted silence.

As soon as they saw him drive into the lot, they were all on their feet; as soon as he got out of the van, they surged around him. Maybe twenty of them, ranging from late teens to late twenties, the girls in tank tops and low-slung jeans and funky eyeliner, the guys in ripped sweatshirts, mesh shirts, work boots, combat boots, some of them also in eyeliner. A general air of dispossession, desperation rank as sweat, voices running into and through each other: *Asha*, they were saying, *Asha, please, let me please, need to see Asha, talk to Asha, she's the only one who can help me—only one—*

"Hey," he said, and then, as someone reached out and grabbed his arm, as someone else grabbed his jacket, "Hey," fire in his voice now. He hated when they touched him.

They fell back and looked at him.

It was like this, now, in every town, the crowds who waited for him backstage or outside or sometimes, like now, where they crashed at night. It was widely understood that the band broke into two parts: Asha and himself, and the professional musicians Lucas had gathered in LA, who had started referring to themselves as the Less Interesting Three, and who instead of being jealous or resentful actually seemed—relieved. They wanted to be part of the music, but they didn't want the kind of attention the music seemed to generate. They stayed in different motels from Lucas and Asha, or crashed at the houses of friends or fans. For a band on tour, they were all managing to spend an astonishing amount of time apart.

It was understood that Lucas was the uncontested leader of the band: he produced and mixed in the studio; he chose the towns, the venues, the dates; he selected the song list; he dealt with the club owners and managers. The other band members took care of themselves and their equipment, showed up on time, did what they were supposed to do, and didn't argue, didn't offer personal opinions. Lucas doubted that any other band in the world so willingly capitulated to the artistic vision and control of one person. But then, no other band had Asha as a lead singer.

He was the one she had chosen.

He protected her, ran interference for her, and controlled all access to her.

This, too, was widely understood.

Now, he scanned the crowd, their faces and eyes, until one girl in particular caught his attention. Lucas didn't know how or why he made his choices; only, there was something inside him that seemed to speak up; *Yes. This one. This one is right,* and Lucas had no choice but to select accordingly. Sometimes that inner voice didn't speak up at all, and Lucas would dismiss all of them, turning his back and walking off, ignoring their cries and catcalls.

The girl he found himself looking at now was the youngest in the group. Lucas judged her to be fourteen, maybe fifteen, her skin dewy and soft beneath the garish makeup. He hadn't seen her in the club the night before, although the fading stamp on the back of her hand told him she'd managed to fake-ID her way in there, watch them perform.

He said to her now, "Do you know what you're doing here?"

Resisting the urge to come right out and say, *Get lost. For your own good. You're too young for this, don't know how bad this shit gets.*

"It's my stepfather," the girl said. "I need to talk to Asha. I know she'll help me. It's my stepfather."

He reached out for her, gathered her cold thin fingers in his own, pulled her forward. He lifted his voice: "Everybody else, good-bye. Come to the desert. We'll see you in the desert."

Some grumbling, swearing, boot heels scuffing on pavement, but the group began to drift apart. People knew how it worked.

The girl said, "Can I wait with you? I won't do anything—" Her fingers clutching his sleeve. She smelled of baby powder, cigarette smoke.

"Just shut up. I mean, just please be quiet. Please. Okay?"

She nodded.

In the room she hunched in the chair in the corner, her knees drawn up against her chest, as if determined to take up as little space as possible. "I appreciate this," she said. "I really do."

"Whatever."

"My name's Carrie."

"Nice to meet you, Carrie. Remember what I said?"

She nodded vigorously. "I'll be totally, perfectly quiet."

He went to the window, drew aside the curtain. He saw his own ghost in the glass. He tried to cast his mind into the night outside, past the parking lot and the shut-down downtown streets to wherever Asha was roaming. It seemed to him, lately, that his body could sense hers, or not his body exactly but his *blood*: when she was close by it actually kind of . . . *hummed,* turned *electric,* as if she had thrown a switch deep inside him (*should have left it turned off,* a voice kept insisting in the back of his mind, *you should have run away from her, killed yourself to get away from her,* and he told that voice to shut the fuck up and get the fuck away from him) and when the singer, *his* singer, was absent for too long he felt twitchy, edgy, nervous. He felt the ground opening beneath him.

But now, the outside dark carried the answering charge of her presence. He looked at the girl and said, "She isn't far."

But then, she never was.

He had felt the change working deep inside him the moment they arrived in LA. His music came back to him. Like an avalanche unleashed in his skull, thundering its way to release. He was writing again, he was on his guitar again, itching for other instruments as well. Asha's shadow ghosting over him, Asha's voice fueling him, as the white fire at the pit of his belly sprang hotter, higher.

One weekend he drove up to Malibu, went walking on the beach. Dolphins came close to shore, cresting just inside the waves. He watched them as long as they would let him. He watched the sun set. He closed his eyes and took lungfuls of air, as if the salt could scour him clean. *I'm clean,* he would think. True—he hadn't touched heroin, had barely *thought* about heroin, since that day her small figure had appeared alongside the highway—and not true. Some new contamination was twisting in his blood cells—but such a small price to pay. The music had come back to him. There was so much more ahead. Music that no one had ever heard before.

Music that could steal your soul. His own soul was already gone, he figured, traded away in that motel room after Brett died—*Because if she isn't the devil, then she is damn close*—and he was surprised by how little this bothered him. Music was the force, the godhead: it spoke every fucking language, it came down through time and crashed apart barriers. What was his soul, what was anyone's, in comparison?

She came to him, sometimes, in the middle of the night; he'd rise awake to find her tangled round him, her body fitted fluidly to his. He'd breathe in the scent that always clung to her, coppery like blood, sour-sweet like carnage. They did not have sex—that wasn't what she wanted from him, if she even wanted it from anyone—although at times he felt as if they were . . . melding; as if he could look down and see her limbs melting into his, her blood pumping through his veins.

He never looked down.

Why me, he would ask her, and he did not know if he spoke those words or if she lifted them from his brain.

Because you were calling me.

His mouth twisted wryly.

I didn't realize.

You've been calling me for centuries.

Her mouth against his throat. The hot touch of her tongue. Tasting him.

You create the music of angels, she said. *Dark angels. It has always been so.*

In the small, dark clubs they played he watched Asha grow as a performer, her voice discovering its range of expression. It was elastic, that voice; it encompassed worlds. Lucas had never heard anything like it. Her voice entered into him, so that soon he couldn't compose anything without imagining that voice as the center. He knew they were feeding off each other. They fattened up, and the performances drained them until they were lean and hungry and desperate all over again, looking at each other, clawing new ways back into that music, that edgy throbbing howling bass-slapping skull-crashing soul-stirring music. And in gig after gig, Lucas felt the reaction from the audience grow stronger and deeper, that connection sometimes so intense he wondered why it just didn't manifest itself in a physical form: a tunnel of flesh and blood rising round them, band and audience both, enclosing them, making them as one. Music was community. Music brought together strangers all looking for the same transcendence and oblivion of self. The song entered you and you entered the song; you and it understood each other. You were no longer alone. Onstage, Lucas scanned the faces of the crowd and saw the rapture overtake them, bodies jumping, arms writhing in the strobe-lit air, eyes turning up in bliss and gratitude and adoration. In those moments, they all understood each other.

From the beginning of their tour, he was surprised by the audience they drew. As if word had raced ahead of them—which he supposed it had—and given people time to prepare for their coming. They did no promotion, no radio shows, not even posters tacked to telephone poles. They showed up and played, and people showed up to listen. They were somewhere in the Midwest when Lucas realized that some of the faces in the audience were familiar.

It was the redhead who clued him in.

He saw her in the front row of a club in Lincoln, Nebraska. She was wearing jeans so low-slung they barely cleared her pubic bone. Her breasts were large, bouncing freely beneath the thin cotton of her T-shirt; her hair was thick and red and wild. He had a five-second fuck fantasy right there, as his hand moved along the fretboard and Asha howled into the microphone, and then he shifted into the next song and the redhead melted into the crowd and he forgot about her.

Until nine days later when he saw her again, this time

in a bar in a town a long way from Lincoln. This time Lucas also recognized her two friends: the towheaded skinny boy with the rings through his eyebrows, the short girl in the lace bustier. Lucas glanced over the crowd and—unless he was imagining it but no, didn't think so—saw other faces that set off echoes of recognition. And he saw, that night, the first painted blue symbol on a girl's cheek, glittering in the half-light.

In the gigs, the places, the nights that followed, he began searching the crowd for faces he knew he'd seen before, and then for the glistening blue shapes and signs and symbols that were showing up, with slow but building regularity, on naked shoulders and arms and midriffs. People were tracking them from gig to gig, Lucas realized, and the wet look of fervent devotion he saw in all those upturned gazes reminded him that *fan* was short for *fanatic*. And he could feel the force beneath the music, ripping into him, tearing up his hands as he played. He would look at Asha, wailing on the lyrics, and think again, *If she isn't the devil, then she is damn close.*

And yet, in the grip of the music, he didn't care.

In the grip of the music, it all seemed worthwhile.

One night, he had just loaded the amps in the back of the van and was heading into the club to settle up with the cheap asshole owner when movement from the alley snagged his attention.

Asha was there, standing just outside the club's side door. There was a small group of people around her, including the redheaded girl; Asha leaned over and kissed her on the mouth, then again on the forehead, and the girl rocked back on her heels. A guy dropped to his knees and hugged Asha's legs. The singer pulled his hair, slapped at his face, and laughed. The guy wouldn't let go of her.

Asha looked over and saw Lucas.

And smiled.

*   *   *

Later that night, she said, "Do you really need so many answers, Lucas? Isn't it enough just to play the music?"

"It was," Lucas said. "But now—"

"—You want knowledge? You want to open up that little box?" She made a tsk-tsking sound. "You might go mad."

"I think I'm already there."

"No. Not quite."

"Where is this leading, Asha? Where is all this—"

She moved too quickly for him to see; suddenly she was crouched on the bed beside him, touching his face with her hand. Her touch was slithery-cool. He wanted to pull away from her, but also to bury his face in the curve of her throat. He did neither.

"—Leading?" he whispered.

"The desert," she said. "My children are heading out there even now."

"Your children."

"In the clubs. Outside the clubs. Now I sow. I cultivate. But soon will be the harvest."

"And I thought they were just our number-one fans."

"But they are. They adore you, Lucas. They'll worship you too, if you let them."

She returned to the motel room just before midnight. Lucas could tell from the lack of color in her eyes and lips that she had not been feeding that night. Her gaze went directly from him to the girl in the chair. "Hello," Asha said brightly, in the way she'd learned off one of her television shows. "What's this?"

The girl was frozen in the chair. Her eyes went wide, her hand gripping the armrest.

Asha clucked her tongue. "Carrie Levin. You should be at home." Her smile turned sly, mocking. "You should be in bed. It's a school night."

The girl scrambled off the chair and came towards her, her head and shoulders bowed in a way that struck

Lucas as odd, unnatural, until he realized the girl was deliberately making herself smaller than the singer.

"My stepfather," she said softly. She glanced up at Asha, peering through hanks of bleached hair. "And my mother does nothing."

"I'm not a counselor or a social worker or a cop, Carrie. What makes you think I can help you?" Her standard response, her ritual.

"Your music," the girl said. "Your music."

"So you have something for me?"

The girl only stared, her mouth working silently.

Asha said, not unkindly, "You have something for me? You are prepared to atone for me?"

The girl nodded, stepped back a little, the color leaching from her face. She opened her purse and fumbled out a steak knife. She looked at Asha and said, "You want . . . You want a finger?"

"Or a toe," Asha said gently. "You decide."

The girl crumpled to the floor and pulled off her shoe, her sock. She positioned the knife above her little toe and did not hesitate. Lucas glanced away, but still heard the crunch of bone. When he looked back, the girl was taking a roll of medical gauze from her purse, wrapping it around her foot. Her eyes were lit up like beacons.

She folded the severed toe in a white cloth and offered it to Asha. "Is it enough?"

Asha touched her thumb to the girl's cheek. She folded up the cloth and slipped it into her jacket pocket. She looked over at Lucas. "Come," she said.

He felt the tidal pull of her presence and knew that *no* was a word he had become incapable of saying.

"Fuck it," Lucas said, and sighed. "I guess I'll drive."

The girl's house surprised him. From her cheap clothes and cheap hair he had expected something much more modest than the Colonial-style house that sat inside its own several acres. A dog was barking behind a high wooden fence. The girl led them up the arc of driveway, through the door into a spacious foyer. A staircase curved up to a second-floor landing. The girl called out, her voice breaking only slightly, "Mom? John?"

No answer.

From upstairs came the thump of techno music.

The girl stood in the foyer, beneath the chandelier, refusing to look at either of them. Asha glanced around her with interest, her hands hooked through the belt loops of her jeans. She wore a ripped and grimy T-shirt, wide leather cuffs on both wrists. She looked calm and very young, innocent inside the clothes, like a suburban teenager playing at being bad.

"Steven!" a man's voice yelled. Footsteps in the hall. A man went to the base of the stairs without noticing any of them. "Steven, would you turn that shit *down*!"

The music went on unabated.

The man turned and saw them. He was middle-forties or so, tall and well built with only a slight paunch, in corduroys and a brown sweater and slippers. He adjusted his glasses, as if to see them better, and said, "Carrie? Who are these people?"

Carrie mumbled something Lucas couldn't hear.

"Carrie? Would you answer me please?"

Carrie hitched in a breath, said, "This is—"

"I'm a friend of your stepdaughter's," Asha said. She smiled at the man and stepped towards him, tilting her head to an unnatural angle.

The man's eyes widened and he took a step back.

"She tells me you've been fucking her," Asha said pleasantly, "very much against her will. True?"

The man's mouth opened. He looked from Asha to Carrie, placed both hands against his stomach.

He said, "What—"

"Oh," Asha whispered, "it is true. It is so true." She drew closer to him and he tried to back away from her, looking at her in open-mouthed amazement, but tripped and fell to the red-gold-blue Persian rug. Asha crouched beside him, fluid and quick, and before the man could react she was grasping his face in both hands.

"You introduced her to fellatio when she was eleven," Asha whispered, "and anal intercourse when she was thirteen. True, true, true."

Carrie looked on, her body swaying like a charmed cobra's.

"I—" The pronoun a guttural syllable in the man's throat. Asha had her hands along his cheeks, was staring into his eyes. Lucas thought of a demented faith healer.

"True, true, true," Asha whispered. Tears were spilling from the man's eyes now: water tinting pink, then turning to blood. "So how do you live in daylight? You shut yourself off to your nature. You pretend you aren't the man who goes into her room, shoves the pillow over her face, says if she tells he'll put her family back in that dingy little trailer park. In daytime you pretend that that nighttime man isn't you. But guess what. It is you. It is you. Daytime or nighttime, you're the same man."

Blood began to gush from the man's nostrils, spilling over his lips, dropping fat red stains on the Persian carpet. Asha pressed her hands against his cheekbones. Lucas heard bones cracking. The man's glasses fell from his face, to the floor, and Asha smiled gently and crunched them beneath her knee.

The man's eyes filled with blood.

He opened his mouth and screamed.

It was a high-pitched, unfurling sound, and there was an answering crash from elsewhere in the house. Footsteps hurried down the hallway. Right away Lucas noticed the resemblance between the girl who'd brought them here and the woman who stood in front of them now; she was surprisingly young, dark blonde hair framing a fine-featured, angelic face. It was the kind of beauty a woman could trade on, Lucas thought, use to negotiate herself into a better life.

"John," she screamed, and Asha whirled on her.

The singer made a sharp, shrieking noise and thrust

out her hand—Lucas thought wildly of a traffic cop—
and the woman's body tilted back until she should have
fallen, yet she hung there suspended, hands flailing comi-
cally at the air, and then her body dragged itself back
along the floor, heels scraping across the carpet, and the
woman screamed again as something invisible, impossible,
picked her off the floor and slammed her high against the
wall. It pinned her there.

Vivid crunching sound of bones, one by one by one,
as the woman's chest imploded beneath her silk blouse.

Asha stood. The man was convulsing by her feet,
hands clutching his face, blood gushing from his eyes
and nose and mouth and ears. Asha ignored the sounds
he was making and turned to his wife. The woman's
breathing was a gurgling, broken thing.

"You lost your girl," Asha said. And Lucas thought,
in that moment, that Asha's voice sounded not vicious
or vengeful but . . . *wistful,* as if part of Asha's mind
was no longer in this house but casting into memory,
addressing not this woman but someone else from a long
time back. "You sold her out. So now she's mine."

The woman's head lolled against her shoulder.

"That's just the way the world works," Asha said.

Asha flicked her fingers.

Lucas saw the life pressed out of the woman's eyes.
Her body turned limp and fell to the floor. Asha knelt
beside it, her hand slipping beneath the woman's blouse,
groping for the heart.

The girl Carrie slumped to the floor. She rocked back
and forth, keening softly. Her stepfather was still thrashing. Lucas glanced up—

—And saw the teenage boy watching from the
landing.

He was pale, lanky, brown hair in his eyes, wearing a
black T-shirt with holes in it. *Jesus,* Lucas had time to
think, *I used to look like that*, before the boy turned and
ran deeper into the house.

Lucas stepped over the bleeding, convulsing man and

took the stairs two at a time. He stepped into a long hallway and paused.

He felt something turn over in his blood—something that felt and tasted like Asha—and in that moment he knew where the boy was. He could feel the boy's presence, a warm and pulsing thing, beyond a door to his right. Lucas pushed it open. A teenage boy's room: messy, smelling of dirty laundry and grilled cheese and stale marijuana, posters of rock bands and women in bikinis on every inch of wall space.

A bathroom, Lucas saw, opened off the left corner. The door was slightly open. He could feel the boy, that hot animal energy, beckoning him from beyond. He strode towards it until he saw a thing that stopped him like a blow to the groin.

The boy's stereo and CD collection. This corner was lovingly organized. The CDs were lined up like little soldiers, or stacked neatly beside the speakers, awaiting selection and usage. Except for one. It had been pulled from the ranks and tossed atop the shelf where it stared up at Lucas now.

His face. His name.

It was Lucas's one solo effort. Recorded in that brief space of time after Paula's suicide and before his own return to Mexico. Released the same week Kurt Cobain killed himself. It had sold few copies.

But this kid had it.

Lucas pushed open the bathroom door, stepped inside.

The boy was on the blue tiled floor, slumped against the tub. His face was slack and blissful. Lucas knew before looking what he would see: the boy's arm tied off, the needle in his flesh like a cigarette hanging off a lip. The boy's eyes rolled towards Lucas. "You," he croaked.

"Yeah," Lucas said. "Me."

He removed the needle and dropped it in the sink. As he knelt beside the boy he couldn't shake the feeling that he was looking at himself, some other version of himself.

"You are so cool," the boy said.

Lucas touched the boy's hand. And he sensed—the same way he had sensed the boy's presence behind that closed bedroom door—the fury of heroin storming through the kid's bloodstream. Too much, too much. But better to die this way, than at the hands of the young woman—

—*Demon*—

—Downstairs, who had slaughtered both parents in minutes.

The boy said, "My dog? He's out back . . ."

"No one's going to hurt the dog."

The boy's eyes fluttered closed. "You're so cool," he said again. And the power of speech left him.

Lucas stayed there, cradling the boy as he died.

He thought: *There is no salvation for me now. This is darkness.*

And yet, amazing how easy it was, how natural, to rejoin Asha and walk back outside. The yard quiet and dewy with night. The teenage girl was standing in the driveway, next to Asha. She looked at Lucas and said, "Where's my brother?"

Lucas shrugged.

She said again, louder, "Where's my brother? Where is he?"

"Hush," Asha said. "You have to pack. Time to go."

Her eyes were wide. "Go where?"

"The desert. With the others. Join the others."

"I'm not going anywhere without my brother."

Lucas blew out air. "He's dead."

For a moment the girl didn't say anything. Then: "What?" The bones in her face seemed to dissolve. She looked to Asha. "What did he say?"

Asha shrugged. "Get your things together. It's time for the desert."

"No," the girl said. She stepped back. "I'm not going anywhere without my brother. Where's my brother?"

"Such defiance," Asha said mildly. The girl took another step back, her head bowing as if Asha's gaze were a crown too heavy to bear. But her eyes took on a hard, shiny look.

"I'm not going," she said again.

Asha said, "You want to be with your brother?"

The girl nodded.

Asha grabbed the girl's head between both hands and wrenched it across the right shoulder. The sound was like a thick branch snapping. They watched the girl's body slump to the driveway.

"Asha," Lucas said.

All his unease, his guilt, breaking open in the syllables of her name.

Asha grinned at him, small teeth gleaming. "Get on your knees."

He stared at her for a moment. "What? I—"

"I have a gift for you."

He did as he was told. Best to do that with Asha.

She lifted a hand to her mouth. Something began to emerge from between her lips, something long and slender and gleaming, undulating into the air, weaving itself through her fingers. A serpent, patterned in red and gold.

"A gift for you," Asha said again, and lowered the snake to his mouth.

He saw the sleek, diamond-shaped head, the eyes like black crystal beads.

"No," he said. "No—"

The creature darted through his mouth with such force that he felt two teeth break against the inside of his cheek; felt the long choking slither down his throat. He fell into damp grass and gagged and gagged again. And then the snake, or whatever it was, transformed into something else, tasting of smoke and sand and ash: filling up his lungs, expanding through him; his blood, his heart, the churn of his brain in his head.

He wretched and spat into the grass; he got to his knees, then doubled over and spat again. "What the *fuck*

was that?" He had the blind animal urge to rise up and
strike her down, rip her throat out, tear her to shreds.

"It was a little piece of my heart," Asha said, and
laughed. "I think you'll like what it does for you."

He turned away from her. He could still feel her moving inside him: he was infected and invigorated at the
same time. He could feel something in his brain starting
to change. *You're a marked man now,* a little voice said
inside him. *You belong to her. She's moving all
through you.*

Staggering just a little as he walked round the side of
the house, he whistled to the dog in the backyard and
then fumbled open the gate. The dog was medium-sized
with some black Lab in him and fringed, feathery ears.
"He's coming with me," Lucas said, offering his hands
for the dog to sniff and lick. He had never owned or
wanted a dog before, but he remembered his promise to
the dying teenager in the upstairs bathroom and suddenly believed the only thing keeping the ground from
opening up and dropping him into hell right *now* was
this one goddamn stupid promise, this one goddamn dog.

The animal pressed its head into his hands.

"No worries," Asha said. Another saying she'd gotten
off the television. She even spoke it with a slight Australian accent. "I have no taste for canines."

Twenty

"Jessamy," Kai said quietly. "Follow me."

He led her through hallways and rooms. She had no sense of how this house was designed; it *had* no design. From the outside, it looked finite and contained, like any other structure—but the interior seemed to ramble on forever, extending its wings deep into the landscape. The light angling in through the windows could have been passing through from another world.

He took her to a small, sunken, high-raftered room empty of furniture, the floor layered with rugs. Kai went to the windows and drew the blinds. A pass of his hand lit the candles in the alcoves. The air took on a faint perfume that was pleasing, soothing. Kai said, "Close your eyes."

She did.

He said, "Del should have given you some kind of training image. A vision of caves, or tunnels, or hallways—"

"One hallway," she said, surprised. "Lined with doors." The image was fresh and vivid as if it had never left her mind, merely waiting for her to go back behind her eyes. The hallway careening off to its vanishing point, the staggered, tilted doors that lined either side, the fierce winds whistling past her.

"Doors," Kai said. His voice sounded far away, although she knew if she opened her eyes he would be right beside her. "And some of them are beginning to open?"

"Some of them."

Opening only slightly, with different tints of light—yellow, purple, pale blue—spilling through. She felt heat flickering over her, breathed in the faint scent of ash.

The demon's voice came riding the winds:

Remember, one of these doors is mine. So give credit where credit is due . . . It is my gift to the prince. And my gift to you.

Her eyes snapped open. The dream-hallway was gone. Back in the chamber with the silk rugs and candlelight.

Jess said, "I heard Del. In my mind. He's still in my mind."

"No," Kai said.

"He's still in my mind."

"Often during a quickening the student's mind produces its own guide-figure," Kai said. "This guide can take the form of a loved one, or someone the student has never met but admires, sometimes even an old enemy. But it's just a deeper part of your mind talking to you, Jess, helping you figure things out." Kai paused. "Like in a dream."

"A dream."

"There is nothing in you of the actual demon himself."

"Del said he gave me something," Jess said, looking at him directly. "Something that you could not foresee or predict."

"He's a trickster and a liar, Jess."

She remembered his cry, refracting off the cold stone walls: *You owe me for this! Remember, remember, sweet prince!*

"All he did," Kai said, his voice hardening, "was unlock the power that belongs to you by birthright. The hallway, the doors, this is your training image. It will help you visualize the magic as it now moves freely through you, as you learn to channel and control it. Do you understand, Jessamy? You are a spellcaster now. Like me. Like the others. Only—"

She saw the flare in his amber eyes.

He said, "Only with the potential to be much more powerful."

She heard the rattle of wind at the windows. There were no chairs, so she sat cross-legged on the layered rugs.

Kai crouched beside her, keeping his eyes level with hers. "The magic takes a different form, a different language, with everyone. Your magic will emerge naturally from inside you. You only have to let those doors open, let each spell rise up through you cloaked in the symbol of its choosing. Try it now. Close your eyes and find the boy."

She looked at him.

He said, gently, "Jess. Close your eyes."

She did.

She stood at the beginning of the uncanny hallway.

"Think on the boy." Kai's voice was soft in her ear. "Can you hear him?"

"No," she said, but then saw a door swinging open down the hall. The light that spilled out was tinted army green. She stepped into that light, spread her arms and lifted her face.

She breathed in, very faintly, the smells of beer, cigarettes, fried meat.

And then a voice:

—I'm looking for this guy calls himself Lizardking?

She whispered to Kai, "I hear him," catching the bright thread of amazement in her voice.

"Good. You've located your psychic connection to him. If you can only—"

"Quiet," Jess said.

— . . . Only name I have for him. He gave this address.

The boy's voice suddenly paused.

And then:

—Did somebody else just come in here?

Jess felt cold wind blow across her face, and then silence. In the hallway of her mind, she stepped forward again, deeper into the light, listening for the boy's voice. Listening. Moments passed, stretched into minutes, and then another fragment:

—I wanted to go see a band with him . . .

But then the boy's voice cut out completely and she heard the song from her dream instead, flooding through her mind, chasing away the light and any trace of the boy's presence. *I can't believe/I'm getting away with this/ Junkies' parade through lover's town . . .*

The door slammed with such violence her bones reverberated.

She opened her eyes and looked at Kai.

"I lost it," she said.

"It takes practice. Each time you tap into the Binding, the connection will last longer, go deeper."

"No," Jess murmured. "No. It's not just lack of practice . . ."

She remembered the way the expression on his face, when he saw her in the parking lot, turned from bewilderment to terror.

"He's scared of me," Jess said. "He's fighting me. Whatever this Binding is, this connection you keep talking about . . ."

She remembered what the boy had said to her . . . *I was promised my release.*

"Kai. He recognized me. He knows me. And he doesn't want anything to do with me."

Kai stood up. "Mina will have some lunch prepared. Then we'll return here, and continue."

"What are you not telling me?"

He whirled on her and said, so sharply she took a step

back, "I'm telling you what you need to know when you need to know it. When I trust that you can handle it. All right?"

She said nothing.

"Now come," he said.

He was already at the door. But instead of following she stayed where she was. "What happened between you and Mina?"

"What?"

"You two have a history—"

"For crying out loud, Jess—"

"Romantic?"

He blew out air, shrugged. "Hundreds of years ago."

"Did you love her?"

"I don't know if you'd call it love, exactly."

"Have you ever loved anyone, exactly?"

"Why are you asking me this?"

"I need to know more about you. I need to feel like I can trust you."

"But you do trust me."

"That could change," she said.

He was silent. He seemed to be pulling inside himself, then said abruptly, "After seven hundred years, love and grief seem synonymous." Then added, as if offering her something: "Mina was my first."

"First love."

"Yes. But now we look at each other and see—We remind each other of everything that went wrong," Kai said. "We were careless, destructive, without realizing it. We were part of a much larger blindness—we were why Bakal Ashika and her followers achieved so much power so quickly. No one thought to watch them the way they were watching us. We were much too fascinated with ourselves—" Kai paused, waved a hand, as if to cut himself off. "It's an old, familiar story."

"And so they brought down the Labyrinth."

"It might have been dying anyway," Kai said, "although we don't talk about that. But *they* took it and killed it and turned it to sand." His expression softened a little. "What did the demon take from you, Jessamy? What memories?"

Now it was her turn to be startled.

Kai said, "Memories of love? Love fascinates them—they find it so strange, so exotic. Memories of someone who made you happy?"

She suddenly didn't trust herself to speak.

Kai answered for her. "Gabe. Your boyfriend in New York."

"Yes," she said. "I didn't know you knew—"

"And so how do you feel about him now . . . after that transaction?"

She called up Gabe's face and felt detachment, as if watching a movie that no longer held interest. *I love this man,* she said to herself, but the words meant nothing.

She said, "He no longer feels real. I mean, obviously he still exists—"

"But not for you. Not like he did before."

"That sounds so harsh."

The candlelight leaped and flickered in the alcoves, tinged the air with their perfume and sulfur.

"Jess. He wasn't for you."

The expression in his eyes did not match the certainty in his voice. She realized that, within what seemed to be a statement, he was actually posing a question.

They watched each other.

"I know," she said. It was her answer.

She could hear the wind beating on the windows. She cleared her throat and said again, "The demon gave me something—"

"So he claimed."

"He did. I can feel it. It's like this pulse inside my brain, very cold but hot at the same time."

"Del plays tricks," Kai said. "Games, mind games. Confusion delights him."

"And if he was telling the truth?"

"Then sooner or later, his so-called gift will make itself known."

"That's not reassuring."

Kai's smile was both gentle and grim. "It isn't."

Jess looked down at her hands. A thought occurred to her. "Make sure there are some paints or markers in my room. Something I could . . ." She heard the fear again, knock-knock-knocking: if she let it in, it would paralyze her. "Something happens when I sleep. I write things. They're like these . . . coded messages, from my sleeping self to my waking self. As if this other self knows things I don't—"

"It does," Kai said. "It always has."

Another morning, Jess told him: "There's someone in my dreams."

"What?"

"I'm not talking about the boy. Someone else."

"Sometimes Ashika is capable of—"

"Not her."

"But this person is a recurring dream element? And he feels—real—to you?"

"He feels familiar," Jess said. "Like someone I knew long ago."

"It could be someone you share a Dreamline with."

"How does that work?"

"When we refer to the Dreamlines, we're talking about the space in between. In between worlds. In between life and death. In between life and life, for those souls compelled to return."

"Reincarnation?"

He shrugged. "A Dreamline is like a pathway of light and energy that cuts through the border-realms, these places of in between. But Dreamlines also link souls."

She frowned. "You mean like . . . soulmates?"

"Some of these links can be forged through deep magic. My Pact, for example—we bound ourselves to each other, as was the practice then, in order to become more powerful as a group than we could be alone." He paused, then said, "And some souls become linked—share Dreamlines—for other reasons."

"Such as?"

"I don't know, Jess. It's one of the mysteries. And maybe sometimes, in the end, there is no reason—maybe it's just a random quirk of the universe."

Time passed. Her watch had stopped. There were no clocks in any of the rooms. All she had to go by was the light outside, shading from day to night and back again. But even that did not coincide with her felt experience of time: how distorted and elongated it seemed, inside this strange rambling puzzle-box of a house.

During her training sessions, it seemed that nothing much was happening. She felt herself relax into the vision of the hallway of doors—could feel that dream-wind against her face, hear laughter in the distance. She knew it was Del—or whatever her mind was presenting as Del. She couldn't shake the unsettling suspicion that Kai was wrong, that Del had, during their time in his underground chamber, sloughed off some part of himself in her head.

She couldn't bring herself to think too closely on it.

Eventually she would tire, and she ended each session exhausted, discouraged, unable to look at Kai, half-convinced and half-afraid that this was useless on both their parts. But when Jess returned to her own room she realized she felt . . .

Exhilarated.

More than that. She felt charged with electricity, attuned to the life in her veins; when she looked in the mirror she saw someone slightly . . . altered. Her nails were taking on an odd, metallic tint.

The magic changes you.

And she knew, then, despite her apparent lack of progress, that the magic was moving inside her, working itself closer to those doors in her mind. Sooner or later, they would all open wide. She felt wild at the thought of it: as if she was speeding down the highway with nothing in her way but moonlight. The other questions—what she would become, where this would lead and what she might find in the aftermath—got kicked aside. Keep your hands on the wheel, your eyes on the road. Sharp curves ahead.

Somewhere in the distance was the boy.

At the end of another session—by now she had lost count of how many they had had together—Jess said, "Tell me how you visit the Dreamlines. It's like mindcasting?"

"No. Mindcasting is when you send part of your mind out from your body, to probe and explore the immediate environment—"

"I realize that. We've been *practicing* that."

He dealt with her impatience the way he usually did: he ignored it. "Soulcasting is an extraordinarily deep level of meditation in which you send your soul into the Dreamlines. It leaves your body extremely vulnerable to attack. And it's possible to lose yourself in the Dreamlines, unable to find your way back."

"Will I be able to do it? Soulcast?"

"Not yet."

"You can do this?"

"I need to be near or inside another presence of magic."

"You need to feed off the power of someone else?"

He didn't answer.

Jess persisted, "So it follows that the stronger this other magic presence is, the deeper into the Dreamlines you can travel?"

"Yes."

"This place," Jess said, "this demon-prison, or whatever you call it . . . there is magic here. The air shimmers with it."

When he didn't answer immediately, she said, "Kai?"

"Yes," he said, and nodded.

*   *   *

And then, something changed. Even as she went behind her closed eyes and moved into the hallway of
doors, things felt so vivid—

—And she was, simply, *there,* the dream-hallway as
solid and real to her as the candles and silk rugs had
been moments earlier. Jess Shepard stared down a long
tilting hallway of shifting multicolored light, the wind
blasting her face. *Kai,* she tried to yell, but the name
caught in her throat like a fishhook. She felt no exhilara-
tion now, only the wild scrambling urge to get back,
where it was safe—

Get it together. The voice of her uncle, the Judge,
spoke up inside her head. *Are you a coward, girl? This
is my house, and I will allow no cowards in my house.*

"You know where you are," said a voice from beside her.

She turned, saw the blue-eyed figure of Delkor Lokk,
the way he must have looked before his demon went
into him. He wore a blue caftan and rough sandals, his
skin the texture of leather.

He said, "Welcome to the wild country of your mind.
It's nice here."

"So you've decided to set up camp?"

"Don't worry, sweet Jess. I'm a *good* houseguest. I
won't leave the bathroom all stinky and messy. I won't
snoop through your most private possessions. Well . . .
not *all* of them."

"I'm not inclined," Jess said wryly, "to trust you."

"Jess Jess Jess." He gave her a leathery grin. "I am
the monkey wrench, clunking around the big bad ma-
chine. See, sweetling child, sweetling friend of my
sweetling prince, I may not be *for* you. But I may not
be *against* you, either."

She was staring at him, trying to recognize him as
some kind of mind-phantom: a fantasy her own deeper,
dreaming self had sent up to her.

Down the hall, one of the doors was swinging open.

Something came swooping, fluttering, into the hallway. It touched ground inside the silvery light-shaft and cocked its head at Jess.

It was a bird. Sleek dark wings tucked against a darker body. Its eyes were the same blue as Jess's own.

"My silly know-nothing child," Del said. "I believe I hear the sound of your cherry finally popping."

Jess knelt and reached out to the bird.

It spread out its wings and flew at her. The sound of wings grew louder, like thunder, as the bird screeched once and wheeled into her face and the black wings covered her eyes—

And the hallway of doors was gone.

Delkor Lokk was gone.

She was awake now, returned to the meditation room, the faded silk weave of the layered rugs beneath her knees, the leaping twisting candlelight. Back in the thumping, flesh-and-blood truth of her body. "Oh my God," she whispered. She was trembling, her shirt damp with perspiration.

Kai was leaning against the doorway.

"Congratulations," he said, low-voiced. "The first spell is the breakthrough. You'll find the others come more quickly."

"It was a bird."

"The bird *is* the spell," Kai said patiently. "It is the form the spell takes in order to announce itself to you. The magic operates through symbols, Jess."

"Like dreams," she said.

"The magic creates its own language. And that language is different for everyone."

"You talk like it's a living, natural force."

"It is," Kai said, and seemed surprised that she hadn't understood. He reached out for her hand, silver nails glinting, and helped her up. Her legs were cramped and shaky. She didn't know how long she had been sitting there. Kai lowered his head, eyes darkening. His grasp on her wrist tightened, then he nodded to himself and let go. "Summoner's eye," he murmured. "Impressive." He began to explain it to her.

Later—again, how to measure time in a place that had no time? Only that it felt like a very long time—Jess sat at the small desk in her bedroom, holding her pen over the leather-bound notebook. She hesitated, then began to write:

This is how the magic comes to me: In bits and pieces. In code.

And still later, the words starting to come more easily:

I don't know how exactly I'm supposed to use this. This book. It appears to be some kind of hybrid between a journal and a spellbook. Or maybe not. Maybe there's no real distinction between the two, not in this strange existence. This new thing my life has become.

Kai gave it to me after my first spell broke. (This is the term he uses—spells "breaking," as if they were eggs).

"I don't keep diaries," I said. As if the notebook was one of those little-girl things with its own lock and key, instead of a lovely leather volume. Empty creamy pages of unlined parchment. I don't like lined pages. Never did.

"You'll need this."

"Need it?"

"You'll need to write in it. Think of your head and body as a container that can only hold so much before threatening to break apart—this" (he nodded at the notebook) "—is how and where you channel that excess energy."

"What, like therapy?"

Kai actually laughed. For a while I wasn't sure he

even had a sense of humor. Now I realize that
yes, it's there, this quiet little glint behind his eyes.
He said, "More practical than that. It's the place
to channel the excess—the overspill—from you into
your book, which will become more and more an
extension of you. The more magical you become, the
more magical your book becomes. It becomes a
part of you. Understand?"

"I'm trying, Kai." And I am. I'm trying to wrap
my head around all of this. "So what exactly do
I write?"

"You'll write exactly what you need to write."

But I think I'm beginning to understand. I feel the
magic building up inside me. It's like electricity . . .
it's both from me, born of me, and from outside me
at the same time . . . like something inside me has
been unlocked and thrown wide, wide open . . . and
the magic within calls to magic without . . . so
magic finds me, enters me and moves inside my
blood, my bones, where it churns and builds and
generates more of itself, and needs release . . . it feels
like swallowing a bolt of lightning. Again and
again and again.

But the magic isn't meant to be gathered and
hoarded, at least not for long. It is meant to be
expressed. It needs to be expressed. As I write this—
my pen moving faster and more frantically across
the page—I can feel how the act of writing this throws
off stray tendrils of magic even now—I can hear
the soft hiss as the magic sinks into these pages, as the
notebook turns into a weird kind of container—my
writing, my magic, and me, all jumbled together in this
book, impossible to pick apart.

How long have I been here? If I tilt my memory
one way, it feels like forever. Tilt my memory
another, and it feels like ten minutes.

*Another spell is about to break. I went into medi-
tation today, went into the training image—the
hallway, the doors—and I can feel this new spell,
waiting behind one of those doors, not quick and
gentle like the first few, but harder, hotter, darker. It
won't slip out from behind the door so much as
batter it down. I think this one might hurt.*

He was stronger here, in this place. He could feel the
magic moving into him and through him and he felt con-
fident enough, for the first time in a very long time, to
send himself into the Dreamlines.

Soulcasting. Jess had tasted the word, moving it
around her tongue for a moment. *And why do you need
to do this?*

*To travel, to look around, to gather information,
mostly. And*—He paused here, because this wasn't an
easy concept to explain. *To regenerate.*

*Visiting the Dreamlines is like getting your battery
recharged?*

It exhausts you and tears you down, he said, *but then,
when you recover, you're stronger for it.*

Like working out, she said. *You damage the muscle so
that it repairs itself into something stronger, bigger.*

Good analogy.

*Then can you damage yourself enough to get all your
power back?*

*For that to happen I would have to travel deep, very
deep, deep enough to touch the source, the heart of magic
itself—and in order for me, or for anyone, to do that . . .*
Kai let his voice trail off. He didn't want to continue,
but Jess was looking at him with too much expectation.
So he said, simply, *Soulcasting isn't enough.*

What is?

He was silent.

Kai, what is? And he didn't know what she saw in his
face, just then, but her voice dropped low and her eyes

turned wary and . . . concerned? Was she concerned for him?

The heart of magic, he said, *is where things begin. And end.*

She said, *Does this involve a bloodprice?*

He was startled. *Bloodprice? Where did you hear that? Kai. How much damage is enough?*

But he couldn't, wouldn't answer.

Now, he closed the door to the stark little chamber and settled himself on the dais. He closed his eyes and plunged into the dark light of himself, until he felt the magic rushing around him, surrounding him, and pulling him through himself and into the Dreamlines.

He let himself drift, to get used to the space and darkness again, to the weird disembodied feeling of being something and nothing at the same time. He had heard that under rare and strange circumstances it was possible to take your physical body into the Dreamlines—to walk through them as you would walk through any hallway—but he had never encountered anyone who had done this and doubted he ever would.

As he became oriented, his vision adjusted and the darkness took on depth and dimension. His gaze picked out the lights, faint at first and then brighter, brighter, like ropes pulled taut through the darkness, out to its very edges. He drifted through the different strands, feeling out the shades and intensities and textures, until he came to one that went through him and tasted familiar, and the name fell inside him like a stone down a well. He said the name: *Eagan.*

It was as if the name swallowed him up completely and spit him out into a completely different place—

—What looked to be some kind of martial-arts studio.

Here, he felt even less substantial than he had been in the Dreamlines; slipping through eddies of air as, below him, a dozen or so kids stood in two neat lines and finished up a punching/kicking drill. The youngest was maybe six, the oldest well into her teens, all of them in neatly pressed white uniforms, belts tied snugly around their middles.

The drill finished, they snapped their legs together and their arms straight against their bodies.

"Kam-sa-ham-ni-da," the instructor said, and bowed.

"Kam-sa-ham-ni-da," they echoed, and returned the bow.

The kids scattered, talking and laughing as they headed off to the changing rooms, then emerged in jeans and coats and spilled out the doors. Kai could imagine the wet, earthy smells blowing in from outside, mingling with the sweat cast off from so many hardworking bodies. The instructor stayed in his office for a bit and then walked over to the punching bag in the corner. His kicks started simple and became more complicated: soon he was jumping, spinning, slamming into the bag. Kai had to smile. Eagan was showing off.

"I know you're about," he said. "You mad dog, you. Doing a little walking on the Dreamlines, eh?"

You look well. Kai relayed his thoughts and could tell, from the way Eagan stood and smirked, that he was picking up clearly. *Last I heard you were still in that mental institution.*

"I was running it, you bastard. No one's seen fit to commit me just yet."

You know why I'm here?

"I can guess."

Bakal Ashika.

"Yes." Eagan did some kind of complex jumping spinning kick combination that Kai couldn't begin to identify. "Six demon pals in six different prison-spheres, and she hasn't made a move on any of them. So far as I can see or tell."

I've been with Del. There's no sign of her here, either.

"So what do you think she's planning?"

Not sure.

"Maybe she's not planning anything."

You believe that?

"Hell no." Eagan cut his eyes towards the place where he guessed Kai to be. He was off by a couple of feet. "But maybe she only wants you. For now."

This obsession she has with atonement.

"Aye. That the suffering of others—especially you— will make up for her own. That some kind of cosmic balance will be restored."

More than that, I think. She draws power from the blood, the pain. It fuels her.

"Strip away the bloodmagic and she's just another sadist."

The demon-hunger.

"It never stops," Eagan agreed. "It never ends. Or so they like to tell us."

I want her spellbooks. Who has them?

Eagan stepped back from the bag and lifted his hands a little. "I kept my hands clean of that," he said. "They should have been destroyed, those things."

That would have been idiotic. Who has them?

"I chose," Eagan said, "not to know. Or else I might have read them myself." His smile was tight and grim.

He found Romany on a train somewhere in eastern Europe. She was sitting in a passenger car with three people she did not appear to know; she was jotting notes in a spiral-bound notebook. In the last fifty years, Romany had developed a reputation as a travel writer who experimented with fiction. The landscape rushing past the windows was green, wooded: a blur of shadowed lace.

He hovered above the splintered door frame, gazing down. She was small for a Sajae, with broad cheekbones and calm, dark eyes, her black hair swept up off her neck. She stood up and walked underneath him, sliding the door behind her. She walked down the corridor. Her body swayed with the motion of the train. A loudspeaker crackled static; the conductor announced upcoming destinations in several different languages.

Romany glanced into the cars she passed, then ducked into an empty one and shut and locked the door.

"Hello, Kai," she said, and smiled.

It's really good to see you.

She stretched out her arms, as if reaching for an embrace or measuring the distance between them. "I'm impressed," she said. "I haven't been able to dreamwalk in ages."

I'm visiting a prison-sphere. Good energy to work with.

She nodded. "The rumors. Are they true?"

Yes.

"I've been having . . ." She paused, then said, "Bakal killed your lover in St. Martin's?"

And her small son. Yes.

"I saw that in my dreams. I'm so sorry, Kai."

I need her spellbooks. Who has them?

"Ask Mak. He had them for a while—don't know if he still does."

Makonnen? He took them? Did he try to read them?

"I think he did. And I think . . ." She paused, then said, "I think it was more than he could handle, Kai. I think his mind . . . Well, maybe it was cracking anyway. Have you checked in on the others?"

Eagan's in Montreal, teaching martial arts—

Romany laughed and rolled her eyes.

Sato's in Australia. Near Alice Springs. Working as a healer.

"*Still?* Doesn't he get *bored*?"

Daki's on a yacht. She's near Tonga, maybe, I couldn't really tell.

"I miss Daki," she said. Then: "How did we all get so cut off from each other?"

I think we wanted to. Lose each other. After all that happened.

She took this in with a small nod. "Mina?"

She's . . . lost her grip a little. Del's guardianship has taken its toll.

She nodded again. "She's not the only one. We're in trouble, aren't we?"

Yes.

"I like this world. I don't want to watch it burn."

Nor do I. He paused, then said, *I want to open a teleportation spell that will bring the Pact together. When and where it's needed.*

"Kai. You can't do that anymore. None of us can."

Not yet, Kai said.

"You would have to—"

Enter the heart of the Dreamlines. I know that.

"Get all the way there, and all the way back? It would smash your soul to bits. Which wouldn't accomplish anything."

But Ashika's in the game, now, and that changes things. If I get close to her . . .

"Ashika wants to kill you."

Not quickly.

She stared into space for several moments, gathering his meaning.

"Bloodmagic," she said. "Sacrifice."

Self-sacrifice.

"Kai," she said, and then stopped. It was clear, as wheels churned in the tracks and wind whistled through the sliver between window and frame, that she didn't know what to say.

Makonnen was the most difficult of them to find; his link in the Dreamlines seemed faint, tenuous. Kai tracked it through to a sun-scorched district of Soweto. South Africa again: he had not been here since his encounter with the child Jess; but this township outside of Johannesburg was very different from the luxury hotels and tourist attractions of Cape Town.

Mak was sitting outside a small brick box of a house, his feet planted in the dirt, his dark body made darker by the sun. He was moving a rag along the barrel of a rifle, cleaning it without conviction, as if looking for something to do with his hands. "You," Makonnen said lazily, and took a moment to angle the weapon across his lap, to extract and light a cigarette. He watched two women in long-sleeved dresses walk past. They pretended not to notice him, as they chatted and smiled at each other, using their hands to steady the plastic buckets balanced on their heads.

I need Ashika's spellbooks.

"I had them," Mak acknowledged.

Small children shrieked down the street, kicking up dirt. A beaten-up taxi idled at the corner.

Mak continued, "Didn't know what to do with them. Didn't know what they were doing to me. Tried to find you. Needed to talk."

I went away.

"No shit."

I didn't know.

"I needed," he said again, running the cloth along the barrel, "to talk to you. Looked, kept looking. No prince."

I am sorry.

He acknowledged the apology with a tilt of his head. "No shit."

Can you tell me where they are?

"You're going to read them?"

I have to try.

"They are foul," Mak said. "Get into your brain. Get under your skin."

I need to read them, Mak.

He flicked ash. "The twins," he said finally.

You gave them to the twins?

"Wouldn't say I *gave* them."

The twins took them?

Mak hunched his shoulders in a long shrug. A woman leaned out from the doorway behind him—soft brown eyes, a red-and-yellow headscarf—and murmured to Mak in a language Kai did not understand.

"Just a ghost, babe," Mak said in loud, pointed English. The woman drew back, not understanding. Mak's eyes were dark and hooded. He flicked aside the cigarette butt and ground it beneath a bare heel. "Talkin' to a ghost."

Kai says that the magic expresses itself through symbols, like dreams. The bird with the brilliant blue eyes, for example, my first spell: the ability to cast yourself into someone else's point of view, to see what they see. "It feels a bit like I'm invading their mind," I told him.

"No," he said. "You know how children ride on their parents' backs sometimes? What do they call that?"

"Piggyback rides."

"It's like their vision is giving your own vision a kind of pig . . . piggyback ride."

"Are they aware of this?"

"Most of them just explain it away as a dizzy spell, or a headache."

Other spells that have emerged from behind those mental dream-doors:

A snake, silver and glittering, flicking its long tongue at me. Inside this meditative state, this dream-state, I picked up the snake and it curled itself around my arm and disappeared through my skin. "Magic often expresses itself through snake images," Kai said, after. "What do you feel?"

I thought for a moment. "Charm."

"A charisma spell," Kai said. "You'll find that very handy."

One spell was simply a sound. I stood in the spill of light that came out through the doorway and heard the sound of a telephone ringing. It repeated itself for what felt like forever as I turned, turned again, looking for the damn phone. "The ability to communicate telepathically," Kai said. "We'll devote some time to practicing this one; it can be tricky."

"Will I ever be able to interpret these spells myself? Will I always need you to explain them for me?"

"I'm your teacher. This is what a teacher does. Eventually you'll be able to read new spells on your own."

"How long have we been here?" I asked him. "If time moved normally here, how long have we been here, training like this? One month? Six months? A year?"

"Jessamy. It's a useless question all around."

"But—"

"Focus. There's still a lot of work to do."

And the newest spell. This one was different from the others. There was nothing: no image, no sound. Yet I saw the door open, felt something opening up deep inside me. I felt myself change. Yet nothing happened. When I emerged from meditation I could only look blankly at Kai.

"It will reveal itself at some point," he said.

Later, in my suite, I was stepping out from the shower. When, from the corner of my eye, I caught myself moving in the mirror. I glanced away—but something had registered in my brain as odd. I looked back to the mirror—just in time to see my reflection smiling at me when I knew that I, myself, was not smiling—in fact, my jaw was dropping open. My reflection in the mirror became its own creature—a thing apart from me—the link between us severed—so that when I moved it stayed still, and when I stood there frozen it came up against the glass and passed through the glass until it was standing in front of me, like a ghost,

*except it looked much more substantial, it looked
like my living breathing twin except it was neither
ghost or twin, it was . . . well, hell. I don't know
what it was.*

It was magic.

*It turned away from me and walked, naked, across
the bathroom until it came to the closed door. I
don't know if it actually dissipated right there or if
it walked right through the door until it came out
the other side . . .*

I had to sit down until I stopped trembling.

The man and the woman made love on the four-poster
bed. The other woman was draped along the chaise
longue, sipping champagne and watching the couple with
lazy, half-closed eyes. A short silk kimono was belted
loosely at her waist. Kai realized his mind no longer held
any name for her—as soon as he saw her, the old name
had been wiped clean from memory—which meant that
she had either changed it or was in the process of changing it, as they all did from time to time.

Hey you.

She ignored him for so long he began to wonder if
the Dreamline had thinned out or snapped without his
realizing. But then she turned onto her other side, facing
away from the lovemaking couple. "Hello, Your Brightness," she said cheerily. "Are you comfortable here or
would you like to move to another room?"

*The couple behind you seems preoccupied enough. I
don't think they'll disturb us.*

"I think you're right." She drained the flute and
reached for the bottle in the standing silver bucket.
"You're in Vegas, in case you're wondering."

Where's your brother?

"In the suite down the hall"—she gestured vaguely
at the dark-haired man on the bed behind her—"with
his wife."

What do you call yourselves these days?

She grinned. "Tristan and Isolde."

Cute.

"I thought so."

Where are Ashika's spelljournals, Isolde?

Isolde's eyes turned narrow. She readjusted her kimono. "Makonnen went through some strange phase with them," she said. "It got ugly. Of course, you were away at the time. You were unavailable for comment." Thin blade of accusation turning through her voice. He let it pass.

Isolde said, "What could you possibly want with them?"

Bakal Ashika. You know this.

"And so? All sorts of evil forces are afoot in this world. Have you read the papers lately?"

Tell me where they are, Isolde. I appreciate how you and your brother helped Makonnen.

"Those books are contaminated."

They might offer up clues to Ashika's intentions.

"She was in jail for five hundred years. Ever think maybe she's just hanging out, having a good time?"

Isolde. I'm way past the point of enjoying this. Tell me.

She sighed. "Safety-deposit box, one of our banks in Sweden. I'll give you the information."

Twenty-one

The Trans website asked:

ARE YOU READY FOR YOUR JOURNEY?

Yes, Ramsey told himself, as he emptied his bank account and stashed the money in his knapsack and bought a bus ticket to get him to the San Francisco address scrawled on the top left-hand corner of Lizardking's envelope, which he had committed to memory. *Yes,* he told himself, as he leaned his forehead against the grime-streaked window and watched the country unfold around him, in its vastness of fields and sky and small nothing towns, farm equipment rusting in the grass by the highway; the freeways and big rigs and fast-food signs; the hills and plains and mountains. *I am ready.*

Lizardking had given his address c/o King's Way. Ramsey expected a small side street or some kind of apartment building, but what he found instead was a pub. It had a wood-and-wrought-iron façade and looked out of place in a neighborhood of noodle shops and massage parlors and crumbling hotels, cigarette butts stamped into the sidewalks, the homeless napping in doorways with their shopping carts parked nearby.

Ramsey pushed open the heavy door and stepped inside.

A dim, cool interior, air smelling of beer and fish and chips. Maybe half a dozen patrons lurked at the scratched-up tables. Feeling scruffy and self-conscious, Ramsey went to the bar. He could still smell the bus on him. He tightened his grip on the duffle bag he'd bought at a Wal-Mart several states ago and said to the guy in the white apron, "I'm looking for this guy calls himself Lizardking?"

The man blinked several times. "Lizardking?"

"That's the only name I have for him. He gave this address."

"I know who he is," the man said. "He's gone."

"What?"

That couldn't be right. That didn't fit the plan.

But it was then a strange cool feeling blew over him, and a pressure began building in his head; he felt a tap on his shoulder and a woman's voice spoke directly into his ear. *"Ramsey,"* she said. *"Ramsey."* He turned around, turned around again. There was no woman. There was no one standing anywhere near him. He looked at the man behind the bar, said, "Did someone else just come in here?"

The man shrugged. He jerked his head towards a corner table, said, "See that kid with the hair? Talk to him."

Ramsey saw a rangy guy in flared jeans, hair red as a valentine, slouching in his chair, stealing French fries from the older man across from him.

Ramsey said, "He knows Lizardking?"

"Hell," the man said, "he *named* him."

The man moved away from Ramsey and went through the swinging door into the kitchen. The redheaded youth was watching the older man count out cash, lay it on the table. "Leave a tip," the kid said loudly. The man paused, then reluctantly let fall another bill. The kid said even louder, "Jesus. A *decent* tip."

The man looked at the kid for a moment, then slapped all his cash on the table and shoved back his chair and grabbed his briefcase. As he hurried to the door, Ramsey caught the expression on his face: hollow, defeated, as if the bones inside his skin had collapsed in self-disgust.

Ramsey looked back to the kid.

Except the guy was already looking at him, his arm slung across the back of his chair, his eyes hooded. He said, "Do you know where you are?"

"What?"

"Do you know *who* you are?" The guy was smirking. " 'Cause you don't look like you have a fuckin' clue."

"I'm looking for Lizardking."

The guy's expression shifted a little. His arm slipped off the backrest. "Lizzie?" he said. "You're one of his?"

"Uh. I wanted to go see a band with him."

"Yeah, yeah," the kid said, "you're one of *those*."

Ramsey looked at him blankly.

"A Trans fan," the youth said, only he blurred the two words together, *transfan*, "a fucking Asha-ite. Myself, I think their music reeks. Pretentious art-house shit, but whatever. Different strokes for different folks, right?" He shrugged his thin shoulders. He had black-painted fingernails, black rubber bracelets on both wrists. "You're Nemesis, right?"

It took Ramsey a moment to connect himself with his darkhouse.com persona. "Yeah," he finally said. "Except my real name's—"

"Fuck that. We don't deal in real names here. I'm Poppy. Lizzie said you might show up."

"You know where he is?"

"No," Poppy said, but Ramsey caught a flicker in the other teenager's eyes, sensed something hiding behind them. "Where you staying?"

Ramsey shrugged. He hadn't thought that far ahead. "Some hostel."

"Nah. You don't want to stay at 'some hostel.' You can crash in Lizzie's room."

"He lives with you?"

Poppy sauntered towards the door, then glanced over his shoulder. Ramsey hadn't moved. Poppy tossed his head. "Dude, you coming or what?"

Ramsey felt the weight of his gathering exhaustion, and something else: a prickling, itching sensation traveling along his shoulder blades, moving down his back.

The kid knelt, lifted a flared pant leg and extracted something from the inside of his cowboy boot. He tossed it to Ramsey, who reached out and caught it without thinking. A jackknife. Ramsey flipped it open.

"If I make any funny moves," Poppy said, "feel free to protect yourself. But don't worry. You ain't my type."

Ramsey felt the heft of the weapon in his hand. "So what makes you think *I'm* not some psycho?"

Poppy rolled his eyes. "Like I said before. You look too fuckin' clueless."

The sunlight flared in his eyes, making him realize all over again how ugly this neighborhood was. Poppy unlocked a door and stepped into a hallway that smelled of urine and old pizza. Rusted mailboxes dangled off the wall. They walked up three flights of stairs. Ramsey heard a television blaring from behind one wall, the flush of a toilet behind another. "Shithole, sweet shithole," Poppy said in singsong, unlocking a door, kicking it open.

The room was larger than Ramsey had expected, with furniture he guessed had been dragged off the streets. Lizzie's room opened off the back and was about the size of a walk-in closet. "You might want to wash that," Poppy said, eyeing the sleeping bag in the corner.

Ramsey said, "So what happened to him anyway? He disappeared?"

Poppy shrugged. "He's the way he is, you know? He was in good with this guy who runs an Internet café and sometimes he'd spend his whole day at a computer, eating biscotti and shit. He could be there right now," but Ramsey sensed again the falseness in Poppy's expression.

Poppy continued, "He was talking about this trip. He was going to hook up with these kids, head out to Nevada. There's some kind of thing happening out there, for, you know, people like you."

Ramsey glanced at him.

Poppy said again, blurring the words together, "*Transfans.* People are, like, *gathering* out there. They're calling it the Bloodangel, or some such shit. You heard of it?"

"Do you know anything about it?" Ramsey heard the urgency in his own voice. Heard the voice, the Asha-voice, from his dreams: *I will give you a gift.* "Did he leave any information? Because—"

Poppy shrugged. "Like I said, I think—"

"—I'm supposed to go there too."

"—Their music is shit. So no. I know nothing."

"I have to get there," Ramsey said. "Lizardking should have waited for me."

"Oh really?" The corners of Poppy's mouth lifted. "Did Lizzie know this?"

Ramsey glanced away.

"Don't look so downcast," Poppy chided. "I know some people you can talk to. You'll figure it out."

A pager was beeping. Poppy plucked the object from his pocket, squinted down at it. "Well," he said, and Ramsey heard the sigh in his voice, "I *am* a popular boy today. There's an extra key hanging up by the door. There's nothing worth stealing, all I ask is don't burn the fucking place down. Or make a fucking mess." The tone of his voice suggested the latter was the greater offense.

"Thanks," Ramsey said again, awkwardly. "You didn't have to do this."

"Look, I'll tell you straight up: I'm kind of a prick. But Lizzie I liked. Lizzie was—*is*—a cool guy. So if I didn't put you up, he'd be pissed."

Ramsey nodded. He didn't trust Poppy, but this was Lizardking's room, Lizardking's stuff, Lizardking's friends—which meant this was Ramsey's path to Trans, and to Asha. This was just another place to pass through.

Bloodangel.

He just had to find out where to go and how to get there.

Poppy left, door banging. Ramsey opened his wallet and took out the photo of Lauren he'd stolen from one of the Campbell photo albums and propped it against the wall. Just seeing it there made him feel better. Ramsey stood in the middle of a stranger's bedroom and weighed his hunger against his fatigue. The fatigue won out. He dropped his duffle bag and fell across the mattress. The sleeping bag held the sour-sweet smell of someone else's body, but he was asleep too fast to notice.

He dreamed of Lauren. She was dancing in a little school uniform, the skirt swishing around her lean thighs, strands of hair slipping across her mouth. She touched the tip of her tongue to her lower lip and said, *The vessel is unfit. You're running out of time,* and before he could ask her what she meant she was walking away from him, calf muscles flexing.

It was the burning that woke him, ripped him back up through the membrane of sleep, of dreams. His back on fire. Ramsey heard someone cry out—a thin, high, agonized sound—and realized it was himself. He ripped off his shirt, stumbled over to the mirror that hung on the back of Lizzie's door.

He turned his back to the glass, and looked over his shoulder at his reflection.

Wounds had opened up along his back, two slashing lines that slanted from the top of his shoulder blades to his waist, forming an inflamed angry *V*. Ramsey stared, feeling something raw and cold move in beneath the pain, that moved his whole body to shaking.

But the wounds were already closing, their vivid red fading to pink, then fading away altogether. Within minutes his back was smooth and unmarked.

Munroe's voice: *Your body tells the story. Bodies often do. Those marks on your back, for example. They serve as a kind of symbol. Stigmata.*

There aren't any marks on my back, Ramsey had said.

Munroe had been silent for a moment. —*Not yet.*

His legs gave way like broken toothpicks. He fell to the floor and hugged his knees to his chest. He touched a hand to his shoulder, where the bullet wound had left a small scar, and remembered the taste of the bullet as it came up through his mouth.

Help me, he thought.

Someone please help me.

Twenty-two

"Are you coming?" Poppy asked.

They headed south of Market Street, the old stone of central San Francisco giving way to wooden buildings and warehouses. Poppy wasn't much of a talker, and Ramsey liked that about him. He suspected the feeling was mutual. "Down here," Poppy said, turning into a street that was little more than an alley, brick walls edged with fire escapes. A sign hung over a door: DANTE GALLERY. CLOSED FOR INSTALLATION.

Poppy stopped, apprehension crossing his face. He banged the knocker three times.

The door opened.

A tall, thin man said, "Poppy. What a completely expected surprise. Come in." The man's eyes were as black as the braid of hair draped over his shoulder. Those eyes lingered on Ramsey for what seemed a very long time. Ramsey ducked his head. The man chuckled. "Is this your *new* friend?"

Poppy grunted. "His name's Ramsey."

"How very nice to meet you, Ramsey. My name is Salik."

"Hi."

Salik's gaze shifted to Poppy. "You must be missing your *old* friend. You must be missing him very much. What did you call him? Lizardboy?"

"Lizardking. 'Cause he thought Jim Morrison was fucking God." Poppy scratched at his neck with both hands, as if he'd developed a rash. "Could we, uh, get on with it?"

"Of course." Salik turned and led them through a passageway into the main gallery. The walls were hung with paintings in tortured colors that made Ramsey flinch even before he saw the subject matter: scenes of death, of torture: writhing bodies trapped in a dozen shades of hell.

Salik paused in front of a man being disemboweled. "May I offer you some tea?"

"No," Poppy said. He didn't react to the paintings. He had seen them before, Ramsey realized; he had been here many times. "We have to get going."

"Of course."

He crossed to a lacquered desk and extracted a notebook from the drawer. Poppy was fidgeting like a little kid. "Here we are," Salik sang out, flipping through the pages. "Yes, here's your account. You owe us a payment soon. You realize."

Poppy mumbled something.

Salik flashed a bright smile. His right hand moved to his left wrist and made a slight unscrewing motion. The gloved hand came away from the jacket sleeve. Salik dropped the prosthesis on the desk. From the dark silk sleeve cuff, another hand emerged: a stunted, secret hand, white as milk, a key slipping down between the tiny fingers. Salik unlocked the cabinet behind him and slid back the door. He looked at Ramsey. "Would you like to take a look?"

A terrarium sat on the shelf just inside the cabinet; and inside the terrarium something writhed, glistening and blue. Ramsey stepped closer to get a better look, just as the creature shifted its head from behind a rock.

As Ramsey's eyes adjusted to the strange play of light and shadow inside the tank, he could make out the black-and-yellow markings, like alien hieroglyphics, that ran up and down the creature's body. One eye opened, flashed fire-bright, looked steadily at Ramsey, then closed again.

"It's not from this world," Salik said. "It's not from any world, really. It seems to have the remarkable ability to move through all the realms, like passing through rooms in a house. Every so often, it sheds its skin. A remarkable thing, that skin. When you crumble it beneath your fingers, add a few choice ingredients and say a few choice words, well . . ." Salik took a silver cigarette case from beneath the shelf and pressed it open. "You have this."

Ramsey looked blankly at the blue powder. "What is it?"

Salik laughed. He shut the case and tossed it to Poppy. "What is it, Poppy?"

"Best high in the whole damn universe."

"Not exactly what it was intended for," Salik said. "But a lucrative side benefit."

He slid shut the cabinet door and locked it. He slipped the small, pale hand back inside his sleeve, cradled it against his chest. "Good night, young gentlemen." To Ramsey: "A pleasure to meet you."

They were at the door when Salik called: "Ramsey?"

Keep going, his inner voice whispered, but Ramsey couldn't help reacting to the sound of his name. He turned.

Salik had set the notebook on the desk, the long thin fingers of his good hand stroking the cover. "Have you ever been to New York?"

Ramsey shook his head.

"Ever posed for a painting? Perhaps a series of paintings?"

He felt a spasm of disgust and said, "Not interested." He turned away from Salik's widening grin and followed

Poppy through the passageway, out the door, into the damp and narrow side street. "What the *hell?*" he said. "What was that?"

"Just Salik. He's weird, I know, but he's harmless."

"He isn't," Ramsey said. "And you know it."

Poppy shrugged.

Ramsey said, "What really happened to Lizardking?"

Poppy shrugged again.

They came to an intersection blazing with traffic lights. Ramsey felt relief to be on a main street again. Poppy approached a man with dreadlocks and a purple baseball cap, slouching beside the convenience store. They spoke for a moment, then Poppy rejoined Ramsey: "We're looking for a guy in a yellow baseball cap two blocks over," he reported.

They walked along the uneven sidewalk, the wind gusting around them, the street gray and noisy with traffic. The guy in the yellow cap was sitting on the curb, blowing into a harmonica. As Poppy approached, the guy paused in mid-note and smirked up at him.

Poppy sauntered back to Ramsey, looking smug. "The password," he announced, "is Hellrider."

The party was in a warehouse down by the railroad tracks, the lines of trains snaking out from the station, shadowed and stilled for the night. They took a freight elevator to the top floor. People, mostly kids, mostly underage, thronged in the corners, gyrated on the dance floor, gathered around the makeshift bars where girls in hot pants and bikini tops served beer and water from vats of ice. Two DJs were set up in a booth in the back. Kids lounged in front of the whirring industrial fans, sipping water, shaking their hair back, sucking on lollipops. A girl brushed past Ramsey, cutting her eyes at him, popping a pill into her red mouth.

Poppy was grinning. "Oh *yeah*."

As they moved through the room, Ramsey began noticing something else: some of the kids had glittering

blue symbols painted on their skin, on bare shoulders
and midriffs and sometimes their faces. They looked at
Ramsey with shining eyes. He was familiar with the
thousand-yard stare of someone high on ecstasy: pupils
wide and pinned and burnt out from within, like a light
bulb exploded at the core. But these kids seemed . . .
lit . . . a moonstone sheen lifting up through their skin.
They looked at Ramsey as he passed among them and
one by one they smiled, and even though they weren't
speaking to him, or each other—were only swaying and
dancing inside the music—Ramsey's head filled with a
whispering, voices overlapping just inside his ears:

Ramsey. You've finally come. Welcome.

Welcome, Ramsey.

Dance with us. Be one of us.

Come feel the love, Ramsey. Be part of us.

Love us and let us love you.

"Are you coming!" Poppy shouted, looking over his
shoulder. His face was damp and glowing. Ramsey
wasn't sure he wanted to be here, but he also wasn't
sure where else he had to go. He didn't want to be
alone. He didn't want the chance to think about those
strange wounds that had opened up along his back—and
then, just as suddenly, healed and closed.

Besides, the music was good.

The music was very good.

And good music always made him stay.

They went through a doorless doorway into a room
lined with beanbag chairs and slouchy purple couches.
It was darker in here, hazed with smoke, fragrant with
weed.

"Poppy," a girl's voice squealed from the end of the
room.

She was skinny and blonde, wearing low-slung jeans,
straps of a thong pulled high on her hips. She was
sprawled on a couch beside another girl, this one short
and deep-breasted, black hair tangling out beneath a

cowboy hat. In the chair across from them slumped a boy in zebra-striped velvet pants, one leg tossed over the armrest.

"Poppy," the blonde girl said, "you finally *showed*. So what is it? Do you like girls or boys tonight?"

Poppy only grinned and sat down beside her.

"Like *me*," the girl said huskily, furling her arms around his neck in what seemed uncomfortably close to a stranglehold. "Like *me* tonight."

"This is Nemesis," Poppy said.

"Hi, Nemesis."

Poppy said, "Nemesis, this is Echo." He squeezed the girl's left breast and she squealed and slapped at his hand. He pointed to the girl in the cowboy hat. "This is Sweetums." To the boy in the zebra-striped pants, "And this is Jacko."

"Hi," Ramsey said.

Sweetums said, "Nemesis. Sit by me." She made space for him on the couch. Echo was whispering and giggling in Poppy's ear.

Jacko showed his teeth in what Ramsey assumed was a smile, then lit a cigarette and, still grinning, put out the match on his tongue. "Poppy," he called. "You got the stuff?"

Poppy slipped the thin silver case from his pocket. He held it up, announced, "Magic. Magic for everyone," and handed it to Echo, who was sucking on her little finger. She yanked it from her mouth with a small popping sound, slipped it in the blue powder. She traced one side, and then the other, of Poppy's face, leaving streaks of blue. "My beautiful boy," she said, and giggled.

"Careful with that stuff," Poppy said, "I don't want to be fucking paralyzed. A little goes a long way."

Sweetums said, ". . . Psycho like him?"

Ramsey's gaze was fixated on the blue streaks on Poppy's face, glittering there like crushed-up diamonds. It took him a moment to realize the girl in the cowboy hat was talking to him. "Sorry?"

Sweetums popped her gum. "I said what's a nice kid

like you doing with some low-class freak-headed shabby slut-psycho like Poppy here?"

Poppy squawked, "Who the *fuck* you calling shabby?"

"I was looking for someone," Ramsey said.

"Let me guess," Sweetums said, and adjusted her cowboy hat. "You were looking for Lizardking."

"Yeah."

" 'Cause everybody's looking for Lizardking."

"What is that stuff called?" Ramsey asked, his eyes intent on the silver case as Poppy handed it to Sweetums.

Sweetums grinned. "It's jax," she said. "You ever done it before?"

"No."

"Wanna try?"

"No."

"Your loss, baby. Believe me when I say that."

Jacko tossed his long body across the end of the couch, dropped his head into Sweetums' lap and closed his eyes submissively. Sweetums dabbed at Jacko's eyelids, painted them blue.

Ramsey said, "So Lizardking—"

"He's dead," Echo said.

Her voice was matter-of-fact. The others looked at her—Sweetums pausing in the act of drawing a fat tear below Jacko's right eye—and Echo shrugged and flipped her hair. "Of course he's dead."

"He went to the desert," Jacko said, nestling the back of his head into Sweetums' plump lap. "He went without us. That's what I think."

Echo shook her head. "No way."

"That's what I think."

"No fucking way."

"People are already heading out there," Jacko said. "Yvonne and her group headed out a few days ago. I think he went with them. He was impatient. You saw how fucking impatient he was. *The early ones will be rewarded.* That's what he said, remember?"

"How?" Echo said. "How will they be rewarded?"

Ramsey interjected, "What, exactly, is happening in the desert?"

Sweetums looked at him. "You really don't know? Isn't that why you came looking for him? You wanted to join us, right? He invited you?"

" 'Cause he invited us," Echo said. "He's the one who hooked us all together. That's why he wouldn't leave us unless he was D-E-A-D."

Jacko folded his arms across his chest and staring up at the ceiling. "This thing in the desert. It's like, you know, an alternative community—"

"*Party*," Echo said, and grinned. "No cops. No laws. No rules."

"Trans is gonna play," Jacko said. "They're gonna put on shows every night. And people are setting up, like, special theme camps and rave tents and stuff. It should be wild."

Echo sighed and snuggled her head on Poppy's shoulder. Her face was turning slack, blissful. There was jax streaked along her inner forearms: shining, glittering: and Ramsey remembered the strange and scaled little creature in Salik's gallery. Poppy was also turning drowsy, relaxing against the couch.

"You should really try it," Sweetums whispered in Ramsey's ear. "You have to know what it's like. Words can't describe it. When you're jaxed up, you can, like, touch the heart of the universe. You can understand things. You can send your thoughts out to other people."

"What, like acid or something?"

"*Not* like acid," Sweetums insisted. "That's what I'm saying. It's not like anything. Just a little bit at first . . . you shouldn't do too much . . . you hang out and be blissful . . . and then the energy hits you . . . and you dance . . ." She reached over and touched his hand. "It's like heaven," she said, and traced a small line of jax on his skin.

Ramsey jerked away. "It burns," he said.

"What?"

"It fucking *burns*—"

"Well it *shouldn't*." Sweetums blinked in puzzlement. Then: "Oh," she said, "Oh, honey," and Ramsey saw her face change. A blissful, drowsy look stole over her features, but it was more than that; as if a light had turned on beneath her skin, flooding up through her eyes. She reached out for him and he moved away from her but she caught hold of his shirt, breathed, "Oh, I see. It works differently for you. I see you now. They took your wings, didn't they? Took them away. And it still hurts so much."

"How . . ."

"So very very much."

"—Do you know this?"

Sweetums smiled dreamily at him. "You have to be careful," she said. "The jax is the net they use to catch a bird like you."

Ramsey whispered, "Who? Lizardking?"

"No. Lizzie was an innocent. He was in love with the music."

"How do you know this? Any of this?"

Her hand fell away from his shirt.

"How did I know what?" Sweetums giggled. "What did I say? You want some gum?"

"The wings—and Lizardking—"

"I have lots of gum."

Ramsey glanced round at the others. They were all zoning out, nodding off, losing themselves in whatever the hell it was this drug did to you. Echo and Poppy were staring intently at each other, Echo smiling and sometimes nodding a little. *You can understand things. You can read minds.* Jacko had his eyes closed, tapping the toes of his boots together to some interior rhythm. Sweetums broke into laughter at what seemed to be nothing, but then Jacko said, "Yeah, girl, that's right," and Sweetums laughed again. They were all connected, Ramsey saw, tangled in a happy invisible web of each

other. He envied them. He looked at the thin silver case
that rested on the couch by Sweetums's plump thigh.

Magic for everyone.

A voice spoke up so suddenly inside Ramsey it was
as if a stone had struck his own bones. *Not for you.
Keep away from it.*

He wrapped his arms around himself, hugged himself tightly.

Keep away from it. Or you will betray yourself.

His back was starting to itch again.

Starting to hurt. To burn.

Oh, honey. They took your wings.

He moved to the end of the couch, away from
Sweetums, so that he wasn't touching anybody. *There's
nothing wrong with you,* he told himself. *You're a little
fucked in the head, maybe, but really no different from
anybody else, not really, not at the core.* He buried his
head in his arms and closed his eyes. He thought of
Lauren. He imagined that she was beside him on the
couch right now, they would go home together, everything would be all right. *There's nothing wrong with you,*
this imaginary Lauren was telling him. *You don't need
to be so alone. Loneliness sucks. It just grinds and grinds
and grinds you down, doesn't it?* He didn't open his eyes
again until what felt like years later, when Poppy was
shaking him and telling him it was time to head out, and
then, when Sweetums offered him the last bit of blue
powder, he felt a thin, pale burst of defiance, of anger,
and took it, even when it burned.

"Shortcut," Poppy said.

He ducked into an alley. Ramsey trailed after him. He
was getting so out of it he could no longer lift his feet,
sneakers dragging in the dirt. Dawn seeped through the
sky, sending weak, watery light into the alley.

"Hold up," Poppy muttered beneath his breath.

Ramsey stopped, lifted his head.

The man stood in silhouette in the mouth of the alley.

His body like a blade, so tall and thin, a silver-tipped walking cane in one hand. He came towards them, passing through patches of shadow and light.

"Hello, my young gentlemen," Salik said.

Fuck this, Ramsey thought, and spun on his heel, about to walk off.

Except a dark van was rolling up, blocking off that end of the alley.

He turned and looked at Salik. His head felt thicker all the time, like someone was stuffing it with rags.

"Poppy," he muttered, injecting scorn in his voice to hide the note of fear, "who exactly is this loser?"

"Shut up," Poppy snapped. "Salik," he called, "Salik, let's just do this and get it over with. Here." He took something from his pocket and held it out to the other man. "It's his." Ramsey realized it was the photograph of Lauren as soon as it exchanged hands—the photograph he had leaned against the wall in Poppy's squalid little apartment.

"Hey," Ramsey said. "What the fuck? What the—"

"Shut up."

Salik cocked his head to one side. He lifted his cane in both hands, tapped the silver tip against his open palm. "You owe me much more than last time," he said pleasantly. "Much more. But I think . . ." His gaze lingered on Ramsey. "Yes. I think this one's quite the treasure."

Ramsey became aware of Poppy stepping away from him, putting distance between them, saying, "So it's enough? We're good, then?"

He heard the sound of a van door sliding open behind him, the heavy thump of feet as someone jumped to the ground.

"Oh," Salik said, "it's enough. But I think this time I'll take you too."

Before Poppy could react Salik swung the cane and struck him in the face. Poppy's nose disintegrated in a spray of blood and cartilage and then Salik was swinging the cane again, the silver tip connecting with Poppy's temple. The boy crumpled.

Salik looked at Ramsey.

"You," he said softly, and then someone was right behind Ramsey, hooking a beefy arm around his throat.

Ramsey didn't struggle, his gaze still locked with Salik's.

"What are you?" he whispered.

"I could ask you the same thing," the man replied. "But I suspect I already know." Salik peeled off a leather glove. His good hand was coated with the blue, glinting powder. Ramsey instinctively jerked back from it, his back pressed against the unseen man who held him, but there was no way he could avoid it: the caress that trailed silken fire along the side of his face, as he felt the crushed, crumbled skin of something from another world slide across his skin, and then go into him.

His vision dimmed. A hot liquid feeling rose through him, robbed all strength from his body so that he sagged against the hold on his throat. Salik watched him, black eyes shining. He took the photograph from his pocket, made a show of studying it, then grinned at Ramsey. "Pretty . . ."

The net they made to catch a bird like you.

The ground opened up and swallowed him whole; he was free-falling, white light blazing behind him.

Twenty-three

Kai waited, glancing idly around the room: the vaulted ceiling, hushed atmosphere, and plush green furniture. The bank clerk returned to the counter with a tall man who looked to be in his mid-forties; his eyes had a bright, penetrating gleam.

"You have to understand," the man said, "that this is an extremely special account. Access is, shall we say, *restricted*."

Kai took a coin from his pocket and flipped it onto the counter: the hammered-silver coin with the bird-and-serpent crest he'd given to Jess for that night at the Masquerade.

"Ah," the man said. He picked up the coin, ran it lightly across his knuckles, glancing up at Kai with a smile of appreciation. "An honor to finally meet you," he said. "Follow me."

Alone in the small, bare room, the safety-deposit box on the table in front of him, Kai could feel the energy rising through the steel lid even as he passed a hand across it, the lid unlocking and lifting into the air. At once he felt the keen drop in temperature, then a cold that slipped into his bones. A wind shaped itself into being and moved across his face, his hair.

Kai. Kai. Welcome back, Kai.

It's been so long, Kai.

They were phantom-voices, illusions, echoes of echoes of stray bits of magic cast up from the hide-bound books. He ignored them. It was part of the cost of reading. These were the books, the records of knowledge and spellcastings, taken from Bakal Ashika and her followers. Many members of his Pact had wanted them destroyed. Kai had fought for their preservation; his insistence, he knew now, had begun his alienation from the same band of spellcasters he had once helped to lead.

No one trusts you.

She is your flesh and blood.

The books were repulsive to touch. They contained pages made from human skin, bearing inks and dyes mixed with both human and animal fluids: saliva, semen, blood. They warmed beneath his touch with a half-life of their own; and the shadow-life thickened in his ears.

It is all so useless, Kai.

In the end, she is all we have left.

Submit to her. Surrender the world to her. It so richly deserves her.

She wants you. She waits for you.

Go to her. Atone for your sins against her.

Atone, atone, atone . . .

He ignored them. He read through each book, the parchment sighing and squirming beneath his touch, as stray phantom-bits crawled off the pages and rose like smoke into the air around him: dark distorted shadow-faces, hollow eyes and gaping mouths, retreating to the corners and watching from the dark. They were nothing, he reminded himself, they were smoke, and in a little while they would dissipate. But the images that crawled into his brain and burrowed and nested there were harder to ignore. Scenes of violence, torture, death, decay. He shut his mind to them, but, released from the pages, they

were eager for an audience, a witness: they battered at
his defenses.

They began to hurt.

The pain began as a dull throb in his temples and
deepened through his body. He detached himself from
it and continued reading, but as he moved through the
books the images and the pain only grew in intensity,
his gaze touching off the text itself so that everything
hiding and living inside it lifted up into his eyes, passed
through his skin, became a part of him.

The hunger.

The last book held such *hunger*.

The appetite stirred inside him, like a beast waking
up jaws unhinged and ready to howl. It would not be
ignored. It pulsed inside him and more of it rose up
from the pages and he tried to block it, to fight it off,
but it leeched onto him, passed through his skin with a
hot scrabbling sensation. He craved mouthfuls of flesh,
warm salty blood, the fat and the muscle, so nice to
chew—he longed for the flush of devoured life inside
him—life after life after life until it filled him up and
filled him up until he was just . . . almost . . . there,
sated and content, he had finally consumed enough, he
could rest. He could rest. Except he was never quite
there, and it was never enough, and he could not stop.
But if he had to live and hunt and feed this way, then
he would move through the world with others of his
kind, and they would follow and worship him, live alongside him, easing the vast, echoing loneliness that went
nearly as deep as the hunger itself—

Kai pushed his chair away from the table, chair legs
screeching across tile. He braced himself against the table,
dropping his head and gasping for air but still the hunger
roared and churned inside him. *This is not me,* he reminded himself, *this hunger is not mine, it belongs to
Ashika, and if I just wait it out it will pass*— But the
images persisted: flesh tearing and yielding between his
teeth, the hot coppery salt-spill of blood, how soon it

was gone, all gone, nothing left but a staleness in the mouth, *need more need more need more—*

Kai looked to the final book, the last few pages remaining. The dark shadow-things moved in the corners, and on impulse he opened his mind to them:

The world needs to burn, Kai.

It needs to be cleansed, purified. Atone atone atone. Needs to hurt. Needs to twist and writhe. Pain will open up like a great dark maw, it will take everything, and then there will be—

There will be silence.

There will be peace.

There will be a new beginning. New masters. New slaves.

They weren't telling him anything helpful. And yet there was something between the voices, behind the hunger, some bit of knowledge raveling itself together and turning itself toward him.

Kai closed the book, gathered breath, gathered strength, cleared his mind. He opened the book again, to the blank sheets at the back. He slid his fingers across their smooth surface. One page was slightly different from the others. It had a warmth to it, an oddly porous surface. This would have been Ashika's final entry, all those centuries ago: her final vision of darkmagic, bloodmagic, the spell shattering loose inside her.

Kai summoned energy, commanded, *"Show me."*

The blank surface of the page seemed to ripple, then deepen: a crude sketch appeared where before there had been nothing. A young man stood with his arms outstretched, his face twisted. There were deep gashes along his arms and his body. Blood gushed from his wounds into the open mouths of the creatures who crouched to either side of him; who knelt, as if worshipfully, by his feet. Kai stared at the drawing, until it seemed he could taste the boy's blood.

He knew what this image depicted: something so arcane

and exotic that Kai had dismissed it long ago as a kind of myth. But he saw, now, how it was possible. Ashika sought Innat for a purpose that went beyond revenge. Ashika would create a new race on this earth.

Del was sleeping, his body curled in a ball inside the prison-sphere. Kai slipped his hands into the pockets of his coat, eyeing him carefully as he walked the length of the curving stone wall.

"Hello, demon," he said.

Del stirred. Slipped his long fingers across his face, opened one flame-red eye. "No pretty trinkets this time?"

Kai said, simply: "Bloodangel."

Del stared at him. Clucked and sighed and stretched his long, pale body. Switched his tail. Rolled his shoulders.

"No pretty bits of glass," he moaned, "no new, pretty humans?"

"Bakal Ashika never intended to release you." Kai heard his voice echo through the cave. "You, or the others. You knew that from the beginning."

Del pressed himself against the sphere. "The blood-angel rites," he agreed. "I bet you never thought you'd see anything like that, hey hey? Such a slippage only happens once or twice a cosmos."

Slippage. When the Dreamlines ruptured, and two or more realities crossed through each other. When many things, dark and light both, became possible. It was like the universe slapping down the ultimate wild card.

The demon blinked his large, bright eyes. "Bakal has no need of us. She kept no loyalty to us. And I, for one, feel no loyalty to her."

"So she will leave you here to rot."

Del unfurled a yawn. "Probably." He switched his tail again, tapped his fingers against his bony chest. "Would *you* ever consider releasing me, my precious princeling prince? I helped with the sweet thing Jessamy. I could help again." He grinned, his teeth jagged. "Oh, I could be loyal to *you*. I could be *devoted*."

"Del."

"Do you really think you can protect the little Jessamy? Being *what* and *who* you are?"

"Del," he chided. "You can't ask me anything I haven't asked myself."

"And how is that pretty one? Is she proving a most gifted pupil?"

Kai didn't answer. Although Jess had no ability to gauge her own progress and was often frustrated—which could make her sarcastic, impatient, and annoying to deal with—she progressed with a speed that startled even him, who expected so much of her.

Del said, "She is just as much my accomplishment, Prince, as she is yours. Perhaps even more. Perhaps, when all is said and done and bled and died, you will find yourself in debt to me." Del shifted in the cage, rippling his tail. "Has she found her little gift yet? I would *so* like to be there when she does."

"What is it you think you have given her?"

"What I think?" Del pressed his face against the side of the sphere. "What I think is that you have a pretty young necromancer on your hands. So I hope you know what to do with her."

"You expect me to be surprised? Her ancestor summoned and bloodbound a war-angel. She's from the most powerful bloodline in the Labyrinth."

Del seemed to consider. "I say I gave it to her . . ." He unfurled one hand, as if weighing the possibility. "You say she possessed it within her all along . . ." He unfurled his other hand. "Well. I guess we'll never know for sure. Or maybe she can shed a little light on the subject. One day. If she survives."

He paused, then asked, "How are your dreams, Kai?"

Kai only looked at him. He should leave now—he

knew he should—but the demon fascinated him. Pent up inside the sphere, radiating his energy outward, picking up stray notes of the modern world outside, its speech and mannerisms, from visitors who brought that world down into his chamber like a blast of fresh air. And Jess—what she must have been to him—a shell cracked open to get at the sweet meat inside, enough material to entertain himself with for another decade or so.

The demon sidled up against the sphere, hissed, "Is there a bird-creature in your dreams, Kai?"

Kai felt his expression slip a little. A cold wind stirred inside him.

"A *wondrous* bird with a hooked and shining *beak?* Bakal brought him down for you long ago. Long ago. It's been waiting for you all this time."

"I know," Kai said.

"Are you scared?" Del clucked his tongue twice, then said, "But I forgot. Everyone dies. It's just a matter of time, place and pain. Don't *quote* me on that or anything—"

"Good-bye, Del."

"She is your blood, Kai"—Del's voice lifted—"and blood calls to blood. It's all about the blood, isn't it? So warm and thick and rich. Blood is life and heat. Blood connects us. Blood is our insides turned outside. Ashika will find you. And through you, she will find Shemayan's heir, his *blood,* the *blood* of old Shemayan."

Kai said, "I'll see you in another hundred years."

Del grinned at him.

"Babe," he called, and even though Kai was familiar with the demon's ways he was startled, the modern world echoing all the way through Del, through the memories he had stolen: "keep in touch. We don't do this often enough."

Mina was curled in the chair by the fireplace, a red fringed shawl wrapped around her shoulders. As he spoke, he could feel the cold winds inside him, blowing harder now, turning his bones to ice. "There's a new, strange rift in the Dreamlines," he said.

Mina only nodded. "You mean—"

"A slippage. It's how Innat fell back into this realm in the first place. And it's how Bakal will call forth her demons. She doesn't need to summon them. They will come pouring through the rift, as many of them who want to. She only has to call them. Point the way. She only needs—"

"Vessels," Mina breathed, "to hold them."

"—Human volunteers. She will use the blood of Innat to feed and bind them, bind demon soul to human body. And they will move out of the borderlands and into the world."

The wood popped and sizzled in the fireplace, releasing a sweet, smoky fragrance.

"Then it is the end of things," Mina said, "and it is her world now."

His voice turned sharp. "You used to be a warrior. All of you. *Warriors.*"

"We were young," Mina snapped. "We had power. We believed."

"And if I could get that power back?"

Her gaze moved slowly across his face.

"I could go to her," he said.

She realized what was in his mind and said, "No. No."

"I could offer myself. The way she wants. I could *atone*. That kind of bloodprice would take me as far into the Dreamlines as I need to go."

"You would go insane. You would—"

"—Send out a summons on the Dreamlines," Kai said. "A call for the others to bond with me. The way they did before."

"They won't come."

"You sound so certain."

"Not enough of them," Mina said. "Not enough."

Her voice caught in her throat.

"What about you, Mina?" Kai said quietly. "Will you come?"

Her lips were moving; she was whispering, to herself or to him, he couldn't tell. "Everything has its own ending," she said. "Everything moves towards—"

"Mina—"

"I'm tired," she said simply. "We all are. Aren't you?"

"Oh, Mina."

"I have something for you." She slipped a hand inside her shawl, then held out a small polished stone, a tiger's eye. He saw its aura immediately—a rustling of warm, orange energy—and recognized it for what it was. A chakura, a guardian-spell, made by some forgotten Summoner a long time ago.

"I thought those were all gone," Kai said.

"I found it in the Libraries. I thought maybe you could make use of it. You," Mina said slowly, "or your girl." Her eyes were dark and grave.

He nodded a thank you. He took it from her and slipped it in his pocket.

As he approached her door he sensed her presence behind it: she was like sun-warmed water, ocean breezes, a touch of siren's song. Kai opened the door with a glance, calling out, "Jess."

He heard her before he saw her: she was whispering to herself. She was hunkered on the floor in the corner of the room, rocking like a child, her hands twisting together. She was in some kind of trance. She was sleepwalking.

She had painted and written all over the bedroom walls, the sharp smell of paint hanging thickly in the room. On one wall, the boy from her *Heir of Nothing* paintings was bound and gagged, his eyes staring sightlessly; HIS BLOOD WILL BIND THEM was written over and over all around the image. On another wall, men on motorcycles were caught, screaming, in some kind of dust storm, as they

were torn to shreds by the things inside it; through the
haze of storm were glimpses of faces, twisted into something crazed and snarling that went beyond human.

Another wall was nothing but text:

*He went to see the King and follow his Way where
Poppy was waiting for him they went to the party
by the railroad tracks the password was hellrider
poppy offered him jacks poppy offered him jax
poppy sells himself and others and everything else
you must listen to the music because I have a gift
for you if you want it or not but Coyote doesn't
think so Coyote knows you must ride like hell
you must be a hellrider to guard your own soul to
keep your own ghost he fell off the balcony Coyote with his dog I left my heart in san Francisco if
she didn't eat it first*

*The hunger never stops never stops NEVER
STOPS*

*—People crucified on telephone poles up and
down the highways—People bleeding from every
orifice and eating the brains of their children—
people melting and twisting in the flames—he said
Don't you know what you are? She's going to use
you, Ramsey she will she will she will—they will
eat what they can and burn it all down and make
slaves of those who survive*

Her face was white, her eyes wide and staring beyond
him and into a dream. "Jess," he said. "Jess."

Her hands were twitching, etching at the air. She was
in the grip of a thing she could not yet control when she
was awake. She turned to him, and he was reminded of
that morning many years ago when a much smaller,
younger girl had also drifted towards him, trusting he
was what she had dreamed he was.

But when she lifted her head and looked at him, with
a sleepwalker's enigmatic gaze, there was nothing child-

like about her or the knowledge she held. "The bird has your flesh in its beak," she said. "I can see it."

"Jess."

"It's circling high above you," Jess continued. "It's watching you. It's been watching you for years."

"Never mind that. The boy, Jess. Where is he? Can you find him?"

Her face twisted and she gave a small cry. Her hands rose up, carved shapes in the air.

"Jess," he said, and caught her wrists in both his hands, held them as she strained to break away. He was suddenly, alarmingly aware of her long lean body in the flimsy cotton nightshirt. "Jess," he said. "You don't need to write it or paint it. You can just reach inside yourself and say it—"

"Sold for the drug," Jess muttered. "The other one, too. Lizardking. Poppy sold him for the drug. To be killed in the Maze while they watch on the screens. Because that's entertainment. That's entertain—"

"Wake up and say it." He resisted the urge to shake her, to keep the anger from his voice. He was so tired of this. "Where is he? Where is Ramsey?"

And he saw her eyes clear as she came back to herself, as her dreamtime knowledge merged with her waking life. He felt, despite himself, a pulse of satisfaction. She was learning. She was growing.

"San Francisco," she said. Jess Shepard's eyes were wide, her voice tinged with wonder. California, he thought. A desert state. "He's in San Francisco."

Twenty-four

It felt strange to punch in Gabe's number, like sending transmissions to an alien planet. He wasn't in. She meant to leave a message on his voice mail, except her voice curled up and died on her. He would only hear the gaps between her words, the things she was not telling. *If you want to keep your secrets,* he had once told her, exasperated, when they were arguing over something now long gone from memory, *keep your secrets.*

Kai had rented a two-bedroom suite on the sixteenth floor of an old Nob Hill hotel. The marble fireplace, landscape paintings, patterned silk-upholstered furniture, were too early-European for her own tastes. But she saw how it suited Kai—how, when they stepped through the door, he stretched and rolled his shoulders and seemed to breathe easier.

She had asked him point-blank, "Just how wealthy are you?"

"I've been in this world for over seven centuries, Jess." He was sweeping back the drapes, studying the view of the city. "That's a lot of time to learn about wealth. How to make it, lose it, make it again. Whether you use magic or no."

"So are all the Summoners like you? Rich like you?"

"No. Some of them don't care."

"But you care."

"I went from utter luxury," Kai said, "to traipsing around Europe in the Dark Ages with little more than my horse. Believe me, I learned to care." He nodded to the view beyond the window, the buildings and hills, the glimpse of bay. "I made some wealth here," he said absently.

"The Gold Rush?"

He nodded. "The ships that delivered food and merchandise to people who came here, stayed here, built a city. Some of those were mine."

Now, she heard him moving in the living room. He seemed restless and distracted in a way that unsettled her, a bleakness gathering in his eyes. She turned her mind away from him, picked up the telephone and called Chelle.

"Getting out of the city to clear your head." Chelle's voice was sharp. "So is it clear yet? What is going on with you?"

"I've been—"

"You don't even know what happened to him. Do you?"

"Something happened to Gabe?" Her voice went thin and high. "Chelle, what happened? Oh my God—"

"He's in a coma."

"*What?*"

"He went out with some friends to party in the Hamptons, drank too much and tried to drive home. And his fucking friends fucking let him. There were two other guys in the car with him, they're fine, some broken bones. Thank God. Thank God. He could have killed them. He could have killed someone else, plowed into some *kid*—vehicular homicide, involuntary manslaughter— assuming he ever *wakes up*."

"So he's—" She didn't know how to finish the sentence. Her throat went tight.

Silence on the other end.

Then: "I don't know, Jess. He's stable. He's stable. But he isn't waking up."

"I can't—" Jess took in a breath. "I don't know when I'm coming back, Chelle. I got caught up in something. I can't leave until it's finished."

"And you can't tell me what it is?"

If you want to keep your secrets, keep your secrets.

"No," Jess said.

"Are you with someone?"

Jess paused.

"Jess."

"Yes. I am. But it's not anything—"

"He is my *brother,* Jess. He got fucked up that night because he was fucked up over *you,* you realize?"

"I never betrayed your brother," Jess said evenly. "It's not like that."

"It's the guy who came into the bar that night. Isn't it?"

She remembered: the across-the-room glimpse of Kai on the stairs, Chelle plucking the cherry from her Manhattan, votive candles flickering light on her face. It seemed a lifetime ago.

"Jess—"

"It's not like that," Jess said. "Whatever you're thinking is wrong. Believe me."

"And if Gabe wakes up and asks after you? What do I tell him?"

"Tell him something came for me," Jess said, "like I told him it would. Like I always knew it would. Tell him I genuinely loved him. Tell him I'll see him when I can."

A silence.

"Play safe," Chelle said, and hung up.

Jess stared at the bedroom wall, cradling the phone in both hands. People moved into your orbit, moved through it, away. She had accepted this long ago.

She thought of Gabe in a hospital bed, gone deep inside himself, beyond anyone's reach. There were things she wanted to say to him. She wanted to explain herself, defend herself. She wanted to talk about how you were supposed to share your feelings. Confess. Go on talk shows, go to a shrink, write a memoir. Jess had never shared that impulse. An over-examined life seemed just as static and worthless as an unexamined one. But if you acted, if you made things happen, then sooner or later your life would change. That's what painting had always been for her: an act, perhaps even a revolutionary one, that could rescue her from shame and secrets and loneliness. Her paintings were her confessions, and she had never felt the need to reveal herself in any other way. *What makes you think you even want to be known?* he had asked her. But she had always assumed that if he looked at her paintings closely enough, he would know everything.

As if it mattered now.

"It's Gabe," she told Kai. "He was in a car accident."

They were sitting on the terrace, a bottle of sake on the table between them. The night air was soft on her skin, the city dropping beneath them: hills rising and falling like breath, all the way down to the Bay, the lights of the Golden Gate Bridge strung across black water.

"He's in a coma," Jess said.

He was staring into the distance, his eyes hooded. But then he turned towards her, and she saw him gather himself out of his own thoughts.

Kai said, "Persist with the teachings, and you'll be able to go back and help him."

"If the magic changes me enough, you mean?"

He turned his sake cup in his long fingers. "Yes."

"What am I changing into?" Jess said. "Like you?"

"Not quite. But if you go deep and far enough into the magic—" He stared at the sake cup. Again, she sensed him slipping off into his own mind, far away from her, from anyone.

"Kai," she said quietly.

The sound of his name seemed to startle him. "Sorry," he muttered. "The magic changes you. And those of us who go deeply into it, as you have the potential to do—"

"So I *could* become one of you." Jess felt oddly detached, like a scientist probing an interesting new artifact. "A Summoner. With the extraordinary life span."

He looked at her carefully, setting the cup back down on the table. He leaned toward her. She sensed everything he had not yet told her swelling against the membrane of his silence. He said: "You would pass over into a whole new kind of existence. Your life in New York. Your friends there. Your career. You would have to die to all of that. It doesn't come easy. It's amazing, how hard and fast we cling to the things we think define us. But that life, that identity, would peel away from you, one skin, one layer, at a time." He paused, then said. "You would lose the ability to have children. I don't know if that's important to you."

She looked at him blankly. "The magic makes you sterile."

"Children bind you into time," Kai said. "The passing of generations. When you step half out of time like we do—No."

"I always assumed I would," Jess mused. Her gaze slipped past him, to the spires of a church across the street below. "At some point. Have a child."

"The more you feed the magic, the greedier it gets. It wants your time, your attention, your love. There's no room in there for a child. Not much room for anyone."

"It sounds lonely."

"Your definition of loneliness changes, along with everything else."

"Kai—"

"It might not be necessary," he said, looking at her in the half-light that spilled through the glass doors. "Most people with Sajae magic, who learn to use it in some form or other, stay safely enfolded in their humanity. It might be that way with you."

"But you don't think so."

He shrugged. "I make no predictions."

He took something from his pocket and placed it on the table between them. It was a polished stone, a tiger's eye, smooth and gleaming. "This is for you," Kai said. "It's a guardian-stone, a kind of talisman. A spell."

"A spell," Jess echoed. She touched it gingerly, as if it might burn her. She picked it up and cupped it in her palm. "It's a stone."

"When you're lost, throw it as hard as you can into the darkness. And someone will come from the Dreamlines to guide you. A ghost, most likely, although sometimes it's a demon."

"A demon?"

He gave a wry smile. "Just a little one."

"Why would I need this? I have you."

Kai took his gaze away from her.

"Kai," she said. She drew breath. "I'll do whatever I need to do. But I'd like to think I still had choices. That everything isn't just . . . predestined." She wasn't sure exactly what she meant by this. But she could feel the weight of the things Kai was keeping from her, threatening to press down and smother them both.

"You have choices," Kai said abruptly. "We always have choices." He stood and picked up the sake bottle and went back into the suite, sliding the door behind him. Jess looked after him, thinking again of that image in her mind: the beach, the tidal wave. She closed her eyes. She could feel it now, crashing over her, cold and fierce and obliterating.

Twenty-five

It was like thunder. Their music rose and hovered, filled the air, exploded. Lucas didn't feel that he was making music so much as he was caught inside the pulsing heart of it. They had always played well, but they had never played like this before: the music from and of them and yet not. It was its own entity. It used their flesh, their bodies. If Lucas lifted his hands from his guitar strings he suspected it might rip them apart.

The crowd was loving it.

They crowded the orchestra-pit-turned-dance-floor of the old renovated theater; they filled the tables that slanted up through the shadows, they spilled through the doors in the back and milled and lounged and listened in the hallway just outside. As the lights flashed and shifted Lucas could look out and see people holding each other, swaying and jumping to the music, the whites of their eyes gleaming like those of creatures in the bush. Empty water bottles littered the tables. Lucas knew that if he got off the stage and moved through the crowd (and they would love that, they would eat him all up), he would see the odd, otherworldly glint of jax-marks: decorating wrists and throats and naked backs and bellies. He would see heaven-starred, bombed-out gazes turning to him with looks of love and devotion and revelation.

Come to the desert.

Join the festival.

Come drink of the bloodangel.

Asha's fans. Or her children, as she liked to call them (and she said it without any irony whatsoever, at least as far as Lucas could tell).

In moments like this, Lucas was tempted to think of them as his children, too.

They were deep into the final song now, Asha's voice howling up through the octaves. She hit the high note and held it and as the moment stretched on he saw the shadow again, as he sometimes did when they were on stage, saw it rise from Asha's body and hover around and over her, saw it slowly unfurl its long whip of shadow-tail—

The moment snapped.

Asha's voice cut out, the lights came down.

Lucas backed up a step, another step. He could feel the audience, out there in the dark, their collective suspended breath. "Come to the desert," Asha called into the microphone. Her voice rang and boomed. "All my children. Come to the Bloodangel."

The darkness erupted with screams and applause.

Afterwards, he found a quiet corner backstage to have a smoke before heading back to the chaos of the dressing rooms. He pulled smoke into his throat and lungs, gazed disdainfully at his shaking hands until he had steadied them enough to perform surgery.

"Intriguing show."

The voice came rolling down the corridor.

Lucas pulled away from the wall, looked in the direction of the voice.

"Hey there," he called.

No response.

He saw movement at the end of the corridor and for

a moment thought it was his own reflection in the mirror that hung there until the same voice came again: "Interesting music. Interesting singer," and its owner stepped into view, boot heels rapping on concrete. Lucas squinted through cigarette smoke, shadow.

He said, "So who the fuck are you? And how the fuck did you get back here?"

The man smiled and produced a card between his first and second fingers (they were unnaturally long, Lucas saw, with silvery nails). He presented the card to Lucas.

"The name is Salik. Your singer knows me. We go back a very long way."

He took the card without looking at it, careful not to let the other man's skin graze his own.

Salik said, "I'll have one of those, if you don't mind."

He could never refuse someone's request for a cigarette; he had bummed so many in his lifetime he couldn't risk the karma. He handed Salik a Lucky and was about to lend him his lighter when he saw the cigarette between the man's lips, already lit.

"The thing about a creature like Asha," Salik said, and Lucas found himself paying attention, "is that she gets lonely. And even homesick, from time to time, which some like myself might consider ironic. Given what she did." He exhaled smoke. "The home, the city, that they turned to sand."

"The Labyrinth," Lucas murmured.

"Ah." The man looked pleased. "So she has educated you, at least a little?"

"Perhaps a little. Who are you?"

"I used to be important," Salik said. "When I was a child, I studied alongside the prince himself, played with him in the royal courtyards. Now I'm just a dealer."

"Dealer of what?"

"Certain pleasures. So I hope you'll take advantage of my invitation." He gestured to the card in Lucas's hand. "Bring the singer. Or come alone. Either way."

"Why come at all?"

"Something has rather miraculously come into my possession. If I'm not mistaken, but I don't believe I am, I'd be honored to make you a gift of it." The black eyes flared a little.

Lucas said, "And if you are, as you say, mistaken?"

"Ah, then." Salik hunched his narrow shoulders, a parody of a shrug. "You will still enjoy yourself. I, too, can put on some good entertainment."

Lucas stubbed out the cigarette and turned from Salik's grinning face.

Twenty-six

Everywhere she went, the city was hollow with his absence. Whatever pulse of him that had drawn her there was gone. Jess went through the Tenderloin, Haight-Ashbury, the Mission: places where young faces, lost faces, found each other, gathered. None of those faces belonged to her boy. She mindcast through the streets as far as she was able, searching for that flicker of presence, that taste, but there was nothing. Only a void of dead air.

But every time she left the hotel, it was like stepping into a new world. She heard fragments of conversation coming from what should have been way beyond earshot (three girls were talking heatedly in Italian as they waited for the light to change, a middle-aged couple at the end of the block were discussing a Russell Crowe movie); and her vision seemed jacked up, amplified. The colors blazed; cars and buildings and people stood out in sharper detail. She felt removed to a place outside the edges, looking in, and yet she also felt plugged into the world like never before, as if it wasn't moving around her but through her, and she was tasting it from the inside for the very first time.

* * *

When Jess returned to the hotel suite, the Do Not Disturb sign was hanging on the door. She let herself in.

Her hands went to her stomach, as if she'd been kicked there.

Kai was kneeling in meditation, his head thrown back, his arms loose at his sides.

He was also levitating off the ground, his head just inches from the high ceiling. His eyes were closed and he seemed oblivious to her presence. She heard someone whispering his name, over and over, then realized that voice was her own.

Kai's suspended body revolved slowly towards her.

He opened his eyes.

His sockets were filled with molten light, a glowing deep amber. It was as if someone had opened up his skull and filled it with flame. He lifted his hands. His skin was luminescent.

Jess backed into her own room and shut the door.

"What you saw," Kai said. "You shouldn't be alarmed. It might appear dramatic, I know, but it's fairly routine."

She had called room service, even though she had little appetite. But it seemed she was taking more and more comfort in mundane rituals: guiding the waiter inside the room, signing the check, wishing him a pleasant evening. Kai emerged from the other bedroom, a folded map beneath his arm. He reached for the glass of cabernet she held out to him, the half-light downplaying the odd shade of his eyes, the glint of his fingernails.

"Routine," Jess said, and laughed. Then she said: "Soulcasting."

He nodded.

"You went into the Dreamlines?"

Kai glanced at her sidelong, his mouth twisting a little. Shadows slanted across the room, across them both. His expression was impossible to read. "Not deep enough," he said. "But I was able to see . . .

This is what I know, now." He unfolded the map and spread it across the table. "The Dreamlines have ruptured somewhere here," Kai said, sweeping his hand across a portion of Nevada desert. "We call it a slippage. The Dreamlines and this world intersect, and the point of intersection becomes what we call a *sorenikan*. A borderland between the two worlds." He paused, then said, "The Labyrinth was founded on such a place."

"And you think Asha will go there."

"She might be there already."

Jess eyed the map, gauging the distances. "Not that far," she said.

"No. Not far."

"How long do these . . . *sorenikans* . . . last?"

Kai shrugged. "Sometimes for minutes, sometimes for thousands of years. But they're never more powerful than in the first days after conception. After that, it's a long slow decline." He smiled wryly. "Like life."

"So the Labyrinth would have died eventually, even if—"

"Everything dies, Jess. But it should be allowed to die on its own. It doesn't need to get shot, beheaded, and burned."

"What does Asha intend to do there, in this . . . this slippage?"

"There's a term," Kai said, " 'bloodangel.' It's the term used for any otherworldly entity that's sacrificed in order to bring power to others." He paused, drank down wine. "It's in a demon's nature to devour," he said. "I thought Asha would consume Innat, absorb whatever power she could of him, and then seek the release of her old followers, her Pact. But no. She plans to turn the boy into a bloodangel. With her to call and lead them, demons will find the rupture and descend down into our world; she will offer up her human followers for them to possess, and she will give them Innat's blood to drink. His blood will bind human body to demon soul. Create a new race of beings who will follow her. As many of them as she can make. It's an act that would normally be impossible for her—for anyone, no matter how powerful—except for two things: Innat is weakened and vulnerable—"

"And the slippage," Jess said.

"This slippage in particular." He paused, then said, "If Asha gets hold of the boy, a mark will appear in the sky. You will know it when you see it. The mark of the bloodangel. It will mean that the rites have begun. So follow that sign, and you will find him."

"We will find him," Jess said.

Kai smiled a little and touched a napkin to his mouth.

"We," Jess said, more loudly now, "will find him."

Kai took the glass from her hand. "No more of this," he said.

Something woke her. Jess opened her eyes and lay quietly, listening for it again. She could smell the cigarette someone was smoking outside and one block down. She could feel the weight of air on her body.

The cry came again.

Jess got out of bed, feet whispering across the rug. Starlight and citylight slanted in through the terrace doors, and she had the dizzying sensation that her wakeing life and dream-life were merging; that the suite was about to transform into the hallway of doors, the ghost-self of Del laughing and mocking her. Kai's bedroom door was closed. She stood there, hearing nothing except the sound of her own heart as one minute turned into the next.

It came again: the low, tortured groan.

She opened the door.

In truth, he kept himself such a mystery she wasn't sure he slept at all. Always he was awake when she retired to her own quarters; he was awake when she rose the next morning, no matter how early. But she saw his

shadowed form supine on the bed. She heard the cry
break loose of him. His body jerked, arched up, and as
she came forward she saw his twisted face. He cried out
again, his voice splintered—

Only dreams, after all. They can't hurt you.

She had once believed that.

She was beginning to know otherwise.

"Kai," she whispered, and touched his shoulder.

His eyes snapped open and he stared with such violence she took a step back.

"It's only me," she said.

He sat up, the sheet falling away from him. She saw
his naked chest and shoulders, the muscles in his arms.
He was beautiful. How was there ever a time she had
not found him beautiful?

"Bad dreams," she said.

"Bad," he agreed.

She got into the bed with him. She didn't have the
nerve to check his reaction, only surrendered herself to
the impulse. She put her arms around him and laid her
head on his shoulder. She could feel the energy lifting
off his skin, a strange mix of hot and cold; she could hear,
deep in his body, the relentless bass of his heart. He
relaxed ever so slightly, and his hand came up to grip
one of hers.

He said, "Bakal Ashika. She's sending me dreams.
She's getting stronger. And she and I . . ." He paused,
and then said, "My father," and his voice faltered.

She could see he was on the verge of a confession,
something deeper and harder than anything else he had
said to her. "My father," he said again.

She brushed her lips against his shoulder. "Tell me."

"We are linked, Bakal and I. My father was her
father."

He was silent. He was looking away from her. She
took a moment to absorb this, to cast it into language.

"Your sister," she said blankly.

He gripped her hand, squeezed it. "Although I never

knew. Never knew. She and her mother—" Jess waited. He took a breath, and said, "You want to know, you need to know, I will tell you. My father was a tyrant and eventually a madman. He became obsessed with his young sister, my aunt. He seduced her, or raped her, I don't know. She became pregnant. He exiled her from the Labyrinth. When he sent out an emissary to learn what had happened to her and the child, reports came back that they were both dead. But the child . . . She was brought back into the Labyrinth and sold as a slave. I saw her, you know, I saw her many times over the years, in the markets, and sometimes at court, I knew the ones who owned her, but—I never knew, never thought—"

He was silent.

"She's coming closer, Jess. I feel her energy. She has followers now, disciples. They are starting to find each other. We're running out of time."

She closed her eyes. She didn't want to feel fear anymore. She kissed his throat. A sigh escaped him and he turned towards her, eyes glinting in the dark.

He moved his face into her throat and they paused, then; she listened to the rise and fall of their breath, taking on the same rhythm. "Jess," he said, "Jess," as if not knowing what more to say, or if he could say anything; she heard the reluctance in his voice, knowledge of this threshold, but she also heard his longing, and it was this longing that she listened to, the rest that she ignored. She looped her legs around his waist and felt him *give,* then, his arms sweeping round her back, pulling her into him. Heat broke around them, and she felt her own desire to be devoured, as long as it was by him, she would let herself be incinerated, as long as it was by him.

He pulled away from her, gasping. "Shit," he said. It was the first time she'd ever heard him use profanity. "I can't do this. I can't—"

"Why not?"

"It's forbidden. You—" Kai rubbed his mouth, pulled slightly away from her, but his hands stayed on her body, rising to her shoulders, compulsively gripping, kneading, as if testing the raw material of her.

"I'm what?"

She saw his rueful smile before he looked away. In that moment she caught a quick glimpse of the younger, reckless man: there had been, she intuited, many, many lovers.

He murmured, "You're not just any woman, Jess. I have to stay detached."

"Why?" Jess whispered. "*Why?* The world could end tomorrow . . ." It was such a corny line, she had to laugh; and yet there was truth in it.

He touched her face, running his thumb along her cheekbone. "Ah," he said, "ah, Jess—"

"You're not detached," Jess said.

His smile faded. She saw the darkening in his eyes, then, and she moved even closer, running her hands across the smooth broad planes of his chest, the softer skin of his belly, daring him now: "You're not detached. Not since you stepped into my loft—"

"No," he said abruptly.

He tilted his head, studying her, as if realizing for the first time.

"Not since Cape Town," he admitted.

Something warm and deep turned over inside her, radiated all through her: something better than any drug, the thing that drugs themselves tried to imitate. "So let it all come down," Jess said, "and we can deal with it after."

He was silent for a moment; he was so still he seemed to stop breathing.

Looking at her.

And then his mouth was on her throat, and he was laying her down amid the pillows. She felt, then, a new touch of fear, something to do with the vast unknown quantity of him, the boundaries between them now thinning, now breaking. This was a new country now. *Not my equal.* And yet: something inside her, more formidable than she had expected, rising up to meet him, taking him on, leading him inside her.

Twenty-seven

She waits for you, Kai.

Those voices, those whispers, had slipped up from Ashika's spellbooks and into his brain, where they clung like leeches and he couldn't shake them, couldn't reach inside and pull them off. He was plagued by his sister. But then, he always had been.

She is your blood, Kai, and blood calls to blood. Blood connects us . . . And through you she will find Shemayan's heir.

He knew this was true.

He heard himself telling Mina: *I could go to her. I could atone . . .*

And he remembered what Jess had asked him: *How much damage is enough?*

He had refused to answer her, and she had not pressed the question. But now, in his mind, he said, *You have to give up everything. You can't be reborn into your power without dying first. And who can say if you'll be allowed to make it back?*

He lay beside Jessamy and watched her sleep. He touched her face and whispered a word and sent her deeper into slumber, fracturing his earlier promise not to use magic on her. But he wanted these long, deep hours of quiet, of gazing on her, before the clouds that had been gathering for so long now finally started to break. He loved the taste and sight-sound and pale silky feel of her, the heedless way she had watched him in the dark—*Let it all come down, let it all come down*—

Jess sighed, eyes moving rapidly beneath the closed lids. "It is a false moon," she murmured. Dreaming, he knew, talking to herself. Or maybe someone else.

"Blood moon," Kai agreed. He himself had only witnessed one, the night before the great destruction of the Labyrinth: like a red hole ripped through the sky.

"It's just another doorway," Jess murmured. "Remember that."

He waited for more, but she rolled away from him and seemed to sleep on.

He dressed in jeans and a T-shirt, checked the time. A little past three a.m. He took some hotel stationery from the rolltop desk and wrote it down for her: *False moon. Another doorway. Remember.* He unfolded the maps of the Mojave—the maps he had meditated and mindshifted over, had marked up with yellow highlighter—and left them atop the desk, the note paperclipped to a corner.

Then he left her.

Time to find what was waiting for him.

Mist rolled in off the bay, the streets stark and deserted. It was a little past four a.m. He walked with no direction. Bakal would find him. He was holding himself out to be found. He felt supremely detached: as if the world and all its history were spinning away from him, and all he could do was watch it recede.

The world still held beauty for him. The world still broke his heart.

The car glided down the street towards him, headlights

carving up the dark. Kai stopped and waited, slipping
his hands in the pockets of his overcoat. The car pulled
up alongside him, the back window sliding down.

"Lucas," Kai said.

The man's eyebrows went up in surprise. "So you
must be the brother."

"Lovely night for a ride."

"Then by all means." The man pushed open the door,
slid back in the seat to make room for him. "Hop in."

Kai took a last glance around him, the Victorian
houses with their dark bay windows climbing both sides
of the hill. He stepped towards the car—then sensed
calm, sun-warmed water, surface rippled by siren's wind,
siren's call.

Jess.

He turned and saw her. She was not much more than
a shadow, keeping well beyond the light from the street
lamps, the hood of her black coat pulled over her head.
She had deflected his sleepspell. She had faked him
out.

Go! He fired the thought at her. *Don't be stupid.*

She wasn't well practiced in this kind of communication; so it surprised him how smoothly her voice came
to him, how shapely the words felt in his mind.

I'll let you go if you tell me why.

The hiss of a breath behind him. Then Lucas was getting out of the car, demanding, "What was that? Who
is that? Who—"

His gaze went to Jess.

He fell silent.

Standing there, watching as Jess and Lucas watched
each other, Kai felt a current pass between them. Jess
came forward one step, two steps, her face registering
disbelief, even shock. Lucas was riveted in place. His
mouth moved but no words came out. Finally he
hummed beneath his breath, then sang, *"You're my little
handful/I'm your handful of dust—"*

Kai felt Jess mindcasting toward him—then felt that mindcast fragment, her concentration dissolving. She called out instead: "*No.* Don't go with him."

Leave. Casting the thought-word towards her with the force of a slingshot. *Now.*

"*—Isn't it ridiculous/What love's done to us?*" Then he called out, in a low, silken voice, "You want to come with?"

Jess turned and faded into the shadows. She was there; she was not there. Kai was impressed, and allowed himself a small smile of pride for his pupil. As Lucas continued to gaze in her direction, Kai said, "Are you going to chase girls or do as your mistress commands?"

The other man's smile was tight and hard. "Get in."

Rich scent of leather, cologne. The back of the driver's head through the dark glass partition. As the car rolled through the silent streets and out of the city, Lucas leaned back in the seat and said, "So who is she?"

Kai glanced at him.

"The girl," Lucas said loudly. "Who is she?"

"A toy."

"A toy?" Lucas grinned. "Would you be willing to share your toy?"

He shrugged.

"She's waiting for you," Lucas said, and he knew they were no longer talking about Jess. "She's eager to see you."

Kai said nothing.

"I've seen you before, you know. In dreams within dreams."

"That so, Lucas?"

The musician leaned back in the seat. His eyes held the kind of luminosity a man's eyes should not possess. He had been marked, Kai saw. Marked deep.

Kai said, "I was hoping you might surprise me."

"And it appears I haven't?"

"You could have been great on your own," Kai told

him. "Any third-rate psychic could have told you that. You didn't need her. You only thought you did. That's one of the reasons she wanted you."

Lucas turned his face away.

"And you know all this," Lucas said.

"Yes."

"Because I'm so special."

"You make the music of angels," Kai said. "We've always been aware of you."

"Have you listened to our music?"

"She used to sing, you know, in the Labyrinth. They forced her. I never liked her voice then, either."

"Maybe she'll sing for you tonight. And you might change your mind."

Kai laughed.

Lucas leaned forward in his seat, clasping his hands between his knees. Kai could sense Bakal Ashika inside him, moving through him, fueling and deepening his already considerable gifts. What an interesting man he could have been.

There was the chance, however slight, that he hadn't been as fully consumed by Bakal as one would think; that some of the ferocity in his gaze was still his own. Kai touched the man's arm. The man was closed off, held perfectly within himself: he was absolutely unreadable. Kai was impressed.

Lucas was smiling at him.

His face held a shard of knowledge, a shared intimacy, that gave Kai pause. Kai sensed that in touching this man he had also touched on a mystery. Something here that went beyond what he knew, or sensed, or expected.

Lucas said, "She's extraordinary, isn't she?"

Asha, of course. He must be referring to Asha.

And yet, as their eyes met within the soft leather dark of the Lincoln, Kai was suddenly uncertain.

Lucas said, "I would like the chance to know her. To see what she becomes."

Jessamy, Kai thought. *Is there something here you*

never told me, or didn't know to tell me? Something I can't see on my own?

Lucas moved back into the seat, his face slipping into shadow. Kai turned in to his own thoughts, controlling his fear the way Shem had taught him lifetimes ago, focusing and preparing his mind for what lay ahead. It was so close now he could taste it. The blood of it.

The car rolled over to the shoulder and stopped. The two men stepped from the air-conditioned interior into the blunt hot world of desert. The sun burned.

Figures stood in the near distance. Kai felt himself falter. The thought crossed his mind very much against his will: *I can't go through with this. Don't make me.*

"Come, now," Lucas said. His voice was not without gentleness. "We've come so far."

He followed Lucas across the hard-packed sand. He fixed the image of Jess in his mind, her eyes, her body, her voice.

Asha was waiting beside a large outcropping of rock. There were others with her, barely more than teenagers.

"So you chose," Asha said, "and you chose me."

Her voice was devoid of the triumph and glee he had expected. Her eyes were flat like a shark's, her body still.

Kai said, "Yes."

"I wanted to kill you, once," Asha said. "And for a long time."

He tipped his head in acknowledgement, then said, lightly, "And now?"

Her eyes flashed bright green. "What do you think?"

"I think you want family, blood ties. Even after all this. I think you got lonely."

She laughed. "You know what loneliness is, Brother? You think you can comment on mine?" She made a gesture, and two of her children moved forward. They were smiling, giggling. The young man, Kai noticed, was missing his little finger, the stump still raw and healing. They touched him, and he let them; they unbuttoned his shirt, drew it off his body. The sun blazed across his skin.

Asha stepped aside.

"Lay yourself down," she whispered. "For me. For me."

He did as he was told, stretching himself on the rock, spread-eagled, the stone sun-warmed and rough against his back. The women drifted around him, fastening the leather cuffs around his wrists and ankles. He was shackled, anchored to rock, made part of the landscape.

"I will be thinking of you," Asha said. She placed a hand against his chest, traced a line across his belly. "Brother."

The sky arced above him, white and empty and blinding. He closed his eyes against it.

Twenty-eight

"Walk with me," Asha said to Lucas. Another phrase she had learned off the television.

He turned and looked back through the heat-shimmered air to the big man bound to the rock. The others had also begun to drift away, back toward the camps, although some of them would return to watch when the bird came. It would be quite a show.

"Is it real?" he asked, although he no longer knew just what the word meant. Here, especially, where reality was slicing open. This was the desert. These were the borderlands, the wastelands, the no-man's-lands.

"Real enough," Asha said. Then: "Thinking of her?"

"What?" Genuinely not understanding.

"The bit from your dreams."

In his surprise—and something else, maybe a brief touch of panic—his first instinct was to lie. "I don't know what you're talking—"

He didn't see her hand move; he just felt the slap, the nails in his flesh and dragged across his cheek. Even as he staggered back, he felt the heat along his skin, the wounds cauterizing; he touched his face and felt not wounds but scars, thin and ridged, laid across his face.

He felt, then, the flare of rebellion he had felt in the
yard after the snake: the same blind urge to destroy her.
As if he could. Asha was staring at him, that acid-green
stare that could burn through everything.

"Why lie to me?" she said. "Why lie over *this?*"

He shrugged again. "I saw her," he muttered. "She
was with Kai."

"Kai."

His name like a cup filled with rage and longing. Lucas
looked at her in the bleached-out landscape, wanting to
understand, but she had turned her face away from him.
She could have killed Kai, yet it seemed as if the thought
had never entered her mind—or Kai's. The expression
on his face inside the car: he knew what lay in wait
for him, yes, but it wasn't extinction. Or wasn't simply
extinction: who knew how these things worked? *Real
enough.* It was possible Asha only killed out of disgust
or annoyance, or to eat; possible she had other fates in
store for those who intrigued her. He thought of the
festival, the large domed tents barely visible from here,
the worn-smooth mountains rising just beyond them;
even as he watched he could see a new line of vehicles
tracing a path towards it, dust billowing up like flags. It
was possible Asha didn't want to kill the world; possible
she wanted to consume and seduce it. Or maybe to her
it was one and the same.

She had stepped away from him and was looking at
her brother in the distance. The sun was now high overhead. *Poor bastard*, Lucas thought. Asha said, her voice
sounding oddly, curiously young: "This woman was
with him?"

"When I picked him up. Yes. I invited her to come
along"—unable to keep the smile from his voice, not
bothering to try—"but she declined."

"I catch glimpses of her," and again Lucas heard puzzlement in her voice, "but I don't know—I don't know—"
She paused again, stark white sunlight falling over her

face, the bone-colored sand stretching beyond her. And then, surprising him, "Do you think he loves her?"

"I don't know," Lucas said. Then, speaking on instinct, not sure why he believed this but absolutely sure it was true: "Yes."

"Like the others?"

Not knowing what she meant by this, but not having to. "Not like the others," Lucas said, and couldn't stop himself: "She's not like anyone."

Asha's face was smooth and blank, the light blazing up behind her eyes. She was studying him, and he let himself open up to her: why lie over this, why conceal? Why, indeed?

"And you," Asha said. "You, also. You want her."

He didn't respond.

"Why this one?"

"I don't know."

"There are so many others. So many."

"I know."

"Is it the competition?" she spoke wryly, disdainfully. "Is she the grand prize?"

The way the man—the prince, fucking *royalty,* if you could believe that—had looked at him in the car, not just at him but all the way through to something small and naked inside. *I was hoping you might surprise me. You could have been great on your own.* Kai's easy assumption of his own superiority. And running beneath everything he said to Lucas had been something else: *I am here because I choose to be. You hold no power over me. You are the personal assistant, running errands, little more.*

You could have been great, Lucas. You could have been great.

"Partly," he admitted.

"I could take her," Asha said. "This woman of my brother's, this prize. I could spend a little time with her. Then give her to you. Would you like that?"

"I don't exactly want to eat her heart, Asha."

Asha laughed. "She'll be yours to play with. She'll do anything you want, as often as you want, with as many people as you want. She'll do it with dogs if you want. Anything to entertain you." She paused for a moment, then added, "And then, when you get tired of her, we can eat her up together."

Twenty-nine

"Excuse me."

A shadow fell across her table. Jess looked up. A twentysomething man in an orange windbreaker hovered over her, backpack sloping off his shoulders. His eyes were hidden behind dark sunglasses, even though he was indoors, even though it was foggy outside.

"Would you mind if I joined you?" he said.

"Actually," Jess said, "I would."

It was six-thirty in the morning. She was sitting in the corner of an all-night doughnut shop, the air rich with yeast and coffee; she had been sitting and staring through the window without seeing anything except that impossible face, that face from her dreams, taking Kai away from her.

Kai. Her hands tightening on the coffee mug. *You withheld too much from me. What the hell is going on? What the hell do I do now?*

But she already knew the answer.

The map he had left behind in the hotel suite.

"I'm just totally starved for, you know, some conversation," the guy said, sliding into the booth opposite her. "I mean, some normal conversation. I've been hitching for forever, feels like, and you wouldn't believe the freaks and weirdos—"

She was about to tell him to get lost—choosing the way she was going to phrase it—when she gave him a second look.

Something about him seemed familiar.

He adjusted his sunglasses, smiled brightly at her.

"So," he said, "let's do it. Let's make small talk. What's your name? Where you from? What you doing here?"

"Would you mind taking off your sunglasses?"

"I'm a little, you might say, I'm, well, I'm *very* sensitive to light. I'm a sensitive, sensitive boy."

Her suspicion broke wide open. She stared at him in wonder, shaking her head, saying quietly, "Bullshit."

His smile faded.

"All right, then." He slipped off his glasses and dropped them on the table. His eyes were very bright, very blue, and she knew them at once.

"Del," she said.

"When are you going to open *my* door, little Jessamy?" He leaned across the table. "It's there, it's waiting for you. You can't avoid it forever. It's my gift. It's your power. I did it from the goodness of my heart—"

She reached out to touch him. Her fingers grazed his sleeve and felt nothing; she grabbed at his arm and her hand went right through him. He was empty air. He glanced down at her hand as it passed through his chest and he lifted his eyebrows and giggled.

"It's my gift," he said again. "Try it, you might like it."

"Tell me what it is," Jess said. She remembered that feeling from his cave: as if a shard of black glass had driven deep inside her brain. She felt it there now, cold and edged, cutting deeper.

"You're running out of time. Out of time. So get ready for a whole new world." He winked at her. "My regards to the handsome prince."

And he vanished.

But he had never even *been,* she realized; at least, not in a physical sense. She glanced around her. The waitress was pouring coffee for the old man at the counter. Two transvestites were clucking over an issue of *People* magazine at a back table. No one was paying attention to her. Jess fumbled money out of her wallet, dropped it on the table, got the hell out of there.

Thirty

The jax took him high and far. Part of him was vaguely aware that he was in the back of a moving vehicle, that Poppy was beside him, but that part was just a flickering of perception—there and gone—before the jax grabbed hold of him again and sent him soaring.

And then he was someplace else entirely.

He was in a realm that was not of the earth he had known; but that was all right, because he himself was not of the earth, not all of him, not fully. It was a realm of peace and white light and harmony, all the more treasured for being so hard-won. But the bloodshed, the wars, were over now, and he and his kind had held this peace for three thousand years. They were warriors no longer.

But then the hole came, ripping through his very existence; when time and place were sucked away and his world dissolved around him and he was falling through space and time; and it was cold, so cold; and his scream echoed through all the eons, all the worlds, but nothing could save him from falling.

And then a deep blue fireball of light exploded around him.

He thought: *This is annihilation.*

My annihilation.

And yet, when he opened his eyes, he found himself beset with new sensations. He was in some kind of stone chamber. His body had altered, taken on a new kind of . . . substance, materialism. He was contained in a flesh-and-bone cage. It was thick and heavy and clumsy. He reared back in panic, flexed his wings—

Except there were no wings.

Only pain, the seared and scorching kind.

He fell to his knees and shivered on the stone.

"You have fallen. You are mine now."

He looked up, blinking. The pale luminescence of his home-realm had been replaced by harsh color, dark colors, and the light that streamed through the windows of this stone tower was yellow and hot. It hurt his eyes, his skin.

"You will get accustomed to it. To everything."

He forced himself in this strange clumsy body to turn toward the voice.

The man who stood in front of him was tall, almost as tall as he himself had been in the other realm, in the other, true body. This man's eyes were very blue.

The man murmured, "You know my name."

And it was true. He felt the name surge up through his body. He tried to hammer it back down inside, knowing if he spoke it this stranger's power over him would be complete.

But it ripped from him anyway: *"Shemayan."*

"Yes," the man said. "I have need of you. But then I will release you. I will send you home. That is my promise to you."

"Jess," he said. "Jessamy."

The man looked at him, blue eyes shading into confusion.

He couldn't stop this other name from tumbling from his throat. "Jessamy. JESSAMY. JESSAMY—"

"Would somebody shut this kid up?"

"Screaming and dreaming as I fell," Ramsey muttered. The part of him still connected to his Ramsey-reality flickered on again: they had stopped, there were hands on him, hauling him out of the back like so much cargo. Fresh, salted air swept over him. He gulped at it like a fish. "Shemayan," he muttered. "Shemayan."

"Would somebody shut—"

"Never mind, Gavin," another voice said. This voice was familiar. "Our boy Ramsey has a lot on his mind."

Salik. His good hand reached out, touched Ramsey's face. And then the jax dealer stepped away, and Ramsey felt himself carried towards the house. Music, laughter, drifted through the open windows.

And then the Ramsey-reality was going away again. He drifted high and sweet, a bliss-feeling, a jax-feeling. He heard voices from a long way away:

"This one's for the Maze?"

"Not this one. The other one. And the girl."

He soared up and away, beyond the voices. For a while Poppy was floating in that space with him. *Nemesis,* he said. *I'm sorry. We're going to die. I'm sorry.*

My name isn't Nemesis, Ramsey said.

Your name is many things. It wasn't Poppy speaking now. It was the voice that had always been with him, that had entered him when he was seven years old and dying. *You are War. You are Annihilation. You are Apocalypse.*

No, Ramsey said. *I'm not any of those. I don't want any of those.*

It was what you were brought here to do. To fight for them. To kill for them.

No, Ramsey said. *Not anymore.*

The voice fell silent. Things turned dark.

And for the longest time, there was nothing.

When he opened his eyes again the scene struck him as so surreal he wasn't sure if he had come down or gone even higher; if he had gone all the way out of his mind.

He was lying on a divan, screened in by drapes of red silk; from beyond the silk came conversation, laughter, set against some kind of world music; there were also shuffling, clicking noises, and the scent of candles and perfume. He tried to reach out, push away the silk so he could see. He couldn't make his body obey. His flesh felt like a spiderweb trapping the real him deep inside.

Ramsey looked down at himself. He was naked from the waist up. His body was covered with glittering blue jax-marks that formed shapes like hieroglyphics.

"You're awake."

The silk curtain swept back. Salik was smiling at him. "I thought a little privacy was called for," he said. He folded his long body on the divan beside Ramsey and gestured to the gap between the curtains. "Isn't it *fun?*"

It was a cavernous, high-ceilinged room. The walls were embedded with oversized video screens that cast a blank glow. Tables were arranged throughout the room, draped in velvet and silk. People dressed in suits, tuxedos, elaborate gowns, were gambling, although from the little that Ramsey could see these were not games he recognized: the cards were oversized and brightly, oddly designed; the roulette wheel was spinning many different balls of different shapes and colors; people were not using chips but what looked to be bits of glass, or maybe, Ramsey thought, they were actually gems, diamonds and rubies and emeralds and sapphires, all riding on the flip of a card, the drop of a ball.

He searched through the crowd. He was looking for Poppy—even though Poppy, he knew, had betrayed him—but Ramsey saw how the people divided into two groups: those like him, young, dazed, marked up (and fucked up) with jax, lounging on the sofas and divans like dogs waiting for their masters. Some of them were mobile, drifting through the room, but they did not join in the gambling; they lingered at the edges, watching.

The ones who gambled were elegant and imperious. Some of them, Ramsey saw, were spectacular: their height, their grace, their finely cut faces, bathed in the eerie glow from the video screens. And yet there was something sinister about them, as if that beauty exuded from their bodies, gathered and rolled through the room, contaminated the very air.

"An elite, handpicked group," Salik whispered into Ramsey's ear. "They bring their money, their beauty, their cruelty, their curiosity." He touched Ramsey's naked shoulders, his throat. Ramsey tried to speak. Could not. The jax-marks winked and gleamed off his skin, speaking their own brutal language.

Salik smiled. "Are you really so weak? So easily contained? Can't you put on a show for me?" He leaned closer, so that Ramsey could smell the wine on his breath. "Come out of hiding," Salik whispered. "It's time. It's finally time."

A voice rose and echoed through the room: "Five minutes till the Game. All bets in. All bets in."

People gathered round the long tables at the far ends of the room. The air darkened; the electric hum of laughter and conversation died away. People were turning toward the screens.

The hush deepened, became complete.

The screens flickered to life.

Poppy's face filled all of them.

He was standing in the center of a small, empty room, hugging himself, looking around him. He was shaking. He didn't walk so much as stumble from the room, still rubbing his arms, passing from the view of one camera into the view of another. Now he was in a narrow hall, turning in a circle, gauging which way to go. There was a pulped, bloody mass where his nose should have been, and every so often his right hand came up to hover over it protectively.

A murmur of anticipation swept through the crowd.

A chill snaked around the base of Ramsey's spine.

On a different video screen, another room flickered into view. A door slid open and a creature shambled out. At first Ramsey assumed it must be a man in a costume, because nothing on earth could look like that.

Because monsters like that didn't exist.

"Isn't it a prize?" Salik whispered, his hand tightening on Ramsey's shoulder. "I made it a long time ago. When I could still make things like that."

The thing had a doglike head and a long thick body but a shuffling, shambling way of moving; one of its forelimbs looked stunted or twisted, tucked in against its chest. Ramsey saw the glint of long, curved talons.

The thing paused. Lifted its large dark head. Sniffed the air.

And then, after a moment, it shambled towards the far wall and passed from one room into another. It passed through a series of small, intersecting rooms even as Poppy, viewed on alternating screens, wandered through hallways, in and out of doorways. Ramsey's eyes skipped from Poppy to the monster that had Poppy's scent in his nostrils.

The creature slipped into the hallway behind the prey.

And Poppy must have heard, smelled, sensed something because his face—blown up larger than life on the oversized screens—blanched of all color; his eyes widened. His mouth formed a single word—*No*—before he turned and saw the thing coming straight for him.

The murmuring from the crowd pitched to a higher, keener note.

Poppy ducked into another little room. He locked the door and backed away. The creature flung himself into the door two, three times, before the wood splintered. Poppy didn't have time to make it across the room. The creature moved with amazing, startling speed: it was a dark shadow passing over the youth, Poppy's body crumpling beneath it.

Someone in the crowd unleashed a wild, triumphant whoop.

"The beast will only eat the soft parts in the belly," Salik murmured to Ramsey. "The body itself will have to be discreetly disposed of. It's a great nuisance. But oh, so worthwhile."

The same droning voice from before announced: "The final death-score is Zone 4, Time 4. Would the victors please collect their winnings."

A handful of people moved towards the tables.

The music started up again.

The screens flicked back to their blank, pale rose glow.

"Ah," Salik said. "There he is."

Abruptly he left the divan, moved through the curtain and into the crowd beyond. Alone, Ramsey clenched and unclenched his hands. There was no strength in his legs. His body felt hollow, insubstantial, as if sculpted from paper. And still, he felt the warm siren pull of the jax at the edges of his mind: all he had to do was surrender to it, let it sweep through him, obliterate him, sweep him away—

No.

He had to get out of here. He had to find a way out of here—

The curtain swept back again. Salik entered with another man.

The stranger stared at Ramsey for several moments; Ramsey could do nothing but stare back. He had the feeling he should know this man, his name. But his mind felt as hollow and wind-tossed as his body. Nothing inside him was working right.

The man said, "He's pretty, Salik, if you're into that kind of thing." His own lip curled in distaste. "But you honestly claim him to be—"

"I know he seems rather sedated," Salik said. He grinned and winked at Ramsey. "But I have a second act that, I think, will persuade him to show his true colors. It's only when we are properly provoked we find the courage to reveal ourselves, hmmm?"

The man sprawled on the opposite divan and studied Ramsey with an expression that was not unkind. But for all the gentle melancholy in the man's brown eyes, Ramsey sensed a deadness in him. A void.

"There is something interesting about him," the man murmured. "And if he is who you say he is—what would you expect to happen? Do you think we would *negotiate* for him?"

"I value my skin," Salik said mildly. "I only wish that you take him to your mistress and tell her where and how you found him. That she might remember this, and look kindly on me in coming days."

"Five minutes till the Game. All bets in. All bets in . . ."

Salik said, "Are you ready for some true entertainment?"

The room grew dark and still.

The screens jumped to life.

Ramsey recognized her as soon as he saw her on screen, crumpled on the floor, still groping her way into consciousness; but something in his mind got stuck. He refused to believe it was she—it was well and truly she—even when she lifted her head and looked into the camera.

"We went across the country to find her," Salik murmured in Ramsey's ear. "Just imagine, sweet boy. All that effort, just for you."

Ramsey swallowed hard. He scraped up enough voice to say, *"Lauren."*

On screen she turned her head, as if she'd heard him.

She pulled herself to her feet, looking around her, hunching her shoulders. She took limping, shaky steps towards the door.

Ramsey said, "No."

He felt Salik's long fingers on his shoulder, felt Salik's breath against his ear.

"Show us," Salik whispered. His lips stretched into a smile. "Show me. I've been waiting so long for something to *happen*. For something *interesting*."

Something hot and fierce turned inside him. He felt it

pushing at his bones. On the screens, the dog-beast that had stalked and slaughtered Poppy was shambling down hallways, while Lauren made her limping, halting way through the rooms, lost, frightened, but still oblivious to what was coming for her.

Until she came to the room that held Poppy's mutilated corpse.

Ramsey could see the shape of her mouth as she screamed, stumbled back; as the door in another wall opened and the beast stooped through; and the creature and the young woman saw each other for the first time.

And then Ramsey heard another, different screaming, only this one was coming from inside him, ripping out through his skin and bones. He felt himself carried by some rushing force inside him. It swept him down the steps, hurled him into the main room.

On screen, the dark shape of the dog-beast bolted towards Lauren; and as the girl fell beneath it, as she died on screen while the crowd in the room watched and murmured and groaned and cheered, Ramsey felt the air around his body turn hot and still. Just like that: she was dead, she was gone, that's all it took, that one brief sound of a neck snapping, while these people watched and waited for the final score. His skin was charged, electric. He tossed back his head and even he was unprepared for the sound that came from him then, the agonized howl that echoed down through realms and centuries, trapped in his flesh for so long. He felt the rise of wind from his body, whipping through his clothes and hair. It funneled round him—

—Then exploded into the room.

It slammed over tables. Gems spilled across the floor like chips of ice. Someone shrieked. Ramsey ran towards the center of the room, his arms held out, the winds whipping round him. The pain blazed across his back but no longer mattered. It was a simple matter, now, to set the room on fire. Fire crawled up the velvet and silk; fire caught at the clothes of those who weren't already rushing for the doors. The screens along the walls imploded, one by one by one, glass shattering and raining to the floor.

"Lauren!" Ramsey screamed. *"LAUREN!"*

Abruptly as it had come, all strength left him. His knees dissolved like sugar in water; he sank to the floor. His back was on fire. He was being ripped apart from the inside, this hot fierce thing inside that thrashed his bones. It would crack him apart, Ramsey knew. It would pound his mind to sand. His body couldn't contain it, wasn't meant to contain it. He was only Ramsey, after all, an ordinary boy who should have died when he was five years old. He was—

—*The vessel is unfit*—

—Never meant for this.

The air was thick with heat and smoke, the ground littered with broken glass.

Ramsey.

His name, riding the air, coming at him through the flames, the screams.

Ramsey.

The boy looked up. Through the rage of smoke and flame he saw a man waiting for him inside the arched doorway.

Come to me, the man said, in the way of speaking that was not speaking. *I can take you to her. To Asha. You want that, don't you?*

A sob escaped him.

You want that very much.

And as the boy made his slow, broken way through the room towards Lucas Maddox, he saw Salik crouched on a divan like an ape, flinging his hands together in manic applause. He was burning. But he kept applauding, grinning at Ramsey, as the flames ate his clothes and peeled and charred his skin and ignited his hair. "Good show," he was screaming. "Good show, good show, good show."

*　　*　　*

The roof was collapsing, now, the flames leaping up towards the sky. Figures were spilling from the doors; some had jumped from the upper-story windows; others had made it to the cars parked along both sides of the road, or were fleeing down the hillside like mice.

The man carried the boy from the house, the flames bending away from them.

And then they were gone.

Only the fire, the heat, the darkness, and the screaming.

III

In the Borderlands

Thirty-one

Harry Robert Jackson, a.k.a. Coyote

Reno, Nevada

Coyote was still thinking about the dream, even now, sitting in the lawn chair in front of his trailer, a cold beer in one hand and Janice off to her shift at the casino and his big dog at his feet and the sunset, all those pinks and purples staining the sky. His favorite hour. The desert heat cooled off and the light turned gentle and the landscape yawned in front of him, never ending, never changing. He shifted his weight in the chair, sprawled his legs, cracked open another Budweiser. Max yawned and snorted and dropped his big head on his big paws. "Hey, boy," Coyote said, and tossed him the last bit of fried chicken from the bucket. Max was going to stay with his sister while Coyote went into the desert, and Coyote would miss him. He thought more highly of dogs than he did of most humans. There was something about a dog that kept you in touch with the better part of yourself. Max gulped down the chicken and snorted again, rolling his brown eyes up at Coyote just to make sure everything was as it should be.

And it was.

Except for that damn dream, the taste it left in his mouth.

It was the urn, Coyote thought. That goddamn urn, sitting inside the goddamn trailer on the goddamn kitchen table. Filled with the goddamn ashes of one Terry Ressi, known as Brutus to the brotherhood, the man who had *founded* the brotherhood, and who had for some mysterious reason seen fit to fall off a goddamn balcony the week before. Coyote had respected the man and struggled to hold on to that respect, even through the growing suspicion that Brutus was one or two cans short of a six-pack—perhaps even, in the last year, three or four or more. His unlikely demise hadn't helped. Who the fuck fell off a balcony, for fuck's sake? *Sober.*

But Brutus had founded the Nevada chapter of the Hellriders, and you had to give the dead man his due. Tomorrow morning the brotherhood would assemble at the clubhouse and head out into the desert, bearing their leader's remains sealed up nice in the red ceramic urn Janice had picked up at a garage sale two weeks ago. They would ride all the way to Gritson Rock, scatter Brutus's ashes to the elements as the man himself had once requested, then set up camp and get drunk and stoned right out of their goddamn minds.

Coyote was looking forward to it. The desert, the brotherhood, the ride, his old lady's thighs riding his on the back of his Harley: these things were why you lived life, why you showed up at work and put in the hours and the labor, why you paid bills and smiled at the cops even when they gave you shit just 'cause of what you wore and what you rode, why you didn't just snatch up your rifle and say hell with it and go into town and blow away every fucking moron who ever got on your fucking nerves. You restrained yourself. You behaved like a reasonably responsible citizen. You did all this, so you could ride in the desert with your brothers.

But he was uneasy.

Something in the air, maybe. He was seeing things from the corners of his vision—weird things—like shadows, falling and moving and writhing in a way that didn't seem . . . normal, or natural, or quite like it should be. When he was dropping off videos at Blockbuster, for example, he had stopped to admire a supple young thing in white terry-cloth shorts, standing outside the kiosk at the gas station across the street, but then he saw . . . or thought he saw . . . some kind of shadow, slipping up around her body and going through her and *into* her, so that Coyote thought he saw her skin *ripple,* as she tossed back her head and smiled at the sky, as if she'd wanted this, expected it, come a long way for it—

Maybe he was going a little nuts. A few too many chemicals rattling around his old battered brain. He wouldn't be surprised.

As long as he didn't fall off any fucking balconies, for Chrissake.

But the dream.

Started out pleasant, at first. He was in a grassy field with a woman, a babe, long dark hair, the kind of gym-toned well-nourished body you didn't often see on the broads who came drifting through the brotherhood. He spent a long time looking at that body. He was showing off for her, showing her his Harley, explaining everything he'd done to it, every tinkering that made it his own: Coyote's heart, Coyote's soul, Coyote's chopper. The only thing Coyote prized almost as much as his bike was his old lady, and then only sometimes.

I might need to borrow this, this hot young thing was saying, *so I better make sure I can ride it.* And Coyote watched, amazed, as this little dark-haired honey took the bike right from under his hands and straddled it with her strong long legs and kicked it to life and went riding. Riding. On *his* fucking chopper.

He woke up feeling like someone had stabbed him in the gut with an icicle.

So now, Coyote sat in his lawn chair and looked out at the sunset and finished off his beer. Yeah, he couldn't help it, he had a bad feeling. Like there was something bad out there and coming right for him—maybe for all of them—the whole goddamn brotherhood.

Thirty-two

He was a teenage boy: yes and no. He was Ramsey Doe: yes. And no. He was—

Innat.

But that was the name of the son, the firstborn son, the first and proper vessel.

He twisted and flailed on the cold smooth floor, reaching for the true name, but it was gone now, along with so much else. He found instead *Nemesis,* and decided that that would have to do.

The back doors opened and a woman stood looking in at him, her body backlit by harsh desert light. He was being kept in the back of a storage van, holes drilled through the roof to allow for light and air. As the sunlight reached long white fingers across the floor towards him, he looked at his arms, his hands, the skin barely visible beneath layer upon layer of blue symbols and scribbles. They kept writing all over him. The air inside the van was sweltering, but he was cold. He couldn't stop shivering.

"Do you remember me?"

She was in the van with him. She crouched so they were at eye level. For a moment he was confused: was she a person or some kind of animal? Her eyes were green, hard, yet not without a strange kindness.

"Do you remember me?" she whispered.

He stretched his hands in front of him and laughed. *Why would I remember you? Are you something special?* He couldn't seem to dig the words out of his throat but she seemed to hear them anyway.

"You came all this way to find me."

Yes. But I don't know why.

"You want answers. I have them."

I don't remember the questions.

She crawled toward him, shoulders undulating beneath the white T-shirt. She stopped a few inches in front of him, rocking back on her heels. This close, he could see the odd, slithery texture of her pale skin, the bloodshot whites of her eyes. "I could have had the world," she mused, "all those years ago. If not for you."

Behind her, beyond the wide-open doors of the truck, he could see the bright shapes of people in the distance, tents and camps on a bleached-out landscape.

Maybe the world isn't meant to be yours.

"Should it belong to someone like you?"

Fuck no. I don't even want to be here.

She acknowledged this with a tilt of her head. "I tore apart that body they put you in. Do you remember?"

Memory flickered in the very back of him: the feel of teeth and nails. The hurt of it. He shut down the memory. Enough to have lived through it once. "And then," she said, "and then, we fought. We fought in the Dreamlines. I tore up your soul. You remember?"

The past is the past. It no longer matters.

"The past is never past. It bleeds all through us."

I have bled enough.

"No," she said. "Not yet. Not you."

He dropped his head back and drifted. The golden waves rose up from beneath him, subsumed him, carried him away.

*   *   *

And then he was a small boy again—he had been so many things, he couldn't help marveling—he was camping in the desert with his parents. They were fighting the way they sometimes did, so he wandered as far away as he dared, the warmth of the fire giving way to the chill in the air. When he saw a sudden brightness flare up in the sky. He stared as hard as he could at the star-splattered sky, the thing streaking through it, a strange writhing thing of blue fire—

"Look!" he yelled. He ran back to the camp, small feet tripping over sagebrush. "Mommy, Daddy, *look*—"

He heard, then, the pop of an exploding firecracker. Confused, he looked back to the sky, but there were no firecrackers; only that writhing burning thing falling steadily towards him. He turned back towards the campfire, the tent and the beat-up Ford parked behind it, both Mommy and Daddy quiet now, good, they were no longer fighting, Daddy was holding Mommy in his arms—

Except then he was pushing her off him; she was slumping to the sand like one of those floppy dolls in the reading corner of his kindergarten.

"Come here," his father said. Looking at him through the firelight. "Come here, Son."

The boy stopped, confused by the tears on his father's face, the broken-down look in his eyes. "Come here," the man said again, and there was another firecracker pop and something punched the boy in the chest, knocked him down on the hard-packed sand. He tried to breathe and couldn't. He saw the gun, then, in the same hand that would tousle the boy's hair or play toy soldiers with him when the man wasn't in one of his dark moods, those times when "the black dog" visited, that's what his mother called it, "the black dog," and although the boy was on a constant lookout he himself never saw such a dog, and didn't know what, exactly, it had to do with his father.

But now, the taste of sand and blood in his mouth, he

felt the black dog's presence looming over them. He felt
it filling up the world. His father put the gun inside his
own mouth like it was a great big lollipop and pulled
the trigger. The back of his head blew off in a spray of
blood and bone and gristle. The boy tried to cry out but
couldn't make any sound at all. He was feeling cold,
and then colder. There was a great weight on his chest,
squeezing the breath right out of him.

His eyes moved to the sky again, and it was still falling, the blue-burning thing, except it was some kind of
creature, it was some kind of *man,* like an angel, a burning angel like nothing he'd ever seen in Sunday school,
dropping down towards him—falling right over him—he
could see the smooth white face now, the dark and panicked eyes, he could hear the screaming, and smell the
ash and cinder—

—You were screaming and dreaming as you fell—
And then he was no longer the boy but that burning
falling figure, flinging himself from the Dreamlines, burning
a hole through the worlds with his own pain and fear and
fury, nothing to hold him or stop him from falling, he
was scrambling, panicked, utterly exposed, the air like
acid eating away at him, and then, across the vast gulf of
space, he saw the boy, a small figure on desert ground—
Falling, falling, straight into the boy.

I'm sorry.
I didn't know what else to do.
You were dying anyway.

He was stumbling to the side of the highway and waiting for a car, a double-souled creature in a human body,
he was waiting to see what would happen next so maybe
then he would know what to do. He couldn't remember
anything. *Who am I?* I don't know. *Where am I?* I don't
know. *Do I have parents?* I don't know. No, don't think
about that. Don't think about that at all.

A lady in a shiny new Toyota found him, fed him, and bought him new clothes. The lady thought she might keep him. She'd always wanted a child of her own, and a boy such as this would do nicely. She took him through several states and told him to call her Mommy. He didn't call her anything. He didn't speak at all.

One morning he started to bleed. The blood soaked through the back of the flannel shirt she had just bought him at a Wal-Mart and she saw it and screamed and ripped the shirt off his body and then screamed again. He couldn't see the wounds on his back, but he could feel them: long and jagged, from shoulder to waist. His wings, trying and failing to assert themselves, to find bodily form in this realm, this body. *So sorry, wings,* he thought, and bid them good-bye. He felt the wounds closing over, the wings giving up. He could feel his blood pumping itself anew inside his body; it was changing, *he* was changing, as the wing-blood caked and crusted on his clothes. It had become strange blood, a stranger's blood. Not his. But the lady no longer wanted him. The blood was on his clothes. She was parking the Toyota in front of a police station, pushing him out of the car: "Go. Just *go*."

The next time the doors opened, the air was grainy with dust and dusk, and no longer warm. Lucas stood over him for several moments, and Nemesis stared at the long slashing scars on the man's face. Lucas muttered, "Poor bastard," and Nemesis thought, *Same to you.*

Nemesis was aware of himself being lifted, but he couldn't feel the other man's arms beneath his back and knees, couldn't feel anything. His body had been jaxed all the way into a dead zone—no longer capable of motion or sensation.

A useless vessel, he.

Lucas carried him for a while. At some point Nemesis sensed rather than saw Asha fall in beside them. They passed through a large collection of camps: domed tents, some RVs, other vehicles, cables snaking along the ground. He caught drifts of music: classic rock from one direction, reggae from another. They put the camps behind them and walked on, toward nothing but a grinning horizon of tumbledown rocky hills.

"Here," Asha whispered.

This place looked familiar. A lifeless sweep of sand, ringed by black rock: this place used to be a lake, once, in ancient times. He could feel that long-gone water echoing up through the alkali. The last gasps of sun churned the horizon to froth. "Here," Asha said again.

The wind kicked up, then, blowing dust around their bodies. He imagined the gritty way it must be feeling on his skin; he imagined the dry chalky taste that must be in his mouth. Lucas continued to stand there, immobile, holding him; when Nemesis glanced at his face he saw the deadness in the man's eyes, the tight rigid line of the man's jaw. But behind that shut-down look, the man seemed to be considering something. Hiding inside himself.

The air was churning and whipping with dust, leaching out what light of the day still remained. And still, the dust storm continued to thicken, the beige-orange sand rising up off the ground, molding itself into high, curved walls. Two doorways appeared in the sand, one to their left and one to their right, and beyond those passageways Nemesis saw more walls climbing the air, sculpting more rooms and hallways.

Nemesis closed his eyes and put his mind out into the Maze. And suddenly he was the Maze, and the Maze was him, spinning itself out of his own bones, his own energy. He was branching out into hallways and sharp turns and dead ends, into domed and long and closet-sized rooms, as the Maze fleshed itself out across this dead ancient lake. It sucked up life from Nemesis, it pulled life up from the ground and down from the sky. As the edges of two different realms brushed up against each other, then crossed. As here, in this place, the boundaries slipped open, and many things became possible, dark and light things both. Here was the Maze. Here was Nemesis at the heart of it.

Nemesis heard their footfalls as the first ones came for him, echoing through the walls of the labyrinth.

He was aware of Asha looking at him; she didn't touch him, no one touched him, but he knew it was she who made him lift from the ground. Like magic. It *was* magic. He hung in the air, suspended, his arms lifted to either side. A pleasant, floating feeling. He saw the figures come through the doorways, approaching with awe in their faces. They were in their late teens and twenties, clothes grungy from the desert, hair matted with dust. Maybe eight or ten of them. He saw the knife in Lucas's hand but he didn't feel the first cut, or the second, or the third. He saw but couldn't feel the mouths pressing against those newborn wounds, licking and sucking at his blood.

Asha crouched on the floor, watching.

And then her voice slipped neatly into his head:

You were their puppet. You were their little war-angel monkey, forced to perform for them. You don't have to fight for them anymore. You can be as you are. At peace.

One of the men who was drinking from him stepped back and wiped his mouth. He grinned, said, "Thanks, kid," and turned to Asha. He dropped to his knees.

"I enjoyed your brother very much," Asha said softly. "Yours was a generous atonement."

The man left the room. In the hallway outside, Nemesis heard him give a shrieking cry of excitement and triumph. A young woman was stepping up to him now; he could see but not feel the tangled mass of blonde hair that fell over his arm, as she lowered her mouth to the wound along his wrist.

Is this fate any worse than what they condemned you to? They made you a slave for eternity.

Asha was looking at him with gentle eyes.

But I will give you sleep. I will give you final peace.

Memory flickered: he remembered slaughter, and screaming. He remembered the magic-user who called himself Shemayan. *I will release you. I will send you home.* But he had not. He had broken every vow, and Nemesis now found himself here.

So let them drink from this body, if they wanted. It wasn't even his. It had been on borrowed time for all these years. Let them drink and eat it all up.

Asha was still looking at him.

I was put in this world to burn it. And so it must be.

He didn't care. This world wasn't even his. And perhaps it, too, had been on borrowed time, was in need of some kind of ending.

And so.

Let it burn.

Thirty-three

She couldn't shake off the feeling of descent. She looked straight ahead, the highway cutting a swath through desert, morning light slanting over leagues of beige-yellow sand and rock. Yet Jess continued to feel that she was going down, that despite all evidence to the contrary the ground kept sloping and sloping beneath her.

Jess pulled over to the side of the road, stopped the car, reached for one of the bottles of water that rolled on the floor. She sat inside the silence for several moments, gulping water, then got out of the car, door slamming, squinting down both sides of the highway.

Straight.

Flat.

No reason to be feeling this weird vertigo.

Heat and dust and silence, the sky hammering itself into the flat white of noon. And again she had that feeling of—

Tilt.

As if her mind were playing tricks on her, as if drugs had skewed her perceptions and the desert were coming at her, into her, from weird angles. She had the feeling of passing into a new land—a strange land—no longer attached to one world or the other.

This, then, must be slippage.

She pulled into a gas station. She was standing with the nozzle in her hand, sunlight glancing off broken glass on the pavement, when she noticed a camper parked in the corner. Two men and two women were hanging out alongside it, passing a joint back and forth. Smoke drifted in the dry air.

As she lifted the nozzle from the tank and replaced the cap she mindcast toward them. When she glanced up again she saw auras surrounding each of them: slithering gray, shot through with bright red. But what struck her was how the auras bled into each other, so that the four of them looked linked together, their energies merged and binding, as if together they made up one creature.

She closed her eyes, cleared her mind, and when she looked again the auras were gone.

"Hey."

She turned. A towheaded man dressed in lace-up zebra pants was coming out of the kiosk, chewing on red licorice. "You headed where we're headed?" There were faded jax-marks on the left side of his face. His eyes were bright, the whites threaded through with blood. "All by yourself in that lonely car. Why don't you join up with us?"

"No thanks," Jess said.

He tore off another piece of licorice, chewed and swallowed and leered. "Suit yourself."

The group got back into the van, doors slamming. Jess turned away, toward the kiosk, to load up on bottled water and PowerBars.

Kai, she thought. *I wish you were here. With me. Right now.*

Out of nowhere an image of a dark bird lifted itself into her mind's eye: she saw the strip of ragged flesh that dangled from its beak. *Kai,* she thought, *Kai, oh, oh, Kai,* and then she drove the car off the road, wheels churning through sand and sagebrush, not even fully braked before Jess was spilling out through the door and vomiting into the sand, the knowledge of her own loneliness, aloneness, driving through her like a javelin.

When she looked up again, lifting a hand to her mouth, she saw the haze of worn-down mountains in the distance.

But something else had appeared, pulling itself up beyond those rocks. A red circle in the sky. A moon where no moon should be. She leaned against the car, staring at that odd red sphere: mark of the bloodangel.

She could hear Kai's voice in her mind:

It has begun.

Time twisted in on itself.

When the sense of descent overcame her again, she was determined to ignore it. But she couldn't shake the feeling that the ordinary highway was the illusion. The ground had opened up and dropped her onto the other road, the true road, now hurtling her downward at greater pitch and speed.

And then the earth began to shake.

Her first thought was that she had a flat tire. Jess pulled over and stopped the car.

Things grew still again, and quiet.

She flung open the door and got out. The dusk had suddenly, savagely deepened, shadows long and thick, sun a smoldering line that rode the horizon. A wind kicked up, blowing sand. The cacti were stunted and spiky in the half-light.

Something was wrong.

She looked out toward the mountains and tentatively mindcast toward them. What she felt was a cold dark thing that slashed her gut and reeled her back, a fierce dark energy tunneling towards her. She got back in the car and drove it off the road, then hunkered down in the seat, trying to make her body, her mind, as small as possible, as if she could wipe away her entire presence and melt into the landscape.

There was a rumble in the distance, like thunder, only it wasn't anything that nature had produced, not in this world. The sound lifted into a scream: rage and fury and pain and the desire to make pain: all mingling, thundering down and around the highway, tearing across the ground. Jess lifted her head just enough to peer out the window.

They were coming from the opposite direction, a convoy of cars and RVs, maybe eight or nine of them. People were leaning out the windows, upper thighs balanced on the frame, upper bodies curved up and back as if made of rubber, arms flailing, hands clawing the air. She heard the high keening and shrieking of wind and realized it wasn't the wind: it was *them,* these people, these howling and contorted faces. As the cars screamed past she saw mouths and chins smeared with blood, she saw a woman holding up a severed head with long brown hair and a bearded face, the neck stump ragged and chewed. She saw more faces pressed against back windows, hollow-eyed faces whipping and bobbing and shaking on stem-like throats; she saw long slithering tongues lashing the air.

These faces.

Looking directly at her.

Grinning.

And then came a great, groaning, subterranean sound, a roar that boomed up through the earth. She felt the ground buckle, the car rear up beneath her, and she braced herself against the dashboard and ceiling. She was pitched sideways, her head slamming back against the window. Red light flared behind her eyes. Then the pounding started, like rocks or blows raining on the car from all around. The roof, the doors, punched in against her body. She curled up, shielding her head, gasping into her arm while she waited for it to end. *What's happening,* the voice in her mind was screaming, *what's happening what's happening what's happening what's happening—*

She opened her eyes to darkness.

She mindcast beyond the car, sensed the empty air of aftermath. The door was twisted in the frame and difficult to push open. She let her body spill to the ground. The scent of desert earth, sharp as chalk, filled her nostrils. She looked at the car, banged up and overturned and useless.

I'm sorry, she thought. *I failed. I failed.*

I'm so sorry, so sorry.

The air had cooled. The blaze of midday now seemed distant as another planet.

She limped to the car and grabbed her jacket from the backseat. As she pulled it on, her fingers touched a small, smooth shape inside the front pocket.

She took out the stone. The tiger's eye.

. . . Someone will come from the Dreamlines to guide you. A ghost, most likely, although sometimes it's a demon.

Jess did not hesitate. She lifted her arm, reared it back, let fly with all the force in her body. The stone slipped through the darkness and disappeared.

Jess stared after it and shivered.

A figure began to emerge from the darkness. It cast off its own light, a slim pale body slicing through the shadows.

Kai, she thought, and hope leaped against her chest. But as the figure drew closer Jess saw that it wasn't, couldn't be him.

It was a woman.

She carried nothing in her hands, yet emanated light like a firefly. She made no sound, no footsteps. She was less than a whisper in the dark.

Ghost.

And then the woman, barely more than a girl, stood in front of her. They eyed each other across a space that looked narrow yet felt deeper than any chasm Jess could imagine: a chasm of death, and knowledge of death. The ghost had a young, dark-eyed face, dark brown hair falling almost to her shoulders. She wore a white dress, gauzy, something a dancer might wear; she wore ballet shoes with the toes blocked off to dance *en pointe*. The shoes were crusted with old blood, even as fresh stains soaked and spread through the satin.

The dancer tilted her head, smiled sadly at Jess.

Jess said, "Do I know you?"

The girl lifted her shoulders, as if to say, *Does it matter?*

She turned and glanced over her shoulder, and Jess realized she was being asked, or told, to follow. They moved off the road and deeper into the landscape, the highway slipping into darkness behind them. Jess stared up at the false moon, the red mark that hung in the sky as if nailed there, that did not move but let the sky move itself around it; it seemed larger than before, more misshapen, and a bolder, more smoldering red. She was mesmerized. It didn't seem . . . solid, like rock, but hollow and filled with red light.

It was then she began to see them: the blurred shapes moving elsewhere in the dark, faint lights of different hues—blues, yellows, lavenders—picking out the forms, the rippling suggestions, of bodies drifting. For a brief moment she thought they were people carrying lanterns; for another moment she thought they were ghosts. She peered harder at them, trying to make out more form, more detail, but they eluded her: they were shadows on shadows, riding air. There and then gone. She rubbed at her eyes, wondering if this was some kind of mirage, the desert equivalent of northern lights; she saw a slender, purplish shape undulating off to the left of her and then it, too, was gone.

—Keep walking, a voice hissed in her ear, and she felt a cold touch on her shoulder, guiding her back toward the ghost, guiding her on.

—You must not get lost. If you do you will never find your way back.

She glanced beside her.

He was the barest suggestion of a man, his form and features faintly sketched against the dark. Yet his presence overwhelmed her, his energy entering inside her so that she could taste him: he was dry and parched, he was dust turned to dust.

Who, she started to ask, but then his name rose up inside her body as if her own blood were echoing it back to him.

She said, "Shemayan."

The mouth carved out a smile.

—The world has slipped open, little one. It does not happen often. But it has happened here. And they—Shem gestured at the oddly lit shapes slipping past them through the dark—they can sideslip into the desert, one by one by one, where Asha's fans are waiting. They will drink of the bloodangel. Human body and demon spirit will be one, and they can leave the borderlands and move into your world.

Jess said, "They're demons?"

—They are looking for form. Some of them have found form already.

Jess flashed back to the highway, the screaming nightmare of a caravan.

It has begun.

She couldn't keep the chord of despair from her voice. "So how do I stop this? I find the boy—what then?"

—Can you give up everything, Jessamy? Strip away everything you think you are, everything you think you care about, and give yourself up for the world?

She didn't, or couldn't, answer this.

—Because that is what we ask of you. Nothing less. Nothing more.

Jess muttered, "This is insane. How did I come to this?"

Shem cast her a cool glance.

—I was too arrogant, he said. His voice was thoughtful. I thought it was my place to command, my power to wield, and to pass on to my children and my children's children. To you. But it was not. It never has been. We are vessels, Jessamy. That is our power and our privilege. Remember that. Remember your nature, and you will rise up through your destruction. I promise you that.

Light appeared in the sky, distorted and rippling, as if filtering through water. The taste of dust in her mouth faded away, and when she looked back to Shemayan he was already gone. The ghost-girl glimmered up ahead of her and the world took shape beneath her feet again, the desert landscape fleshing itself into view. Dawn sifted through the ridges in the distance; beneath the cooling breeze the heat was beginning to gather, the first strokes of it on her skin.

And riding the edge of the breeze came the stench: she breathed it in as her eyes connected with its source.

The thought flashed again through her mind: *How did I come to this?*

They were walking toward a massacre.

Bikers, maybe eighty or a hundred, were strewn across the landscape like broken puppets. Their heavyset bodies were clawed and slashed, their leather vests with HELLRIDERS—NEVADA club insignias encrusted with blood. Light glittered off metal rings on stiffened fingers, pendants and medallions on torn-open chests, light struck the chrome and steel of the overturned Harley-Davidsons that littered the ground like blasted dusty tombstones. Jess could only turn and turn again, staggered by the sight, the stench of the carnage—metallic, overripe, too-sweet.

She knew, then, what she had been brought here to do and the knowledge and sight and smell were like three rivers crashing into her. Her body crunched in on itself and she heaved and retched into the scrubby ground, but nothing came out of her. She was empty, void.

She looked up at the ghost, who was still and silent and not quite real, a negative form imposed upon the landscape. "Goddammit," Jess yelled, "I can't do this! Do you hear me? *I can't do this!*"

The ghost made no response. Her form was thin and unsteady, shimmering the air like waves of heat. Her eyes were brown and deep and anxious, and for a moment Jess saw through to the young woman she had been, to the quality of human that had not left her completely.

"You knew him," Jess said. "Ramsey."

The ghost moved her head. The expression that shifted through her eyes looked suddenly, amazingly, like love.

"Oh," Jess breathed.

Her fear and repulsion fell away, husked off like an old skin that shamed her. She closed her eyes and turned her mind away from the surrounding carnage and reached through her mind's eye for the hallway of doors—

Except this time she stood at the end of the hallway, and there was only one door.

It was different from the others.

It was larger, and darker, and had a sheen to it, as if black light were trapped inside the material. She stepped closer, and realized: this door was glass. Glass from the floor of the demon's cave.

"That's my door," a voice hissed.

Del was by her side. His blue eyes flashed bright and turned red, and a shadow lifted from his body to hover above and around him. A shadow in the shape of the demon in the cave, the long tail flicking round Del-the-man's sandaled feet. She stared at them, the one self imposed upon the other.

"That's my door," Del said again. "The thing, the gift, the power, that they tried to forbid us. The great dark art they made taboo. This power is for you. It is of you. And now you'll have to use it."

"Tell me—"

Del hissed, *"Necromancer,"* and then vanished.

She was alone in the hallway. She stared at the door, the black-glass door, and she knew, then, that she couldn't stop it from opening even if she wanted to (and part of her still wanted to, part of her was still fighting). The door creaked and shifted in its hinges, and Jess said, "All right, then," the words snatched by the winds, and as the door opened and black light bled through and enveloped her she felt the ache spread through her body and into her head, she felt the warm slip of blood from both nostrils.

The door opened—

—And she blasted right through it, to the Dreamlines beyond.

She felt her mind flexing and shifting and then expanding, as if her consciousness had blasted free from not just her body but her self, her sense of any limits or boundaries that defined her. She was floating high and free from everything she had ever known.

And in this place, this vast cold infinite place of in between, voices called out to her and she listened to them all, heard the uncanny song of the recently dead. She tracked their song, hunted out the longing for life that had not yet left them, made them open and vulnerable to her. She used that to draw them even as another world—higher and sweeter—reached out and beckoned. But she cast herself in front of that beckoning, blocked it with the force of her own shadow, and answered these dead with a song of her own. *Come to me. Come back with me. Serve me. Just for a little while.*

They howled for her and gathered around her and as her mind began the long downward shift into her body, their song followed. The song of the Dreamlines: she gathered it close and brought it down and into her. It wracked her bones with such violence she thought they might shatter: for they were only bones and this song was so vast and cold and ancient, so beautiful and brutal, how could she not break in the face of it? How could she not be annihilated?

And yet, she was not.

That was her power, she realized. To hear this song, to rise in answer with a song of her own; to do this, and survive.

When she opened her eyes, the sun had climbed and the air gone blunt with heat. A Hellrider stood in front of her, his eyes fever-bright. He was tall, thick-shouldered, and cradled against his chest a motorcycle helmet covered in fur. *Coyote,* Jess thought, the name like a weed she pulled from the air, or maybe a dream. She spoke it aloud, testing it: "Coyote."

He looked at her and waited. His skin gave off a moonstone sheen, as if lit from within; perhaps he was, Jess thought, by whatever forces now working through him. He moved his helmet to his other hand and she saw the deep wounds in his chest, clawed right through his leather vest and deep into flesh; they were long, gaping shapes, the color of raw meat yet bloodless. They looked odd, arti-ficial, as if carved from wax.

"Give me your chopper," she said.

Naked horror twisted his face. She bit back a smile, chided, "Coyote," and watched as he struggled. To give his bike to anyone, but especially a woman: it cut against every fiber of his not-quite-fully-dead being. "Coyote," she said again, the third and last time, and he blew air through his beard and handed her the keys.

Around them, she could hear stirrings of motion: boots scraping on ground, bones realigning themselves inside shifting, creaking leather. She could feel the cold, steady weight of gazes collecting on her body. She didn't have to see them—in fact, she kept her eyes averted—to know the fierce light that had entered their eyes now: the light of the Dreamlines. She imagined it piercing their bones, their skin, like sunlight through pinpricks in a photograph.

"When they are ready, bring them to me," Jess said. "Fight for me."

Coyote crossed his arms. His eyes were slanted and hazel; when he moved his head again she saw more of those red, waxen wounds crossing his throat. His voice was like loose gravel. "Of course."

Thirty-four

The first time the bird came upon him he was not prepared for it. The creature circled above him, wings outstretched, its shadow falling dark and cold along Kai's
body. It perched on the edge of the rock in a flurry of
black feathers. He could smell it: sharp and wet like
gasoline. It cocked its head, gauging his body from deep
within its glittering hole of an eye, then dashed its beak
into his belly, again and again, ripping through flesh and
sinew. His back arched with the sensation, his wrists
pulling at the rough leather cuffs; he felt the bird pulling
at him, the insides of him, felt his liver ripping away.
The bird lingered there, a piece of Kai in its daggerlike
beak, then exploded upward in a violence of wings. He
closed his eyes and turned his head. Already he could
feel the wound closing, healing, his liver regenerating
itself inside his body.

The bird returned some time later. Again the long
slow spiral downward, its body a large black shape that
blocked out the sun. Again, it perched at the edge of
the rock. Again, it hacked into his body and tore out his
liver, and this time he screamed, couldn't stop the sound
uncoiling from his mouth. The bird cocked its head at

him, the dripping organ caught in its beak; then it ruffled its wings and leaped into the sky.

Stray feathers drifted in the air, settled on his chest and belly.

The wound healed.

The bird came again.

The wound healed.

The bird came again.

The pain cycled through different stages. First the violence of the act itself, followed by the raw, searing aftermath, the wound exposed to sun and air. Then the itch as the wound closed and healed, an itch so intense it threatened to drive him insane, made him fantasize about digging his fingers into his skin so he could scratch it out. Then for a brief space of time he was returned to other sensations: the heat, the glare, the scrape of rock against his back, the roaring quiet. He lay in his cuffs and watched for the bird, for the moment the silhouette edged into his vision again and circled downward. For the pain to begin all over again.

He didn't know when the bird began to speak to him. He didn't know if he was even sane at this point, only that there came a time when the creature's voice spoke inside his head, thin and high and alien:

There is no redemption in this world, not for you. The sins of the fathers pass to the sons to the sons to the sons. And the daughters.

The bird's eye deepened, darkened; it was a quicksand of nothingness and he felt himself, what remained of him, disappearing inside. The bird told him calmly:

It's all a lie. There is nothing more.

"No," he said. His protest was feeble. His voice scraped like rusted wire; his lips felt as cracked as splintered glass.

The world is lies and maggots and cruelty and war. You know this yourself. The world is disease. The world is shit.

"No."

Let it burn. Give it to the demons and the fires and the hells. There, in the flames, the world shall be cleansed, and purged. It shall find atonement.

"You're insane."

First, destruction. Then, rebirth. It is the way of things.

"You're insane."

It is the way of things.

The bird tore out his liver. But this time it did not stop there; it repositioned itself on the rock, then cracked open his rib cage. He felt his heart pulled out, saw the motion of the bird's throat as it swallowed. He saw the golden beak coming for his face; and then pain shot through his skull as the creature took his eyes—

He was nothing but darkness, and brute animal pain, his inner vision churning from bloodstained to black.

But he held on to himself just enough to think, *Now.*

And he cast himself, his soul, up into the darkness: a blind clumsy leap. He felt the rustle of the bird's wings, the coldness of the bird's dead gaze, and he went through that gaze, plunging into the dark light beyond with a ferocity of speed that made him realize how wrong he had been, to think he could handle this.

And then thought dissolved and there was nothing but the falling.

And the fire.

It was like hands of white flame reaching out through the darkness, towards him, seizing him, pulling him inside, white light streaking past his vision and then closing in and consuming him utterly. Blowing him up. Blowing him apart. *It would smash your soul*, Romany had said on the train, and he could not only feel his own death but reach all the way through it. He felt himself turned to ash and scattered. He let himself go. He let it all go . . . and a voice moved over him like a bath of warm light.

The voice, and he did not know whose it was or where it came from, said: *You can rest now. You've done all you can . . . You're not required to do anything more.*

The light flowed around him. He saw, then, how he could drift into it, and give himself over to it, and become part of it, how the hurt and loneliness of so many centuries would fall away like discarded clothing. This was dying, then? So peaceful. So lovely. How ironic, that people feared something like death when the true horror and brutality were to be found in their own world, where she was—

Where she still was. Where she would be without him.

Jess, he thought.

Just that. Her name, her memory: a different kind of light.

Jess.

Her name, over and over again, the one cry his mind was still capable of, whether it could be answered or no. He focused himself on that cry, he bent himself around it.

You're not required to do anything more. You can rest now, but the voice—and the light it wore around itself— was already fading.

Then the other names came to him, like comets in the dark, and he folded himself around each one and summoned them, and summoned them, until he was thinning all the way into nothing, and a different kind of darkness closed around him, shut him down.

Early morning in the desert.

Mist drifted over the sand. He felt it on his skin, cool and gentle. Figures moved deep inside it. He lifted his head the best he could, to see. One by one they stepped from the mist as if rising from water, until they stood, eleven of them, forming a circle around him.

One of them stepped forward: Mina. And then she was unshackling him, drawing her body against his, rocking him. He could not remember the last time he'd cried, but he seemed to be doing it now.

Thirty-five

She saw the fires from a distance, and then she heard the drumming, stark and tribal, and the metallic gongs rippling out through desert air. She saw canvas domes rising against the smooth black ridges of rock in the background, saw large twisted sculptures of metal. She also caught snatches of different kinds of music, an overlapping progression of sound that marked the passage from one part of the festival to another.

It was huge. She didn't feel that she was riding towards it; she felt that it was bearing down on her.

It was a dense mosaic of tents, cars, and campers, sun stabbing down on metallic roofs. She heard the faint drone of an airplane and glanced up. A little Cessna swerved into its downturn, puttering towards a landing strip somewhere in the distance. And in the patch of sky directly above hung the sign of the bloodangel. The false moon. It was low and swollen and dark, like an overripe fruit, poison for plucking. She felt a breeze against her cheek, and the thought came into her head out of nowhere: *Time to come home.* Red light shining towards her. *Bloodangel. Time to come home.* She frowned a moment—tried to hold on to that feeling, that thought, a little longer, but it slipped through and away like an alien wind. She didn't know what it meant.

Another doorway.

She didn't know what that meant, either.

She left Coyote's chopper behind and approached the playa on foot, threading through the outer rim of camps. People were sitting out on chairs, drinking and talking, some of them glancing at Jess as she passed. Strips of sand served as makeshift streets, and she looked into the spaces between the camps that offered glimpses of the ancient lake bed that swept on for several miles: hard-packed white sand, scent of alkali hanging like chalk in the air. People drifted across it, looking small and lost in comparison.

As she moved deeper into the network of camps the scene began to change: people were wearing increasingly flamboyant costumes, or nothing at all save for glitter or henna or body paint. A man in a loincloth with a crown of thorns jammed low on his head sat on the step of his battered RV, cutting lines of white powder on a CD case; a group of baby-faced women in schoolgirl outfits sat on beanbag chairs, giggling, swigging vodka, and passing around a revolver in some kind of game, slipping it between their skirted thighs; a bearded man in a dusty tuxedo stood in the center of a ring of spectators, making lavish gestures with his hands; as Jess drew closer she realized he was eating razor blades. He caught eyes with Jess and grinned at her, and stuck out his tongue: it was forked at the tip, blood dripping slowly to the sand. She passed a tent with silk scarves tied around the cords, hanging limp in the nonexistent breeze; men and women in garters and stiletto boots lounged on silken cushions, smoking antique opium pipes, their bodies lavishly painted in kohl.

She was being followed.

She looked behind her and saw the people from the gas station. The dark-haired woman in the cowboy hat, the towheaded teenager in the zebra-striped pants, the three or four others clustered behind them. The blond man smiled at her and blew her a kiss.

She didn't have to think about it; she ducked behind an RV, slipped the mirror from her pocket and dropped it on the ground. She felt her mind flex as she drew breath and summoned. Moments passed. Her own reflection rose up from the mirror and drifted off, like smoke, like a ghost, into the crowd. The blond man and his friends followed the false Jess, slipping away through the intricate tangle of the camps.

A female voice from beside her murmured, "Have you been in it yet?"

Jess glanced over.

The woman beside her was staring glassily into the distance. "The Maze," she said. "Have you been in it yet?"

Jess said, "Where is it?"

The woman pointed past the camps, deep into the lake bed. Jess, frowned, seeing nothing—

But then, as her eyes adjusted, the high, molded walls of some kind of structure resolved into view, shaped from the sand itself so that it was difficult to distinguish from the landscape behind and around it. There was something built atop it—what looked like some kind of stage, constructed out of wood, primitive and makeshift and yet visually powerful.

"How far do you think it is?" Jess said.

"Maybe a mile. Maybe two. I haven't been out that way yet. You have to be invited," the woman said, "but they say we'll all get invited. One by one by one."

"What's so special about the Maze?"

But the woman looked at her with such naked incredulity that Jess knew the question was a mistake. She mind-reached for a charisma spell, then gave the woman her brightest smile. She wasn't sure if it would work. The woman stepped back, as if she'd been stung, then blinked again at Jess.

She said, "Is there . . . is there some way I can help you?"

"I need a change of clothes," Jess said.

"I think you look great."

"I need to look like I belong."

"Come with me," the woman said. She paused, then said, with a tentative smile, "My name's Cecilia."

She led Jess past a blue canvas dome; through the wide openings Jess saw psychedelic images playing across the canvas while people nodded off on dirty couches; one girl crouched between a man's legs, her head bobbing in his lap while his hands played in her hair. Several RVs were parked in a neat row behind the dome. A group of burly, naked men hooted at them from one of the rooftops. Cecilia waved at them, taking the key from her pocket and unlocking the door.

The air inside the camper held the smell of garbage and urine. Cecilia disappeared behind a curtain, came out with bright scraps of clothing. "You can have any of them you want," Cecilia said, smiling hopefully. "You can have all of them. You can keep them." She dangled each small piece for Jess's approval. Jess chose black velvet hot pants, a halter, a black cap that had ANGEL printed in rhinestones above the visor.

"Can I get you anything else? You want some water? Some beer? I've got—" She opened the fridge, scanned the contents. "I've got cheese," she offered hopefully, "and leftover chicken, if you're hungry. I've got—"

"No thanks."

"—A few hits of E," the woman continued, "and some coke, and a little bit of jax, if you need—"

"I'm fine," Jess said. "But thank you."

"Anytime." The woman looked at her with the naked, bleeding devotion the charisma spell had wrought; soon the spell would fade, Jess knew, and this woman would wonder what the hell she had been doing, offering clothes and drugs to a stranger. But now she wanted only to please, and even as Jess felt repulsed by the clinging, tendrilous quality in the woman's eyes, she also sensed the seductive edge of it. The pull of being looked at as if you were a god.

"Please stay," the girl said now. "Please stay. Stay with me. Stay—"

Jess left the camper, the screen door slapping shut behind her, the woman's entreaties in her ears.

A dog was sitting in the dirt, right in front of her. Medium-sized black dog with fringed ears. The animal cocked its head as if in recognition, gave a cheery wave of its tail, then trotted away.

People were smiling at her. Jess smiled back, arranging her features into a dreamy, drifting expression, just another pretty girl in provocative costume. "Hi, Angel," some of the men and women said, reading the rhinestones off her cap.

One by one, Jess reached out and touched them.

They cast pleased, startled looks at her . . . then slipped off into the crowd, in different directions, taking a small piece of her along inside them. One by one, Jess tuned in to the different gazes of the men, for a brief moment seeing what they saw: three men in a tent painting glitter polish on their toes; thirtysomethings with yuppie haircuts sitting around an RV, chopping vegetables; fire-dancers spinning wands of flame as the sun sank into the jagged rise of rocks behind them; a yellow dog digging behind a truck. Her perspective had splintered all across the festival but she saw no sign of Ramsey.

She could feel him out there, his presence galling her, pulling at her, but he was like fog. He was everywhere and nowhere. Her gaze went, again and again, to the glimpse of the sand-sculpted structure at the other side of the lake bed. The Maze.

We'll all get invited.

One by one by one.

The red sphere throbbed in the sky, so swollen and

low that Jess imagined she could throw a spear right into
the heart of it . . . and it would explode into blood.
Staring at it, she felt a cool wind sweep down over her,
and she thought she heard a whisper in her ear.

Come home.

Bloodangel.

And then, the barest whisper of a name:

Zakrial . . .

But then it was gone.

Something new entered the air, slowly creeping
through the festival: silence. The different threads of
music from the different camps were fading out. They
were replaced by a low hum of anticipation, expectation,
rolling electric through the air. The random drifts of people began to coalesce, began to move away from the
camps, deeper into the lake bed. Jess kept to the edge of
the crowd, watching. People were coming out of tents
and campers, chatting to each other, but their voices
were muted, their expressions reverential, as if they felt
themselves crossing onto holy ground. It was as if a sig-
nal had gone out through the air, summoning everyone,
but Jess had missed it.

She asked a girl, "Where's everyone going?"

The girl looked at her oddly. "It's time."

"Time for what?"

The girl shrugged. She seemed about to say something
else, then changed her mind and repeated, "It's time."

At the edge of Jess's vision something exploded into
light and flame. She wheeled toward it, but it took another moment to comprehend what she was seeing. Two
of the fire-dancers were kneeling on the sand. One of
them was burning. The other one raised a metal can
over his own head, poured liquid on himself, and then,
grinning, struck a match and dropped it in his lap. The
flames swam up his body.

Someone started screaming. "Put them out! SOME-
ONE PLEASE! PLEASE! Put them out! Put them out!"
Arms reached out from the passing crowd, wrapped round

the screaming man, and pulled him back into the flow of people.

The fire-dancers continued to burn. One of them threw up his arms, his screaming resolving itself into a single word: "ATONE," he screamed. "ATONE—" before he collapsed on his side, still burning.

The wave of people surged over them, swallowing them up.

The camps and vehicles soon thinned into nothing. Out here there was only the desert, the wind kicking up veils of sand. Jess blinked and rubbed the grit from her eyes. The dust storm thickened until she could only see a few feet in front of her. Etched inside the blowing sand were suggestions of people, hints of the crowd that moved all around her. She surrendered to their current, let herself move along with them, into the sand and wind and dazzling whiteness until the winds died, and the sand settled, and she could see again.

The only thing out here was the Maze.

Sculpted from the desert, seared and baked in the sun, the walls rising fifteen, maybe twenty feet, the wooden stage elevated a few feet above that, a strip of twilit sky visible through the narrow space between. Jess scanned the walls for entrances, but the thing looked as impenetrable as a medieval fortress. Illusion, quite possibly: any doorway would be camouflaged, sand walls opening onto more sand walls.

No one was approaching the Maze; the front lines of the crowd kept their distance, as if respecting an invisible barrier. Jess flashed back to the ring of broken glass in Del's chamber, marking out the space that belonged to the demon alone.

Once more, the winds picked up, flinging dust. The sun slipped down the sky, slowly melting against the horizon. Floodlights switched on, carving great paths of light through the dust storm. Jess heard the distant hum of a generator.

And then, a figure appeared on the stage above the roof of the Maze, emerging from the wind-whipped dust as if born from it.

A murmuring swept through the crowd, then intensified as other figures took their places behind the singer, their shapes barely discernible in the dust. And despite herself, Jess felt a thud of excitement; whatever this was, this was also a rock concert. Anticipation ripped through the crowd and set the air vibrating.

A woman's voice said, "Thank you for coming. I'm in love with you all," and the band broke into the first song, the opening chords like waves that gathered, crested, crashed across the desert.

Asha.

Asha and her band, belting out the music inside the drifting veils of sand. It was a primal, stripped-down sound, Asha's voice against guitar and drums. Spotlights came on, cutting white swaths of light across the stage, picking out the shapes of the drummer, the guitarists. Cheers and yells went up from the crowd. The song ended, and the dust storm calmed as if on cue, sand sifting to ground like a curtain coming down. Asha moved to the edge of the stage, into clear open view, and the audience responded with a ferocity of its own: stomping in the sand, arms outstretched and hands turned to fists as if beating the music from the air.

Asha said, coyly, like a young vixen on a television show: "So you came. I knew you would."

The roar that answered her was deafening.

There were no microphones, Jess realized, and yet Asha's voice rose and rolled across the desert as if the air itself caught and amplified it. Asha lifted her arms and said, "You've brought me such a gift. The gift of yourselves," and the audience screamed. Asha waited for the roar to subside, and when it showed no sign of doing so made calming gestures with her arms. "People come into the desert to find God. Are you looking for a god? For any god?"

The roar rolled through the crowd, peaked—

"Are you looking for trans . . ."—Asha paused, and grinned—" . . . *cendence?*"

—And descended on the desert in an avalanche of sound, shouts and cries and whistling, palms beating together—

"Look at me." Asha's voice rising, the sound of pure majesty. She wasn't just playing rock star, Jess realized; now she was prophet as well. Or perhaps she didn't distinguish between them. "Look into me. And I will give you—"

—Feet stamping the ground, people shifting and twisting against each other—

"—Yourselves. You want God? You want to *be* gods? Look in the mirror. Look into your own eyes and see into infinity. The infinity of you. That is your beauty. That is your truth. There is nothing else. Only a world that will enslave you."

The crowd was chanting, fists pumping air: you. The word shaped itself out of the air, rising from those upturned faces. You.

"And we are not slaves," Asha yelled.

The chant took on a metronome beat: you. You. You.

"I've brought you a gift."

A stillness swept down through the crowd, eyes fixed on the Maze and the small, bright-haired woman who stood atop it.

"The best gift. Some of you have tasted it already. But first . . ." Asha came to the edge of the stage, looked into the crowd. "But first," she said again, and grinned. "Who has her? Where is she?"

"Hello, sweet thing," a voice said in Jess's ear.

The man from the gas station was suddenly beside her. He was still wearing the zebra-striped pants. He grinned into her face, then made a quick gesture. The crowd closed in on her.

And as they closed in on her body, she felt them closing in on her mind. Hands pulling and lifting her into the air, until she was stretched out as if on a sacrificial altar. She reached into her mind, for the magic, and for the first time since her training it was denied her; it was like opening a door onto a brick wall. She could feel the hum rising up from the crowd, like a foul odor permeating her body, its outstretched arms like waving tentacles, clasping her limbs, her torso, passing her across and among themselves to the stage. Then: she wasn't sure how it happened, darkness dropping across her eyes, the cold strange feel of a different set of hands on her, lifting her up—and for a panicky moment, the feel of nothing around or beneath her—*am I levitating? Am I*—but then the moment was over, she was dumped onto a hard rough surface. Beneath her, people were laughing.

She was onstage.

She stood up shakily. The world was spinning; she took a moment for it to right itself, for her eyes to adjust to this new vantage point. Sun-liquid horizon, black tumbledown ridge and dense mosaic of cars and tents in the distance. And beneath her, all around her, was the mob. The audience. The bright, violent merging of bodies, faces upturned like rows on rows of small moons, gazes collecting in a laser beam of attention that impaled her, kept her in place. They were screaming, jeering, yelling at her; but in that shocked moment all sound went away and she saw only those mouths—all those mouths—twisting open.

Feed us.

Again. And again. And again.

She was in motion then she was reeling back, spinning—

And then she saw Lucas.

He stood near the back of the stage, in beat-up jeans and a dirty white T-shirt, his guitar hanging slack off his body; his eyes, as he looked at her, were flat and dark and hard.

She backed away from him. Her mind felt clouded and she fought to clear it, shaking her head, but she only felt increasingly disoriented. He watched her, playing a quick riff on his guitar, then said, quietly, as if answering a question Asha hadn't asked, "That's her."

Asha. Jess turned, turned again, but couldn't see her. The fog in her head thickened, crowding out all thought, all ability to make a plan—

It was as if an invisible noose were tossed round her throat and yanked. Jess's hands flew to her neck; she gasped, felt herself stumbling forward. And now she saw Asha at the front of the stage. Asha cut her hand through the air and Jess felt a force drive her to her knees, in front of Lucas.

He continued staring at her, then smiled a little, lifting his guitar off his body and setting it down beside him. Jess tried to move, but it was as if she were clamped in place; it was an effort to draw in air. Lucas gazed down at her, then ran callused fingers along her jawline, pressed the backs of his knuckles against her mouth. She tried to turn her face away and could not.

"So pretty," Lucas said.

There was a force pressing down on her shoulders, nailing her knees to the stage; there was a force that trapped her voice in her throat. She could not speak, could not move, could not find anything from her training with Kai that would counter this. She could only flick her eyes to Asha.

"Take her, if you want her," Asha said.

Lucas looked back to Jess with that flat, dead gaze she had never seen in her dreams. But that was dream, and this was the real Lucas: the man who nodded at Asha now, his hands whispering against his belt buckle, Jess pinned to the ground in front of him, horror turning over in her gut and other images flashing through her brain:

Twelve-year-old girl on her hands and knees

That's entertainment. That's entertainment—

"This isn't quite how I pictured it," Lucas said. A smile cracked across his mouth. "But still—"

It was as if a bomb went off. The floor rocked up beneath her and sent her tumbling. She landed hard, taking the impact on both forearms, but realized she could move again. Her limbs were her own again.

Asha had turned away from her.

A collective sigh rose up from the audience, and then came the sound of voices hissing. People either surged back or were forced back as a group of figures stepped forth, staring calmly at the stage. One man stood at their center, and Jess knew him before he even slipped off his hood; knew him from the way he moved and held himself; knew his height and shoulders and cool deep presence that flowed up from his body.

"This is mine," Asha said. Her own voice was measured, but Jess picked up on something red and pulsing and chaotic, pushing against that self-possession. "I am owed this. Brother."

"The world owes you less than nothing," Kai said.

He raised his hand, and pale blue lightning arced from his palm and slammed into the stage. There was a cracking, sizzling sound, and the air took on the smell of singed wood. Vibrations rolled like waves across the stage, knocking Jess off balance.

A murmur of delight swept through the crowd.

"My brother," Asha whispered. "You should have stayed on the rock." She gestured with one hand, and the drummer lifted into the air, as if an invisible hand had picked him up by the collar of his shirt and swung him out above the stage. For a moment he dangled there, suspended, and Jess saw the expression on his face. He seemed not just resigned but enraptured, his eyes closed, his face turned and offered to Asha.

He burst—neatly and calmly—into flame. Asha flicked her wrist and the human fireball slammed toward Kai. Kai deflected it just in time and people scattered as it blasted into the sand. Flames leaped and retreated and the blackening corpse became visible. People were screaming, and Jess saw the edges of the crowd breaking away, dissolving, as people pushed and stumbled their way back from the Labyrinth. They began streaming across the lake bed in the direction of the camps. But even as some began their exodus the vast majority of the audience was drawing closer, tightening in on Kai and the tall ones who encircled him. Jess could feel the hunger, the greed, the eagerness to see what happened next. This spectacle. This entertainment. From the mingled screaming, one voice rose and shaped itself. Jess realized it was Asha herself. Her voice spiraling up through the octaves, her head tossed back: a shadow slipped out from Asha's body and rose above and around her like the hood of a cobra. Asha lifted both hands and fire streamed out from her palms, toward the Summoners. Fire slammed into the ground and spread like water across the desert surface, glowing bloodred: unholy, unnatural fire.

"You knew," Asha hissed. "The first time you saw me, you knew. You only had to recognize me. I was yours, and you were mine. Family. Blood calls to blood."

Kai was silent a moment, his head bowed; then he lifted his face towards her and said: "Not always."

"Stay alive, Kai. Stay alive, and let me kill everyone around you. There must be atonement. Hear me? There must be atonement."

"This has nothing to do with atonement."

Asha smiled. "Even better."

The crowd was surging towards Kai and his companions—his Pact, Jess recalled, her mind seizing the word—lifted their arms, forming a circle around him with a foot of space between each figure; Jess saw pale blue light leap from hand to outstretched hand, gathering speed and intensity as it slipped from figure to figure, and then it was slipping through and around them, blue light spiraling up around each body and slipping down along outstretched arms, crackling from hand to hand, until the circle of Summoners formed a barrier of blue, snapping energy. A man threw himself into the space between two Summoners, then screamed and leaped backwards, his face and arms laid with welts, as blue light sizzled in his hair.

Protected, at least for the moment, inside his Pact, Kai seemed focused entirely on Asha. The pale blue energy was dancing through his body, streaming from his hands with the force and bolt of lightning, slamming into the Maze, tearing holes in the walls and roof, sand crumbling to sand, as Jess felt the stage roll and tilt and shudder beneath her. Asha stood on the edge of the stage, laughing; she bent her body backward until her hands touched wood and she crept along the edge of the stage as easily as an insect. Kai's spells were blasting all around her but nowhere near her; it was as if she had surrounded herself with an invisible wall. Kai turned his hand palm-up to the sky and the lightning changed to what looked like blue darts, curving through the air, raining across the Maze, exploding into bursts of flame wherever they made contact. The crowd was surging and pushing towards the perimeter of spellcasters, not quite daring to touch them, daring only to get so close and no closer, but Jess saw their longing to tear Kai to pieces or die trying, and Jess saw the strain on the other Summoners' faces and knew they could only protect him for so long. Asha lifted a hand and gestured, and smiled; she was playing with him. She was playing with all of them, and Kai was playing along, to distract her from the real task at hand.

Find the boy. Release the boy.

It was time for her to get moving.

The whole stage shuddered and shifted. She couldn't keep herself from falling, she tumbled and scraped along the rough surface. Someone screamed: a high, piercing note, hovering in the air, clear as glass. Jess looked to the desert floor far below her and saw cracks webbing out across the hard-packed earth like a shattering windshield; loose sand slipped into the widening crevices.

From between them, from deep inside the earth, shadows rose, pulling themselves up into air: formless things seeking form, moving into the crowd. Someone screamed again, and then was silenced. Jess felt the change in the air, the change in the audience below her, as shadows played across faces and bodies, probing, hunting; some were left alone, and others were penetrated, shadows hovering on their skin and then absorbed.

Asha screamed something unintelligible at Kai, her lips wrinkling back from her teeth. She flipped back onto her feet, lifted her arms. Shadow streamed out from her body. "Try not to die, my brother, even as everyone around you—as we kill them and eat them—"

The sound was faint at first but then louder. The high keening cry of battle. It lingered in the air, then gathered intensity, ferocity. And then they were appearing from behind the ridge, roaring through the bloody twilight, engines revving, and they descended, the Hellriders, rows on rows of them, their wheels churning up the desert as they ripped into the crowd, whooping and hollering, some of them standing up on their bikes in unnatural feats of strength and balance, some of them whipping tire chains. Their eyes were like burning holes, their skin gleaming-pale against black leather. The dead, Jess thought. They were dead. They were undead.

And they were hers.

And, as if sensing this, people were falling back and away from them: from the chains and knives and spinning tires. The mass of crowd broke apart into groups, the Hellriders circling round and through them, howling and keening; there was the pop-pop of gunfire as someone shot out the tires of one bike, the Hellrider who rode it leaping up onto the seat, then springing off the bike and into the air and onto the back of the man who still wielded the gun, driving him into the ground. Shadows swarmed over them like piranha.

"Demons?"

Lucas had materialized beside her. He spoke casually, as if they were high in the bleachers watching baseball.

"No," she said, "they're mine," and couldn't help the pride in her voice. She said it again: "Mine," as the wheels churned up sand, as gunfire sounded again and a Hellrider at the far edge of the crowd slumped in his seat, motorcycle crashing to ground and skidding into the audience. People were leaping away from it, screaming and laughing. Shadows slithered through the air. Many Hellriders were on the ground now, with brass-knuckled fists and knives and tire irons. Fire swarmed across the desert floor. She said to Lucas: "Take me to the boy. Do it now."

He laughed. "You think I'm gonna make it that easy?"

She considered what to say next: *I don't think Asha owns you. Not truly,* but then she noticed the marks on his face that she had never seen in her dreams. She spoke on instinct, threading her voice with contempt: "Nice scars."

His punch caught her on the edge of the jaw and sent her wheeling. She feinted more disorientation than she felt, saw him coming from the corner of her vision and shifted into magic, the mind-blow hitting him squarely in the chest and sending him back, stumbling, but not as far or as hard as she hoped. When he came at her again he was limping, surprised, grinning. "Come on," he said. "Come on, little girl." As the air filled with smoke and screams and the smell of endless burning, Jess focused on the man from her dreams. She lifted her hand and summoned again, felt an odd painless scorching rip through her as blue fire formed at her hand and streaked towards Lucas. *Holy shit,* Jess couldn't help thinking, *it works,* and she tried it again, the fireball forming more quickly this time. Lucas was coming at her, ducking and twisting, but blue fire scorched the side of his T-shirt: he dropped and rolled, extinguishing the flame, and was up again with such grace and speed that Jess could sense the magic in him: different from her own, but guiding and protecting him all the same. "Not bad," Lucas was yelling, teasing, "for a girl." Gunfire sounded again, bullets slamming into the stage around her. She saw Lucas move, again with that astonishing speed, and she moved too late; he grabbed her, forced her up, swung her towards Asha.

"Watch," he hissed, his arm clamped around her throat. "See what my lady can do."

Asha had lifted her hands towards the sky. The clouds opened up and poured out rain. Not just rain: Jess saw the dark color, tasted salt as hot thick drops fell on her lips. Blood. The sky was raining hot blood. The ground churned into thick, red mud. The flames only leaped higher, as if the rain were fuel. She twisted inside Lucas's grip, pulling both their bodies around; a Hellrider passed through her line of vision, bike crashing and skidding in the mud; at once people fell on him, blades flashing; someone had an axe; within moments they had hacked off his legs, his arms. The Hellrider did not scream or cry out. He lay there and waited.

Lucas said, "It's not too late to change sides—"

She looked to Kai in time to see the perimeter fading, the blue light dimming in intensity, one Summoner falling to his knees. A handful of people slipped through into the Summoner circle and hurled themselves at Kai. He blocked them with ease, pointing at each person, using the magic to fling them back into the audience. A large man in leather S/M gear with shadows clinging and rippling over his body came at Kai from behind, whipping a chain; Kai turned before Jess had a chance to scream a warning, and sent lightning into the big man's body. The shadows scattered up and away from him, dissipating into air; the man stared at Kai and dropped to his knees, blood gushing from his mouth. Kai turned to face other attackers. He would last a while, Jess knew, but eventually all the Summoners would fall. Sheer num-

bers would overwhelm them. *We are not what we were.*
She looked into the scene below her. Fires raged and
burned even as blood soaked the ground; members of
the audience were fighting the Hellriders, the Summoners and, in places, each other. Their bodies made twisting, writhing shapes in the near-dark. One of the cracks
in the ground was slowly widening; two men wrestling
in the mud cried out in surprise and terror as they were
sucked into the earth. The air filled with shouts and
screams, scattered gunfire, the thump of bodies slammed
to ground, and a low atonal humming that came from
everywhere and nowhere, rising up from the very earth.

Jess scanned the stage for Asha and realized she was gone.

"Where's the boy?" she said to Lucas. She wasn't
fighting him anymore, choosing to relax into his grip.
"Where is he?"

Lucas hissed into her ear, "We can all hang out. We
can party like rock stars." He spun her around, still gripping her by the throat; she clawed at his hands, but she
could sense the magic moving in and around him and
felt her own power dissolving. She forced herself not to
panic. They stared at each other; and the dead expression in his eyes began to splinter, something else shining
through it: glee, Jess thought. Elation. He was getting
off on this.

He kissed her on the mouth, hard, his tongue slipping
between her lips and she bit down but he was too quick
for her, his body rocking away from hers as he threw her
to the ground. She landed on elbow and hip. He was
loping along the edge of the stage, then dropping to his
knees and lifting a trapdoor. He paused—looked back at
her and grinned—then disappeared down through it. Jess
ran after him, skidding and sliding on the bloody stage,
her eyes connecting for one brief moment with Kai's as
he stood below her. *I love you,* Jess thought. Flinging
the words out towards him, as the crowd fell on him,
and she threw herself beneath the stage after Lucas.

*   *   *

A blind plunge into a claustrophobic space. The walls were too high and narrow. It felt as if they were closing in on her.

She forced herself to slow down, calm down. She mindcast into the space around her, searching for any sign of the boy, and felt the jerk of his presence like a fish on a line. He was not far.

"Jess . . ."

A hissing, drawn-out female voice.

A figure moved in the shadows just ahead.

She said: "Who are you?"

"Jess . . ."

Something was . . . off. Jess mindcast again, probing this presence for any information, but came up against a flat cold feeling that made her step back in revulsion.

She heard a faint click, and then blue light swarmed the narrow corridors. The figure she had half-glimpsed in the shadows turned out to be herself. She was staring at her own startled expression in the mirrored wall at the end of the corridor.

But then her reflection smiled at her, murmured, *"Jess . . ."* and faded. It was not her own magic; it was something, someone else.

A different, familiar voice said: "I want to apologize."

This voice came from all around, as if it on loudspeaker, but at the same time possessed a sly, warm undertone, a lover's tone, rubbing up against her ear.

"Lucas," she said. "Where are you?"

"Oh," he said breezily, "I'm around. The question is, sweet thing, where are *you?*"

She was backtracking down the corridor. She saw an opening to her right and stepped through it. The hallway branched in three directions, her scattered reflections gliding out along the walls. *"Jess,"* the reflections were saying, *"Jess."* She tried to shut her mind to them. It was difficult. They moved and shifted all around her, these splintered images of her own self, grinning and waving and leering at her, beckoning her onward.

She cast her mind out again, toward the boy, felt his warm jerking pull from elsewhere in the Labyrinth. She chose the left opening.

"I want to apologize for what happened on that stage," Lucas was saying. "Not our little tussle, which I enjoyed. I hope we get to do that again. But before that. For that incident that had you . . . well, you know. On your knees."

"Don't worry about it," she muttered. She stopped again, glanced at her choices. Left, right, or straight ahead? She chose the latter, following the darkened corridor as it veered slightly left. One of her reflections— this one a gaunt, sallow version, as if in the last stages of cancer—was hissing at her as she passed.

"It's not like I *wanted* you to give me a blow job in front of thousands," Lucas was saying, and she could hear the grin in his voice. "On this one thing, Asha was wrong. I'm not looking for that kind of puppet. At least, not with you."

She was now choosing her direction with more confidence. She knew she was angling in toward the center, where the boy was, his presence like a hot wind she was walking straight into.

"Even if you find what you're looking for," the disembodied voice mused from all around her, "you think you're going to get back out of here? Do you have a *plan,* Jess?"

She didn't answer.

"What exactly do you think is going to happen to *you?*"

"I'll probably die," she said.

"And you're okay with that?"

She came to another intersection and veered right. The reflection that confronted her was bloated and blue, floating high inside its mirror-space. Jess tried not to cringe.

She said, "Where are you, Lucas?"

"I can offer an alternative option."

"Why are you hiding from me?"

"Hiding," he echoed, and laughed.

Another faint click, and the light disappeared.

She stood enfolded within a deep and perfect blackness.

Lucas said, huskily, "Come find me."

The light came back on.

She was no longer in a labyrinth of any kind.

People roamed around her, sleekly and expensively dressed, holding glasses of red wine, champagne. There was laughter and conversation. The walls were white and pristine and hung with art; through breaks in the crowd she glimpsed bold, striking paintings. The style was familiar, and even though—or because—she had never seen those works before, she turned away with a coldness in her stomach.

"Champagne?"

A waiter stood before her with a tray, the light dancing off the flutes.

"No," Jess said. "What is this place?"

The waiter blinked at her. His face remained carefully polite. "The Museum of Modern Art."

"In New York?"

Just the slightest touch of wryness. "That would be the one."

"What . . ." Her mouth had gone dry. "What show is this?"

"Hers," he said, and gestured to a tall slender woman in blue who stood with her back to them, engaged in conversation with a circle of admirers, gesturing with her glass of red wine to make a point. She had silver hair pinned up in a chic, untidy knot.

"Who—" Jess said, but the waiter was gone. She moved through the crowd, toward the silver-haired woman, but then paused. Her chest felt hot and tight.

She turned instead to the paintings.

Portraits done in flat, bold colors, unexpected angles: arresting, incisive, exploding off the canvas. And then she came to the one of the youth in the desert, jagged rock rising behind him, sun bleeding through sky. She knew the title before she read the small card affixed to the wall beside it: *Heir of Nothing*.

"Nice," Jess murmured, lifting her voice to whoever might be listening. "Nice trick. Well done." She glanced again at the woman, the artist, near the center of the room, now posing for a photograph.

"No trick," Lucas said. "Only you."

He was beside her. He wore jeans and a black leather coat; he held a glass of red wine in one hand and a stuffed-mushroom appetizer in the other.

"Is this . . ." Jess was looking around her: the vivid, concrete detail. "Is this real?" The question slipped out before she could stop it. "This is just illusion. This is . . ."

"It's real enough," Lucas murmured. He nodded towards the silver-haired woman in blue. "That person—that fifty-five-year-old woman you were on track to become—revitalized the American art scene, brought it back down to the people. Well," Lucas muttered, glancing around at the well-heeled attendees around him, "some of the people." Juice squirted as he bit into the mushroom.

The artist turned, and her face came fully into view.

Fifty-five, Lucas had said. Her gaze glanced off Jess . . . and then came back again in shocked recognition.

They stared at each other across the room.

Just an illusion, Jess told herself.

And yet it was hard to believe this wasn't real as concrete: the air-conditioned room that thrummed with conversation, the glint of wine in Lucas's glass, the loose tread of footsteps as people passed from painting to painting, and this other woman, this strange, older version of herself: her stance, her expression: the mingled arrogance, defiance, and melancholy that Jess recognized as very much her own.

"This was all for you," Lucas whispered in her ear.

"This was the path your life was supposed to take. You could still have it. If you were to join me."

She was feeling dizzy. She took a step back, and suddenly had to fight to catch her breath. The woman was still staring at her, the blue eyes turning flat, cold, accusatory. As if to say, *Who are you to deny me this. Who are you—*

"All you have to do is say yes," Lucas said.

—To deny me?

"Say yes to Asha. Say yes to me." He had his hand on her arm.

Yes. It was, Jess thought, such an overripe syllable.

"No," she said, as if arming herself with the word and shrinking behind it, protecting herself from her own desire for what she saw around her. The beauty. Such beauty broken out from her own mind and heart and talent.

"Shame," Lucas said softly, and then it was all gone.

They stood in darkness again.

Jess closed her eyes. She counted off the beats of her own heart. When she felt centered enough to speak, she said, "Is that how Asha got you, Lucas?"

He didn't answer.

"With promises of beauty and greatness?"

"I have something else to show you," he said.

The lights came on again.

A voice, amazed, said, "Jessie?"

She stood in her uncle's study, in the town house in Georgetown: oak-paneled walls and crowded bookshelves, including the rows set aside for his prized first editions; the inlaid, never-changing men's-club smell of leather and cologne and tobacco. She recognized the model cars on the shelves, the pen-and-ink sketches in their silver frames clustered on the wall beside the fireplace.

The Judge was sitting in the leather chair behind his desk. "Oh my God," he said softly, and stood up.

In her memories of him he was a strong, towering

figure; but now she saw that he was not quite six feet, only a couple of inches taller than she was. He was thin, with a slight stoop to his shoulders, his dress pants and cashmere sweater hanging off his frame.

He came round the desk, his arms held out to her.

She backed away from him.

His arms fell to his sides like broken wings. "I understand," he said. "Jessamy, sweet girl, I'm so sorry."

"You're . . ."

This is not real, she told herself, yet the dizziness was storming through her skull again, whipping all her thoughts to hell.

"Sorry," the Judge said, "for all the pain I caused you. I was so wrong, Jessamy. And that . . . that knowledge has tortured me. Never a day goes by when I don't think of you. You are my family."

Not real. Not . . .

"So very deeply sorry," the Judge said. "Apologies are useless, I know, but this one is sincerely meant. Please believe me. Do me the honor of believing me."

He dropped to his knees in front of her.

Not real, she thought again, but those words were like a neon sign slowly flickering out of power. She stared at the old, familiar figure kneeling before her. In her encounters with men those first years in New York, part of her was always waiting for the insult, the blow, the taste of blood in her mouth. It took a long time before she could trust that her own compass was directing her to the gentle ones, the ones like Gabe.

And now the Judge was at her feet. She could see his pale scalp through the tufts of white hair, see the faint trembling of his hands as he lifted them towards her. He was holding a whip. As Jess watched, he took off his sweater and cracked the whip across his chest, across his back, across his chest again, scoring deep red welts.

"Please," he said.

Blood streamed down his skin, matting the fine silver hairs on his chest.

"Please," Claude Harker said, and Jess jerked away from him, taking deep, gasping breaths like a diver breaking the surface. "Now you," he said, and held the whip out to her. "Hurt me. Hurt me the way I hurt you."

Not real not real not real—

"No," she said, and again, "no," even as she was tempted to take it, take hold of the whip and find out what it was like, just once, to strike the Judge, she would only do it once, then drop the whip at his feet because she was better than that—so only one blow, deep and lasting, to make him bleed just a little bit more—

"No."

Her uncle was gone. She was alone in the study, the fire churning quietly within the fireplace. "Lucas," she said, "get me out of here. Lucas—"

No answer.

"Lucas!" she yelled again. She felt herself beginning to break, beginning to panic, but this time couldn't stop herself: *"Lucas!"*

And then darkness.
Surrounding her. Enfolding her. Lifting her up.
She was floating.
Am I dead, she thought, *or only dreaming?*
And then a man said, "Wake up."

Jess Shepard opened her eyes.

Thirty-six

"Good morning," Gabe said. He grinned at her. He was standing by the window of his studio apartment, in his boxers, smoking his first cigarette of the day. The rumble and blare of Chinatown traffic drifted up from the streets below. "How's the head?"

". . . What?"

Jess pushed aside the sheets, pushed herself up against the headboard. She was naked, and there was a faint stickiness along her inner thighs. She looked at Gabe, looked down at her own pale body. Something felt off, not right, but she couldn't remember what it was. Her head felt stuffed with cotton. Had they made love? Why couldn't she remember? Had they been that drunk?

"Your head," Gabe said again, patiently. "Last night. There was much tequila. Remember?"

"Shit," Jess whispered. "No." She touched her hands to her temples. There was a foul taste at the back of her throat. But something wasn't right. "I'm not that much of a drinker," she muttered. She was talking to Gabe, but she also needed to clarify something to herself. "Not anymore."

"You were last night," Gabe said. He stubbed out the

cigarette, chuckling a little. "You were smoking, too. That opening really undid you, didn't it?"

"The show," Jess said.

The show was last night, and yet the memory felt as if it were coming from a long way away.

"Did you see the expression on your dealer's face? She was fucking *orgasmic*. Especially when that collector—what's his name? David Salik?—walked in the room."

She remembered drinking the red wine at the show, then the talk with Gabe in that piano bar and then . . . ? What had come after? Barhopping, slamming down tequila shots, stumbling in her heels. She didn't remember smoking—she hadn't smoked in twenty-three months. But her throat did taste like . . . ash, and she caught the scent of smoke in her long hair.

"Jesus," she muttered. "Tell me I didn't—"

She couldn't complete the sentence—*Tell me I didn't do any C*—but Gabe lifted a hand and said, smiling a little, "No coke."

She blew out air, relieved. "Well," she muttered, "only two vices out of three."

"Last night was great," Gabe said. "You were wild."

Jess said, "I don't . . ." She looked at him again, said, "What's with the goofy smile on your face?"

The smile widened. He raked both hands through his hair, came forward, and dropped to his knees beside the bed. "I didn't think you'd remember," he said. "You were pretty trashed. So I took it back and figured we'd do it again."

"Took what back?"

He slipped his hand into the back pocket of his jeans. "Jess Shepard," he said, and she stared at him in amazement. "Oh, you're kidding me," she said, and his smile broke into a grin, the slightly off-center grin that she loved and he said, "Marry me."

"Marry you," she said.

Something not right about this. Not right . . .

"Jess," Gabe said. He lowered his head for a moment, as if reconsidering his approach, then muttered, "Last night you said yes. You were pretty goddamn thrilled about it, actually."

"I . . ." This damn hangover. It was harder and harder to think. "Marriage isn't for everyone," Jess said. "It might not be for—"

Gabe lifted his head and stared at her directly. "You want to marry me. Have a baby. My baby."

"A baby," Jess murmured. Well, yes. Although motherhood didn't fit with the way she saw herself, neither could she deny that longing, the way it tugged inside her as if tiny hands had already grabbed hold.

A tiny boy, she thought. A tiny girl. She'd take either.

"You want a home," Gabe whispered, "a family, a place to belong. I can give that to you. I'll be warm strong arms to hold you. You'll never be lonely again."

His eyes were ocean-colored, thickly lashed—*Such a shame,* Chelle had said more than once, *to waste lashes like that on a guy.* You could dive all the way inside eyes like that. Let yourself get swept away.

"Let me be your home, Jess."

"I thought I'd lost you," Jess murmured.

"Belong to me."

"For some reason, I thought—I thought it was over."

"Silly girl," Gabe said, still smiling. "Say yes to me. Say yes."

"There's something I need to remember. There's something I need—"

"Everything you need is right here. Right here in this room. All you have to do is say yes." He held up the ring. The diamond was at least a couple of carats, sharp-edged and filled with its own white light, glittering on the smooth platinum band.

"Say yes."

She was struggling to find her way through the hangover, the wave of emotion swelling inside her. Yes. The word pulsed beneath her skin. *Yes* was the word that made everything easy. *Yes* made the world feel so good.

Gabe shifted his knees on the floor. He was beginning to look uncomfortable. Sweat slipped from beneath his hairline, curved a slow path down his cheek.

"I'll give you everything you want," Gabe said. "Everything. I love you, Jess. Don't you get it? I would die for you."

The last words caught at her. Her head was throbbing. *Something not right. Not right. So very very wrong—*

His eyes widened slightly, as if he realized he'd made a mistake.

Another drop of moisture slipped down his cheek, a small ruby glimmer.

It snapped into place, then, blasting out the strange sticky webs that someone had spun in her head. "You were in a car accident," Jess said.

Gabe fell back from her, eyes widening.

"You're in a coma," Jess said.

Blood was streaming out from his hairline now, pouring down his cheek; the right part of his skull assumed a sunken appearance. He stared at her for another moment, his breath whistling in his throat; then his eyes closed and he slumped to the floor.

She got out of the bed. She realized she wasn't naked after all; she was in the outfit she'd taken off the girl in the trailer, knee-high boots caked with orange dust. She turned away from Gabe's slumped and bleeding body— *Not real,* she told herself, even as she took in the smell of his blood, the rasp of his breathing—*not real not real not real—*

The bedroom door was closed and locked. She struggled with the knob, then stepped back and stared at it.

She summoned.

"You lose, Lucas," Jess muttered, and the door blasted open as if she'd detonated an explosive.

Pale red light spilled into the bedroom. The wind

howled in, stroked her hair back from her face. Jess
crossed the threshold—

—And stepped into the center of the Maze.

A large room, red light flowing from the sconces set
along the slanted walls. Figures moved inside the shadows, their eyes crawling across Jess as she walked deeper
into the room, her own gaze riveted on the couple just
ahead of her. The woman and the boy.

Bakal Ashika lounged on a raised dais, a naked teenage boy sprawled limply in her arms. The pale skin of
his legs and arms were slashed with bright red lesions.
As Jess watched a figure detached itself from the shadows, stepped up onto the dias and knelt before Ashika
and the boy. He carried an oversized wine glass in both
hands. Ashika nodded at him. The man placed the glass
beneath the boy's wrist. Ashika's lips moved as she mur-
mered words that Jess couldn't hear. Blood spilled from
the wound, filled the glass, and then stopped as neatly
as if a valve had closed. The man drank deeply and
swiftly, then bowed again to Ashika and retreated down
the steps.

Ashika looked at Jess and smiled lazily.

"You can't have him," Jess said.

"Oh, Jessamy," and she was startled to hear her name
coming from this woman's mouth, "I claimed this one a
long, long time ago."

"He wasn't yours to claim."

"Oh?"

Another figure emerged from the shadows, stepped up
to the dais, knelt before the boy. This one held out a
heavy silver goblet, like something from a medieval ritual. Blood splashed. In Asha's arms, the boy was mo-
tionless, his head turned against her body.

Look at me, Jess thought. *Look at me.*

"So he's yours?" Asha said. "Why? Because Shemayan used him first?" She paused, then said, "Come
here, Jessamy. Have a taste. Lucas seems fond of you."

Her smile widened a little. "As does my brother. I could find some real use for you."

Where was Lucas? She scanned the shadows, but didn't see him anywhere.

"So come, Jessamy, and drink. Is that so much to ask? I can give you so much."

"Nothing real," Jess said.

"Oh," Asha said, "it's real. It's all very real."

Look at me.

She saw—or thought she saw—the boy stir, ever so slightly, in Asha's arms.

"Your life," Asha said. "Your future."

Look at me.

"Or . . ." Asha said, and her mouth curled at the corners, "mercy."

The blow struck Jess from behind. It sent her to her knees. Red light bloomed around her, and she was trapped in the center. There was a high-pitched sound that vibrated through the light and then went into her, going all through her, until it felt as if her bones would splinter.

"I can make it stop," Asha said, as the pain intensified and she fought back a scream, "or I can make it go on for centuries. Is that real enough for you?"

But she was looking at the boy.

Ramsey was lifting his head, looking toward her.

Their eyes locked.

Jess said, "I release you."

His head lifted.

"I release you," Jess said again. "As you were promised long ago. Go home."

The boy fell from Asha's body to the stage. Something lifted out of him: a long, lean shape of white shimmering energy, hovering over the boy. The creature lifted its head. Black eyes bore directly into Jess.

The entity shot towards her, the red sphere of light that imprisoned her shattering like water.

It was like a thousand strokes of lightning slamming

into her. It whipped her back—whipped her head back—
and tore a scream from her throat that was so high and
pure it was unlike anything she'd ever heard. Her mind
filled with alien memories—pale flickering shapes gliding
against a white sky—and the knowledge of her own power,
unleashed fully for the first time.

She felt herself dissolving, and she was no longer afraid
of that, either.

You. Asha's lip had curled. *You want to fight me? You
don't even know your own name.*

Jess felt another, alien voice, speaking through her:

My name is Zakrial.

Jess gave herself over, folded herself down so that she
was taking up as little space inside herself as possible.
She reached her mind toward the Labyrinth walls and
they dissolved, the high rounded edges softening, crumbling, the walls falling away in chunks of mud, collapsing in on themselves; she felt the cold ancient power
that was Zakrial radiate through and out from her
body. The walls and roof exploded. Suddenly there was
sky and wind and blood-rain; the air was thick and
churning. Asha shrieked. A shadow erupted from her
skin, moved across her body, and transformed human
skin into glinting silver scales. Asha's eyes glowed, the
sockets widening and deepening, filling with an acid
green; her blonde hair stiffened into chunks of yellow
bone, giving her scalp a rough and studded appearance.
She turned, and Zakrial saw the tail, long and thin with
a studded tip, and even as Zakrial recognized both it
and its purpose Bakal Ashika lashed it toward him. He
heard the hiss as it cut through wet air and he moved a
half-second too late; he felt the bite of it across his back,
and then the searing pain.

Bakal said, *Must we do this again?*

He felt, then, a different pain move across his back.
He felt a shifting pressure inside his bones, pressing up
against the skin of this borrowed body. His wings,

searching for form the way they had so many times during his time in this world—searching, never finding it.

Until now.

They erupted up through his skin with a sound like tumbling water; he felt the liquid flexing motion of them unfurling above him, sending long pulses of wind into the blowing mud and rain. He lost the earth beneath his feet; he was airborne again, and for the one sweet moment he was so distracted by the joy of it he forgot about Bakal, almost ignored the whipping tail. In the last half-moment he twisted his body away from it, felt the tip catch and whistle across his cheek. He climbed the air, then looked below: the swarming fires, the air filled with screams and gunshots and cries of pain, motorcycle wheels spraying mud.

He found Bakal's acid eyes, staring up at him, Bakal's mouth wrinkled back from rows on rows of jagged teeth.

Zakrial said: *Come to me. It is time.*

She moved into a crouch and then sprang, her arms reaching for him. She slammed into him, the force of impact tumbling them both through the air, her teeth snapping at his throat. This was what she wanted: close, intimate contact, skin on skin, blood on teeth, not the distant sparring of spellcasters. He flexed his wings, pulled them higher into the air, the desert dropping away below. Blood-rain slashed at them, hot and wet, salty tang on his lips and in his mouth. He head-butted her and felt her grip on him slacken; he gauged the distance to the ground—good enough—then pulled his wings against his body and went spinning into free fall, disorienting her, before abruptly jerking out of it, wings flexing long and smooth and easy, the ground disappearing beneath him once again as they rose, and rose.

Zakrial.

A different voice, not Bakal's. A new voice. He turned, and found himself staring at that strange, red moon, pulsing right above him. Except, this close, he

could see it was not a moon after all; it was not even
solid. He was beating the air with his wings, something
pulling at his memory. There was something he was
supposed to remember. When a burning pain slashed
across his wings and then slashed him again: Bakal
was whipping him with her tail, squirming against his
body, raking her claws across his torso. He caught her
arms in his own, felt that odd silvery skin against his
palms, and folded his wings and plunged again into
free fall.

And suddenly, Bakal twisted in his grip and came
loose of him, dropping long and easy to the ground as
he unfurled his wings and skimmed across the desert,
across the crowd, people crying out and scattering away
from him, yelling at him, pointing, his nostrils filling with
the smells of burning and carnage. He curved upward
through the air, went higher, looking down for Bakal.
She was on all fours now, loping through the crowd and
then away from it, moving across the vast pale stretch
of dead lake, keeping pace with him. A man was in her
path, didn't get out of her way quick enough, and she
raked her claws across him, tearing away part of his arm
as she tossed him aside. Zakrial saw her gather her legs
beneath her, saw her spring towards him, and as she rose
up he twisted back and to the side, her hands closing on
nothing but blood-rain. She fell back to the earth, landed
smoothly, legs bending deep, tail lashing the ground in
frustration. Zakrial rolled over on his back and hovered,
grabbing a moment to look again at the red moon.

Not a moon.

It was . . . concave.

Zakrial. A cool wind of a voice, blowing in from another realm, blowing through the—

Something he was supposed to remember.

False moon. Not a moon.

Just another doorway.

Not a moon. An exit.

His wings beating long and hard now, lifting himself towards it—

Zakrial. Time to come home.

—And then, for one moment, staring into the rich red expanse of it, seeing how it reached through the sky, tunneled between worlds. And, deep at the other end, he saw the long slim silhouette, saw the rise and flex of wings like his own.

Come home, come home, come home.

Zakrial turned again and gazed at the scene spread out below. It was like something from hell; maybe it *was* one of the hells. He locked eyes again with Bakal, and made his decision. He dropped toward the ground even as the other chose her moment, then, and leaped for him, her arms stretched out toward him, and in the half-moment before they met he cast his mind out toward her, saw his opening, and took it.

He reached into her soul before she could even realize his intentions. It was like falling into an inferno. No room to think or breathe, no oasis here, no water anywhere—she was raging, raging, no longer knowing why—she was pain, and fury, and hunger, and blind twisted instinct. *I was put in this world to burn it.* But she was the one who'd been burning all this time. And he had someplace cool and quiet to offer her: a realm gone beyond war, beyond apocalypse, where even a thirst such as hers could be obliterated.

Kill you, she said. *Kill you.*

He said: *Come with me.*

He had his arms around her, crushing her against him. He pulled them both up through the sky, the blood-rain, and she was squirming and slippery in his arms; he rose up against the false moon, his own shadow falling into the face of it. And then he flung them through. He felt the vessel-body drop away from him, felt the red light close itself around both him and the demon he carried, the demon he held by the very soul, the

two of them lashed together so tightly they could have
been one.

She was aware of herself falling, cold air streaming
past, and pain that blazed through her body in a dozen
different places. She was falling and she didn't know
how to stop herself; she was falling to her death and too
battered to care.

But it was then she felt gentle hands on her body, a
voice whispering in her ear: *My love. My love.* Her descent began to slow as invisible arms caught and held
her, slowly bringing her to the ground.

She looked down and saw Kai far below. She closed
her eyes and focused her mind on him, focused on moving her body more deeply into his magic, to make his
task as smooth and effortless as possible. And then her
feet were touching the earth as gently as if stepping
down from a plane.

And then he was there for her to fall against, his real
arms wrapping around her: flesh and blood had never
felt this good, this warm, this loving. She nestled into
him. He said nothing; he stood there and held her.

It was truly raining now, clear cold natural rain drumming the desert. Mutilated bodies slipped into crevices
that were slowly but surely rumbling closed. The survivors
were scattering in all directions: some were taking down
their camps, packing cars, driving off; others were wandering into the horizon, looking for a road, a highway,
a group to join. Jess didn't know what would be left of
this night, or how people would begin to explain it, make
sense of it.

Across the lake bed a near-giant of a man in a ripped
leather jacket caught her eye. They held gazes for a moment, as the rain slashed down between them, and the
man lifted his motorcycle helmet in a kind of salute. A
helmet, Jess knew, that was covered with coyote fur. She
watched as he turned and walked away, and she won-

dered where on this huge plain of nothing he was headed.

"What will happen to the Hellriders?" Jess asked.

Kai thought for a moment, then said, "I don't know. Some of them will find a place to sit down and expire; they'll be eager to go back into death. And others . . ." He shrugged. "The others might last for a while. They'll find some old spark of themselves to hold on to, they'll take it as far as they can. Life tends to have that kind of character. It insists on persisting." He put his arm around her shoulder and turned her around, to face the figures approaching them.

"This is my Pact," he said.

They stood around her, the other Summoners, tall and imperious, and nodded at her as their names were announced. Makonnen. Daki. Romany. Eagan. Isolde. Javiera. Sato. Asadel. Tristan. Adrian.

And Mina.

"Hello, Jess," Mina said. There was a deep scratch along her right cheek.

The one named Eagan, a tall burly man with dark hair and blue eyes, turned to Kai. "We didn't contain all of them. The early ones, the first ones who drank from the bloodangel—they'll be moving through the borderlands, into the real world."

Kai nodded. "We'll have to hunt them down."

A broad grin split Eagan's face. "Aye," he said. "It will be fun."

Isolde was the one who brought her to the boy. They had placed him in a nest of sleeping bags in one of the tents, rain pattering off the canvas roof. Ramsey's skin was blanched of all color, his legs and arms crisscrossed with wounds. She wasn't sure if he was even breathing. Jess laid her hand on his chest. "Don't die," she whispered. "Stay in this world for as long as you can."

She felt, rather than saw, the presence manifest itself on the other side of the unconscious youth. It was the girl, the ghost, who had led her in the night. She looked at Jess with deep brown eyes, and placed her own hand possessively on the boy's chest.

"Let him stay a while longer," Jess murmured.

They held gazes for a moment that felt never-ending. The girl gave a slight nod, then faded from view.

Ramsey gasped for air. "Sleep," Jess said, and touched his forehead. "Sleep deeply, and heal." She didn't move from his side until Kai Youngblood knelt beside her, and put his arms around her, and kissed her throat and face.

Thirty-seven

Gabe had been in these rooms for a long time, ever since, drunk, he veered into the wrong lane and headlights came blaring into him. His world filled with sound—the crash and screech of metal on metal—and one of the guys in the backseat, screaming—and then turned to dark.

When he woke up—

Except he hadn't. What he had done, instead, was like opening your eyes deep underwater. He had come back to a sense of himself, but it was the thinnest and palest of senses.

He drifted.

Every so often sounds filtered down from the world outside him—voices—he caught snatches of medical terms he didn't understand and, once, Chelle's voice. She was talking to him (he couldn't make out the words) and crying. He wanted to comfort her. He wanted to say something, anything. But then he was descending again, down through all the layers of himself until there was nowhere deeper left to go, and little hope he'd find his way out.

*   *   *

Down here, there were many rooms. He could spend the rest of his life drifting through them (and recognized that as a likely possibility). Every room he had experienced throughout his lifetime was down here, and more: rooms from television shows and favorite movies; rooms glimpsed through strangers' windows; rooms seen in magazines and read about in books; rooms taken from his own imagination, never existing anywhere else except here, inside him. Eventually, he sensed, he would open a door that led not into a room but his own death. He didn't know if that would be ten days or ten years from now; he had no way of counting off time.

So he drifted.

Beyond every door he opened, in each room he stepped into, he expected the pale final face of his own mortality.

He did not expect Jess Shepard.

"Hello," she said.

She was sitting on the silk-upholstered couch in his parents' Long Island living room, dressed in jeans and a black tank top, her hair in a loose, untidy knot.

He was too stunned to speak.

"I'm sorry," Jess said, "that I couldn't get here any sooner."

It was the first time he'd ever tried to speak, down here in the bottom of himself. His words sounded echoey and hollow, as if he were speaking in two different tones at once. "That's okay," he managed.

"Not much time for talk. We have to go before I forget."

"Forget what?"

"The way out. You have to understand. I'm new at this."

He was bewildered.

Jess smiled and stood up and stepped around the coffee table towards him. As he leaned into the scent of her, a sense of loss cut through him, even though she was right in the room with him, they were together.

Jess stood on tiptoe and kissed him on the throat.

"Let's go," she whispered.

She took his hand and led him back through the rooms, all the rooms through which he'd wandered. He wanted to speak, but she was intent on their direction, stopping several times to consider this door or that door. But she chose with confidence, and although Gabe didn't know how or why this was happening, he never lacked belief in her.

So it came as no real surprise when Jess stood in front of the last door with her hand resting lightly on the knob. She turned to him and said, "Gabe . . ."

He touched her shoulder.

She said, "I wasn't the one for you."

He thought about this a moment, then said, "I know."

"Now go," Jess said, and opened the door for him.

Not taking his eyes away from her, Gabe stepped across the threshold.

Simple enough to open his eyes. He sat up in the hospital bed, the frame creaking beneath him, and spent a moment examining the tubes that ran in and out of his body, the bandages and bruises on his forearms and the backs of his hands. The light that came through the window was the watery, early-morning kind. From below he heard the grind of a large vehicle downshifting. Traffic noise. He was in love with traffic noise. It meant he was back in the world.

He looked up in time to see a nurse pass by the doorway. A moment passed, and then the nurse doubled back and stood in the doorway and stared at him. She was holding a clipboard. She stared at him some more and he smiled at her and waved. She dropped the clipboard.

*   *   *

Later in the week, after Chelle's tears had dried up a little and she could start to think about such things, she would tell him the strange thing that happened to her the day after he woke up. How she was coming up from the hospital cafeteria, looking forward to hearing her brother's voice again, watching the expression in his open eyes, when she passed a woman in the hallway. The woman wore a dark hooded coat hanging open over faded jeans. Something about her height, the way she moved, was familiar. Chelle turned, in time to see the woman also turning, looking at her.

The woman said, "Chelle."

It was Jess Shepard. Or rather, Chelle told her brother, it was and it wasn't. This woman was leaner and harder than the friend Chelle remembered; her skin, the kind of pale, sunburn-friendly skin that never tanned, had darkened to a light gold color, and her *eyes*. Chelle paused, and when she spoke again her voice held an edge of awe. Jess's eyes were a fierce, electric blue, and there was a moment when they flashed so bright that Chelle had a thought—

—*She's no longer fully human*—

—An absolutely impossible thought.

She was too startled to say or do anything. She could only stand there like a tall piece of furniture as Jess came up to her and hugged her fiercely. "Go to your brother," Jess whispered in her ear. "I'll see you around."

"Jess—"

But then Jess Shepard was gone, striding down the corridor. She slipped through a door and it banged shut behind her.

"Jess," Chelle said. There was a mystery here she wanted—needed—to crack open. In less than a second she made her decision and was through the door, down stairs, down another hallway, until she pushed through a fire door and ran out into an uncertain New York morning. Jess was at the corner on the other side of the parking lot, and she wasn't alone. Chelle saw—when she came to this part, she hesitated a moment, then took a breath and continued—she saw a tall man in a light wool overcoat and a teenage boy carrying a skateboard. They were standing together, the teenager saying something to the older man, as they waited for Jess to join them. Then the three of them crossed the street and turned the corner, out of view.

"Jess," Chelle yelled one final time. She had competed in track all through high school and college and although she wasn't in that kind of shape anymore, she was still fast when she wanted to be. But by the time she reached that corner and looked in all directions, Jess and her companions were gone.

Epilogue

The man came from nowhere.

That was how it seemed to him now, stepping along the sun-scorched highway. His skin had darkened to a deep tan it had never been before, a shade that still surprised him—stunned him—when he saw himself reflected in the grimy mirrors of gas-station restrooms. He came from nowhere; he was no one; he had nothing.

Nothing, except an open vista of possibility.

Nothing, except possession of himself.

Nothing, except the ability to create music that could tear your heart out.

And the dog, trudging beside him, panting in the heat, tail held rather daintily at half-mast. The black dog with the fringed ears that he'd named Ronin. Lucas had him too.

The world had changed, even if the world itself didn't know it. But *he* knew. The first, early demons *(the early ones will be rewarded)* had been given physical expression, had slipped all the way out through the slippage borderlands. He was looking forward to meeting a few. It was just a matter of time. What would happen after that—what he would choose to do after that—Lucas didn't know.

For now, it was enough to walk, and feel the sun on his skin, and dream.

He thought a lot about the painter. He had dreamed about her the night before; neither of them had said anything, she only turned her back to him and slipped off her shirt so he could see her new scars. Narrow white ridges ran from her shoulder blades to the small of her back. He found them quite beautiful. He had the urge to touch them, but she was already stepping away from him.

He told her: *This thing with us will go on and on. The way it always has.*

Because she was out there too, in the world, moving through it; and they would find each other again, the way they so often had, in life after life after life.

Roc Science Fiction & Fantasy
COMING IN NOVEMBER 2005

DAYS OF INFAMY by Harry Turtledove
0-451-46056-1

The master of alternate history takes on Pearl Harbor Day. What if the Japanese followed their air attack with an occupation of Hawaii? What if they were prepared to use the island to launch a military attack on America's western coast?

WINDFALL by Rachel Caine
0-451-46057-X

In Book Four of the Weather Warden series, Joanne Baldwin's stormy personal life is taking a toll on her patience—and her powers. Now Joanne is torn between saving her lover, saving her powers—or saving humanity.

SHADOWRUN #1: BORN TO RUN
by Stephen Kenson
0-451-46058-8

This all-new trilogy begins on Earth, 2063. Magical forces have awakened and the world is changed. Kellan Colt has come to Seattle only to learn that in this world, there is only one law: survival.